LORD OF THE SHADOWS

A Medieval Romance

By Kathryn Le Veque

Printed by Dragonblade Publishing in the United States of America

Library of Congress Control Number 2014-009
ISBN 1494927500

Kathryn Le Veque Novels

Medieval Romance:

The de Russe Legacy:
The White Lord of Wellesbourne
The Dark One: Dark Knight
Beast
Lord of War: Black Angel
The Falls of Erith

The de Lohr Dynasty:
While Angels Slept (Lords of East Anglia)
Rise of the Defender
Steelheart
Spectre of the Sword
Archangel
Unending Love
Shadowmoor
Silversword

Great Lords of le Bec:
Great Protector
To the Lady Born (House of de Royans)

Lords of Eire:
The Darkland (Master Knights of Connaught)
Black Sword
Echoes of Ancient Dreams (time travel)

De Wolfe Pack Series:
The Wolfe
Serpent
Scorpion (Saxon Lords of Hage – Also related to The Questing)
Walls of Babylon
The Lion of the North
Dark Destroyer

Ancient Kings of Anglecynn:
The Whispering Night
Netherworld

Battle Lords of de Velt:
The Dark Lord
Devil's Dominion

Reign of the House of de Winter:
Lespada
Swords and Shields (also related to The Questing, While Angels Slept)

De Reyne Domination:
Guardian of Darkness
The Fallen One (part of Dragonblade Series)

Unrelated characters or family groups:
The Gorgon (Also related to Lords of Thunder)
The Warrior Poet (St. John and de Gare)
Tender is the Knight (House of d'Vant)
Lord of Light
The Questing (related to The Dark Lord, Scorpion)
The Legend (House of Summerlin)

The Dragonblade Series: (Great Marcher Lords of de Lara)
Dragonblade
Island of Glass (House of St. Hever)
The Savage Curtain (Lords of Pembury)
The Fallen One (De Reyne Domination)
Fragments of Grace (House of St. Hever)
Lord of the Shadows
Queen of Lost Stars (House of St. Hever)

Lords of Thunder: The de Shera Brotherhood Trilogy
The Thunder Lord
The Thunder Warrior
The Thunder Knight

Time Travel Romance: (Saxon Lords of Hage)
The Crusader
Kingdom Come

Contemporary Romance:

Kathlyn Trent/Marcus Burton Series:
Valley of the Shadow
The Eden Factor
Canyon of the Sphinx

The American Heroes Series:
The Lucius Robe
Fires of Autumn
Evenshade
Sea of Dreams
Purgatory

Other Contemporary Romance:
Lady of Heaven
Darkling, I Listen

Multi-author Collections/Anthologies:
With Dreams Only of You (USA Today bestseller)
Sirens of the Northern Seas (Viking romance)
Ever My Love (sequel to With Dreams Only Of You) July 2016

Note: All Kathryn's novels are designed to be read as stand-alones, although many have cross-over characters or cross-over family groups. Novels that are grouped together have related characters or family groups.

Series are clearly marked. All series contain the same characters or family groups except the American Heroes Series, which is an anthology with unrelated characters.

There is NO particular chronological order for any of the novels because they can all be read as stand-alones, even the series.

For more information, find it in **A Reader's Guide to the Medieval World of Le Veque**.

TABLE OF CONTENTS

CHAPTER ONE

".... I should have known from the beginning not to concern myself. We have so many choices in life, in every situation. One choice can mean the difference between life and death. This choice, for me, would come to mean both...."

The Chronicles of Sir Sean de Lara

1206 – 1215 A.D.

Tower of London
January, Year of our Lord 1215

HE SHOULDN'T HAVE bothered. He knew from the moment he observed the situation that he should have walked the other way and pretended not to notice. He was hidden by the fortified entrance of the White Tower from the group that had gathered near the newly constructed buildings on the eastern wall. It would have been so easy for him to slip away. But for some idiotic reason, he remained.

A drama was unfolding in the morning hours of the ninth day of January of the New Year. A young woman with bright red hair was hanging from a second story window of the structure as someone desperately attempted to pull her inside. Through all the screaming and drama, he could see that the red-haired girl was determined to leap to a nasty death below. He left the safety of the shadows, morbidly intrigued by the life and death struggle. Like the allure of a good beheading, it was pure entertainment.

The closer he moved, the more the players came into focus. It was frenzied and dangerous. The redhead was half out of the window, set upon a narrow protuberance of the stone that comprised the exterior of the building. She was howling, struggling to break free of the hands that held her. He couldn't hear what she was saying but, being female, he surmised that it probably wasn't terribly important. Better to let her jump and be done with it.

His attention then moved to the woman attempting to prevent the suicide; he couldn't make out the features at this distance, but he could certainly distinguish the blond hair that shimmered against the afternoon sky as gold would shimmer against the sun. He found himself more intrigued by the beauty of the hair than by the chaos unfolding around it.

He moved closer still, the hair luring him. As he arrived on scene, the few people that were standing about noticed his presence and quickly moved away from him. The movement was innate, like oil parting from water. No one with a sane thought in their head would dare stand within proximity of Sean de Lara. Like cockroaches, they scattered.

He didn't notice when the group shifted away from him. That was a normal happening and not worthy of his regard. Furthermore, he was looking overhead; the redhead was most of the way out of the window by now, the woman with the blond hair pleading urgently for her to come inside. Surely things were not as bad as they seemed, she said. But the red-headed woman was lamenting loudly. She was apparently unworthy, unloved, and wholly unsuited to remain in the land of the living. The blond assured her that none of this was true. She loved her dearly. *Please come inside, Alys!*

He maneuvered himself towards the window. He didn't know why, but he could see what was coming. The fall wouldn't kill her, but it could seriously injure her. He didn't know why he should bother with this idiocy. Perhaps to make up for all of the evil he had done in his life, there would be one good thing he could list as a contribution to Mankind. He saved a silly girl from breaking her neck. He could imagine St. Peter laughing him all the way back to the depths of Hell for that natty little side note to an otherwise problematical life.

He was almost directly beneath the window now. The redhead

slithered out onto the narrowed shelf but the stone was slippery and she was unable to gain a foothold. Just as he reached the base of the window, her grip slipped and she plunged straight down.

She was still screaming when he caught her. She wasn't heavy in the least and he had stopped her fall with ease. But her flailing hands had clipped his nose and he could feel a trickle of blood. The girl stopped screaming, her mouth still open, when she realized that she was not a messy, broken blotch on the ground. Her startled blue eyes looked at her rescuer with such surprise that, for a moment, he actually thought he might crack a smile. He'd not done that in years. In his profession, there was nothing to smile over. He was sure he'd lost the ability long ago.

She must have stopped breathing at some point, because she suddenly took a huge gasp of air with her wide-open mouth. It was like looking at a fish. Without a word, Sean set the woman to her feet. She was shaken and her legs did not seem to work correctly. He steadied her when she couldn't seem to stand. Her mouth finally closed and she looked at him with a sickeningly yearning expression.

"My lord," she gasped. "I… I do not know what to say. Thank God you were here to save me, else… else I do not know what would have become of me."

He couldn't help responding. Stupidity always provoked his irritation. "You would have seriously injured yourself just as you were attempting to do. God had nothing to do with my appearance."

She clutched him for support. "But… my lord, I am sure that God sent you to save me. I am positive of this!"

"He did nothing of the kind, my lady."

"I am in your debt, forever and ever."

"Unwarranted, my lady."

"But I am your *slave*."

He was thinking that he should perhaps disengage her hands and leave quickly. He did not like the way she was looking at him.

"I assure you that is not necessary," he removed one of her hands and was in the process of removing the other. "I would suggest you stay away from windows until the urge to climb out of them leaves you."

The young woman would not let go. She continued to clutch at him, re-grasping him every time he peeled her fingers away. For every digit he removed, two would take its place. He swore she had nine hands.

"Please, my lord," she gasped softly. "I must know the name of the man who has saved my life."

"Suffice it to say that I am a knight who has done his duty. No more thanks or obligation is necessary."

The redhead was still pawing him when he caught a glimpse out of the corner of his eye. The blond hair he had seen two stories above his head was suddenly in his midst and for a moment, it was as if time itself stood still. Startled, he found himself staring into the magnificent face of the woman with the hair of gold. Nothing about her was foul or defective. She was, in a word, perfect. For a moment, he thought he might actually be gazing upon an angel. He could think of no other explanation.

But the exquisite woman wasn't focused on him. She was out of breath, evidence that she had run the entire way from the apartments above. From her expression, it was clear she had not known what to expect. Seeing the other woman alive, when she had presumed otherwise, was nearly too much to bear.

She grasped the hands of the hysterical redhead. "Alys," she breathed. "Are you hurt?"

Alys shook her head. "Nay," she suddenly seemed weak and faint, dramatically so. "This brave knight saved my life. He is my redeemer, I tell you. He snatched me from the very jaws of death."

The blond woman turned her attention to Sean and his heart began to thump loudly against his ribs. She was an incredibly lovely creature with luminous blue eyes and long, dusky lashes. Her skin was creamy, her nose pert. He tried to get past his fascination with her beauty, struggling to focus on her softly uttered words.

"My lord," she said. "My sister and I cannot adequately express our thanks. We are forever in your debt."

So they were sisters. *Strange,* he thought. When the redhead had expressed her indebtedness, it held no attraction to him. But with this sister....

"Obligation is not necessary, my lady," he said quietly.

She smiled the most beautiful smile he had ever seen. "You are too kind," she said in a sweet, lilting voice. "Consider the House of St. James your loyal servants, my lord. No favor you would ask of us is too great."

Something in Sean's expression grew dim. It was like a shadow falling over the sun, imperceptible to all but the experienced eye. But whatever warmth had been brewing was instantly quelled.

"St. James?"

"Aye, my lord."

"And your names?"

"I am the Lady Sheridan St. James and this is my sister, the Lady Alys."

His response was to gaze at the pair a moment longer before silently, yet politely, excusing himself. It was nothing more than a slight bow and he was off across the compound, an enormous man with arms the size of tree limbs. He walked with the stealth of a cat, disappearing into the shadows from whence he came. As quickly as he had appeared, he was gone.

The girls watched him go, puzzled by his swift retreat. Alys was positively crestfallen.

"You frightened him away," she said accusingly. "He said that no obligation was necessary. Why did you press him?"

Sheridan's lovely face darkened as she looked at her sister. "You silly cow," she snatched the girl by the wrist. "You frightened him with your insane behavior. What on earth possessed you to climb out of the window? Had he not caught you, you more than likely would have fallen on his head."

"That's not true!"

"He had no choice but to catch you."

Alys' pale face flushed. "How *dare* you. God sent him to save me!"

"Blasphemer," Sheridan hissed. "Be silent and come back inside with me. We will speak no more of this day or of your behavior. Mother would have your head if she knew what you have done."

Alys rose to the fight, but her face suddenly crumpled. She became overdramatic again.

"But he left me," she moaned. "He left in the night. His steward said so. What choice did I have but to end my disgrace?"

Sheridan tried to retain her dignity in the face of the crowd that still lingered. They pointed and whispered, but no one approached. She put her arm around her sister, hustling her back towards the entrance to the apartments.

"I do not know why he left, Alys," she said quietly. "Perhaps we shall never know. But that is no reason to kill yourself."

"But… but he said he loved me."

"Perhaps he was mistaken."

"How can you mistake love? And… and I believed him. I allowed him to…"

"Hush. We will speak no more of this, Alys. Not another word, do you hear?"

"But I am so humiliated," Alys wept softly.

Sheridan did not want to speak of her sister's plight. This wasn't the first time she had fallen for a man of unscrupulous character that had taken advantage of her. She was always falling in love with one man or another, pliable to their whims and lust. And this wasn't the first time she had threatened to end her suffering.

"You must be strong," Sheridan did not know what more to say. They had been through this too many times in the last few years of Alys' young life. "You must be strong and wait for the proper man to come to you."

Alys' expression brightened with unnatural rapidity. "Perhaps God sent the man who saved me to replace him. Perhaps it was fate, Dani. God sent my savior to save my life and mend my broken heart. Do you believe in love at first sight?"

"I do not."

Alys' tears faded as they entered the dark, cool corridors near the Flint Tower. "My savior must have felt something for me. Why else would he risk his life to save me?"

Sheridan could only roll her eyes in disbelief.

ଓ

NESTLED DEEP IN a long stretch of ancient stone and mortar, the solar of the king was a dark place at any given time. In the day, it was gloomy, but in the night, it was positively sinister. Phantoms lingered in the shadows and the heavy smell of alcohol reeked throughout the room. The king liked his drink and had a tendency to pass out with tankards in his hand, which then spilled upon the floor and seeped into the expensive carpets.

Tonight was no exception to the usual dreariness and stench. The dinner hour was swiftly approaching and the hall of St. George was filled with servants, vassals, and the finest food that England could provide her people. But the king's solar was reserved for Henry II's youngest son and the most prominent members of the king's circle to attend him in conference.

It was a somber group that gathered this eve around their king, John Softsword. William Fitz Osbern of Monmouth lingered by the hearth, while the volatile pair of Humphrey de Bohun of Caldicot and Walter Clifford of Clun huddled a few feet away. Lesser lords with minor titles and lands completed the evening's royal guest list; Bernard de Newmarch, Richard Fitz Pons, and Payn St. Maur. These men, and their immediate retainers which could number four or five additional men each, filled the solar to near capacity.

It made John feel secure to have these men around him. He was tortured by inner demons, hounded by a lifetime of failure and insecurities brought on by an insecure upbringing. He was essentially weak-minded and needed those of strong mind and opinions hovering close. Physically, he was a man of small stature, bad hygiene, and one heavily lidded left eye that gave him a rather dull appearance.

"Henry St. James, 3rd Earl of Bath and Glastonbury, died last year," Monmouth continued the conversation they had been involved in since entering the private solar. "I was aware that the Bishop of Bath was in London on the widowed countess' behalf, but not the daughters."

"He fought with my father," the king said, his usual cup of wine in hand. He was getting drunker by the minute. "He did, in fact, fight always on the side of my father. He has ever been against me."

"There are many in London at this time that raise opposition to you, sire," Monmouth replied. "We have kept watch of them, have no fear. Ask your Shadow; he will tell all."

Attention turned to the darkened recesses of the room near the servant's entrance. Back there, in the depths, lingered the king's bodyguards. These two men were sworn to protect the king, sworn to do his will and fulfill every perverted and outrageous whim. To speak of them struck fear in the hearts of even the bravest of men. Gerard d'Athée and Sean de Lara were strong-arm men without an ounce of compassion if it ran contrary to their sworn duty.

"De Lara," the king spoke to one of the two lingering in the blackness. "This news of the St. James' women has come from you. Tell us all you know so that we may assess the threat."

Sean came into the light. His deep blue eyes were fixed on the king, unwavering, cold and calculating. He was an enormous man, even larger than d'Athée and twice the size of any other in the room. He had been rumored to kill men with his bare hands, appendages as large as trenchers, and there wasn't one in the room who did not disbelieve that. He had been with John for several years, far more feared than his bear-like counterpart Gerard, because there was one great difference between them: Sean had intelligence. A dangerous man with a brain was a dreadful prospect. And he had the ear of the king.

"My lords," Sean spoke with a voice that seemed to rise up from his feet to exit his mouth. "I can tell you that we have seen a collection of opposing barons gather in London in the past few weeks, much more than we have ever seen before. The House of St. James is merely one of many."

"Who else is here that we may not know about?" Fitz Pons demanded. He jabbed a finger in Sean's direction. "We know you have spies that report to you, de Lara."

"I have spies," Monmouth muttered, out of turn.

"We *all* have spies," Clifford interjected impatiently. "But our spies are spread out over our lands as well as in London. They run thin at times." He glanced at Sean, his old eyes sharp and wise. "De Lara knows all, sees all. He knew that the House of St. James was at the Tower and told us so, last week. Today he has met the daughters, which is of no consequence to us. I care not for the women, but I do care for Jocelin. That is where the true power lies."

The mood of the chamber was growing uncomfortable. Jocelin, Bishop of Bath, was an influential man with a tremendous voice within the church. The House of St. James was allied with the man and, consequently, most of the West Country. With all of England in civil war and conflict, alliances and enemies were of supreme importance at this time.

"The Earl of Lincoln arrived yesterday," Sean continued. "Worcester, Coventry and Rochester have been here for weeks. I am also told that Salisbury, de Warenne and Arundel are on the road and due to arrive within days. De Braose rides with Salisbury."

One could have heard a pin drop. It was more than they had imagined. The mood turned from uncomfortable to ominous as the shock of the information sank deep.

"De Braose is the most powerful lord on the marches. As we speak, he is waging war against the Welsh," the king's voice was tinged with bitterness. "Why does he come to London?"

"Reginald is on the marches, sire," de Lara replied. "His son Guy rides with Salisbury."

"God's Bones," Fitz Pons hissed through clenched teeth. "Two of the three most powerful marcher lords ride to London, not to mention Arundel. What does this all mean? Why are they all converging on London?"

"They ride against the king, of course," de Lara said steadily. He paused, eyeing the crowd, wondering if they were ready for the rest of his report. "There is more, my lords."

John glanced up from his nearly empty chalice. "What more?"

"I am also told that Fitz Gerold, Fitz Herbert, Fitz Hugh and de Neville are expected from the north, though I cannot be sure. The information is unclear and several weeks old. And then there is the matter of de Burgh…"

"Hugh de Burgh," John slammed his chalice to a table, missed it, and it clattered to the floor. "I will punish that man, I swear on my father's grave. He defies me, my old tutor. I will strip him of everything my father ever granted him and call it swift justice."

John's rage was up. If it became worse, he would throw himself down on the rushes in fits. It was important that he remain in control, important for his cause that he put on a strong appearance. No doubt nearly every man de Lara named would be in attendance at the feast tonight and they must see nothing other than a collected monarch. Sean glanced at Gerard, the great hairy beast of a man, and with a silent gesture sent him in search of the physic. He was well aware of the signs of impending convulsions.

The nobles sensed this as well. De Lara took a step towards the group and immediately the men moved to vacate the chamber. There was a feast awaiting and much plotting to attend to. They would leave de Lara to calm the king.

When the room was empty and John sat twitching in his chair, Sean took a moment to study the man. He was attempting to assess just how close he was to seizures.

"Sire," he said quietly. "You needn't worry over those who would oppose you. Your loyalists are just as strong. This is an old story and an old issue. We have dealt with worse. The monarchy will prevail, I assure you. It always has."

"But the church stands against me," John was salivating as he spoke. "Worcester, Coventry and Bath are in London, no doubt to assist the barons in plotting my downfall."

"They are men of the church, sire. Perhaps they are merely in London on papal business."

John grunted. "The church has ever been against me. And that nasty little business a few years ago…"

"Your excommunication was short-lived, sire."

"But I had to prostitute myself and my country in order to please that bastard, our gracious, sympathetic and illustrious pope," John's rage was gaining again. "He damn near emptied our coffers with his demand for tribute. But it was of no avail. The man is *still* against me."

"Even if that is the case, sire, you count the bishops of York, Northumberland and Chester among your allies. They understand your vision for England and for her holdings."

"Pah. They understand nothing but tribute and penance. I must pay for the sins of my father and those before him. That is the foundation of their hatred, you know. The sins of my entire family. 'Tis not just my political stance that has provoked the abhorrence of the church."

He was speaking with the petulance of a child, exaggerated, with dribble flying from his lips. Sean knew that paroxysms were imminent. His next words were specifically designed.

"As you say, sire."

"Of course I say. The church is full of idiots and mercenaries."

"The church favors those who pay well for its loyalty, sire. And I have heard that Northumberland has been well-courted by William Marshall as of late."

John's eyes widened. "My brother's chancellor? He lures my greatest supporter?"

"Money is sometimes greater than faith, my lord. Or the love of a king."

John's rage exploded and he was twitching on the rushes by the time the royal physic arrived.

CHAPTER TWO

"... Lo, there did I see my destiny when I gazed across the room on that fateful night...."

The Chronicles of Sir Sean de Lara

1206 – 1215 A.D.

"DID YOU EVER imagine what Adonis must look like?"

Alys was lying horizontal on the great bed that she shared with her sister. She was half-dressed for the evening meal, most of her time having been spent in the land of silly daydreams. Sheridan had been attempting to hurry her up for the better part of two hours. But Alys moved, as always, on her own time.

"No," Sheridan was gazing into a polished bronze mirror that was strategically affixed to the chamber wall. "I have not imagined that. And you should not waste your time. You must finish dressing or I swear that I will leave without you. The bishop will be here at any moment."

Alys turned to watch her sister as she pulled a bonecomb through her silky dark-blond tresses. Sheridan's hair was thick and straight, while Alys had more natural curl than she could handle. Still, Sheridan was able to roll her hair with strips of cloth at night, resulting in cascades of curls for the following day. In a world where beauty was judged on natural attributes, Sheridan often felt inadequate as far as her hair was concerned. But she did possess the loveliness of face and figure so as not to feel completely unattractive.

Alys never thought her sister was unattractive. In fact, she was proud and jealous of her beauty at the same time. She finally decided to push herself off the bed and go in search of her hose, which could take some time to locate. She was a messy girl and her clothes were generally strewn all over the room.

"Surely my savior has the face meant for Adonis, do not you think?" Alys bent over when she came across her shoe. "Did you not notice how handsome he was?"

Sheridan was in the process of pulling the front section of her hair back and securing it with an enormous comb in the shape of a butterfly. "I noticed how big he was, to be certain. The man was three times your size."

"But he was beautiful," Alys sighed.

Sheridan had not given him a second thought, but she did seem to recall unnaturally clear blue eyes and a square, firm jaw. Upon deeper reflection, she supposed he had been rather handsome in a rugged sort of way.

"I presume so. I did not give much notice."

Alys found her hose. "Do you suppose he will be at the feast tonight?"

"If he is one of John's vassals, I am sure he will be."

That prompted Alys to move faster. She yanked on her hose, affixed the garters, and put on her shoes. Then she snatched the comb that Sheridan had been using and began furiously brushing her hair.

Sheridan frowned at her sister's pushy demeanor. Fortunately, she had finished securing her own hair and moved aside so that Alys could have full control of the mirror. She went to the wardrobe to collect her slippers.

"Good Lord," she grunted as she bent over for the shoes. "She cinched my corset far too tightly."

"Who?"

"The maid."

"Oh." Alys had brushed her hair so roughly that it was turning into a giant frizzy ball of red hair. She smoothed her hands over it furiously. "Look, now. What do I do?"

Sheridan went to her rescue. They had been through this routine before, too many times. She put beeswax and a slight amount of oil on her hands and smoothed them over her sister's hair, again and again. Most of the strands tamed, but some clung to her as if alive. It was like trying to tame a wild beast.

"If he is there tonight, do not make a fool of yourself," she muttered as she smoothed Alys' hair. "You already thanked him. There is no need to throw yourself at his feet."

Alys was appalled. "I would do no such thing."

Sheridan worked the oil into the ends of the hair until it was absorbed. "I know you far too well, baby sister. What have I told you before? You must be cool and pleasant. 'Twill make you more appealing than if you lay at his feet like a door mat."

Alys made a face, rolling her eyes. Then she yelped as her sister pulled a single, painful strand. "I am sure he will want to dine with me if he is there, do not you think?"

It was Sheridan's turn to make a face. Alys never listened to reason, from anyone. Finished with the hair-salvage, she fastened a delicate black hairnet over Alys' head to compliment the red dress with black accents that she was wearing. When all was said and done, Alys' wild mane was nicely contained.

"There," Sheridan said. "Now you look presentable. Have the maid beat the wrinkles from the dress before we leave."

The little maid they had brought with them from their home at Lansdown Castle was in the larger antechamber airing out the heavy cloaks her mistresses would wear. The woman came when Alys beckoned, bearing the large paddle made from water reeds normally used to beat bed linens and rugs. The red-haired sister put her arms up and the servant girl went to work, smacking out the wrinkles from the linen that had formed when Alys had lain all over the bed during her daydreams.

With Alys finished, Sheridan returned to her final touches so that she would be presentable before the finest courtiers in England. It was, in truth, intimidating. She gazed at herself in the mirror, assessing her reflection; she wore a gown of iridescent green, like the color of the sea on a warm summer day. The sleeves were long with trailing cuffs, the neckline daringly low, and the bodice tapered at the waist to emphasize her slender torso. A lovely necklace of rough-cut emeralds finished the look.

As she inspected her face, she noticed that her lips were chapped again. She had to constantly rub a solution of beeswax and salve on them to keep them from cracking and bleeding. On special occasions, she added a touch of ocher to the mix and turned her lips a delightful shade of red. It was perhaps a bit much, and a little daring, but she liked the result when she was brave enough to do it. Tonight, she decided, was just such a night.

She wasn't aware that Alys was also watching her as she went through her closing preparations. Alys' blue eyes grazed her sister, from head to toe, wishing yet again that she had been blessed with even half the beauty her sister had. Though their facial features were similar, Sheridan's were refined and delicate and Alys' tended to be broader. Sheridan had lovely white teeth, with slightly protruding canines, that added charm and character to her beautiful smile. Alys had slightly protruding front teeth that made her look like a rabbit. Sheridan also had a slender neck and shapely shoulders, whereas Alys' neck was a bit thick. In fact, her entire body was a bit thick; not fat, but full. Sheridan had a trim waist made even more slender with the corset, which only made her breasts appear rounder and firmer.

Alys often wished she had been born in Sheridan's figure. Perhaps it would have made a difference with the men she had fallen in love with. Perhaps they would have stayed. But she wasn't bitter, strangely enough. It was simply something she lived with.

A knock on the door sent their hearts racing with excitement. The little maid flew into the antechamber and opened the door for Jocelin, Bishop of Bath and Glastonbury. A rotund man who had been close friends with their father, Jocelin had taken it upon himself to assume the paternal role for the girls when their father passed away suddenly the year before. Lillian, their mother, had not fared well with the death of her husband and the family had been in emotional need. Jocelin had stepped in, not only for the family's requirements, but also as a promise to Henry St. James.

The men had been united in their alliance against the oppressive monarchy that had driven a bitter wedge through the heart of the country. Henry's death was unfortunate, as there was still much to accomplish in that arena and Jocelin knew they were well on their way. Tonight, the first festival feast of the year would be an excellent opportunity to assess the growing opposition and reaffirm alliances. The king, allies and enemies alike would be in attendance and Jocelin was eager to gauge the playing field.

Unfortunately, the notion was on Sheridan's mind as well. He knew the moment he looked into her angelic face that she was thinking the same thing he was. Henry St. James had no sons, and Sheridan had been inevitably directed into the role. She was the eldest child, intelligent and wise, and like her father in every way. She would have made a fine son and heir, and Henry had raised her as if she had been male. Truth be known, part of the reason Jocelin had assumed Henry's mantel to keep Sheridan out of trouble. As Lady Bath's daughter, she wielded the power of an important earldom and in these days of political upheaval, wise council was needed more than ever.

"Greetings, ladies," Jocelin said in his great booming voice. "How lovely you look this eve."

Alys grinned and spun about to display herself. Sheridan shrugged off the comment and accepted her cloak from the maid.

"I am told de Warenne is on his way to London," she said. "He was an old friend of my father's. When he arrives, I should like to see him."

Jocelin helped her with the heavy, fur-trimmed garment. "We will both see him upon his arrival. Tonight, I have arranged for us to be seated with the Bishop of Coventry. William is a very old friend and a strong supporter of our cause." When Sheridan turned to face him, adjusting the neck of the cloak, he lowered his voice so Alys would not hear. "We will speak to him about arranging a meeting with the other allies."

"How soon can this be done?"

"I do not know. There are many we must arrange this with, and it must be done in all secrecy. Should the king discover our plans…."

"He'll arrest us all and execute us for treason."

Jocelin bobbed his head with resignation. "It is possible. I also understand that William Marshall will be at the feast tonight, another mark in our favor."

"William Marshall?" There was excitement in her tone. "Do you think we could arrange to sit with his party? No offense meant to the Bishop of Coventry, but William Marshall is legendary. The man has served three kings and I, for one, would be eager to bask in his presence."

Jocelin patted her shoulder patiently. "In time, little one. You do not invite yourself to the Marshall's table. You wait to be summoned."

"But…"

"Tut," he held up a finger, cutting her off. Now was not the time to continue this discussion. To change the subject, he lifted his voice to Alys. "Are you ready, my dear? There is much food and festivity awaiting us. We must hurry before it is all over with."

Alys bolted from the door with Jocelin and Sheridan close behind. A small contingent of the Bishop's men and of St. James' men await in the hall, commanded by a knight who had been Henry's captain for many years. Neely de Moreville was a powerful man with an unspectacular face, but of calm and good character. He bowed to the ladies, paying particular attention to Sheridan.

"If my lady is ready," he extended an elbow.

Sheridan took his offered arm and followed him down the corridor. Jocelin and Alys were immediately behind them, followed by four St. James guards and four Ecclesiastical guards.

The Tower of London was a labyrinth of dark corridors, a grand hall and cramped rooms. It had recently seen some expansion; a new moat had been added, filled by water from the Thames, and several buildings and apartments were added on the south side of the White Tower. The largest addition, however, was the Bell Tower that loomed high above the fortress.

The group left the east apartments and crossed the bailey towards the White Tower. The feast would be in the keep's great hall. Sheridan's gaze moved over the new, enlarged surroundings.

"I have never seen such a large structure," she said. "Surely this is the strongest and most impregnable fortress in the world."

Neely took any opportunity to speak with Sheridan. Being his liege's daughter, he had watched her grow from a sweet child into a dazzling young woman. But he knew his place, well aware of their difference in station.

"It has quite a history, my lady," he said. "Especially over the past few years with the contention of power between King John and his brother, Richard."

"I heard tale that John laid siege to the tower several years ago while Richard was in the Holy Land."

Neely nodded. "Richard's chancellor, William Longchamp, initiated a massive expansion project, the results of which you see now. John took advantage of his brother's absence and attacked the new defenses. Longchamp was forced to surrender not because the fortifications failed, but because the Tower ran out of supplies."

Sheridan thought on that a moment. "'Twould seem that John will stop at nothing to gain what he wants."

"Keep that in mind, my lady."

Having served the House of St. James as long as he had, Neely had been trusted with their innermost secrets. He was well aware of Henry and Sheridan's position on John. He was, in fact, extraordinarily uncomfortable that she was here at the core of King John's wickedness. It had been, in his opinion, foolish of her to come, but this journey had been planned for a long time and nothing would stop Sheridan from accompanying Jocelin in her father's stead.

Neely knew more than he let on about the king, as did Jocelin. They both knew the man had no morality. He had been known to seduce the wives of his advisors while the men were powerless to stop him. For those who tried to resist him, he had them thrown in the vault and took the women anyway. Sometimes the men were left in the Tower to rot. One did not refuse the king and live to tell the tale.

Which was why they were particularly fearful for Sheridan. She was a magnificent creature and it would only be a matter of time before John saw her. When that time came and the royal summons arrived, Neely was still uncertain to what he should do. Jocelin wanted to whisk her to a convent if and when the occasion came. Not even the king, with as much trouble as he had historically experienced with the church, would violate the sanctity of a convent. But the problem was that once she was committed, she would have to remain. For a beautiful young woman and the heiress to a massive earldom, that was not an attractive option. Therefore, being in London, at this moment in time, was risky in more ways than one.

Sheridan knew none of this, of course. They had decided not to tell her for fear of upsetting her. Though she was a stable and wise girl, still, they were attempting to protect her. No use in worrying over something that they could not control. But they could be on their guard.

The entrance to the White Tower loomed ahead. The keep was constructed of pale stone that gave it a ghostly glow in the moonlight. It was so tall that it appeared to touch the night sky. The St. James party mounted the steps and entered the small foyer immediately inside the structure. There were two stewards there to greet them, ushering them further down the corridor and into the great hall beyond.

Lansdown Castle was a grand enough place with a large hall. But even the homey fires of Lansdown's hospitality could not compare to what they soon witnessed. It was as if they had entered an entirely new world; never had Sheridan seen so many tapers, slender beams with gracefully lit tips. They gave the hall an unearthly glow. The room was also very warm, not only from the amount of people in it, but because there was an enormous fire in the two massive hearths that bordered the east and west walls of the room.

More servants greeted them, dressed in finery affordable only in the house of the king. There were several long tables, all decorated with phials of wine and seasonal fruit. Nobles, such as they do, sat on benches, tables, and all around the room. They were everywhere, the men who harbored such power in England. On Neely's arm, Sheridan watched it all quite closely. It was an intimidating sight.

Power and wealth reeked from every facet of the massive, fragrant hall. While Neely deposited Sheridan at the table and faded into the shadows, as other knights did as their masters took seat, Jocelin sat between Sheridan and Alys. Their soldier escort fell back against the wall directly behind them. The party was barely settled as Alys snatched her goblet and held it aloft for wine.

A servant was at her side almost immediately, filling the goblet. Alys downed her allotment and demanded more. Sheridan settled herself on the bench, smoothing her gown and kicking off the dried rushes that had adhered themselves to her slippers. All around the room gathered groups of men and women, the gaiety of laughter filling the warm, stale air. In the gallery above, a group of minstrels played a haunting tune. Sheridan twisted her head around, watching the group overhead for a moment, before returning her attention to the brilliant room.

"Do you see anyone that you recognize?" she whispered to Jocelin.

Jocelin's sharp eyes scanned the hall. It was like being in a roomful of predators; each man had the look of both killer and prey. There was an odd air about the place, of both suspicion and friendship. His gaze came to rest on a group several yards to their left and he visibly perked. "See there," he said quietly. "The Bishop of Rochester and his party. And I also see with him the barons Fitz Gerold and Fitz Herbert, men from the Welsh marches."

"Do you see de Warenne?"

"Nay."

"Coventry or Rochester?"

"Not yet."

Sheridan tried not to be too obvious about staring. "If you point out these men to me so that I may recognize them," she whispered, "perhaps I will be able to set up the meeting we've all longed for. No one will suspect a lady in these circumstances of subversion."

Jocelin cocked an eyebrow. "'Tis only subversion if what we are attempting to accomplish is thwarted. If successful, we shall be loyalists."

"There is no one that disputes our rightness," her voice grew stronger. "No one on earth that would dare to…"

Jocelin cut her off. "Look," he almost gestured but caught himself in time. "There is the Earl of Arundel. I haven't seen the man in years."

Sheridan caught sight of a short, red-haired man as he disappeared into a well-dressed crowd. Before she could comment, Jocelin crowed again.

"And look there," he bordered on excitement. "William Marshall in the flesh."

Sheridan found herself gazing at a man that was relatively close. He was tall and lanky, with thinning gray hair. When he turned in her direction, she was struck by the sharpness of his gaze. His eyes fell upon Jocelin and he walked straight for him. Jocelin rose to his feet and extended a hand.

"My lord," Jocelin said. "It's been a long time."

William Marshall brushed his lips against Jocelin's papal ring. His dark eyes twinkled. "Too long," he said. "I am surprised you have managed to stay out of trouble since the last I saw you."

Jocelin grinned. "Who has been spreading such lies? Trouble is my bed fellow. We're good friends and keep each other company."

William laughed softly. Then his gaze fell on Sheridan and he bowed gallantly. "My lady."

Jocelin took the opportunity to introduce her. "My lord William Marshall, may I present the Lady Sheridan St. James, eldest daughter and heiress of the late Henry St. James, 3rd Earl of Bath and Glastonbury."

The Marshall appraised her courteously. But Sheridan felt as if God himself was scrutinizing her. She curtsied before the man and he took her hand chivalrously.

"My lady," he greeted. "I knew your father. He was a righteous and cunning man."

She smiled, mortified that her lips were twitching with nerves. "Thank you, my lord. May I say that it is indeed an honor to finally meet you."

"And you."

"May I introduce my sister, the Lady Alys."

William turned to the redhead. "My lady."

He took her hand in a gentlemanly fashion and touched his lips to her fingers. But that was the end of it. With a lingering glance at Sheridan, the Marshall turned to Jocelin and the two of them lowered their voice in private conversation. Sheridan looked over at her sister, now on her third goblet of wine. Alys was gazing adoringly at the Marshall.

Sheridan went pale.

"Oh, no…."

ଓ

THE FEAST COMMENCED when the king entered the hall. It was with great pomp and ceremony, as befitting the monarch. Barons called to him, women waved at him. John, a short man with a droopy eye and noticeably bad hygiene, gestured benevolently to the group in the hall. It was reminiscent of the Pope making his rounds among his admiring subject, with all the flair of a holy parade. Some of the older men who had served his father were less friendly towards him, yet there was respect as due the king.

It took several minutes for the king to make his way to the dais where the royal table was lodged. Festooned with a variety of fine goblets and a huge centerpiece of marzipan sculpted into naked cherubs, John took his leisure time in reaching his seat. He was more intent to linger over the adoration of his subjects.

Jocelin watched him with disgust.

"He is not his father's son," he grumbled. "Henry was ruthless and deceitful, but at least he could call himself a man. His son lacks even that privilege."

Sheridan leaned in to him. "I hear they call him John Softsword because of the loss of all of his holdings in France."

"'Twas ten years ago that he acquired that name," Jocelin said. "That name and a few others."

Sheridan suppressed a grin. "I was not allowed to hear those other names, Your Grace."

"If I know Henry's mouth, then I doubt that is true."

Her smile broke through and she lowered her head so that the others would not suspect her joviality was at the expense of the king. She collected her goblet and took a long sip of the tart wine. Glancing up just as the king took his seat, she noticed several soldiers and retainers to the rear of the royal dais. Though most were finely dressed nobles, some wore weapons and armor. One man in particular looked familiar; he was so enormous that he was twice the size of nearly every man in the room. About the time she began to realize where she had seen him, Alys grabbed her arm.

"Look, there," she hissed. "The knight behind the king, dressed in full armor. Do you see him?"

Sheridan's initial shock sharply cooled. "I do."

Alys' fingers dug into her flesh. "My savior! He is behind the king!"

Jocelin couldn't help but hear the commotion between the girls. Alys had jostled him about in her excitement. "Here, here, what's this? Who are you two talking about?"

The girls leaned close on either side of him, their focus on the royal party. "The massive knight that stands to the king's right hand," Alys was pointing and Jocelin took her hand and put it in her lap. "Do you see him?"

Jocelin found the source of their curiosity. His eyes narrowed. "Aye," he said slowly. "I see him."

"Who is he?" Alys demanded.

Jocelin watched the large man for a moment before answering. "Why do you wish to know?"

"Because he saved my life today," Alys said, oblivious to the tone of Jocelin's voice. "I… I had an accident."

Jocelin looked at her then, sharply. "An accident?"

Alys didn't want to explain herself. "Aye, I… I fell. He saved me. Who is he?"

By this time, Jocelin's behavior had Sheridan's attention. She wondered why he suddenly looked so tense. She tugged on his sleeve gently.

"Do you know him?"

The bishop shook his head. "I do not know him, but I know of him." He lifted his cup, regarding the ruby liquid inside. "If you must know, the barons call him the Lord of the Shadows."

The disclosure caused both girls to look back to the royal platform. "Lord of the Shadows," Alys repeated dreamily. "That's marvelous."

Jocelin gulped from his chalice. "Nay, young Alys, that is *not* marvelous. The man is a demon."

She was indignant. "What do you mean?"

"What I mean is that he is the Devil's disciple. He is the king's protector and used by the king for the most evil of purposes. There is no man in this kingdom that does not fear him. His presence, his very name, is synonymous with pain and death. If you see the man, run for your life."

The girls looked at the dais with a bit more recognition and dread. "What do you mean when you say that the king uses him for evil purposes?" Sheridan almost didn't want to know.

Jocelin debated whether or not to tell her; de Lara would be the one to come for her should she catch the king's eye. "Evil, Dani," he said quietly. "The king sends de Lara to commandeer women for his conquests."

Sheridan tried not to appear too horrified, but Alys was unimpressed. "But what's his name?" she insisted.

"Sean de Lara."

"Sean," Alys whispered, feeling it roll across her tongue. "Sir Sean de Lara. What a beautiful name."

Jocelin turned on her. "Listen to me now, Alys. I know your penchant for the opposite sex. I know of your naïve views and your trusting ways. Though I do not know the circumstances of de Lara's involvement in your accident, I will tell you this; stay clear of him. Remove him from your thoughts. He is no prince to sweep you away nor a man to be trifled with. I promise you that the only reason John still sits upon that throne is because of de Lara. No one is brave enough to attempt his removal, and the man is deadly in more ways than one. Not only is he physical power, but he has intelligence. His tactical knowledge is without compare. No army will go up against John during these times because of de Lara's very presence. You will, therefore, heed my words; forget him. Harbor no false notions of his good character."

Alys' eyes were wide with disappointment. Her gaze moved from the bishop to the dais and back again. "Are you sure? He didn't seem that way to me."

Jocelin patted her hand. "I am sure, little Alys."

She didn't look convinced, but to her credit, said nothing more. During Jocelin and Alys' conversation, Sheridan's gaze never left de Lara's distant face; she had remembered the man from their afternoon encounter. He was three times her size, that was true, but he wasn't misshapen or ugly as a giant would be. He had crystal-blue eyes, the clearest she had ever seen, and a square jaw that projected power and astuteness. His features had been even and extraordinarily attractive. In fact, the man positively reeked of masculinity. He was striking.

Nor had he been impolite or unkind to them. He had, after all, saved Alys' life. At no time did she receive the impression of death or hazard from him. He seemed polite and chivalrous. Puzzled, yet resigned to Jocelin's words, she returned to her goblet and put the notion of the mysterious Sean de Lara out of her mind.

The meal was lavish and plentiful. Huge slabs of pork and mutton were on display, served by the fancily-dressed servants. William, Bishop of Coventry, eventually showed himself; a slight man that reeked of alcohol, he seated himself and several retainers across the table from Jocelin and the St. James women. He greeted Jocelin amiably, introduced himself to the ladies, and spoke well of Henry St. James. He seemed congenial enough. But he finished the otherwise normal conversation by running an inviting foot against Sheridan's leg.

Strange that his gesture did not shock her. She had heard tale of men of the church seducing women and had seen a few questionable actions in her lifetime, enough to know that these men were not entirely celibate. It was well known that they could be quite corrupt. She casually shifted so that her leg was not within reach of his dirty toes, but it seemed the bishop had long legs and managed to stroke her ankle once again with his cold digits. When she cast him a baleful glance, he ran his tongue over his lips and grinned.

Disgusted, she rose from the table with the whispered excuse to Jocelin that she was in need of the privy. She couldn't even look at the Bishop of Coventry, infuriated that his leering attention had forced her from the table. He had managed to unnerve her enough so that she needed to collect herself. That was not a usual occurrence with her; Sheridan was normally steady in a world filled with flighty women. But the events of the day and the excitement of the evening had shaken her otherwise steady constitution. She needed a breath of air. When Neely tried to follow her, she called him off.

She walked from the warm, fragrant hall and out into the corridor. It was several degrees cooler in the long hall. There were an abundance of guards and servants about, each one of them asking to assist her. Sheridan shook the first two off but allowed the third, a young lad dressed in red bloomers, to show her to the door. He took her to a small exit seldom used that led out into the yard just south of the Tower. Long, stone steps led down to the dirt below.

The moonlight illuminated her way, a bright silver disc against the night sky. As she reached the bottom of the stairs, she glanced up to admire the evening. It was a lovely night and she inhaled deeply of the winter fragrance. From the cloying warmth of the hall to the airy chill of the evening, it was refreshing. She thought over the bishop's actions for a moment longer before putting it out of her mind. The man was a supporter of their cause and she could not let anything interfere, not his apparent lust or her distain. If it happened again, she would be forced to speak to him in no uncertain terms. She hoped it would be enough.

It was actually quite cold for January and Sheridan was without her cloak. But she enjoyed the cold, unlike most. She found it invigorating. She moved away from the steps, strolling into the yard and gazing at the Wakefield Tower several hundred yards to her right. It was a massive cylinder framed against the black sky. Now and again she could see the guards upon the wall walk, going about their rounds. It was a busy place, this living, breathing heart of England. Another few steps had her at a large oak tree that stood solitary and alone in the vastness of the empty yard. Glancing into the thick branches above, she heard a voice behind her.

"My lady is without a cloak," the tone was so low that it was a growl. "'Tis cold this eve to be taking a stroll without cover."

Startled, she whirled around. De Lara was standing a few feet away. She had never even heard him approach. All of the things that Jocelin had told her about the man suddenly came crashing down and it was an effort to keep steady.

"I… I enjoy the cold, my lord," she hoped her voice didn't sound as startled as she felt. "This is nothing but a balmy eve."

Sean stood his ground, his clear blue eyes focused on her face. Never did they wander in an evil or suggestive manner. Nevertheless, Sheridan was on pins and needles as they confronted one another.

"Bravely spoken," he said. "Where is your cloak?"

"Inside."

"Then I shall go and retrieve it for you."

"That is not necessary, my lord," she said quickly; *too* quickly. "I shall return to the hall. You needn't trouble yourself."

The glimmer in his eyes changed, though his expression remained unreadable. "No trouble at all, Lady Sheridan. 'Twould be my pleasure."

Sheridan could see that he would not be deterred. Remembering Jocelin's words, panic began to snatch at her. "No need, I assure you. I shall return to the hall this instant."

She was halfway to the steps by the time he replied. "Why would you want to return to that den of depravity and gluttony? You are in much better company out here with the moon and stars."

She paused although she knew, even as she did it, that she should probably continue running and never look back. "It is a lovely evening, of course."

He began walking towards her, slowly. "Then why do you run like a frightened rabbit? This is not the woman I met this afternoon. She was far more controlled and coherent."

The panic that pulled at her suddenly gripped her full force. She threw out a hand as if to stop his forward progression. "Come no closer. If you try to take me to the king, I'll scream as you have never heard screams before. I'll fight as you have never seen a woman fight. I'll… I'll kill you if you try, do you hear me?"

It all came out as a rapid stream of high-pitched threats. Sean stopped in his tracks and his eyes widened. After a moment, he broke out in laughter. In all his years, he'd never seen or heard anything so hilarious. For a man who had not openly laughed in ages, it was a liberating experience.

"So that is why you run?" he said, sobering. "My lady, I assure you that I have no intention of taking you to the king."

Sheridan's heart was thumping in her chest. She could hardly catch her breath out of sheer fright. But above her racing emotions, she realized one thing; de Lara had an amazing smile. His straight, white teeth were bright against the moonlight and dimples that carved deep channels into both cheeks. Had she not been so terrified, she would have been completely entranced.

"What...?" she swallowed, torn between wanting to trust him and the inherent instinct to run. "You mean you have not come here to abduct me for the king's... the king's...?"

He shook his head. "Nay." His voice was a rumble. "I saw you leave alone. I came to make sure that you did not come to harm."

There was something in his manner that put her at ease. It was probably foolish, but she felt it nonetheless. "But I am not your concern, my lord. Why would you do this?"

"Because a woman wandering alone is not safe," he said. "However, after your threats of great bodily harm, I would hazard to say that you are no ordinary female."

"I am not."

"You can more than likely take care of yourself."

"I have been known to win a fight in my time."

"Is that so?" He appeared genuinely interested. "Against what mighty warrior, may I ask?"

She pursed her lips reluctantly. "Only my sister. But she packs a wallop."

"Of course, I have no doubt," he said sincerely. "She seems the fighting type."

"She is."

The conversation died for the moment, but it wasn't an uncomfortable pause. Sean stood several feet away, watching the reflection of the moon off the lady's fine features. As he had noted in his initial impression of her, there was nothing imperfect about the woman. He shouldn't have followed her outside, he knew that; but he had seen her from the moment he'd entered the great feasting hall and, try as he might, he couldn't seem to ignore her. When she left, he had followed. He didn't know why. He didn't even know what he was going to say to her should he have the chance. But here he was and the conversation had come easily.

"Are you really going back inside?" he asked.

She shrugged. "I probably should. My family will wonder what has become of me."

"I would be deeply honored if you would walk with me for a few moments."

If you see the man, run. She couldn't shake Jocelin's words. But the knight standing before her didn't seem the death and destruction type, at least not at the moment. His manner was quite gentle. It emboldened her. Never one to shy away from the truth, she looked him squarely in the eye.

"For what purpose?"

He was silent for a moment. Then, a well-shaped eyebrow slowly lifted. "Because it is a lovely evening and I should enjoy the company of a lovely lady."

She considered his kind request. "Won't the king be looking for you? I am told that you are his protector."

He could see where this was leading and he wasn't surprised. For the first time in his long, illustrious and hazardous career, he felt a twinge of shame. For once, he wished he could keep his chosen profession out of this. He'd never wished that before and it was a strange awareness.

"Our king is amply protected," he said simply.

He extended an enormous mailed elbow. She gazed at it a moment, her deliberation evident. Then, she looked at him. "May I ask a question?"

"If that is your pleasure, my lady."

"Very well. If I was your daughter and a man of your reputation asked permission to take me on an unchaperoned walk through the Tower grounds, what would you, as my father, say?"

A twinkle came to his eye. "What do you know of my reputation?"

"Probably more than I should."

He didn't lower his elbow. "Walk with me and we shall discuss it."

"We shall discuss it now or I will go back inside."

The twinkle in his eye grew and he lowered his arm. "As you wish, my lady. What would you like to know?"

She felt comfortable enough to ask him. Besides, she was still close enough to the Tower to make a run for it should she anger him. "Are you really as malicious as I have been told?"

His expression didn't waver. "I would not know. What have you been told?"

She didn't want to offend him. But she wasn't sure if she trusted him, either. Surely Jocelin would not lie to her. Brow furrowed in thought, she began to walk. Sean took pace beside her.

"We must be honest, my lord," she said after a moment. "It would appear that you and I are on opposite sides."

"'Twould seem that way."

"Then I am your enemy."

"In theory."

"I had not heard of you before this day. What I was told was quite unflattering."

"To you or to me?"

She looked at him. "To you, of course. I was told that you are not only the king's protector, but that you assist him in his… his dastardly and distasteful deeds. Everyone is afraid of you. Is this true?"

He drew in a long, deep breath. Thoughtfully, he gazed up at the sky. "It is far more complicated than that. Politics always are."

"But you are kind to me. I do not fear you even though I am told that I should. Why are you kind to me?"

"Because you were kind to me."

She stopped walking, lifting her hands in a confused gesture. "How would you know that? I only met you this afternoon. I said but a few sentences to you."

He looked down at her, so diminutive and sweet against his massive size. "It wasn't what you said, but how you said it. Your manner was kind."

There was something in his expression, barely perceptible, that brought her an odd sense of pity. "You are unused to people being kind to you."

His reply was to lift an eyebrow. When he put his elbow out, this time, she took it. They resumed their walk.

"I suppose there are those that would call me foolish for even speaking to you," she said.

He was enjoying the feel of her on his arm. It had been ages since he'd last experienced such satisfaction. "Absolutely."

"And if my family were to see me at this moment, I would be in for a row."

He glanced at her. "They will not beat you, will they?"

She met his gaze. "That is a strange question coming from a man..."

"Of my reputation."

She smiled sheepishly. "I should have worded that more carefully."

He just smiled at her and they resumed their walking in silence. Sheridan was beginning to grow cold in spite of her assertion that she was immune to such a thing.

"You did not answer my question," she said.

"What question was that, my lady?"

"If a man of your reputation were to take your daughter on an unescorted walk, what would you do?"

"Kill him."

He wasn't joking. She knew from the tone of his voice that he had never been more serious. It wasn't a boast, but a fact. In that statement, she could see that everything Jocelin had told her about him was true. He was a man of deeds bred of evil. Still, she did not sense that Sean was an evil man. In their first meeting and now their second, she had never received such an impression.

But the mood threatened to grow odd and strained. She did not want that. Instead, she chose to make light of his comment.

"Do you plan to kill yourself, then?"

He gave her a crooked smile. "Nay, my lady. I intend to behave as a chivalrous knight should."

She stopped walking again and looked at him with the utmost seriousness. "Sir Sean, you have been nothing but chivalrous since our first meeting this afternoon. And for saving my sister, I will always show you kindness no matter… well, no matter what our politics."

Sean was genuinely touched. His life was full of subversion and deadly threats and he truly couldn't remember, in recent times, when he'd had a moment that had been even remotely pleasant. There was no comfort in his life. As wrong as it was, he was finding comfort with an enemy.

"I thank you," he said quietly.

The moment was sweetly awkward. At a loss for words, Sheridan resumed their walk yet again. She could have walked all night on his arm, letting the conversation flow as easily as honeyed wine.

A cold breeze suddenly blew off the river and enveloped them both, swirling with frenzied intensity. When it died as abruptly as it came, Sheridan shivered. Sean noticed immediately.

"My lady is chilled," he said with concern. "I shall return you to the hall."

"I am not cold, truly," she insisted. "I would rather walk."

He looked at her. "Your lips are gray."

She lifted an eyebrow. "We're standing in moonlight. Everything is gray."

The normally unreadable expression turned suspicious. "Even as you speak, your lips quiver. That is not my imagination."

He was right, but she made a face that suggested it was a reluctant surrender. Feeling somewhat pleased with his victory, he turned her around in time to see a figure emerging from the shadows of the White Tower. He caught the glint of a blade and knew before the shape came fully into view that it was an assassin sent to kill him. In his world, it could be nothing else.

Normally, he took a sadistic pride in proving his worth as an adversary. He was the living example that no man could kill the Lord of the Shadows. But this time it was different; he had Sheridan on his arm and his heart lurched with fear for her safety. Sheridan saw the approaching blade and let out a strangled cry a half-second before Sean shoved her out of harm's way.

The assassin wielded the light-weight blade with practiced agility. It sang an eerie cry of death as it sailed through the air, three successive thrusts at Sean's head. Weaponless, de Lara stood his ground as the weapon hurled in his direction. With a defensive move that had him spinning rapidly to his left flank, he ended up behind his attacker. Reaching down, he grabbed the hilt of the sword and used the palm of his right hand to strike a brutal blow to the back of the man's neck. The force of the jolt was hard enough to snap his spine. The man fell to the ground, dead, with his blade in Sean's left hand.

Sean stood there, gazing impassively at the corpse. This was not an unusual occurrence and he had faced better. Sheridan, however, stood several feet away, her mouth gaping in shock. It took Sean a moment to remember that she was still there.

"Are you all right?" he tossed the blade down and went to her. "I did not mean to be rough with you, but I did not want you in the line of fire. I pray that I did not hurt you."

She just stood there. "My lady?" he prodded gently.

She blinked. Then her knees buckled and she threw out her hands as if to grab hold of something to steady herself. Sean was the nearest object and he took hold of her so that she wouldn't fall.

"I think I need to sit down," she whispered tightly.

He looked around but there were no benches within walking distance. He put one arm around her slender torso and took firm grasp of her right arm, holding her fast.

"You'll be all right, my lady," he said with quiet assurance. "I'll not let you fall."

They took a few slow steps in silence. He could feel Sheridan quivering like a leaf and guilt swept him. He held her tighter.

"That man," she gasped. "He was… he tried to *kill* you."

"Aye," he said steadily.

"But why?"

He lifted an eyebrow. "If you know anything of my reputation as you have said, then you can answer that question."

She took a deep breath, struggling to regain her composure. "I know, but that was so… so bold, so brutal."

"I know."

She looked up at him; he had not even worked up a good sweat. He looked completely unruffled, the same as he had appeared the moment they realized the man was upon them. It infuriated her. "And you are so calm?"

He shrugged. "Panic is deadly. One must think clearly in order to survive."

She stared at him a moment longer before shaking her head. "Then surely I would have died because I cannot imagine being calm in the face of a deadly attack."

"It is an acquired calm, I assure you."

Her eyebrows flew up. "Are you saying this sort of thing has happened before?"

He didn't answer. He continued to walk with her, holding her against him so that she would not collapse. Even when he thought she might be stronger, he continued to hold her simply because he liked it. As they neared the narrow steps that led back up into the Tower, a herd of men came flying through the doorway and down the narrow stairs. Even in the moonlight, Sean recognized the St. James colors.

Neely came rushing at them with his sword leveled. Shaken but not senseless, Sheridan could see what was about to happen and threw up her hands.

"Neely, no," she cried. "Put the weapon down."

He came to a halt several feet away. His dark eyes were twitching with alarm and anger. "Let her go," he shouted at Sean.

Sean was completely calm, completely impassive. "The lady has had a fright." His voice was as cold as ice. "If I release her, she may fall."

Sheridan could see that there was no easy way out of this for any of them unless she took action. She patted Sean gently on the arm that held her. "It's all right," she told him. "I am well now. You may release me as he has asked."

He did as she bade, but his eyes never left Neely. It was like a marauder tracking its quarry. Sheridan sensed the deadly tension as she went over to Neely.

"Put the sword down," she ordered quietly. "Sir Sean has committed no wrong. He has saved me from an assassin."

She pointed to the body several feet away in the shadow of the White Tower. Neely could see it faintly in the dark and he looked at her, puzzled as well as frightened.

"We heard the scream," he looked her up and down. "Are you well?"

"Indeed," she didn't like his hovering manner. "As I said, Sir Sean saved my life. He should be commended."

Neely looked at Sean. The last thing he would do was praise the man. After a long pause filled with hostility, he spoke tersely. "We are grateful."

Sean didn't reply. Though he was watching Neely, his peripheral senses were reaching out to every man around him. There were at least eight. With a lingering glance at Sheridan, he took several backwards steps, fading back into the shadows where the assassin lay. Sheridan held his gaze until he disappeared into the blackness.

When he was sure de Lara had left, Neely turned his full attention on her. "What happened?" he demanded softly. "How did you end up out here? You said that you were…"

She put up an impatient hand. "I know what I said," she snapped, heading back towards the narrow stone steps. "I needed a breath of air. I was attacked and Sir Sean saved my life. Leave it at that, Neely. No more questions."

He shut his mouth, but he wasn't happy in the least. They both knew this would get back to Jocelin and there would be hell to pay.

CHAPTER THREE

"...Not to act on my thoughts would have been the wiser. My error was in the act of doing...."

The Chronicles of Sir Sean de Lara

1206 – 1215 A.D.

"DID SHE SAY anything of value, then?"

"Nothing that I would consider, my lord."

"But you conversed for some time."

"It was light conversation, I assure you. Politics barely entered into it."

These meetings were always clandestine; dark alleys, dark rooms, stables, anywhere they would not be easily recognized. Such had been the way for years, since Sean's induction into the service of the king.

The meetings were no more than once every three months or so. To attempt a more frequent encounter would be to invite suspicion. As it was, Sean had to make sure his schedule and activities were nothing out of the ordinary. It was the middle of the night, after the king had retired for the evening, and Sean was in the stable bent over the hoof of his immense charger. The other half of the conversation came from the loft above, well hidden in the mounds of freshly dried grass. They never spoke face to face.

"I am truly not sure how much she knows," the voice said. "Her father died last year and left her with a great earldom. From what I understand, she has assumed his mantel in every way. What Jocelin knows, she knows. If there is imminent rebellion in the wind, she will know it."

Sean used an iron pick to clean dirt out of the horse's hoof. "If there is imminent rebellion in the wind, then you would know it, too."

The voice grunted. "Not necessarily. Some of the barons believe I am too far removed from their cause and that my head is swept up in the storm of politics. Some believe my time came and went with Richard. In any case, I wield power, aye, but only within my own troops and close vassals. I do not have the pulse of the common man."

"And you believe that she may?"

"'Tis possible. She is rooted to the rebellion on a much more grounded level."

"Then what would you have me do, my lord?"

"You have made contact. Perhaps you should maintain it, simply to see if she will provide you with anything useful."

Sean had planned on doing that regardless. "She has a security force. It will not be a simple thing to communicate with her."

"You are the Lord of the Shadows. Stealth is your gift."

Sean was silent a moment as he dropped one hoof in favor of the other. Although there were stable boys to do this work, none of them would go near his charger for fear of being trampled. Bred in Galicia by a man whose family had been breeding big-boned war horses for a hundred years, the animal's military reputation was beyond compare. Sean was the only one who could get near the beast.

"What else do you know of her?" he asked casually.

The voice hissed, the gesture of an individual with strong opinions. "That she will make some man a very wealthy husband. She is quite lovely as well, but I am sure that escaped your notice."

Sean knew it was a jab but he chose to ignore it. "Does she have suitors?"

"Nay. Jocelin has told me that she has refused every man her father attempted to contract with. Now it is the bishop's duty to find her a husband, which will be no easy task. The man actually listens to her opinion. He is a fool."

Sean didn't reply. The voice continued. "Has the king seen her?"

"Not yet."

"It is only a matter of time. He will demand her, you know."

Sean's movements slowed. "That is possible."

"You will have to bring her to him as you have the others."

Sean remained silent. The voice spoke more loudly. "Sean? Did you hear me?"

"I heard you."

"Why do you not respond?"

"Because I have nothing to say on the matter."

The tone of the voice turned to one of disbelief. "You cannot actually be thinking of refusing him?"

"As I said, I have nothing to say on the matter."

"I have listened to you speak of the St. James woman for the past half hour. I know you, Sean. I have known you for thirteen years. If I did not know better, I would say that you have an interest in her."

"Think what you will."

The voice fell still for a moment. "No matter what you feel, you cannot refuse him. You have not refused him for nine years."

Sean let the hoof fall. He leaned up against the horse, his gaze moving out into the darkness of the stables. His manner, normally steady, suddenly turned bitter.

"Aye," he muttered. "For nine years I have catered to his every repulsive whim. For nine years, I have kidnapped men's wives and delivered them to the king like a gift on Christmas morning. For nine years, I have cleaned up his leavings, disposing of the women who have died as a result of his lust and delivering those who managed to survive back to their homes." He tossed the iron hook against the wall, so hard that it lodged in the wood. "No matter how much I have convinced myself that the king's behavior was of no consequence, deep inside, I knew that it was. For the women that died as a result of his lust, I made sure they had a Christian burial. For the women who survived, I made sure they were cleaned and fed and delivered to those who would care for them. For every evil I helped create, I also tried to right it. No one knows that I orchestrated anything other than the evil, of course, other than God. The king's sins are my sins in the eyes of men."

The voice in the loft was silent. Long moments ticked by before it spoke again. "Though I have always suspected your feelings on the matter, this is the first I have heard you speak openly of them."

"I am getting foolish in my old age."

The voice snorted softly. "Take care, then. You are as we had always hoped for you; the most feared man in the kingdom. Your reputation is without equal. You are finally where you can accomplish the most good. Be strong, de Lara. The day will come when you will be rewarded for your loyalty."

Sean broke from his cynical, thoughtful stance and moved around the horse. He picked up a currycomb and ran it across the silver hide. "I hope that day will come soon. I grow weary of being seated by the Devil's right hand."

"As would any rational man, but you are by far the strongest of us all." The straw in the loft shifted, raining down on the horse's back. "Keep your focus, Sean. You are where you are most valuable now. The barons are clearly amassing and I sense that John's days are numbered. But you are critical to this success. Is that clear?"

"It is, my lord."

"If anything crucial happens, you know how to contact me. Otherwise, I will contact you again in a month or two. We shall meet again."

Sean didn't answer. The straw stopped falling on the horse's back and he knew his contact had slipped from the loft, out into the dead of night. He normally left these meetings feeling a new sense of purpose. Tonight, he left feeling disheartened.

When he finally slept in the last hour before dawn, his dreams were of luminous blue eyes.

CB

"WHAT DID I tell you about him?" Jocelin exploded. "Did you not hear a word I said? The man is dangerous!"

Neely had waited eight whole hours before confessing the evening's events to the bishop. Sheridan had been rudely awakened by Jocelin's shouting shortly after dawn. Now, in the antechamber of their apartments, she found herself on the defensive. Completely missing the point of Jocelin's rage, as usual, Alys sulked in the corner because her sister had gotten to speak to the mysterious Sean de Lara and she had not.

"I have told you twice what happened," Sheridan said evenly. "And I know what you told me about de Lara. But he was a complete gentleman, I assure you."

"He is a wolf in sheep's clothing," he fumed. "What possessed you to go outside the Tower in the first place? You are mad, girl, mad."

She lifted an eyebrow at him. "If you are going to insult me, then this conversation is over. I should like to wash and dress for the day."

"You are not dressing just yet," he jabbed a finger at her. "You will provide me with satisfactory answers."

She sighed with exasperation. "What would you have me say? That I was tired of being preyed upon by your friend, the Bishop of Coventry? That I was, in fact, disgusted by the man rubbing his feet on my leg, so much so that I was compelled to get a breath of fresh air or vomit?"

Jocelin looked at her with shock and she nodded her head, firmly. "Aye, he did that, the old fool," she insisted. "So I had to take a walk to clear my thoughts. As I was walking, a man tried to attack me. Had it not been for de Lara, I would not be here at this moment. Now, may I please dress?"

Some of the wind went out of Jocelin's sails. "Oh, Dani," he whispered. "Why didn't you say something to me? Why not tell me about William where I could have confronted him?"

She waved him off. "I would have told you, eventually. I simply did not want to embarrass your friend in front of you."

Jocelin sat his bulk down in the fine sling-back chair adjacent to the hearth. There was peace now where there had been fury seconds before. "It is not a matter of embarrassment," he muttered. "I cannot believe that he would betray me so."

He seemed genuinely distressed. Sheridan went to him, leaning over to kiss his bald head. “He did not betray you. He rubbed his toes on my ankle. Perhaps it was an accident and he really meant to rub the table leg. In any case, you needn’t feel bad. It’s over and done with.”

Jocelin grunted. “Over and done with, aye. But at what cost? Putting you at the mercy of de Lara.”

She pursed her lips with frustration. “How many times do I have to tell you that he was a perfect gentleman?”

He didn’t have an answer. He was much more concerned with entertaining the horrible scenarios. Leaving Alys half-asleep and still pouting on the chair opposite the silently brooding Jocelin, she retreated into the bedroom.

Her maid had a porcelain bowl of warm water waiting for her. Rose petals floated on the surface. Removing her night shift, she washed her face and used a soft linen rag to run warm water over her body. She always felt better when she washed in the morning. The maid briskly dried her and rubbed rose-scented oil on her skin to soften it. Just as her lips were constantly dry, her skin was also. The oil helped.

Her favorite dress was a soft blue linen sheath with long sleeves and a simple belt that draped around her hips. With it, she wore the silver and sapphire cross that her father had given her. The maid brushed her silken hair and wove it into one long braid, draping it over a shoulder. Sheridan finished her toilette by rubbing beeswax on her lips from her ever-present pot of the stuff.

The window of her chamber was open and she could hear the birds beyond. She went to the opening, leaning out over the yard below and remembering the previous day when Alys had nearly plunged to her death from the same window. Thoughts of the event brought thoughts of Sean de Lara.

She leaned against the windowsill, gazing into the gentle blue sky and wondering if de Lara would ever speak to her again. The way Neely had chased him away last night, she wondered if she had made an enemy. She’d never seen Neely so edgy, which only lent credence to

Jocelin's tales of de Lara's dark reputation. Her father's captain had known of the man; that much was apparent. She would have wagered that every male of political awareness knew of the man. Still, she continued to doubt what everyone seemed to know.

"If you are thinking of jumping, I wouldn't."

The voice came from below. Startled, she looked down to see Sean leaning against the wall directly below her. It was the first time she had seen him without his armor; he wore a bleached linen tunic, heavy leather breeches and massive boots. Without his helm, he had light brown hair, close cropped and riddled with flecks of gold.

The full lips set within his square jaw were twitching with a smile and the clear blue eyes were glimmering, as if he knew something she did not. It was an amused expression. He was, in fact, excruciatingly handsome now that she had a chance to see him in broad daylight. He looked nothing like the horrible Shadow Lord she had been warned about. She realized that she was glad to see him.

"What are you doing down there?" she asked.

"Waiting for a St. James sister to fall into my arms," he replied with a twinkle in his eye.

"Ah, I see," she smiled down at him. "Which one?"

He pushed himself off the wall, turning around so that he could see her lovely features better. "Must you really ask that question?" He held out his arms. "It is your turn."

She laughed. "No, thank you, my lord. I have no desire to see if your strength will hold out a second time."

He smiled broadly at her, resting his fists on his hips. "Then allow me to say good morn to you, my lady," he bowed gallantly. "I do hope you slept well after your harrowing experience last night."

"I did, thank you for asking," she said. "And you?"

"I never sleep."

"That's terrible. How do you survive?"

"By my wits alone."

"That must be terribly difficult."

He lifted an eyebrow. "Are you suggesting my wits aren't up to the task?"

She laughed, a dazzling display of lovely teeth and tinkling gales. Before she could reply, the door to her bedchamber opened.

"Dani?" It was Alys. "Who are you talking to?"

Sheridan quickly stood up, wondering why she suddenly felt so horribly guilty. "I...," she faced her sister. "A... person was passing by as I was looking out of the window and I simply said good morn."

Alys was at the window and pushed her head through. Sheridan was positive she would see Sean and the entire morning would be filled with lectures and angry exchanges. Sheridan turned back to the window, her eyes falling upon the last place she had seen Sean and fully prepared to make excuses to her sister.

But a strange thing occurred; Sean had disappeared and there was nothing below but dirt and stones. Curious, not to mention disappointed, Sheridan scanned the area but saw nothing. It was, yet again, as if he had simply disappeared. Alys, bored with the featureless view, went over to the bed and threw herself onto the mattress.

"I am so miserable, Dani," she threw her arm over her forehead. "The only man I was every truly attracted to has apparently decided he is interested in you."

It occurred to Sheridan that her patience for Alys' self pity was very thin. An unselfish sister would have been happy that she had found some interest in male companionship. But Alys could see nothing but her own disappointment.

"If you are speaking of de Lara, then I would suggest you find another subject," she said. "Jocelin warned us about him. My encounter with him last night had, shall we say, brutal moments. You'd best forget about him." Alys peered at her. "What about you? Will you forget about him?"

Something in Sheridan changed at that moment. She had never lied to her sister in her life. But she decided in that flash of time to keep her feelings about de Lara to herself. Alys would only create misery if she knew that her sister actually had some curiosity towards the man. And it wasn't the fact that it was de Lara; Alys created misery if her sister showed interest in any man. If Alys could not be the center of male attention, she had always been determined to ruin her sister's chances.

But Sheridan said nothing of what she was thinking. She promised herself at that moment that she would keep her feelings to herself. It would be safer for all of them if she did. Moreover, if her bizarre interest in de Lara was something to last for only a day or two, she did not want to be embarrassed. Alys created quite enough embarrassment to go around with her own dalliances.

"He is forgotten," she said simply. "Now, what will we do today, darling? What is your preference?"

Alys shrugged. "I do not feel like doing anything. I do not want to see anyone or be seen. Perhaps we will stay to the apartments and contemplate our pitiful existence."

Sheridan didn't feel like staying to the apartments. She felt like walking out on the grounds on the off-chance that de Lara might find her again.

"As you say," she said as lightly as she could, heading for the massive wardrobe against the wall. "I plan on going to the chapel this day and having the priest say mass for father."

They all knew how Alys hated attending mass. Too often, she fell asleep in the middle of it and snored like an old dog. "You go ahead," the redhead snorted. "I will wait for your return."

Sheridan dug through the wardrobe, coming across the delicate black mass shawl that had belonged to her grandmother. She really had not planned on paying for mass today, but it was as good an excuse as any. Her stomach twitched with an odd, giddy excitement and she knew in the same breath that she was being foolish. De Lara was more than likely long gone, maybe forever. But she didn't care. The urge to see him again, to speak with him, was strangely overwhelming.

She blew into the antechamber where Jocelin was still glowering. She was mildly startled to see another body present; she'd never even heard him enter.

"My lord Marshall," she dipped into a polite curtsy. "I did not know you were here, my lord."

William Marshall sat opposite Jocelin, his gray eyes piercing as they gazed at her. "I have only just arrived, my lady," he stood up. "My old friend and I barely had time to speak last night. I went to his chamber and they told me he had come here. I apologize if I have intruded."

"You have not," Sheridan assured him, thinking he looked different from when she had met him last night. He looked as if he'd slept in a field; there was hay in his hair and on his tunic. He looked exhausted. But those thoughts were cast aside as she realized that she was very glad to have Jocelin occupied, as he would not insist on accompanying her.

"If you will excuse me, I plan to have mass said for father this morning," she said. "I am on my way to the chapel."

"What of Alys?" Jocelin asked.

"She prefers to say here." Sheridan tossed the shawl over her shoulders and went to the door. "I shall take an escort, have no fear."

She was halfway through the door as Jocelin called to her. "Neely is in the hall."

Sheridan acknowledged him with a wave. She didn't want Neely escorting her, of all people, especially if they ran into de Lara. In the dim, cool hall near the Flint Tower, she caught sight of the knight several feet away in a small alcove. His dark eyes fixed curiously on her.

"My lady is leaving?" he asked.

She couldn't decide if she was still angry with him for spilling the evening's events to Jocelin. Neely had only done what he felt he should do, and that was to protect the St. James family even when they could not, or would not, protect themselves. For as many years as she had known him, he was more like family to her, and family always forgave family. But she still did not want him escorting her.

"I am going to church," she said. "Give me a guard and I'll be on my way."

"I will take you myself."

"Nay, you will stay here," she lifted an eyebrow. "Alys is in one of her moods and I need you here should she decide to jump from the window again. I will depend upon you, Neely."

He knew what had happened yesterday but, to his credit, had not said anything to Jocelin. Whatever Alys St. James did anymore didn't surprise him.

"Is it bad?" he asked.

"Bad enough," Sheridan replied. "Please do me this favor. I do not want Jocelin catching wind of her antics."

Neely nodded in resignation. He and Sheridan had spent a good deal of time over the past few years concealing Alys' peculiar behavior. He motioned to two of the guards standing against the wall. "Lady Sheridan wishes to go to church," he said. "See that she is amply protected."

It was more escort than she wanted, but she didn't argue. Leaving the cold halls of the apartment tower, she descended the steps into the cool, bright January sunshine. The Tower grounds were fairly alive with activity, mostly soldiers as they went about their business. There were, in fact, many different Houses on the grounds, probably more than the Tower had seen in quite some time.

People tended to keep to themselves, however. There weren't great social gatherings due to the tense political climate between the king and most of his barons. It was a heady world of intrigue and enemy, of suspicion and loyalty, and no one could be certain that their ally of the moment would be their ally tomorrow. Lives often depended upon silence. Therefore, nearly everyone Sheridan passed barely acknowledged her.

The Chapel of St. Peter was on the opposite side of the compound against the west wall. She walked past the White Tower on her way to the chapel, gazing up at the massive structure and remembering the previous evening with clarity. The yard in which she had met Sean was on the opposite side of the building and she was unable to catch a glimpse of it. Instead, she walked through the dry, cold grounds, thinking the whole place to feel rather desolate.

When she reached the chapel, she left the guards outside. The chapel itself was a long, slender chamber with a soaring ceiling and massive support columns. Long, needle-thin lancet windows lined the walls, running nearly floor to ceiling. There were no pews or benches, only a bare floor of hard-packed dirt. At the back of the chapel, near the door, stood the prayer candles, lit by those who paid a pence for a priestly prayer.

It was an empty chamber for the most part. Sheridan put the shawl over her head and began to walk towards the front of the hall, keeping an eye out for a priest or acolyte. As she drew near the altar, she caught sight of two priests in the shadows, conversing with each other. Taking a quick knee in a show of respect for the altar before her, she folded her hands in prayer.

It wasn't long before she heard footfalls approach. Opening her eyes, she gazed into the face of a young man who could not have been much older than she. His hair was cut in the traditional priestly fashion, the crown of his head shaved bare in piety. He wore rough, if not slightly dirty, brown robes with a large wooden crucifix hanging around his neck. His blue eyes were kindly.

"I am Father Simon," he said softly. "May I be of assistance to my lady?"

She stood up. "I would like a mass said for my father."

"Of course. A shilling it will cost."

She fumbled around in the small purse she had attached to her wrist. All the while, she wondered if it had been foolish for her to think de Lara even went near the chapel. This whole thing had been a ruse. Perhaps it had been a wasted one, and now it would cost her a shilling. Well, perhaps not a wasted trip, but she had truly hoped to catch sight of him again. The Lord of the Shadows more than likely did not suffer the illumination of God's house. She was beginning to feel foolish.

She handed over the money. Father Simon smiled. "Mass will be said at Vespers. Your father's name?"

"Henry St. James."

"Of course. Good day to you, my lady."

As he turned and walked away, Sheridan noticed straw on his robes, embedded near his shoulders, as if he had been laying in the stuff. It stuck her odd that William Marshall had been covered in the same substance. With a shrug, she gave it no further thought. Perhaps all men at the Tower suffered the affliction of mysterious straw.

Sheridan returned to her apartments near the tall, dark Flint Tower without catching another glimpse of Sean de Lara that day.

CHAPTER FOUR

"... The defining moment came as swiftly as a thief in the night. Before I realized the time had come to pass, the cost was already higher than I'd ever dared to dream..."

The Chronicles of Sir Sean de Lara

1206 – 1215 A.D.

"WHERE HAVE YOU been, de Lara?" the king was still in bed, his latest conquest cowering beside him with the filthy bedcovers pulled to her neck. "I called for you earlier and was told you were not to be found."

The room was dark and smelled like painful sex. Sean had long since gotten over the shock of seeing a terrified, naked woman in the king's bed. He had learned to ignore it.

"Even I must eat, sire," he said steadily. "My apologies for not being available when you called. You know that is not the norm."

John threw off the covers, his skinny, naked body for the world to see. He made no move to cover his nudity or conceal the virginal blood on his large, flaccid member. Again, Sean saw none of this; he made a habit of always looking the king in the eye, for a variety of reasons.

"Summon my chamberlain," he said to Sean, who moved to do his bidding even before the command left the king's mouth. "Today is a great day. Do you know why?"

Sean eyed the small, wiry Master of the Chamber as the man scampered into the king's bower. He oft felt pity for the man, having been abused by the fickle monarch for the majority of his adult life. Even though Sean knew the answer to the questions, it was never a good idea to let on that he was indeed aware. It took the joy away from

John of being able to tell him again. And to upset the king was not on his agenda at this moment.

"Pray tell, sire."

John's black eyes flashed. "Today is the day of the battle of Tours, whereupon my father died."

"A glorious day, sire."

The king threw up his arms as the chamberlain put his large, coarse linen shift over his head. "Tonight will be a feast like none other. And that is why I summoned you earlier."

"What is your wish, sire?"

D'Athée joined them at that point. Sean swore the man looked more grizzled and uncivilized by the day. He held a tray with food for the king; as was usual, one of John's Protectors retrieved the food from the kitchen and picked one person at random to taste the meal. This discouraged poisoning the food. Over the years, Sean had been confronted with more than one person who refused to touch the food. Such refusal always led to death. But it had discouraged many from tainting the king's meals.

Gerard set the tray down, eyeing the woman in the bed as the king dressed. It wasn't unusual for the unkempt knight to help himself to the king's leavings and by his expression, his thoughts on the woman were clear. But Sean maintained his focus on the king; never would he imagine himself stooping to d'Athée's actions though he had made it a strict policy never to comment on the other's behavior. Such opinions could be contentious, and in his position, he could not afford conflict with someone he often had to trust his life to. He had to let it be.

"I feel a trip to the Avenue of the Jewelers is in order," John said as he examined the multitude of colored tunics presented to him by the chamberlain. "I would gift myself with something befitting today's celebration."

"As you say, sire. When would you like to leave?"

"As soon as I am finished with my meal. See to it, de Lara."

"It shall be done."

"And another thing," John stopped him before he could leave. "The other night, in the hall, I saw a woman who has whet my interest."

"A name or a description, sire?"

John stood still as his chamberlain, now assisted by the Master of the Wardrobe, fit him with a heavy red tunic. "I cannot give you a name, but she was very young, seated with Jocelin, Bishop of Bath and Glastonbury."

Sean felt a wave of apprehension sweep him. "Those were the daughters of Henry St. James. Which one do you refer to?"

"There were two? I only saw one. The redhead."

An avalanche of relief descended upon him, followed instantly by a fire of guilt. The king must have seen the girl seated there when her sister wasn't present, for surely had he seen Sheridan, his request would have been much different. He shouldn't have been glad that the king's attention was diverted to the other sister, but he was. Now he faced a peculiar dilemma. He did something at that moment that he had never done before, at least not with the king. He bargained.

"Sire, if I may make a suggestion," he said.

John let his arms down as his servants finished securing the golden, lion-themed sash at his waist. "What is it?"

"Forgive my impertinence, but I would offer food for thought in this matter. It may not be a good idea for you to bestow your attention upon the St. James girl at this time."

John looked at him, a flicker of annoyance in his black eyes. "Why not?"

"Because her father was at the heart of the baron's rebellion against the crown. Since his death, his family has the pity of his allies. To summon the daughter, to take your rights as king, may inflame the barons even more. They will not view your bedding the daughter of their beloved dead ally kindly. You may be inviting more than you wish to deal with at this time." He moved towards the king, his blue eyes full of the grim reality of the situation. "The rebellion is like a simmering pot, waiting to boil over. One small incident and it could explode. But if you still desire the girl, I will bring her."

John sniffled, wiping his nose on the sleeve of his tunic. It was apparent that he was contemplating Sean's words. John trusted very few people and de Lara was one of them. The man had never steered him wrong in all of the years he had been in his service. He could see the implications as explained.

"I will consider your words," he said after a moment. The king was never one to agree with his advisors outright. He always manipulated the situation to make it appear as if they were agreeing with him. "Go, now. Prepare my litter."

Sean left without another word, listening to the cries of the woman in the king's bed as d'Athée raped her in the presence of the monarch.

☙

THREE DAYS LATER, Sheridan still had not caught another glimpse of the enigmatic Sean de Lara. She faced the realization that de Lara had no more interest in her than a honey bee had in a wilted flower. Aye, she had been a pretty thing to flatter for an evening, but that was evidently the extent of it. She was coming to feel like Alys did at times, that men were non-committal and easily distracted creatures. It was the first time she had ever felt the sting of rejection.

It wasn't even a sting. It was more like a foolish feeling. No man had ever captured her attention enough to warrant more than a passing thought. But de Lara had. Moderately depressed, she had decided by the third day that she wasn't going to linger on him any longer. Moreover, Jocelin had plans for a clandestine assembly by the end of the week and that was where her focus needed to be. All of the hopes and dreams her father had provided for were finally coming to fruition and her sense of optimism was palpable. She couldn't let thoughts of a man sidetrack her.

But hopes for a new day for England could wait, at least for the moment. Today, she decided that a visit to the Street of the Merchants would be in order. There had been rare times that she had been let out of Lansdown to shop in Glastonbury or in Trowbridge, and she had discovered that she was something of a lavish spender. If she liked what she saw, she bought it. Unfortunately, she'd not learned the art of bartering, as her rich father had simply advised her to make the purchase regardless.

Her mood improved with the prospect of shopping. Alys, after having slept until late morning, barely awoke in time to join her. Alys wasn't a spender, however; she was interested in the food rather than the merchandise. The Street of the Merchants was bordered by the Street of the Bakers, which was convenient for both sisters. The Avenue of the Jewelers, in the Jewish sector to the north and east, wasn't far off, either.

It was a cool day. The fog had rolled in sometime during dawn and had not yet abated. There was mist in the air, enough to make Alys' hair frizz but not enough to truly dampen. Sheridan dressed carefully for the day in a gown of undyed lamb's wool, soft and clinging, accentuating every curve. She wore a belt of silver thread and uncut citrine stones, the tassels of which trailed to her knees. The cloak she wore was heavy wool, of the same undyed color, with a stiff, protective collar and a rabbit fur lining. Her hair was pulled into a single thick braid that draped delicately over one shoulder.

Alys, as usual, was a mess until her sister stepped in to help. In short time, she was dressed in dark blue wool to protect against the chill. Her hair, however, was unmanageable with the mist in the air but, given her maiden status, she let it flow down her back like a giant frizzy mess. All she could speak of, as they left the apartments with their maid and escort, was the bread she would soon be tasting. All Sheridan could think of was the fabric she would soon be buying.

There was another great feast tonight in the Tower in honor of some victory the king accomplished against his brother, Richard, many years ago. Sheridan didn't keep track of such things, for they were petty family squabbles as far as she was concerned. What mattered was the here and now. There was, however, one benefit to this victory feast; as much as she pretended not to care otherwise, she knew de Lara would be somewhere in the hall. If she were to purchase a wonderful fabric and have it back to the apartments by the nooning hour, her maid could baste together an acceptable gown by suppertime.

Her thoughts were idiotic. She knew that even as she climbed into the litter that her men had brought from the stables. With her sister beside her and the maid on a small gray palfrey behind them, they moved from the Tower grounds through the new gate in the Lanthorn Tower and proceeded out to the avenue along the edge of the Thames.

The river was shrouded in mist as the sun struggled to penetrate. Sheridan was glad for her cloak, as the temperature had dropped considerably now that they were outside the protective walls of the Tower. They were nearing the massive bridge that led over the Thames when she caught sight of what she thought was a rat. It was certainly not an unusual site. But as her caravan grew closer, she saw that it was a tiny little dog. As her litter passed, the little dog sat on the edge of the road, its tiny tail wagging. She sat bolt-upright on the litter.

"Stop," she commanded. "Neely, bring me that pup."

Neely was on his charger at the head of the column. Those closest to him heard his audible, impatient sigh. He lifted his three-point visor, of the latest style, and fixed upon the little mutt. His initial reaction was to contest the request, but he wisely kept his mouth shut. Whatever the lady wanted, he would oblige without question. It had long been a policy with him in the hopes that someday, the lady would see him for more than the captain of the guard. He was convinced that blind obedience and kindness would someday be the key to Lady Sheridan's heart.

Armor groaning, he dismounted his steed and clanged to the edge of the dirty avenue. The little dog didn't run; he merely gazed up at Neely with his big black doggy eyes. He was a white beast with little legs, short hair, and a big brown spot on his back. Neely reached down and scooped the mutt into one hand.

He walked over to the litter and extended the hand that held the puppy. Sheridan gently took the dog from his mailed grip.

"Look at him," she cooed. "He is freezing, poor little thing."

The dog wagged his tail happily and licked her furiously on the chin. She laughed out loud as Alys, not strangely, began to complain.

"'Tis cold, Dani," she said. "We must keep moving."

Sheridan was consumed with her happy little acquisition. Neely gave the order to move out and the procession continued to the road that led from the bridge and deep into the bowels of London.

The streets leading to the merchant district were cold, dirty and, at times, dangerous. Neely was on his guard as they made their way through the narrow avenues, passing by citizens of London whose faces were dark with suspicion and curiosity. By the time they reached the busier merchant district, the sun was starting to peek through the fog. Sheridan, having fallen in love with her little pet in the short trek from the Tower to the commercial quarter, perked up at the sight of the merchant stalls.

She climbed off the litter, leaving the dog enfolded within the heavy woolen blanket that had covered her. Though the sun threatened, the air was still cold and she pulled her cloak tightly about her. Her eyes fairly glittered at the sight before her.

Neely approached. "If it pleases my lady, I will have the litter bearers wait here. I will escort you into the avenue."

Sheridan nodded. "You'd better bring another man. I intend to purchase many items today and may need another pair of arms."

Neely emitted a low whistle and motioned to one of his more seasoned soldiers. As the man stepped forward, he turned back to Sheridan.

"If my lady is ready?"

She grinned. "Always."

He and the soldier followed several feet behind Sheridan and Alys. Their very first shop was a perfume den, a place that stank like a sheik's harem. Exotic oils from all over the known world filled the shelves of the dingy little shop and it wasn't long before Alys smelled in horrible combination. Sheridan was wise enough not to rub the oil on herself, but Alys got caught up in the goods and found herself a victim of her sister's enthusiasm.

Neely stood by the door, watching Sheridan forcibly rub scented oil on Alys' arm and grinning when Alys would snort and howl. As he watched, he thought to himself that it was good to see Sheridan smile again. She'd smiled so little since her father's death. Today was the first time in months he'd actually seen shades of the old Sheridan return.

It seemed like ages passed as he stood and watched them. Finally, Sheridan settled on Gardenia and Lilac and paid extra to have the oils placed in lovely glass phials. Alys couldn't remember which fragrance she liked best so she settled for something that smelled like Apple Blossoms. The perfume miser wrapped the goods in dried grass and an envelope of fabric, handing them off to the happy women. As Sheridan left the shop, she handed the packages to Neely and continued on down the avenue.

Nearing the second shop, this one of fabric goods, Alys spotted a vendor across the street selling apples cooked in honey and spices. She tore off across the street.

"Go with her," Sheridan told Neely. "Don't let her buy more than one. And for heaven sakes, don't let her wander further away. There are smells all over this street that will lure her."

Neely didn't like leaving Sheridan, but did as he was asked. The seasoned soldier remained behind with Sheridan, posted just outside the stall door of the fabric merchant.

This stall was bigger than the perfume miser's. It was lined with bolts of fabric from every part of the world. Sheridan started at one end and inspected every piece, every thread, in every bolt, until she reached the other side. The merchant had spied her early on and had taken to following her through the accounting of his wares, answering any questions she may have. Her questions were intelligent, usually about the country of origin and the materials used.

A fabric called Albatross was a particular favorite; it was very fine, all-wool, and favored by women in the cloister for their wimples. Another favorite fabric was called Brocaded Brilliantine – a silk and wool mix styled in a brocade pattern. Lastly, the merchant showed her something new from Paris called French Crepon, a delicate yet durable weave.

In a relatively short span of time, she had selected three fabrics – a Brocaded Brilliantine of deep green with a golden undertone, an Albatross of pale yellow, and a French Crepon of ruby. The merchant also had all manner of notions to accompany the fabrics such as thread and faux decorations. One such decoration was a bird made from sawdust and real feathers. It looked positively alive. Delighted, Sheridan purchased it with the intent of having it paired with the ruby satin.

She also purchased a variety of delicate Irish lace, woven with golden thread as fine as a spider's web. Sheridan appreciated good craftsmanship, as she herself had never had a particular talent for needlework. Handing the fabric off to the soldier waiting outside the door, she proceeded down the avenue.

The street was quite crowded by now, mostly with nobles seeking finery whilst visiting London. For many of those from the far reaches of England, a visit to the Street of the Merchants was required lest their reputation suffer. Street vendors dotted the street, selling soft wheat cakes, honey candy, fruit, and meat on a stick. Sheridan looked around for Alys and finally found her at the cart of another street vendor who was selling fruited cakes. Even across the distance, Neely caught her eye and she simply shook her head in a combination of disgust and resignation. She didn't blame Neely for not keeping a rein on her sister's appetite; she'd never been able to do it very well, either. Alys would eat herself to death some day and they'd all be to blame.

Sheridan became aware of a rumble of noise, gradually increasing in intensity. There seemed to be some commotion on the opposite end of the street, but she couldn't clearly see what was happening. It looked to her as if there were a great many soldiers about. But passing notice was all she gave it as her attention fell on the next stall. In addition to more fabric, there were also a variety of items that had been brought from the Continent – carved wooden figurines from the land of the Norse, beaded jewelry from Greece, and little blocks of incense that looked like dirt but that, when lit, created smoke of the most wonderful scent.

She couldn't keep her hands off the finery. Her fingers soon smelled of myrrh and sandalwood as she handled the little blocks of incense and put them to her nose. Then they made her sneeze and she had to put them back. The bolts of material were of less variety than the previous stall, but she rifled through them nonetheless. She did manage to come across a very fine blue wool from Scotland, which she promptly put on her purchase list. Alys would look wonderful in the color. Noticing that there was a shelf of material next to the front door that she had missed, she went to inspect a bolt of thin, gauzy linen when a shadow moved through the doorway. She saw no more than that before someone abruptly pulled her away from the door and back against the wall.

It was dark, as whoever had her against the wall was quite a bit larger than she and covered her with his entire body. Startled, not to mention terrified, she opened her mouth to protest when a mailed glove covered her lips.

"My apologies, my lady," a quiet, very deep voice rumbled. "I did not mean to startle you, but you must stay here, just for a moment."

She recognized de Lara's voice immediately. Looking up, she was able to discern his features in the weak light of the shop. He dropped his hand from her mouth and she was able to speak.

"What's wrong?" she demanded. "Why have you restrained me?"

His clear blue eyes were steady and appraising as he gazed upon her. He was in his armor, an enormous man made even larger by the protection he wore. All she could see was the face beneath the raised visor, the features everyone had told her to be terrified of. Even now, she could not summon the will.

"I saw your sister outside and assumed you were somewhere close by," he said. His tone turned serious. "Please do as I ask; stay here and do not leave until the king clears this avenue."

She was torn between the thrill of seeing him and the frightening ambiguity of his words. "I do not understand."

His hands gripped her upper arms; she could feel his strength through his mail, her fabric. It was the most powerful, wonderful feeling she had ever known. "I mean that you should not," he said quietly. "But I would ask that you trust me in this matter."

She wasn't sure how to take him. She could hear the commotion outside as the king approached. "You do not think… you do not believe that I would try to harm the king somehow? Is that what you think?"

His eyes flickered with humor. "Nay."

"Then why do you wrest me against the wall like a common criminal?"

"What I do is for your protection, not the king's."

An idea occurred to her and she was coming to understand what he meant. The light of comprehension dawned. "You do not want him to see me, is that it?"

He didn't answer. He continued to gaze down at her, thinking he'd never in his life seen a lovelier creature. Three days of not seeing her, of not witnessing her beauty or coming to know her wit, had left him starving like a man without food. But he had been the shadow of the king and the king had been busy, affording him no opportunity to break away.

"I would express my deep regret at not having been given the opportunity to see you for the past few days," he changed the subject as delicately as he could. "I hope you have been well."

Part of her wanted to hear his words very much. The other part of her did not want to be sucked into the mysterious games he liked to play.

"I have," she replied, rather casually. "A pity that you have been so busy."

"More than you know. But I would like to remedy that."

"What do you mean?"

A grin played on his lips. "Must I be plain?"

"I am afraid so."

He lifted an eyebrow with feigned reluctance. "Very well. I have been thinking on this subject since the night we walked together in the yard so I may as well spell it out. But first, you should know that I am not a man given to whims. I do not make swift decisions."

She cocked her head. "That makes no sense. You are a knight. Sometimes you must make split-second decisions that will affect your very life. And now you say that you do not make swift decisions?"

Now his eyebrows furrowed. "Cheeky wench. That is not what I mean."

"You said you were going to be plain. You have not been plain."

He gave her a look that suggested she was in for a spanking if she didn't curb her mouth. "You have not let me be plain, nor have you allowed me to explain myself. Do you want to hear this or not?"

"If I must."

An expression of momentary outrage was replaced by a reluctant grin. "You are not going to make this easy for me, are you?"

She returned his smile, a radiant gesture that lit up the room. "Did you expect any less?"

"God help me, I did not."

"Then pray continue."

"I will if you will shut up."

She pressed her lips together in a gesture of complete silence. His eyes twinkled at her. "Now, if I may continue," he went on. "What I was going to say was that I would like to…."

He suddenly trailed off. There was a small window for ventilation over Sheridan's head. Sean caught sight of the king's procession passing by the stall, tracking every sound, every movement. He remained as unmoving as stone; the only indication that he was not a statue was the slight movement of his eyes. She felt his grip tighten on her arm before he finally looked down at her once again. His manner was suddenly very serious.

"Stay here," he whispered. "Do not leave until the king has gone. Do you comprehend?"

There was something in his tone that frightened her. She nodded her head. "Aye."

He thought to give her a smile of encouragement but stopped short. He took both of her hands in his massive gloves, holding them gently, urgently. "I am going to ask that you trust me, Lady Sheridan."

She was thoroughly puzzled. "What…?"

"As you once trusted me with your sister's life, I am asking you to do so again."

She had no idea what he meant. He suddenly kissed both of her hands and was gone. The man moved so swiftly that the sharp action took her breath away. Her heart thumping with fear, and a bit of excitement from his kiss, she hid behind the fabric bolts enough to be able to peer from the open door to see what was happening. Powerful curiosity had the better of her.

The king was speaking with Alys.

CB

SEATED IN A fine chair in the antechamber of her borrowed apartments at the Tower, Sheridan stared into the weak fire. The flames licked at the blackened brick, crackling unsteadily as the sun waned. Soon, night would be upon them all and the celebratory feast would commence. But Sheridan had no thoughts of feasting this night. All she could think of was the horrors of the afternoon.

Alys had been commandeered by the king. Nay, not by the king; by Sean himself. Sheridan had heard her sister screaming as she was taken from the Street of the Merchants, the sounds of horror echoing in her brain. When Neely had tried to intervene, he had been hit from behind by a massive, burly man and hauled away, unconscious. Someone had told her that he had been taken back to the Tower and thrown in the vault. She didn't even know Neely's fate and the trepidation of it ate at her.

Horrified, Sheridan had been escorted back to her Tower apartment by what was left of her guard. She had sent for Jocelin immediately and, in a rage, the bishop had set off in search of Alys. That had been several hours ago and she had yet to receive any word. Though she could have very easily collapsed into tears, she had to remain strong until she knew the fate of both her sister and Neely. Crying would not accomplish anything.

Her new little puppy would have been a joyous diversion had she not been so troubled. After feeding the animal some scraps from the morning meal, the little dog had slept beside her the entire afternoon. She petted the dog absently now and again, but her mind was clearly elsewhere. And with the onset of night, her anxiety was growing.

Trust me, de Lara had said. She had up until the moment she saw him take Alys away. Now she didn't know what to think. All she could hear was Alys' screams rattling in her head. She had to close her eyes to erase the pain. Maybe she should have listened to what everyone had tried to tell her. *The man is pure evil.*

"M'lady," her little maid was standing in the bedchamber door. "What… what do you wish to wear this night?"

Sheridan looked at the woman as if she had gone mad. But in the same breath, she knew that the king would be at the feast. If the king was there, then de Lara would also be there, and possibly even Alys. She had to go, no matter how much she did not want to.

"My white silk that Father brought from France," she said. "I would wear the gold girdle with it."

The maid fled to prepare the garment. It was the most expensive gown Sheridan owned, a magnificent white piece that hung off her shoulders with a wide, rounded neck, a long waistline, and huge belled sleeves. Gold and white embroidery lined the neckline, edge of the sleeves, and the entire hemline of the gown. It was, in a word, spectacular. For some reason, she wanted to look her best tonight. One must always look their best when challenging the king.

She dressed carefully. The Gardenia oil she had purchased that day was used liberally. She left her long, silken hair unbound and flowing down her back in soft curls. Beeswax with a hint of ocher colored her lips. Gazing at herself in the polished bronze mirror, she saw someone different gazing back at her. It was hard to pinpoint, but somehow the reflection had matured. There was wisdom to the gaze, stiffness to the back that suggested an unwavering drive. She also realized, at that moment, that she would trade herself for Alys if she had to. Perhaps that was what she was attempting to do; strike a bargain with the man her father hated most. She wanted to make herself tempting. She hoped that Henry would forgive her.

There was a knock at the door. Snapped from her thoughts, Sheridan practically ran to the panel, throwing it open and fully expecting to see Jocelin and, hopefully, Neely and Alys too. Instead, her eyes widened with surprise and horror. Sean de Lara stood in the hall.

"*You*!" she gasped.

She tried to slam the door but Sean caught it before it could close. He wedged himself between the door and the frame as she struggled to shove it closed. He could have easily burst into the room, tossing Sheridan halfway across the floor in the process. But he simply held his ground.

"My lady," he said steadily. "I come with news. Please let me in."

She did something at that moment that she hadn't done since her father's passing. She unexpectedly burst into tears and Sean gently pushed the door open. She didn't resist. He stepped in and shut the panel behind him.

He stood there a moment, watching her sob. She looked absolutely radiant in the white gown. He wanted very much to pull her into his arms and comfort her.

"Lady," he said in a soft, gentle growl. "Please do not cry. There are things we must discuss."

She looked at him, furiously wiping the tears from her eyes. "You… you told me to trust you and then you took my sister."

He did put his hands on her, then. "I know," he murmured, steering her towards the nearest chair. "I had to."

She allowed him to seat her. He pulled up a stool from the hearth and sat in front of her. He gently took one of her hands into his great palm.

"Alys is fine," he said. "She will see you at the feast tonight."

She wiped a stray tear, her luminous eyes glimmering like a clear blue lake. "She… she is well? She is unharmed?"

He brought her hand to his mouth. "Aye," his lips brushed against her flesh as he spoke. "She is quite well. She had an afternoon of sweets and conversation with the king."

The tears faded and she experienced the sensation of his warm lips against her skin. It sent bolts of excitement through her veins. But his words garnered her focus at the moment. "Sweets and conversation?" she repeated. "But… I do not understand. Everyone knows that the king… when he sees a maiden he wishes, that he simply… or you…."

He smiled, his lips still against her hand. It was as much as he dared do though he very much wanted to do more.

"That is why I asked you to stay in the merchant stall, for your own safety," he said. "The king has not seen you yet. But he has seen Alys already. I am sorry for my methods, but it was imperative that I act as I did in order to keep her safe. Suffice it to say that she is untouched."

Sheridan was still puzzled. "I do not understand any of this," she muttered. "If she is well, why did you not bring her back to me? And what of Neely? Where is he?"

"Your captain is in the vault," he replied. "I shall release him tomorrow. Other than an aching head, he too is well enough. But I have other news regarding the bishop."

"Jocelin?" she said, her voice laced with panic. "What has happened to him?"

Sean took a long, deep breath. He had only just calmed her and did not want to upset her again, but he was forced to speak the truth. "The bishop came to the king's apartments demanding Alys. I am afraid he was rather aggressive. I could not intervene, you understand. I was busy making sure that Alys did not come to harm."

This time, she gripped his hand. It was the first time she had done so. Feeling her soft, warm fingers against his flesh was a sensation he'd not felt in years. He'd forgotten how much he'd missed it.

"What happened to him?" she asked softly. "Please tell me."

"He is also in the vault."

Her eyebrows lifted. "The king threw a man of the church in the vault?"

His reply was strangely impassive. "It is of little consequence. The king has a long history of contention with the Church. They cannot do any more to him than they already have."

"But Jocelin is a bishop," she insisted. "Why did this happen?"

Sean cocked an eyebrow. "When he started swinging his staff at the king's guard, there was little more to do. Even bishops must know that they cannot take to violence against the king."

She just sat there, dumbfounded. It seemed as if there was no point in arguing, for she knew what Jocelin was capable of. She'd seen it herself on occasion. When he had left her apartment hours before, he had been angry enough to kill.

"So what now?" she asked softly. "What will become of him?"

Sean pursed his lips thoughtfully, looking down at her hand enclosed within his. He stroked her fingers for a moment. "When the king's anger cools, he will most likely be released."

She was still as he rubbed her fingers, half of her thrilled with the newness of the sensation, the other half embroiled in the mayhem that was enveloping her.

"Jocelin gave John a convenient excuse to be rid of him," she said quietly. "The king knows that Jocelin is one of the leaders of the opposition against his tyranny. He took advantage of Jocelin's rage and used the excuse to jail him. With Jocelin out of the way, there is one less powerful foe to align against him."

Sean stopped rubbing her fingers and looked at her. His clear blue eyes were impassive. "I would not know, my lady."

She gently, but firmly, pulled her fingers from his grasp. "I think that you do," she murmured. "And perhaps it is best that you leave now."

"Why?"

"Because I ask it."

He stood up without another word and went to the door. Sheridan remained seated, staring at the lancet windows across the room, wondering why she felt so utterly horrible at the moment. He was leaving, yet he said he had saved Alys from the king's lust. Politics came into play and she grew scared. Her mind began whirling with doubt, fear, and finally hope. Abruptly, she stood.

"Sir Sean," she said.

He paused, his hand on the door latch. "My lady?"

She hated apologizing; it had never been one of her strong suits. "I… I do not mean to be cruel, for if what you say is true, then I owe you my gratitude for saving my sister yet again." She twisted her fingers as she approached him, confusion on her lovely face. "But there is so much about this world we find ourselves a part of that I do not understand. You, for instance; you are my enemy. Everyone tells me to fear you, yet you have been nothing but kind to me. When you had no reason whatsoever for protecting my sister, it seems that you did so. You have no reason to release Neely, yet you say that you will. And finally, you come to my apartment, kiss my hand and tell me that all will be well as if you and I are fighting for the same cause. I find you tremendously puzzling, Sir Sean. I am unsure how to read you."

He took his hand off the latch, a faint smile on his lips. He made no move to take her hand again or move closer to her.

"As well you should be," his voice was a gentle growl. "I can only tell you this; when I look at you, I do not see politics."

She lifted an eyebrow. "What is it that you see?"

The corner of his mouth twitched. "I see the most beautiful woman I have ever had the fortune to witness. And she has wit, charm and grace."

She was flattered. "So… is it your wish that we should be friends?"

He gave her an expression, gently done, that suggested she was mad. "Oh, no, my lady," he said softly. "Not friends."

"Then I do not understand."

His clear blue eyes gazed steadily at her, never wavering. "More than friends."

She comprehended his meaning; at least she thought she did. "If you think that our acquaintance should be something clandestine and disgraceful, think again. I'll have no part in being a… a concubine."

He laughed at her. "Nothing so scandalous."

"Is that so? Well, I still do not understand. But, then again, I have not understood anything about you since the day we met."

"I wouldn't worry overly. You'll have the rest of your life to understand me."

"The rest of *my* life?"

"That is usual when people marry."

Her mouth popped open. "Marry?"

He shook his head as if she was the most unintelligent creature on the face of the earth. Throwing caution to the wind, he threw an arm around her slender waist and pulled her hard against him. Sheridan gasped at the swiftness of the movement, at the shock and delight of being pressed up against his massive torso. He held her fast, a great warm embrace, his face lingering an inch above her own.

"Aye, you silly wench," he growled. "In case you have not yet understood my meaning, you will marry me. There is no one else on earth worthy of you."

She'd never been held by a man in this fashion before; the heat, the excitement, was nearly too much to bear. Her heart was racing and her mouth was dry, but all she could think, feel or hear was Sean's presence around her. It was an all-encompassing, all-consuming sensation.

His lips came down on her mouth, softly at first, but more insistently by the second. It was hot, warm, and deliciously wet. When he spoke, his lips were against her own.

"Agree with me," he commanded softly.

"I cannot," she breathed.

He kissed her again, hard. "Aye, you can. Agree to marry me."

His kisses had her head swimming. "Agree?" she repeated stupidly.

"Aye," he kissed her again, his tongue moving along her lower lip. "Say yes."

"Yes?"

He gently suckled her lower lip when his tongue was done playing with her. "Good girl," he murmured. "Now, I will see you at the feast tonight."

With one more succulent kiss, he was gone. The door closed and Sheridan stood there for one solid minute before she realized that he had left. The only thought she could manage to grasp was one of shock.

What have I done?

☙

WHEN SEAN RETURNED to John's apartments, he lingered out of sight for a nominal amount of time before making his presence known. It was his usual method of operation so that the king, and others, would not know his pattern of coming and going. There was far too much spying going on between noble and king, soldiers and officers, and he did not want to get caught up in that foolishness. There were those who had tried to watch his movements over the years but they had only come to embarrassment or, in some cases, harm. Sean de Lara was not a man to be watched or monitored. It was best if no one tried.

Even as he lingered in John's receiving room, watching the king hold audience with some of his more loyal barons, his mind was elsewhere. Thoughts of the fairest maiden in all the land filled his brain, numbing him to the activities going on in the room. The king was angry about something; that much was obvious. Sean watched his furious actions but did not hear his words. The only words he could hear, at the moment, were his own.

You will marry me.

He wasn't sure where those words sprang from, but they had come nonetheless. He was not sorry in the least, though he was still rather surprised. He'd never considered himself the marriageable type. His work was his wife, the needs of the king his mistress, and there was no room for anything else. He hadn't even thought on the implications of his proposal or command, whichever one chose to call it. Sheridan St. James was an heiress, and a very wealthy one at that. She was governed by the Bishop of Bath and Glastonbury, the very man who was in the vault at the moment under arrest. Sean could only imagine how the bishop would react when all of this came to light. He knew that Sheridan would not be the one to tell him. It would be Sean.

What he refused to entertain at the moment were thoughts of what it would mean to the king. The term traitor came to mind. He suspected the king would never fully trust him again, yet he also knew that the man would eventually see the political benefit of such a union. He was also fully aware that John would view his wife as something of communal property; it was the thought that disturbed him the most. The political aspect, he could deal with. But his wife would most certainly not be communal property. For that reason, and that reason alone, he would be more than willing to keep the union secret. The less John knew the safer Sheridan would be.

But he could not ignore the fact that the political connotations were almost unfathomable. For a man that had made politics his life's work, it was strange that the politics of such a union, at the moment, did not overly concern him. Sheridan St. James could have nothing but the clothes on her back for all he cared; he wasn't interested in her wealth or political connections. All he knew was that, from the moment he first spoke to the woman, she cleared all else from his mind like a divine flood, washing away the old in favor of the new. He'd hardly spent more than an hour of combined time with her, but still, that time had been nothing like he'd ever experienced. She made him feel alive and warm. She made him feel that life was worth living. He wanted to feel that way forever.

He was distracted from his thoughts as the king abruptly rose from his gilded chair and began stomping around the room. Sean paid attention, thinking perhaps that it might be wise.

"It will do no good to smack the answer out of Jocelin," the king was saying. "He'll not tell us anything and I do not want to risk the wrath of the Church. Already I have pushed them by tossing their bishop in the vault. Even now, I wait for a decree informing me that they have sent word of my actions to Rome."

Fitz Pons was on the opposite end of the conversation. He tended to be the most cowering, the most acquiescent, so the nobles would use him like a shield when dealing with the king. His submissive disposition usually buffered the king's unpredictable temperament.

"Sire," Fitz Pons said. "We know that de Braose arrived this afternoon. I have been told by several reliable sources that he has already met with Hugh de Burgh and the Earl of Salisbury. Given the swiftness of this meeting, I can only surmise that whatever they are planning, they are planning quickly."

"But what?" John exploded. "I employ legions of spies, the best in the world. Why can no one tell me what this means?"

Sean knew he meant him. But he waited until the king actually addressed him before offering any information.

"De Lara," he said. "What do you know of this?"

Sean stepped forward, watching the room of men instinctively shift away from him. "I know that when de Braose arrived, Salisbury and de Burgh were waiting for him. They met at a tavern on St. Ciles hoping that they would not be noticed."

John seemed pleased that his most reliable emissary had current information. "Excellent," his black eyes glittered. "Do we know what transpired?"

Sean shook his head. "It is not known, sire. But at the conclusion of their meeting, Salisbury set off for Billingsgate House."

"Was he followed?"

"He was followed. We discovered he went straight for Rochester, who is supposed to be at St. Bartholomew's with the other bishops. Rochester, interestingly enough, was in disguise. Once Salisbury left, Rochester sent out four riders, all four in different directions. We were unable to track them beyond the city limits."

John's eyes narrowed. "Something is amiss, I can feel it," he hissed. There was panic in his features. "What do you intend to do about it, de Lara? The waves of dissention are growing. They are organizing now!"

Sean lifted an eyebrow. "One of the main pieces to the puzzle is in our vault at this moment. Though we cannot coax truths from the Bishop of Bath and Glastonbury as we would like, there is perhaps someone we can coax."

"Who?"

His reply was as impassive as always, the features on his powerful face without emotion or care. Every man in the room was frighteningly thankful that the name from his lips was not their own. They'd all heard tale of de Lara's methods of torture. They were legendary. Agony was too tame a word.

"Neely de Moreville."

The king's features suffered happy illumination. "Henry St. James' captain," he breathed. "I'd forgotten he was in our vault along with Jocelin. Surely he would know the heart of the matter."

"It is possible, sire," Sean said. "But, then again, he is a mere knight and perhaps not privy to the private dealings of his lords."

John was animated with glee, paranoia. "Find out. By whatever means necessary. And take Gerard with you; his methods of persuasion can be quite barbaric."

"By your command, sire."

Uglier words were never uttered.

ଓଃ

SHERIDAN SAT ALONE at the table in the great feasting hall. There was no Alys, no Jocelin, and no Neely. She felt exposed and apprehensive. After her encounter with Sean earlier, she also felt disoriented. Four hours later, thoughts of his kisses still clouded her mind.

The great hall was warm, well-lit and fragrant with fresh rushes. Much wine had already been served. She had imbibed more than she should have out of sheer nerves. She could only pray that William did not join the table; she was in no mood for his flirting tonight. What she wanted more than anything, at the moment, was to see Alys.

"Lady Sheridan St. James?" a male voice spoke. "Excuse me, but are you the Lady Sheridan?"

Sheridan shook herself from her lonely thoughts, glancing across the table. A man in pieces of armor stood there, short of stature, clean-shaven, with black hair and nearly black eyes. He smiled kindly.

"May I know who asks?" she answered.

His smile broadened. "I am Guy de Braose. I believe our fathers were friends."

She blinked as the name registered. "Of course," she said. "I was told you were coming to London."

He gestured to the bench before him. "May I sit, my lady?"

"Of course."

"Thank you." He settled himself down in the chair; he was, truthfully, not much bigger than Sheridan. He had a very youthful, handsome face with big dark eyes. "I do apologize for not being here earlier. We ran into some foul weather which delayed our arrival."

"No apologies necessary," she assured him. "We are glad you have arrived safe."

Guy smiled his thanks and glanced around. "Is Jocelin arrived yet?"

"Aye," she said, wondering how much she should tell him. But she knew he was a trusted ally so she told him what she knew. "There was a bit of trouble this afternoon, I am afraid. Jocelin will not be attending our feast this night."

"Oh," Guy's expression washed with disappointment. "I pray his health is good."

"It is," she assured him. "Sir Guy, I shall be frank. The king somewhat forcibly demanded my sister's company today and when Jocelin found out, he went to the king and created something of a ruckus. I am afraid that he was put in the vault."

Guy's eyebrows rose. "He threw the bishop in the vault?"

She nodded. "My captain of the guard is also there."

"And your sister?"

"I am told she will be joining us this evening, unharmed."

Guy puffed out his cheeks. It was a lot to absorb. "My God," he breathed. "I wish I had been here sooner. Perhaps I could have helped."

"I appreciate your support, but I am sure there is nothing you could have done," she said.

Guy smiled at her, a bashful gesture. He seemed mildly awkward at ease, like a shy adolescent. "Would… would you mind if I sat next to you, my lady? I feel as if we are shouting at each other across the table and I suspect this conversation is not something we would want others to hear."

She saw no harm in it. "I'd be pleased."

He wasted no time in rounding the table and taking a seat next to her. With another shy smile, he collected his goblet and took a healthy drink of his wine. As the conversation stalled, Sheridan looked around the room, seeking her sister.

"I was sorry to hear about your father's passing," Guy said. "My father was very distressed."

She looked at him, forcing a smile. "Thank you," she said. "I know my father thought very highly of Sir Reginald. Did he come with you?"

Guy shook his head. "We've problems on the Marches. He is needed more there."

"Ah," she understood. "I have heard from my father that you have had much trouble as of late."

Guy shrugged. "They wish to rule their own lands. We wish to rule it for them."

She shook her head, taking another sip of her wine. "It seems that war and rebellion are everywhere."

Guy did not respond directly. He changed the subject. "Salisbury should be joining us shortly. Truthfully, I thought he would be here by now."

It occurred to them both that the room seemed to be oddly absent of the king's opponents. Sheridan and Guy seemed to be the only pair with the exception of Hugh de Burgh on the opposite side of the room. He'd not acknowledged them; in fact, Sheridan didn't know him on sight but Guy did. He had pointed the man out to her. Sheridan was coming to wonder if Alys would ever join them, and she was furthermore coming to feel nervous about the atmosphere of the entire room. As the celebration of King Henry's death twenty years earlier, it was naturally full of John's supporters. Her uneasiness grew.

If Guy felt it, he did not say so. Though seemingly a slip of a man, he nonetheless had a great maturity about him. Growing up in the ruthless House of de Braose had done that for him. The family had a history of brutes and deviants, interspersed with men of good character. According to her father, Guy was one of those blessed with such noble traits. Sheridan could sense that.

The clear sound of coronets suddenly pealed throughout the room, announcing the arrival of the king. The entire chamber jumped in anticipation. As Sheridan and Guy rose to their feet, Sheridan heard someone hissing behind her.

She turned, seeing her little maid cowering against the wall. The girl looked terrified and Sheridan immediately went to her.

"What is it?" she demanded. "What's wrong?"

The girl looked as if she'd been weeping. "My lady," she whispered. "Sir Neely… he is come back."

"Where is he?"

"At the apartment, my lady. He is badly hurt."

Sheridan's heart lodged in her throat. "Hurt?" she repeated, shocked. "What happened?"

The girl shook her head, wiping her nose. "He would not say. He is on the floor of the chamber. I think he is dying!"

Sheridan fought her panic. Guy had walked up behind her, listening. When she turned around, he was standing there.

"I must leave," she said to him.

"I heard," he replied. "Who is Sir Neely?"

Sheridan realized that she was actually shaking. "The captain of my guard. He was in the vault this afternoon."

Guy's features tightened. "It sounds as if the king's men have had a little fun with him."

Sheridan couldn't manage a reply. She was heading for a side exit just as the king was entering the hall. Guy thought perhaps it would be the chivalrous thing to escort her. He had no idea it was the worst move he could ever make.

Sean was watching them from the shadows.

CHAPTER FIVE

"... War is a man's game, though no one thought to tell her that. She was not only playing with fire, she was seducing it...."

The Chronicles of Sir Sean de Lara

1206 – 1215 A.D.

THE CORRIDOR OUTSIDE of her apartment was dark and void of the usual guard. Sheridan should have thought that to be strange, but she was too concerned for Neely. When the door to her chambers finally opened, she walked headlong into a room full of the unexpected.

The Earl of Salisbury sat near the blazing hearth along with the bishops of Rochester, Lincoln, Worcester and Coventry. William Marshall stood near a bowl of winter fruit, gorging himself on ripe pears and throwing the cores to the puppy, who was dancing at his feet.

Shocked, she delved further into the room and was greeted by the Earl of Warenne. The Earl of Arundel was back in a corner, conversing quietly with Henry de Neville. The barons Fitz Herbert and Fitz Hugh rounded out the company, older men who had seen much fighting with Henry the Second and Henry St. James. The most powerful men in England filled her antechamber, all quite calmly, and all quite deliberately.

Sheridan's surprise was full-blown. She had no idea how to react. But it was especially evident when the Bishop of Bath and Glastonbury took her by the arm.

"Jocelin," she gasped, hugging him fiercely. "When were you released?"

He kissed her hand. "Earlier this afternoon by Neely."

Her head jerked towards the bedchamber door; Neely stood there, not a bloody mark on him, his dark eyes glittering at her. He bowed chivalrously.

"Oh, my," she sighed heavily, trying to get a grasp on the situation. "But who released Neely? I do not understand any of this. I was told that Neely was...."

"I know," Jocelin patted her hand. "We had to get you back to your apartment without raising suspicions. 'Twas I who sent Millie after you with tales of death."

Her gaze was still on Neely. "Are you well? How did you get out?"

Neely moved to stand next to her. "It was quite strange, actually," he said. "A bear of a man opened my cell and grabbed me by the arm, took me to Jocelin's cell one flight up, and then told us both to leave. I don't know who he was or why he let us go. But I did not ask questions."

Another surprise in a night that had been full of them. She mulled over Neely and Jocelin's release for a few moments until the activity in the room caught her attention again. She looked around the room, awed by the company therein.

"All of these men," she whispered to Jocelin. "There was no indication in the corridor of their presence. No guards at all."

"Better not to raise suspicions with a collage of sentinels from all over England announcing a room full of nobles."

She understood, somewhat. "But why are they here?"

Jocelin's eyes twinkled. "With the king celebrating the anniversary of his father's death, certainly he did not expect any of us to attend. So, while he is occupied, so are we. Under his very nose."

Sheridan could see the strategy now. Shock fading, she was coming to understand the brilliance of such an assembly. No guards in the hall to announce their meeting, and assembling as the king himself was else occupied.

"The last I saw, he was entering the great hall as Jesus entered Jerusalem on Palm Sunday," she said. "Everyone was at his feet."

"Then he shall be occupied for some time," Jocelin took her by the elbow and pulled her into the center of the room. "No better time to start than the present. Gentle nobles, if you please. Now that Glastonbury has arrived, let us begin."

The men around the room put aside their small conversations and Jocelin stepped into the center.

"Thank you for your attention," he said. "I suspect our time is limited to the duration of John's degenerate feast, so I shall come to the point. Henry?"

De Neville moved forward. A thin, wiry man, his family had been a fixture in Northumberland since the days of William the Conqueror. He was cunning and he was wise.

"Good men of England," he began. "There is no need to go into the details of why we are here; we've know this time has been long in coming. With John's recent defeat in France to reclaim his northern territories, he has once again returned to London and to levy more taxes against us and our properties. There was a time when the king would consult with his barons for such a thing, but that time is over. John views himself as an omnipotent emperor, not a king with responsibilities towards his people. We all know that he will tax us into the ground if we do not act."

The nobles glanced at each other, some knowingly, some nervously. Sheridan knew exactly what they were referring to; she and her father had had long discussions about the consensus of the allies. Though as a woman she should have kept silent, as Henry St. James' heiress, she controlled the powers of the earldom. She would speak on behalf of her father.

"I have fifteen hundred retainers camped ten miles to the east along the Thames," she said. "The Bishop of Bath and Glastonbury commands another four hundred. All of these men are awaiting the command to move."

The room was silent with the heaviness of the realization. Everything they had been planning, the secret happenings of months past, was finally coming to bear. They were perhaps a bit ashamed that a woman had been the first one to offer arms. Arundel finally spoke.

"I have two thousand men just north of the city," he said. "They can be ready to march at dawn provided we are all in agreement."

Guy had been relatively unnoticed since the moment he entered the room. He, too, had been shocked by the men unexpectedly receiving him in the St. James antechamber, but his shock had just as quickly disappeared. His father had told him to expect something like this and he was moderately prepared.

"I speak for my father, gentlemen," he said, his voice wise beyond his years. "If London is to be taken, you have de Braose support. Though we've war on the Marches, I have brought five hundred men with me. My father sends his approval for this action."

"It's not merely the action," Sheridan said, still hesitant to speak her mind in such auspicious company but feeling strongly that she should. "Once London is captured, what then? Where is this document I have heard tale of from my father, a charter that will ensure the monarchy will treat the barons with fairness?"

"I have it," William Marshall spoke, like the voice of God. "As Earl of Pembroke, I have appointed myself constable of the document. It has been worded mostly by Stephen, Archbishop of Canterbury and William, Bishop of London, but certainly we have all had a say in the content."

"Is it complete, my lord?" Sheridan asked. "Is it something that will justify our actions should we decide to move forward?"

William shook his head. "It is not yet absolute, my lady. That is why we've met here this night, to complete this document that the king will be bound to govern by."

William snapped his long, gnarled fingers and a man emerged from the shadows, a steward bearing the Marshall cross. From the folds of the man's tunic appeared a long, cylindrical tube, from which he pulled forth a fragile, yellowed vellum. The steward set it upon the table in the center of the room and the others looked at it with varied degrees of interest. It was a large document, full of careful writing.

Sheridan watched the others vie for a better look at the manuscript. She stood back, out of the way, her mind churning with thoughts that Henry St. James planted in her head. She could not rest until she had answers.

"My lord Marshall," she said. "I mean no disrespect, of course, but if I am to order my army to march on London and in essence, create an act of treachery, then I would have my deed supported by a valid foundation from this body of men. That is to say, if I am to march, then let it be for a reason. Let the king be able to behold that reason and fulfill it as required. I will not march for marching's sake. I will not be a traitor for traitor's sake."

As she finished, nearly every man in the room was looking at her. Arundel actually smiled but deferred all comments to the Marshall. He was, after all, the one she had addressed.

"Well said, little Henry," the Marshall said after a moment. The men around the table chuckled softly, as did Sheridan. "The reason is before you. We are reviewing it as you speak. But you will draw your own conclusion; if this document is not sufficient reason for you to march on our king, then I shall not require it, nor will I be disappointed if you do not. You must make your choice."

"Then if we approve the contents of this charter, we will move immediately to secure London in an effort to force the king into agreeing to our terms?"

"London is our hostage. By agreeing to our terms, the king can save her. By saving her, we can thereby save all of England."

"You make it sound simple, my lord."

"Simple, no. But necessary."

Sheridan had no more questions at the moment. William's gaze drifted over her, carefully; he had a good deal of respect for her as Henry's daughter. But there was something more to Lady Sheridan than met the eye; they could all see that. She had intelligence and she was well-thought. Henry had raised a sensible child.

Sheridan could feel his gaze, hoping he didn't think that she was an idiot. Here she was, surrounded by some of the most powerful men in England, all of whom were treating her with a great deal of respect. She supposed it was because of her father, never imagining it was because she was in the process of establishing her own foundation of support. Eyeing the men around the table, she walked towards the document, her gaze running over the yellowed parchment. She finally looked to the Marshall.

"I cannot read, my lord," she admitted. "Would you be so kind as to read what the document says?"

William smiled at her and wedged himself in between Fitz Herbert and Salisbury. His gaze focused on the first clause.

"First, that we have granted to God, and by this present charter have confirmed for us and our heirs in perpetuity, that the English Church shall be free, and shall have its rights undiminished…"

A knock at the door interrupted him. The mood of the room turned black with apprehension as Jocelin spoke quickly to Sheridan.

"Do not open the door," he instructed firmly. "Ask who it is and send them away."

She nodded and went to the door, followed by Neely with a dagger in his hand. He stood to the left of the door as Sheridan spoke through the panel.

"Who calls?" she asked.

"'Tis me," Alys' voice filtered through. "Let me in!"

Before Jocelin could stop her, Sheridan threw open the door. Alys stood there, looking perfectly safe, whole and sound. Sheridan was about to throw her arms around her when she saw a figure lingering behind her, nearly obscured by the dark shadows of the hall. The figure, in fact, had hold of Alys' arm as an escort would. It took Sheridan a moment to realize that it was de Lara.

And he could see everyone in the room beyond.

ଓ

THE SUN WAS brilliant and the birds in the January-dead trees sang a happy tune. Spring was months away, but the weather seemed to be encouraging a quick approach. Being January, snowfall and the moisture it brought would have been good for the earth. But the sun was good for the people that ventured into the outdoors to bask in the cold, bright rays.

Sheridan was no exception. Seated on a chair her maid had brought in the yard outside of the Flint Tower, she held a piece of needlework that she had been attempting to complete for the better part of a year. It was an ambitious piece her mother had designed, with hummingbirds and flowers and little bees. Sheridan's slender fingers had never been good with a needle and the fabric was covered in little brown spots where she had poked herself and bled. Even now, she was attempting the piece to keep her mind off the other events that seemed to have embedded themselves into the fabric of her life. Nothing was simple any more. Things only seemed to grow worse.

Alys hadn't gotten out of bed for three solid days, ever since Sean had escorted her back to their apartments following her afternoon with the king. She had decided that she wanted to be a royal consort and was convinced that the king was in love with her. When Sheridan had, not so nicely, told her she was mad for even entertaining such a thought, Alys had taken to her bed, miserable. Sheridan and Neely had taken turns watching out for her, making sure she didn't try to leap from the window again or make an attempt to contact the king. She was essentially a prisoner. But a miserable sister was better than a dead one.

It was Sheridan's turn to take a break from guard duty. She wanted out of the apartments and into the sunshine for as long as it would last. While Neely grudgingly stayed with Alys, Sheridan, the puppy and her maid retreated to cool daylight of the Tower yard. While the puppy ran off and the maid gave chase, Sheridan attempted the needlework, her mind mulling over the millions of thoughts that had succeeding in robbing her of sleep as of late.

Her most prevalent thought was of Sean. He hadn't said a word when he'd dropped Alys off three days prior. His clear blue eyes had perused the face of every man in the antechamber before he left in complete silence. Shortly thereafter, the meeting had hastily disbanded. She knew that short of the king showing up at her door and catching them all in perfidious conference, having been seen by Sean de Lara had been the worst possible scenario. The nobles were clearly terrified and she felt as if they somehow blamed her for the event. Arrests were expected and some of them had even gone into hiding. But, so far, nothing had happened.

It was like waiting for the other shoe to drop, the hammer of the Gods that would smash them all into oblivion. Sheridan was afraid for herself, of course, but she was more afraid for Jocelin. Not even the Church could protect him were he labeled a traitor.

But more than that, she was concerned for what Sean thought. It wasn't as if he hadn't known her loyalties were not to John. They had discussed that at the onset. But she suspected, somehow, he knew her for what she was; a conspirator. Her loyalties lay with England, not with a deviant king. Still, she knew he did not see it that way. As the personal protector of the king, there was no way he could not understand that she was the worst sort of enemy.

It was a depressing thought. De Lara had always shown her such courtesy, such regard. She had enjoyed their encounters and the way in which he spoke to her. He did not speak to her as some men spoke to women, as if the female barely had a brain. Sean spoke to her with respect. She would miss that. She would miss him, too.

She went back to her needlework, stabbing herself for the tenth time that day. With a yelp, she put the sore finger in her mouth to suck away the blood. She needed a thimble but did not want to return to her apartment to get one. A shadow suddenly fell across her and a massive hand reached down to take the finger from her mouth.

"Let me see," Sean's voice was soft, deep. He glanced at the material in her hand. "From the looks of that, this isn't the first time you have done this."

Sheridan was more than startled. She nearly fell off her chair with surprise. "My lord," she struggled to catch her breath. "Forgive me. I did not hear your approach."

He wiped at the small dot of blood on her finger. "I meant that you should not." He kissed the fingertip and gave her back her hand. "There, now. Better?"

She looked between her finger and his twinkling eyes. "Much," she said. Then, she didn't know what to say other than the obvious. "Are you here to arrest me?"

He crouched down beside her chair, his blue eyes scanning the compound around them. "Why would I do that?"

"For the unlawful assembly you saw in my apartment. If you are here to take me, I shall go peacefully."

He pursed his lips, slowly shaking his head. "A memorial."

"Excuse me?"

"All of those men I saw in your apartment were friends of your father, having come to pay tribute to you and to his memory. All I saw was a memorial."

She just stared at him. Feeling her confused gaze, he turned to look at her. "Did you have something more to say to that?" he asked.

Sheridan was baffled, relieved, and overjoyed at the same time. She had no idea how to react. "Do I?"

"Nay, you do not."

"Are you sure?"

"I am."

"As you wish, then. But I would like to ask a question."

"What is that?"

"Why would you do this?"

"Do what?"

She wasn't sure how to word her thoughts, not wanting to contradict him when they both knew very well that he had taken the time, effort and thought to cover actions that would have brought anyone else immediate imprisonment. In that instant, the blossoming relationship between them deepened. The path, for them, was chosen. It was a defining moment.

"Oh… I do not know," she finally gave up, her luminous eyes moving over his strong features. "I suppose I am simply wondering why you would be so good to me."

A smile played on his lips. "Because you are my betrothed."

"Am I still?"

His brow furrowed. "What would make you think that you are not?"

She put the needlework in her lap. "Must everything with you be so evasive? Do you realize that you have answered almost all of my questions with another question?"

"Have I?"

She growled in frustration and he chuckled softly. "'Tis not my intention to be evasive, my lady. But the answers you seek to your questions are ones that you can just as easily answer yourself."

Her gaze locked with his. A strange heat filled the space between them, a warmth that bloomed in her chest and spread outward into her arms and legs and fingers. Everything was tingling. The longer she looked at him, the stronger the warmth became.

"You are perhaps correct in some respects," she said softly. "But there are times when I would like an answer from your own lips."

He felt the heat, too. He was positively melting the longer he looked at her. "As you wish, my lady. What answer would you like to hear?"

She could not have pulled away from his gaze if she tried. She didn't want to try. But she could not have assumptions and conjecture between them.

"I would have total truth between us, Sir Sean," she said softly. "I expect nothing less and will accept nothing more. If I ask you a question, will you answer me honestly?"

"I will."

"Do you know what was transpiring in my apartment the night you brought Alys back to me?"

"Aye."

He didn't hesitate with his answer. Her heart leapt into her throat, thinking of all the men who were undoubtedly in danger. "Did you tell the king?"

"You said only one question."

Frustrated, she stood up and the needlework fell to the ground. "Do you have any idea how horrible it has been for me, knowing you saw all of those men in my apartment and knowing that because of me, their very lives are at stake? They're terrified and suspicious, and I do not blame them. And it is my fault!"

He stood up, too. Taking her hand, the one she had poked, he tucked it in to the crook of his elbow.

"Walk with me," he commanded quietly.

Dumbly, she obeyed. Sean walked her over to the wall, west of the Flint Tower. It was cool in the shadows, out of the view of most. Slowly, they paced the dirt as it stretched along the enormous expanse of masonry.

"As you said when we first met, you and I could be considered enemies," his voice was low, guarded. "If I chose to believe that, it would be easy. You have made it easy for me."

"I am not your enemy," she replied. "But I do not hold the same loyalties as you."

"Loyalties are perception. They are not always truth."

"What does that mean?"

"It means that you should not believe everything you see or everything you are told." He came to a stop and faced her, his eyes scanning the walls before focusing on her. "I will say this once and then speak no more of it. You are a young, naïve kitten caught up in a game played by ferocious lions. They will eat you if you are not careful. Your father was a lion like the rest of them and knew the game well. I cannot believe he has left you so defenseless in this den of animals."

She could sense concern in his voice. "What do you mean?"

He grasped her gently by the arms. "What I mean is that you must get out while you can. Take Alys and go home. I will come for you when I am able."

She lifted an eyebrow. "Do you know something that I do not? Are we in danger?"

"You have fifteen hundred men within a two hour march of London."

She struggled not to react. "Who told you that?"

"It is my duty to know that and more."

It wasn't his tone that scared her as much as his words. Her heart began to thump heavily against her ribs. She pulled from his grasp, stepping back to give some space between them. She was afraid and defiant at the same time.

"If you have spent the past week attempting to woo me so that you can get information out of me, then you have wasted your time. I'll not tell you anything."

"If you think that is the only reason I have wooed you, then you are more naïve than I suspected."

Her fear and fury took hold and she turned away from him, unsure of what to say, unsure of what to do. She hadn't taken two steps when he grabbed her, spinning her around to face him. His body was pressed against hers, his face filling up her entire field of vision. The heat, the power, was overpowering.

"What I feel for you has nothing to do with politics," he growled. "What I feel for you is purely between a man and a woman. Do not believe for one minute that I do not know why you are here, or who your companions are, or even those passing in and out of your apartment. It is my responsibility to know all, see all, for the protection and information of the king. My eyes are his eyes in all things. I will admit this to you; I escorted Alys back to your apartment that night not for the reason you think. I did it because I saw you leave with young de Braose. Had I found him alone with you in your apartment, I would have killed him. Instead, I found you with a roomful of men conspiring around a table. I could have told the king the verity of my observations, but I chose not to. Politics, at that moment, did not come into play. I was simply glad that you were safe and adequately chaperoned regardless of the disloyal circumstances."

It was a shocking admission from John's most ferocious protector. She had never seen such passion from him, a palpable thing that reached out to embrace her. Her small hands found their way around his waist, hesitantly at first. His flesh, through his tunic, was firm and warm beneath her fingers.

"What did you tell him?" she whispered.

"That I saw old friends paying respect to the family of their deceased colleague."

Now that his admission was finally clear, she could hardly believe her ears. "You lied to protect me? My God, Sean… why would you do that?"

He could feel her hands and the power those small appendages had over him was unexpected. He would have done almost anything for her at that moment, just to feel her tender warmth, her response, against him.

"I told you why," he growled gently. "And you ask too many questions."

His lips descended on her, softly at first, but more persistent by the moment. The heat that had been smoldering between them ignited into a roaring inferno and Sean pulled her into his savage embrace, feeling her yielding body collapse against him. She was sweet, soft, delicious, and he kissed her as he had never kissed a woman in his life. Up until this moment, he wasn't sure if he really ever had. At least, not like this.

Sheridan's thoughts, as nebulous as they were at the moment, followed a similar path. The only tale of men's kisses she had ever heard had come from Alys, sloppy things that had left a chord of distaste in her mind. But Sean's kiss was nothing as she had been told; it was powerful and tender at the same time, warm and passionate. Being held by him, consumed by him, was nothing she had ever experienced before. She knew within the first few moments of delight that it was something she could learn to crave. Perhaps Alys hadn't been too terribly wrong about the allure of men, after all. Perhaps there was something to it.

"God," Sean breathed, his lips moving to her cheek. "I cannot go a moment of the day without thinking of you."

"Strange," she whispered, feeling his mouth against her skin. "We go for days without seeing one another."

"Not by choice, I assure you," he said. "The king keeps me quite busy."

She pulled back, gazing up at him. Strands of her long hair were caught on his mail and he carefully pulled them free.

"This is all so wonderful," she murmured. "But it is also so confusing. We've known each other a matter of days and already we are betrothed and…."

She couldn't finish her sentence. He tapped her tenderly on her chin. "And… what?"

She shook her head. "I was going to say mad for each other, but I am not sure that's true. Perhaps it is the newness of all of this causing me to speak before I think. I feel as if I am going to faint, yet I am so happy that I could shout it to the world." She put her hand to her forehead. "I do not know what I am saying, Sean. Forgive me."

He smiled at her, a delicious gesture wrought with delight and tenderness. "There is nothing to forgive. I feel as you do, though you'll not hear me admit it again. 'Tis wrong for a man to admit he feels faint and giddy."

She giggled, her wits returning after his kiss had drained her of them. Gazing up at his handsome face, she tenderly touched his forehead, his cheek, as if studying a fine piece of sculpture. There was so much character and strength in those powerful lines.

"I have never been mad for anyone," she whispered. "This is all so new to me."

He closed his eyes as her hand moved across his face. "Nor I. But I do know one thing; we will never be without one another. This I swear."

Her hand fell from his face, her features softening with concern. "But our situations are so different. Sean, I must ask you honestly; when you insisted on marriage, did you even think about my station, about yours, and how it would affect us both? The reality of the other night when you brought Alys back to the apartment only served to underscore that difference. Do you think any of those men would ever trust me again if they knew that you and I were speaking of betrothal? Do you think....?"

He put a finger to her lips. "I am aware of the implications, even more than you are. Do not think for one moment that those very thoughts have not crossed my mind a thousand times. And do not think for one moment that the king would not have me executed if he discovered our ties."

Her eyes widened. "Executed?" she gasped. "Oh, Sean, that cannot happen. You cannot...!"

He kissed her to silence her, a passionately urgent gesture. "Have no fear, my lovely little angel. As long as we keep this secret safe between us, for the time being, there is no danger."

She was torn between responding to his kisses and the verity of her fears. "But someone might see us together," she said. "Even now, someone might be watching. 'Tis not safe."

He sighed, kissing her a final time. "I know," he replied with regret. "Which is why our meetings have been irregular and, at times, brief. I do not know when I will see you next. It may be tomorrow, or it may be weeks away. Even now, I have been gone overlong from my post. But I consider the risk well worth the reward."

She shook her head. "You must go back immediately."

"I will, in time."

It was obvious he had no intention of releasing her any time soon. She pulled from his embrace, grasped his arm, and tried to turn him around. "You will go *now*. Please."

He grinned, allowing her to lead him away from the shadows of the wall. "Aye, captain."

By the time they were halfway into the winter-dry yard, she had taken her hands from him and they were a respectable distance apart. There could very well be eyes on them now and they were both acutely aware.

"The king will announce a masque to be given in honor of his wife's birthday sometime next week," he said, his demeanor having returned to that of a predator as they crossed the compound. His gaze was everywhere, scanning. "You will attend this masque."

She glanced sidelong at him. "I will?"

"Aye. As will I. In costume, 'twill be a simple thing to steal a dance or a kiss. And I should enjoy the time with you."

"I will not see you between now and then?"

"I did not say that. You will indeed see me, at some point."

They walked in silence, nearing the Flint Tower. Finally, she came to a halt. "Sean, I must say something."

He paused. "What?"

Her face grew serious. "I… I would rather not see you again if the discovery of our association would lead to your execution. As much as it would pain me, I would rather have you alive and untouchable than a dead memory."

The mood between them grew solemn. His gaze lingered on her a moment, choosing his words carefully before he spoke.

"I told you once that the one trait that ignited my interest in you, other than your beauty, was your kindness. You were kind to me from the very first moment you looked into my eyes. Before you even knew my name, you were gracious, and even after you knew who I was, your civility continued. Even if you had been a plain, unassuming woman, I would have found your depth of character extraordinarily attractive. You, my lady, have a beautiful heart."

Her lovely cheeks flushed. "Your words humble me, my lord. But you must know that I mean what I say. I cannot even fathom the agony and guilt that your demise would bring me. I would be like Alys, attempting to throw myself from a window simply to rid myself of the anguish."

The corners of his mouth twitched. "I have no intention of allowing death to claim me any time soon. To not have you in my life, at my side, would be more painful than any death I can imagine." He took her hand and brought it to his lips. "Have no fear, Lady Sheridan St. James. We will both live long, healthy lives together."

His kiss brought tears to her eyes. She'd known the man's affections hardly a few days and already she could not imagine being without him. With a wink, he left her standing there, watching him disappear into one of the doors that lead to the barracks flanking the Flint Tower.

☙

"SIEGE IS IMMINENT. We are withdrawing the nobles from the Tower so that they may join their troops."

"Even Sheridan St. James?"

"Especially Sheridan St. James. God only knows what would happen to her should she be left behind. It is imperative that she get out immediately."

The bell tower of Winchester Cathedral had been a convenient meeting place time and time again. The king was in the sanctuary at Vespers and Sean, as usual, was prowling the grounds in search of any threat against the monarch. That was usual wherever the king went. Only this time, he had paused in his duties long enough to make a pre-arranged contact. It had been conveniently arranged to coincide with the mass. What he heard so far had him ill to his stomach.

He signed heavily. "I told her to leave."

"Did you tell her why?"

"Of course not."

"Did she agree?"

Sean leaned back against the ceiling truss in the low-ceilinged room. "She did not have the opportunity. We became… sidetracked."

The figure behind the bell, well off in the shadows, would not have hay on his clothing tonight. The last time they had met, he'd neglected to see the grass until someone had pointed it out to him, hours later. It had been a foolish error. Tonight there would be no such opportunity for one.

"Sean," the shadow-figure began. "I do not know the extent of your involvement with Lady Sheridan, but if it is what I believe it is, then you must curb yourself. We have reached a critical point in our endeavors and I cannot have you distracted."

"It is not a distraction," Sean replied steadily. "We are to be wed when all of this madness is finished."

"Wed?" the figure repeated, incredulous. "Are you mad? You cannot marry the woman."

"I can and I will."

"Jocelin will never allow it."

"Jocelin will approve when all is said and done."

There was fidgeting and grunts of disbelief coming from the shadows. "So you believe that your service warrants the earldom of Bath and Glastonbury? Not that I disagree, but you picked a mighty difficult goal. To aim for Sheridan St. James is, shall we say, reaching for the heavens. She is gloriously wealthy and well supported by the Bishop."

Sean picked at the beam above his head. "This isn't about the damn earldom," he said, disgust in his voice. "She could have only the clothes on her back for all I care. She is a deeply compassionate and courageous woman, and I greatly admire her. That is why I am marrying her, and for no other reason."

"Don't tell me that you believe yourself in love with her?" the voice was cold.

"If not now, then I very shortly will be."

"Sean, Sean," the voice moaned, sing-song. "We cannot have this complication. Twenty thousand men are preparing to capture London as we speak. I need your head clear, not addled like a foolish child's. I swear on the grave of St. George that I'll remove Sheridan St. James myself and hide her from you until this is all over if you do not focus on the tasks at hand. You have come too far to fail now."

"I'll not fail," Sean said evenly. "And you'll not touch Sheridan. If I catch wind of you so much as looking at her, you'll rue the day you were born. She is not a pawn to be trifled with."

"Even as your threats fill my ears, that statement alone tells me that you are already in love with her," the voice replied. He sighed deeply, shifting in the shadows as he collected more pressing thoughts. "All that aside, she must leave the Tower. She will probably take it more seriously if Jocelin or one of the other nobles forces her to move."

Sean nodded. "That is where the directive must come. When I told her, I simply sounded like a jealous lover."

"Are you?"

"What?"

"Jealous?"

Sean hissed, running his fingers through his hair. "Probably. I saw young de Braose escort her back to her apartment the other night and was fully prepared gut him."

There was a pregnant pause, long and solemn. "Then you should know that Reginald was in negotiations with Henry St. James before his death to marry Guy to Sheridan, though she does not know it. Since she had refused all suitors up until that point, Henry thought it best not to tell her."

Sean felt as if he'd been slapped. "Who told you this?"

"Jocelin."

"Are negotiations still ongoing?"

"Aye. That is why Reginald sent Guy to London, among other reasons. It was Reginald and Henry's hope that once Sheridan met Guy, she would more readily accept him as a suitor."

Sean didn't have a ready reply. He just stood there. After a moment, he hit the beam above his head so hard that the entire bell tower shook. Sawdust and other flotsam floated down in the still air, landing on the floor, in his hair, on the bell. His jaw flexed dangerously, the clear blue eyes distant and hard.

"Never in my life have I ever wanted anything other than to serve the cause," he growled. "Since I was seventeen years of age, I have been completely selfless and dedicated to my task. You have seen nothing but flawless duty from me and it was because I had convinced myself that someday, I would be rewarded for my service. I knew this world would pass away and a new England would take hold where I would not have to stay to the shadows, where I would not be feared and loathed, and where I would not have to defend my life every moment of every day. Now, when I can see the light at the end of the road and I have found the only thing I have ever wanted, you are telling me that I am going to have to fight for this, too?"

The tone of the voice was patient, understanding. "I am not saying you will have to fight for this. I am simply telling you that there is competition. Did you suspect for one moment that there was not? Sheridan St. James is a beautiful, wealthy woman."

"She has a sister," Sean snapped softly. "Give Alys to de Braose. He'll still gain a fortune."

"In spite of what you may think, Guy de Braose is a fine young man. He is brave and level-headed. And from what Jocelin has told me, he is quite enamored with Sheridan."

Sean growled and the voice spoke quickly. "It's not his fault, Sean. He does not know of your interest, as no one does. I suspect you intend it that way, do you not?"

Sean stood there a moment, pounding the beam absently as he mulled over his thoughts and the words of wisdom from the shadows. "It is," he finally said. "No one can know, for obvious reasons."

"Then do not be hard on de Braose. You cannot fault the man his good taste."

Sean just rolled his eyes. There was resignation in his posture as he stepped away from the beam. "It is not as if my family is not as old or prestigious as the House of de Braose," he muttered. "My family, in fact, has been here far longer than the Norman usurpers."

The man behind the voice knew Sean well. He knew that de Lara was a man of impeccable character, of flawless devotion, and of singular mind when it came to King and duty. He'd never once asked for compensation or reward for the deadly task he had undertaken nine years ago. The words coming forth from de Lara at the moment were words of self-pity, of emotion. The man behind the voice was shocked at the depth he was witnessing.

"I know that very well," he said. "You can trace your lineage back six hundred years to the ancient kings of Deira. Your father was Viscount Darlington and your elder sister married into the Umfravilles of Prudhoe Castle, heirs to Northumberland. Your father's title and lands have passed to you since his death, including Stonegrave Castle. But because of your devotion to duty, the castle has stood unoccupied for six years, alone, waiting for your return."

Sean slapped the beam again, unexpectedly and sharply. "Exactly. Because my commitment to the cause was more important to me than assuming my rights as Viscount Darlington. And for what? To be told that all of this has been for naught, that what I truly want in reward for my service might very well be denied to me because you apparently don't trust that I can keep my focus on the cause? I find that offensive. I have given up more than anyone for what I believe in. You have no right to deny me what I want."

"No one is denying you," the voice said calmly. "But you must look at all angles. Your timing is poor. We must focus on what is most important right now."

"Is my sense of duty being called into question?"

"Most certainly not."

"I will not give up Lady Sheridan."

The voice, once again, sighed heavily. There was no getting around the subject. Men in love could be the most stubborn creatures on the face of the earth.

"As you say," the voice said. "But she must leave the Tower at once, for her own safety. I will instruct Jocelin to make it so. Now, may we speak on other matters?"

Sean was broodingly silent, his mind a clutter of thought and emotions. He was unused to such disorder. "Aye," he finally said.

"Tell me of the king."

"He knows that something is amiss. He knows of Rochester's meeting with Salisbury."

"Has he gone so far as to rally his troops?"

"Not yet."

"You cannot let him, Sean. And you cannot let him leave the Tower."

"Understood."

"What is his troop strength?"

Sean pushed himself off the wall, crossing his massive arms as he spoke. "Warwick and Percy have a massive contingency from the north between them. They are nearing Coventry from what I am told, at least one week away. Suffolk has a thousand men to the east within a day's ride, as does Norfolk. William Fitz Osbern has brought his entire regiment from Monmouth, about eight hundred men. Plus the royal troops, there are nearly five thousand men in or around London that will oppose the siege."

The voice snorted. "We will crush them."

"You must be vigilant of Warwick and Percy from the north. They will be able to attack you from behind and create a second front."

"We can position men to prevent the main body of our army from being disrupted," he said. "Unless… unless we wait for Warwick and Percy to reach London and bed within her walls."

"I would advise against it. Take London now while she is weak. Call in reinforcements from the Marches to occupy Warwick and Percy."

The voice grew serious. "Then I must speak with de Warenne. He will know his loyal March allies."

"We cannot expect any more support from de Braose. He is raging war right now with the Welsh."

"Not the Welsh, Sean," the voice said softly. "Against Clifford. Reginald is going after Kington Castle on the Marches in an effort to wrest it from Walter Clifford."

Sean hadn't heard that bit of information, and he usually knew everything through his network of informants and spies. "But Clifford is here, in London."

"I know."

"Surely he is aware of the siege?"

"Possibly not yet. He has been here for some time. It takes time for news to travel."

"Then how do you know?"

"Young de Braose confided in a few."

Sean shook his head at the irony of it. "Revenge is sweet. Clifford stole it from the de Braose clan and now they want it back. Young de Braose has been telling everyone his father isn't here because he is fighting rebels."

"He is, in sorts, just not Welsh rebels."

There was a humor to the irony of political agendas and the petty wars of barons. Sean lingered the information a moment longer before tucking it away.

"We should meet by sunset tomorrow to follow any progress that has been made," he said. "The king will not be leaving the Tower anytime soon that I can see. We will have to rendezvous on the grounds."

"The well house near the barracks."

They had been in the bell tower overlong. Sean brushed the dust off his arms and made for the narrow, spiral stairs that led to the parapet below. He knew the king would soon be looking for him.

"Sean," the voice said. "The meeting you saw in Lady Sheridan's apartment the other night..."

Sean held up a hand. "No worries. I told the king it was a wake for Henry."

"I know." The voice paused. "My secondary sources tell me that he did not believe you. You should be aware."

Sean leaned against the wooden rail. After a moment, he smiled dryly. "It is not because he does not believe me personally. It is because he is suspicious of everything regardless of what we all tell him. He lives in a world of paranoia that the rest of us can only imagine."

"Are you certain?"

"Nine years of experience tells me this."

"Be cautious, anyway. You are our best, strongest asset in this war against tyranny."

Sean nodded, took another stair, and suddenly paused again. "I nearly forgot to ask. The document I wrote; did you receive it?"

"Father Simon delivered it. That is what we were examining the other night when you saw us in the St. James' apartment."

"I thought as much. Did it incorporate everything it should?"

"That and more. Your text is brilliant. You clearly have a talent with written prose."

"Under your direction, of course. But remember; I do not want my name mentioned anywhere. I am not responsible for this document that will change the course of this country. I would rather be an invisible contributor. Leave the glory to those who wish it."

"Have no fear. The impression was given that the Bishop of Canterbury and the Bishop of London were the authors. No one will ever know that you are the true creator of the Magna Carta."

"Is that what you are calling it?"

"Fitting, is it not?" The voice suddenly took on a concerned tone. "And speaking of writing, are you still keeping your journals?"

"I am."

"Take care that they do not fall into the wrong hands."

"The priest keeps them for me in the chapel. They are safe."

"See that they are. I have always disagreed that you keep a log of your years with the king."

"Perhaps someday they will give historians an insight into his madness and the turbulence of the times. Besides, you know that I have always been fond of writing. It keeps me sane."

"You should stick to treaty writing. It is safer."

Sean snorted with humor as he reflected on the title of the treaty that had taken a year out of his life to write. The *Magna Carta*. Sean quit the bell tower and disappeared into the shadows below. When the cathedral was sufficiently vacant, the Voice disappeared as well.

Time was running short.

CHAPTER SIX

"... I found myself wishing my time and life were my own so that I would be better able to focus on the amazing events unfolding before me. I would have given all that I'd worked for if just one afternoon could have been given to us where I did not have to worry about death and impending destruction... the storm was approaching swiftly...."

The Chronicles of Sir Sean de Lara

1206 – 1215 A.D.

"I WANT TO see the king."

The guards in Plantagenet crimson gazed down at the round, red-headed young maiden standing before them. It wasn't usual to have visitors to the royal wing unless summoned, either under their own will or kicking and screaming. But this young lady, clad in a pretty red gown, seemed quite determined. One of the guards recognized her as having been in the king's chambers a few days prior. He immediately sent a page to the king's secretary.

So Alys waited in the sumptuous surroundings. She knew the king would grant her audience. She was certain he had been thinking of her just as she had been thinking of him. She knew that he was married, but it was of little consequence. She could still be a royal ward. She wanted the same attention he had lavished on her before, the same undivided consideration and compliments to her beauty that he had given her. So many people, including Sheridan, had said so many terrible things about him, but she did not believe it. He had been completely kind to her. She knew he had feelings for her.

It wasn't long before she heard a set of doors open down the long corridor. They banged into the wall, giving her a start. Looking up, she saw a massive figure coming towards her, silhouetted by the sun pouring in through the large lancet window at the far end of the hall. It took her a moment to realize it was Sean de Lara.

Her face lit up.

"Sir Sean!" she said happily. "You have come to…"

Sean reached out and snatched her around the arm, practically dragging her down the corridor. Alys' momentary glee turned to alarm.

"You are hurting me," she said. "Let go of my arm."

Sean acted as if he hadn't heard her. He yanked her all the way down the corridor, ignoring her increasing pleas, until he reached the room he had come from. He literally threw her inside and Alys lost her balance, tripping to her knees. Frustrated, terrified, she looked up to see him bearing down on her.

"What are you doing here?" he growled.

She was petrified. "I… I came to see the king."

His jaw was flexing so hard that it looked as if he was going to snap his jawbone. "Does your sister know you are here?"

"Nay," Alys didn't realize she had her hands up as if protecting herself from de Lara's wrath. "She is in bed, tending a sick headache."

His jaw stopped ticking and he peered more closely at her. "Sick headache? Is she ill?"

Alys slowly lowered her hands. "She gets them sometimes. She cannot eat or stand for a few days until it goes away. Sometimes she vomits if there is too much light in her chamber."

Sean's fury at Alys was suddenly turned to grave concern for Sheridan. She had seemed fine when he saw her yesterday. But he had to keep his focus. "Get out of here," he reached down and picked her up off the floor. "Go back to your apartment and stay there. Never return, Alys. Do you understand?"

Alys didn't. "But why? The king was so kind to me the other day."

His expression clouded, a terrifying vision of death and intimidation. "The king wants nothing more than to rob you of your maidenhood and violate you as you cannot even possibly imagine that a man could do. I could tell you horror stories that would give you nightmares for the rest of your life, but I will refrain simply for the fact that I would protect your dignity as a lady. But I swear that if you ever come back here again, I will spank you within an inch of your life. Do you comprehend me?"

Her big green eyes were wide with terror. "Aye," she whispered.

"Then go home. Stay there."

She was out in the corridor by this time. Without another word, she turned to leave the same way she had come when another set of doors opened and she found herself walking straight into d'Athée. His grizzled face twisted with delight at the sight of her.

"Ah," he said. "The Lady Alys. The king will be delighted to see you."

Sean was several paces behind Alys. He could do nothing but gaze impassively at her as Gerard took her by the arm and led her back into the open room. Feeling sick to his stomach, he followed.

John sat before his elegant dressing table, watching his chamberlain cut the front of his hair with a very sharp dagger. He glanced into the polished bronze mirror, seeing Alys' reflection, Gerard's, and in the doorway, Sean. Shoving the chamberlain aside and nearly losing an ear in the process, he turned to his guest.

"Lady Alys," he rose from his chair. "I heard you had come to see me. How kind."

Alys smiled timidly. "I…I thought perhaps to thank you for the delightful afternoon we spent together, sire."

John took her hand gently, a gesture that was as sickening as it was forced. "Ah," he said sweetly. "A lady with manners. I was about to have my morning meal. Will you join me?"

Alys glanced hesitantly at Sean, fearfully at Gerard, before answering. "I would be honored, sire."

Sean was starting to feel the distinct twinges of panic. He'd seen that expression on the king, too many times. He knew where it would lead. He had held the king off once with warnings of unified opponents should he violate a St. James woman, but he suspected that warning would only hold good once. Alys had walked right back into the jaws of the lion and he was very quickly realizing there was nothing he could do about it. She was going to be eaten.

As he watched Alys sit at the private table in the king's bower, he could see the familiar pattern forming. D'Athée faded into the shadows as he, too, was expected to do. If he didn't follow the pattern, the king would wonder why. If the king began to ask questions, then Sean's entire position could be in doubt. If his position was in doubt, then nine long, horrible years of his life would be wasted, never to be regained again. He could not blow his cover. The king could not realize that a traitor lay closer to him than he had ever dared imagine.

He could not risk his position, not when everything was so close at hand.

Stupid girl!

He left the room and shut the door. There were guards in the corridor, watching him, and he would not react. He retired back into the large chamber that belonged to him adjacent to the king's apartments. Of all of the turmoil he had ever felt about his position, this was the worst. It was a nightmare. He knew what he had to do, but he also knew what he should do. Holding his breath, he waited for the first screams. They were not long in coming.

Damn her!

Sean burst through the connecting door, into the king's chamber. The king had Alys on the floor near the table, the top of her gown ripped away to reveal snow-white flesh. She was sobbing hysterically. The king looked at Sean, his expression between fear and annoyance.

"De Lara?" he said through clenched teeth. "What manner of crisis is this?"

Sean reached around the king and yanked Alys off the floor, so hard that he heard a bone snap. She screamed, clutching her wrist. Sean shoved her back through the doors and into the adjoining chamber, slamming the heavy oak panels behind her hard enough to rattle the walls. Furious, bordering on a loss of control, he faced off against the king.

"Sire," he was struggling to maintain his composure. "I told you that attacking a St. James woman would be foolish. With all of the allied nobles in London at this time, and particularly those paying tribute at Henry's Wake earlier this week, can you not see the folly of your actions? I forbid you to deliberately incite a riot against the crown when we have worked so hard to contain it. Surely there are other women you can entertain yourself with."

John gazed at him with his droopy-eyed, piercing stare. He fidgeted with the tunic that was askew on his torso. After an eternity of horrid, tension-filled silence, during which Sean was positive the man was going to have him arrested, the king suddenly broke into an unexpected, completely abashed, grin.

"De Lara," he grunted, slapping Sean on the arm. "My most loyal servant. How on earth do you tolerate me? I am trying to destroy myself even as you try to save me. Are we such a foolish pair, you and I?"

Even at those words, Sean could not relax. He was so furious that he had bitten his tongue; he could taste the blood. "If it is a woman you want, I shall find one for you," he said. "But I will not let you provoke the opposition as you seem so willing to do. I will not let you commit political suicide."

John was still grinning as he made his way, lazily, back over to his dressing table. "Very good, de Lara, very good," he spoke like a man who clearly understood his mistake. "I would prefer a blond. Not too thin."

As quickly as his lust roused, it was as quickly forgotten. From somewhere, the chamberlain appeared and resumed cutting the king's hair with a razor-sharp dagger. It was as if nothing had ever been. It looked the same as it did when Sean had entered the chamber.

But Sean was used to that. John could be bitterly confusing in that sense. Without further thought. Sean retreated back to his adjoining room where Alys was huddled against the wall, holding her wrist. When she saw Sean approach, she began to cry loudly. He knelt beside her, swiftly, putting his hand on her head in a comforting gesture.

"I am sorry, Alys," he muttered. "Truly, I am sorry. It was an accident. But I had to get you out of there and I apologize if I was brutal. Do you understand that?"

She was sobbing pathetically. "He… he tried to…"

"I know," he felt so badly for her that he kissed her on the forehead. "Come, let me see what I have done. Please know I wouldn't have intentionally hurt you for the world. I did not mean to."

She sniffled, wincing when he ran his fingers over her forearm. "It hurts."

"I know. I can feel the broken bone through your skin. Let's get you out of here and to a physic."

Sean went to the wall and pushed on one of the massive decorative panels that lined the perimeter; it swung open, revealing a steep, narrow staircase that disappeared into the darkness below. He took a taper in one hand and Alys in the other.

"Come along," he said. "Watch the steps; they're steep."

Tears fading, left arm held tight against her body, Alys allowed him to lead her down the dark stairs.

As the secret panel closed softly behind them, the doors on the opposite side of the chamber softly opened. The king was standing in the archway with Gerard. The men gazed unemotionally at the wall with the hidden panel, each man thinking his own thoughts of what he had just witnessed. It was difficult to know their conclusions. It was the king who finally spoke, a great deal of reluctance in his tone.

"Follow him," he said to d'Athée. "See where he goes."

"He goes to take her to the physic, sire," Gerard said. "You heard the bone snap yourself."

The king mulled over the situation, Sean's words. His weak mind was torn with suspicion and jealousy. "Indeed I did," he said. "But I have seen him do worse and show no compassion. Why this time? Why with her? Perhaps he wants her for himself."

D'Athée could only shake his head. The king waved a finger in the general direction of the concealed panel. "Follow them. Report back to me."

Gerard, against his better judgment, obeyed.

ଓ

"SHE IS HURT enough," Sean had Sheridan by the waist. "Go – sit over there, away from her. There will be no battles today in my presence."

Sheridan wasn't listening. She was so furious and terrified that she was crying. She wanted to take her sister's head off but Sean wouldn't let her.

"Ooooo," she shook both of her fists at a weeping Alys. "You are a fool, do you hear me? A fool! I should kill you and be done with it!"

Sean bodily picked her up and carried her to the opposite side of the room. There was a chair; he set her down in it, gently, and grasped her face, forcing her to look at him.

"Calm yourself," he commanded softly. "Alys needs your comfort, not your anger."

Sheridan's eyes were filled with tears. Then, she closed her eyes tightly and refused to look at any of them.

"She'll not get any from me," she hissed. "Please, I need to lie down. I feel horribly ill."

Sean swept her into his arms and put her right back onto the bed where he had found her a few minutes earlier. She had looked as if she was dying, lying in a dark room with a cloth over her eyes. But a brief story of Alys' morning to explain her splinted wrist had Sheridan leaping out of bed like a madwoman. It had, in hindsight, not been the brightest of ideas. Her sick headache was worse than before.

"What can I do for you?" he leaned over her, his powerful arms braced on either side of her.

She put her arm over her eyes, blocking out the light. "Nothing," she whispered. "Darkness and quiet are the only things I need. This will pass."

He gently touched her arm, a comforting gesture, wishing he could do more. "Shall I send for the physic?"

"Nay," she rasped. "He can do nothing."

"Can I at least try? I cannot stomach seeing you like this."

She grunted in response. If it wasn't a direct denial, he took it as an affirmative. He turned to go, pausing at the door. "If I leave, can I be assured that you will not attack your sister in my absence?"

Sheridan's arm flopped from her face in an irritated gesture. "Do you think I would wait until you go to rip her apart? I would be doing it right now if I felt any better."

He grinned, quitting the apartment. The little maid came out of hiding and went to her mistresses, Sheridan first to put another cool cloth on her face, and Alys second to inspect the splint on her arm. Alys waved the woman away, sending her for food. When the door closed softly behind her, Alys sank wearily into the sling-back chair near the smoldering hearth. Already, it had been a long and eventful day.

"Where was Neely when this madness was going on?" Sheridan whispered from the bed. "Why is he not here even now?"

Alys gazed at the lancet window, covered by the heavy oilcloth. "I sent him on an errand. He will be gone for some time."

"You did *what*?" Sheridan ripped the cloth off, her red eyes glaring at her sister. "Where is he?"

Alys was torn between shame and defiance. "You needn't yell."

"Yes, I must," Sheridan seethed. "Where did you send Neely?"

"To Gunnarsbury."

"What on earth for?"

Alys was starting to loosen her insolence. "Because when we were at the Street of the Merchants the other day, a vendor told me about his shop in Gunnarsbury and he said he had the most marvelous delicacy from an ancient recipe from the Holy Land, and that I positively must have some." She came to a sudden stop and her lip stuck out in a pout. "So I sent Neely to get it for me."

Sheridan was dumbfounded. "You sent the captain of the guard to Gunnarsbury for food?"

"Not food. A marvelous sweet paste made from Almonds and sugar. They call it Marzipan. Isn't that a wonderful name?"

Sheridan stared at her sister for a sharp, brief moment before leaping off the bed again and beating Alys over the head with the wet cloth that had been on her eyes.

"Nay," she screeched. "It is not marvelous. How could you be so foolish? You sent Neely away just so you could be wild and disobedient, and I'll have none of this, do you hear?"

Alys put her good arm up, trying to protect herself. "Dani, I am sorry. Please do not be so angry at me. I am truly sorry. I promise that I will not do it again!"

Sheridan's head was about to explode. With a final good smack to her sister's head, she suddenly fell to the floor, laying down against the cold wooden planks and putting her cheek against the coolness of it. The room was swaying and she felt so ill that she was sure she was going to die.

"Leave me alone, Alys," she groaned. "You will be the death of me, I swear it. Go away and leave me."

Alys tried to pick her up from the floor. "Let me help you back to bed."

"Nay," Sheridan slapped at her. "Leave me. Go. Please."

Alys stood over her, uncertain what to do. "But…"

"Go. I shall be fine. I need to lie here quietly."

Reluctantly, Alys did as she was asked. She opened the door to the antechamber and the little puppy scampered in, racing to Sheridan on the floor and licking her face furiously. Alys watched as her sister calmed the dog and eventually bade it to lie beside her. Leaving Sheridan on the floor was a difficult decision, but she'd seen this before. There were times when her sister had laid on the cold floor for an entire day with a pounding head simply because it felt more comfortable than on a sticky, lumpy bed.

She closed the door to the bower and wandered aimlessly into the antechamber. She stood there for some time until the servant returned. The maid had a tray of bread and cheese and Alys sat, eating dejectedly. All of that energy from her sister had been over only half the story; she hadn't even told her about Sean breaking her wrist. It had been an accident, of course, but he had still hurt her.

Gazing down at the heavily bandaged arm, it throbbed considerably. The physic had given her a bitter willow brew to drink to ease the pain, but it wasn't helping. She took another bite of cheese and chewed, lost in self-pity.

A soft rap sounded on the entry. Alys set the cheese down and went to the door. Opening it, she came face to face with a slight young man with deep brown hair and a handsome face. He smiled timidly.

"My apologies for disturbing you, my lady," he said. "I saw you the other night but we were not formally introduced. I am Guy de Broase."

Alys swallowed the bite in her mouth, forgetting all about her horrendous morning. Sir Guy's youthful attractiveness sucked all of the self-pity and confusion right out of her.

"My lord," she bowed deeply. "I am the Lady Alys St. James."

"I know." His smile broadened. "It seems that all of the St. James women are exceedingly beautiful."

She blushed furiously. "Thank you, my lord."

"Is Lady Sheridan at home?"

Alys thought of her sister lying on the floor in the next room. "She is indisposed at the moment," she opened the door wider. "Would you like to come in?"

"Thank you."

Guy entered the room respectfully, taking the chair that Alys indicated for him. She offered him some bread and cheese, which he declined. But he did take some wine. It was rapidly apparent, however, that Guy had come for one purpose alone; he had come to see Sheridan.

"I am sorry your sister is unavailable," he said. "Will she return soon? I hate to burden you with my presence."

"No burden at all, my lord," Alys said. She was thrilled to have the opportunity to sit with a handsome young man. "In truth, my sister is ill. She is resting in her bedchamber as we speak."

Guy instinctively looked at the closed panel. "I see," he said. "Nothing serious, I hope?"

"A sick headache."

"I see," he repeated. Then, he quickly stood. "I do not want to disturb her with our conversation. Perhaps I should leave and come back at another time."

Alys was quick to assure him. "We will not disturb her unless we shout. The walls are thick."

He smiled weakly and sat back down. He was coming to suspect that the Lady Alys wanted him to stay and chat. But he was uncomfortable with the look in her eye; sort of as a cat watches a mouse. She was ravenous. His gaze began to dart about nervously, unsure what to say, now wanting to leave.

He was saved by Neely throwing open the antechamber door. Neely's face was ruddy from the chill weather outside, but a fire of annoyance blazed in his dark eyes. He was about to vent his frustrations on Alys when he caught sight of Guy. Respectfully, he saluted.

"My lord," he said. "I apologize for my hasty entry; I did not know you were here."

"No apologies necessary," Guy said, moving for the door. "I was just leaving. Lady Alys, thank you very much for your hospitality. If you will give my compliments to Lady Sheridan and wish her a swift recovery."

Guy was at the door before Alys could protest. He almost seemed panicked to leave. But he wasn't clear yet; in his haste, he opened the door and ran headlong into a small man with unkempt white hair and a gnarled face.

"Forgive me," Guy apologized. "I did not see you, my lord."

The old man brushed at the front of his tunic for no real reason. In his hand, he held a big leather satchel.

"I am Lott Gilby, the physic. I have come for the Lady Sheridan." His sharp eyes fell on Alys. "You there, lady. Where is the Lady Sheridan?"

Alys recognized the physic who had bandaged her wrist. She motioned him inside. In the course of the exchange, Guy slipped out without being noticed.

"In there," Alys pointed at the bedchamber door.

The little man shuffled in, very business-like. Neely, having been gone since sunrise, had no idea Sheridan was ill.

"What's wrong with her?" he asked Alys.

"Sick headache," she told him.

It wasn't a new story with Sheridan. Neely had seen many of these episodes. He opened the chamber door for the physic, immediately spying Sheridan on the floor. He burst into the room, almost knocking the old man down in his haste.

"My lady," he knelt beside her. "Can you hear me? Are you all right?"

She stirred and the puppy jumped up, trying to lick Neely's face. "I have not hurt myself, if that's what you mean," she said quietly. "I just need to be left alone."

Neely was about to tell her that a physic had been summoned but the old man pushed forward and knelt beside Sheridan.

"My lady," he said. "De Lara sent me. Can you tell me what is wrong?"

Sheridan peeped an eye open, looking at him. "A sick headache. There is naught you can do for me. This has happened before."

The physic grunted, digging in the satchel he brought. He pulled out some phials of liquid, pouring some of this and some of that into a small pewter cup. As Alys and Neely watched curiously, he tossed a measure of white powder into it and stirred the concoction. It was like watching a witch make a brew and they were properly awed by the mystery.

"Drink this," he instructed to Sheridan.

With Neely's help, she sat up and drank the bitter brew. As she wiped her mouth and made a face of disgust, the physic turned to Neely.

"Put her on the bed," he said. "She will sleep like the dead for a day and night, but it should cure her."

Neely picked her up and lay her gently on the bed. Sheridan was still wiping her mouth. The puppy jumped up on the bed beside her, wriggling happily and burrowing in her covers.

"Sleep now, my lady," the physic instructed. "I shall return tomorrow to see how you are faring."

He was concise and business-like. And it was apparent that he had no time for pleasantries now that his task was complete. Neely escorted the physic from the apartment. When he returned, his expression was guarded. Sheridan was on her back once again, a cool cloth over her eyes.

"My lady," he began hesitantly. "I must ask you a question."

"Neely…" she was exasperated; would no one let her sleep? "What is it, then?"

Neely glanced at Alys, on the opposite side of the bed, and noted her bandaged wrist. His jaw began to flex.

"May I ask what has gone on this morning?" he said.

"What do you mean?"

He lifted an eyebrow, speaking mostly to Alys. "I am not a fool. I know I was sent on a ruse because Lady Alys apparently did not want me around. I will not argue the point, as it is my duty to serve the House of St. James. However, upon my return I find Lady Sheridan huddled on the floor in distress and Lady Alys with an injured hand. I would appreciate a logical explanation of why I was sent away and why everyone seems injured."

Sheridan lifted the cloth off her eyes. "I will let Alys explain why her wrist is injured. As for me, it is nothing quite so spectacular. You have seen me like this time and time again."

"If that is so, why did the physic say that de Lara sent him?"

Sheridan had hoped Neely had missed that part of it, but she wasn't surprised that he hadn't. Neely was, if nothing else, extremely sharp. And he was voraciously protective of both her and Alys. Her fury in her sister's actions returned, for a myriad of reasons.

"Because de Lara once again saved Alys' foolish hide today," she snapped. "When he saw that I was ill, he was thoughtful enough to send a physic."

Neely glanced at Alys, his dark eyes full of doubt and resentment. "What did you do while you had me out running circles for you?"

Alys refused to look him in the eye. "You have no right to ask me such things. I am above your reproach."

"But you are not above mine," Sheridan said. "Tell him, Alys. Tell him or I will. Tell him how you went to the royal apartment to see the king because you think he is in love with you. Tell him how the king tried to ravage you and how de Lara saved your life. Tell him!"

Alys was red in the face by now. She stood up, stomping to the door. Neely reached out and grabbed her good arm.

"Not so fast, my lady," he was as close to furious as either of the girls had ever seen him. "Is this true? Is that why you sent me away, so that I would not stop you?"

Alys yanked her arm away. "You are not my father, Neely de Moreville. You are a mere knight. You have no charge over me. We pay you well, we feed you, and therefore you do as we say. I'll not have you questioning me."

Sheridan sat up, shocked and incensed by her sister's diatribe. "How dare you speak to him like that," she hissed. "Neely is one of the family. He is part of us. You will apologize immediately or you will suffer the consequences."

"Suffer what?" Alys was gaining in momentum. "The both of you have done nothing but spy on me and suppress me for as long as I can recall. But, of course, no one watches you, Sheridan. You are so pretty and perfect. But I know otherwise." She thrust a finger in Neely's face. "Do you know that Sheridan has been sneaking out and meeting Sean de Lara? It's true!"

Neely's head snapped to Sheridan, whose eyes bugged with the shock of hearing such secretive information come blasting forth from her sister's big mouth. A storm was brewing, bigger than any of them could have guessed.

"Alys," she snapped. "I will never forgive you for lying about that. I have never done anything of the sort."

Neely was off of his tirade against Alys and focused on Sheridan now. "Is this true?" he asked. "Have you been meeting de Lara? My God, Dani, you know who he is and what he is. How can you risk yourself like that?"

He called her Dani. He hadn't called her Dani in years. There was pain in his voice. Sheridan wasn't so naïve that she didn't know how Neely felt about her. She'd always known. But it was unfortunate that she could not, and would not, return his feelings. Still, she couldn't look him in the eye and lie to him. It would have been disrespectful to all he'd ever meant to her family.

"I have met Sean on a few occasions," she said quietly. "He had been kind and gracious and delightful."

"De Lara?" Neely said incredulously. "The man is terror personified. Are you mad?"

"I'll not have you speak of him so."

"Why not? It's true. I cannot fathom why you have allowed yourself to play games with the Devil."

"He is not the Devil, Neely. I forbid you to speak ill of him."

Neely was beside himself, eaten with jealousy and rage. "I have never known you to be stupid, but I suppose I was wrong. You have the weight and trust of the good allies of England upon your shoulders, yet you cavort with the enemy."

She snapped. "Still your tongue, man. My father has worked harder than anyone to ensure that England sees a new age and my loyalties lie with my father's work. Question my trustworthiness again and I will send you along your way."

Neely froze, his dark eyes glittering with ferocity and distress. "I wasn't questioning your faithfulness," he said quietly. "I was questioning your sanity in keeping company with Sean de Lara."

"I know exactly what you were doing. Take care that your jealousy does not consume you, Neely. What you desire can never be and I will not allow you to discourage others who may vie for what you want for yourself."

That was enough for Neely; like a dog that had been beaten one too many times, he quit the bedchamber with his head down. His injured heart was evident. Alys still stood at the foot of the bed, shocked by the exchange, shocked that the focus had veered away from her so violently.

"Oh, Dani," she murmured. "You have hurt him."

Sheridan didn't want to talk anymore, to anyone. "Get out," she told her sister. "I do not want to see you again today."

Alys left the room, but not before she began weeping. She was sniffling as she quit the chamber and softly closed the door. When she was gone, Sheridan lay back down upon her pillows and cried.

CHAPTER SEVEN

"… when it became obvious that nothing we had planned for would come to pass, other ideals took shape. It was necessary. A man of experience knows his limitations. I refused to accept mine…."

The Chronicles of Sir Sean de Lara

1206 – 1215 A.D.

THE CORRIDORS OF the royal wing were quiet at this time of day. As dusk fell and shadows waned, the royal guard were changing shifts and the king was taking his usual late-afternoon slumber so that he would be able to stand an evening of food and drink without retiring early. It spoiled his fun. De Lara and d'Athée were in their usual room, in the chamber off of the king's main bower. This time of day was like the calm before the storm. Sean was sharpening a small dagger; d'Athée was trying to make heads or tails out of a map of the Welsh Marches.

He wasn't an educated man. Gerard's strength lay in the physical realm. He was as strong as a bear but as shallow as a cat. There wasn't much he knew or cared about other than enough liquor to drink and enough women to bed. He relied on Sean's intellect where it really mattered. The two of them had worked side by side, day and night, for five years. To date, it had been a compatible relationship though they could hardly be called close. It was simply the way of things.

"De Lara," Gerard scratched his loused head, his frustrated expression fixed upon the map. "Kington; where is it?"

Sean glanced up from the dagger. "South of Montgomery."

"Where?"

Sean stood up, still rubbing the dagger against the stone, and walked over to where Gerard stood against the table. He looked at the map and thumped a finger on the spot.

"There," he said.

Gerard squinted at the map. "Is it a big castle?"

"Big enough. Clifford holds it, plus he also holds Clifford Castle and Hay-on-Wye Castle."

Gerard shook his head. "Not so."

"What do you mean?"

"Clifford came to see the king while you were off with the red-haired chit. De Braose is laying siege to Kington as we speak. He had it before and now he wants it back."

Sean lifted an eyebrow but did not respond further. He walked away from the table, back to his chair. Gerard was still focused on the map.

"He wants you to ride for Kington," he said. "He'll be sending you within the week."

"Who?"

"The king."

Sean had to consciously prevent himself from reacting. He took his seat casually, spit on the stone, and continued sharpening the dagger. "Did he tell you this?"

"Aye." Gerard looked up from the map. "De Lara, 'tis your business what you do with the red-head. God knows, I have done enough with women to warrant a fine place in Hell. But at least I take them after our king has had his fill. I think your actions have concerned him."

"Is that so?" Sean knew that Gerard could hardly keep a secret, or his opinions, to himself. With Gerard, sometimes it was difficult to separate the two. "What actions are those?"

"That you took the woman away from him. He doesn't like competition."

"So he is sending me to fight Clifford's war in punishment?" Sean snorted. "I would hardly believe that."

"He is sending you to smash de Braose."

Sean continued the steady grind of metal against stone, although his thoughts were racing. "That," he said slowly, "I would believe. Did he say this?"

Gerard nodded. "He is furious with the de Braose clan. With the final father and son remaining from that great dynasty, he is determined to crush them once and for all. Were the king to confiscate their holdings along the Marches, it would greatly enrich his coffers."

"Indeed," Sean sighed, trying to appear as if the information really did not concern him. "The House of de Braose has been a Norman fixture in England since the conquest. I am almost sorry to see the last of the line go."

"Don't be," Gerard said. "If I were you, I'd worry about the House of St. James."

Sean's heart skipped a beat. "What in the hell for?"

Gerard made his way over to where Sean was seated. "Because our king is mulling over the possibility of razing Lansdown Castle on your way to the Marches."

Sean stopped sharpening. He stared at Gerard, struggling not to overtly respond. "Why would he do that?"

"Why not?"

Sean held Gerard's gaze a moment longer, trying to read him. But the man's expression was characteristically stupid. He slowly went back to his blade. "Then he'd better send me with a large army. Lansdown is nearly impenetrable."

Gerard lingered around the chair for the moment. Sean could feel him breathing down his neck. He wasn't so sure why the man was being so solicitous, but he didn't like it. He was suspicious. The blade in his hand suddenly ended up at Gerard's throat.

D'Athée threw his hands up in response to the threatening action. There was a glimmer of humor in his dark eyes.

"Not me, my friend," he said with a smile. "I am not your enemy."

Sean's clear blue eyes were laced with venom. "Tell me everything you have heard and tell me why you feel the need to be so solicitous."

Gerard continued to grin at him in the hopes of infuriating Sean. It didn't work. After a moment, his smug grin faded.

"He had me follow you this afternoon," he rumbled. "He wanted to see where you took the St. James girl. I followed you to the physic and back to the St. James apartments. Then I followed you back to the physic again, where you sent the man back to the St. James' chambers. And now, here we are, cozy comrades."

Sean had the point of the blade aimed right at his major artery. One flick and the man would bleed to death right in front of him. They both knew that it was not out of the realm of possibility; they'd both seen Sean do far worse.

"Why did he have you follow me?" Sean's tone was as deadly as the wicked gleam of the blade.

"Because you stopped him from having his way with the red-haired girl. You have never done that before."

A split-second of uncertainty crossed Sean's eyes, but Gerard was too dense to see it. "I told him why. There is no mystery to it."

Gerard shook his head, rubbing his neck against the blade. Spots of blood appeared. "But you took her to the physic and escorted her home."

Sean lifted an eyebrow. "I have done that before, too, and well you know it. In fact, you have accompanied me on such outings. I did nothing with the St. James woman that I haven't done before."

"Except stopped the king from taking her. You know as well as I do that no one does that and escapes his wrath, or his suspicions."

"So what has he sent you to do? Watch every move I make? Kill me as I sleep?"

Gerard shook his head, carefully. "No, my friend. Nothing so drastic. You are a favorite of our king. But you placed doubt in his mind with your actions. He will demand a show of your loyalty now."

Sean could see where he was leading. "To destroy Lansdown?"

"To prove you are more loyal to him than to the House of St. James."

With a hiss, Sean dropped the knife and turned away. "So that's it," he said. "He needs affirmation of my fealty."

"Aye."

Sean turned to him. "Does he really think I have loyalties to the opposition? For Christ's sake, I have spent nine years in his personal service. Does he really believe I would jeopardize my standing for a stupid wench hardly out of swaddling clothes?"

Gerard shrugged. "All I know is what I have heard. He has not told me anything directly. I would expect he would do that, to you, very shortly."

Sean's jaw was ticking, a million thoughts rolling through his mind. "He wants me out of London and off to the wilds," he muttered to himself. There was tremendous irony in his voice as he slowly shook his head. "Oh, sweet mercy."

Gerard left him alone. Sean didn't know where the man went, but he suspected it was to tell the king of their conversation. Of that, he was unconcerned. But he was deeply concerned with the course the last few minutes had taken.

So he would be ordered to ride to Kington, destroying Lansdown along the way. It didn't even matter that Lansdown would be his own when he married Sheridan. It had nothing to do with that. What mattered was making sure Sheridan was safe before he left, and there was no doubt he would go. He had to. Nine years had come to this point and he would not risk everything, at least not now.

Everything now hinged on the attack on London. It had to be before he left for the Marches so that he did not have to go. He would undoubtedly be required to stay and protect the city. Consequently, he had to get Sheridan out of London now and send her home for her own safety. However, if the attack on London was delayed and he found himself mobilizing for the Marches with Lansdown in his path, then he would find himself attacking the castle with Sheridan within its walls.

It was an appalling prospect.

A FEW HOURS before dawn found Alys wandering the halls of the royal apartments again. Roused from a deep sleep, Sean could hear her distant weeping. With a start, he threw himself out of the chair he had been dozing on and tossed open the doors from his chamber so hard that one of them actually unhinged. He was in the corridor, marching towards the sounds of her weeping.

She was disheveled and hysterical, attempting to tell a crimson-clad guard the purpose of her visit. Sean marched upon her and she cried out the moment she saw him. But he knew, whatever she said, could not be beneficial to anyone so he slapped a massive hand over her mouth and physically carried her back down the hall in the direction that she had come. He didn't want her anywhere near the royal apartments. She had already cost him much. He would not let her cost him everything.

Halfway down a servant's stair, he set her down. Her face was red and damp from weeping.

"I told you never to come back here again," he growled. "It was not a request but a command. I told you that if I saw you again that I would…."

"Sir Sean, please," Alys sobbed. "I came to find you. My sister is very ill."

He forgot his anger. "What is wrong?"

Alys shook her head. "I do not know. I cannot wake her. She breathes harsh and labored, as if she is dying. I am afraid that she is!"

He didn't ask her any more. Grasping her arm, far more gently this time, he led the way back to the St. James apartment. The corridors were quiet and still at this hours with oil lamps burning every so often so as not to create total darkness. He could feel royal soldiers around him, guarding the different wings that they passed through, but he ignored them. By the time they reached the apartment, his panic had blossomed while Alys' had calmed. They made an odd combination.

There were two St. James soldiers in the hall protecting the door. Alys waved them aside as the little maid unbolted the panel from the inside. Once inside, the little puppy jumped all over his feet and it was an effort not to step on the beast. The room was warm and dimly lit. Avoiding the dog, Sean went straight to the bower.

It was nearly pitch dark in the room, but he could hear Sheridan's breathing the moment he entered the door. It sounded like a death rattle.

"Bring some light," he commanded quietly as he went for the bed. He could barely see her in the darkness and he felt for a pulse. It was fast and weak, and his heart sank. "How long has she been like this?"

Alys hovered behind him as the maid brought forth a fish oil lamp. Immediately, they could see how pale Sheridan was.

"A few hours," Alys said. "The physic gave her some medicine and she fell asleep, and now I cannot wake her."

Sean put both hands on her face, enormous appendages that swallowed up Sheridan's entire head. His fingers were in his hair, his flesh against her. Stabs of longing, of angst, filled his chest as he touched her.

"Sheridan," he whispered. "Sheridan, can you hear me?"

She was limp, like a corpse. He stroked her cheeks with his thumbs. "Wake up, angel. Hear my voice and awaken."

"She won't." The panic returned to Alys' tone. "What shall we do?"

Sean didn't hesitate. "Send for Gilby," he snapped softly. "Tell your guards in the hall to go for him; he is near the barracks. Tell them to hurry."

Both Alys and the maid fled. Alone in the room, with a small lamp casting an eerie white light on Sheridan's features, Sean gazed at her with a tremendous amount of sorrow. His thumbs continued to stroke her cheeks, his forehead finally coming to rest on her own. It was a helpless gesture. Never in his life had he felt so powerless, listening to her labor to breathe, terrified that she was indeed going to die right in front of him. The thought nearly brought tears to his eyes, and it was a shocking realization.

Pulling her limp body up against him, he cradled her against his massive chest, rocking her gently with the inborn instinct of all human beings. It was a deliciously painful gesture, her fragile warmth against his strength.

He was still holding her when Gilby came. The old man had to practically pry her out of Sean's arms. Sean had known Gilby for many years and trusted the man's discretion. He knew that no word of his actions or behavior would reach the ears of others. Sean, Alys and the little maid watched with baited breath as the old physic examined Sheridan. He listened to her chest, checked her pulse, checked her eyes. He even looked in her ears. Finally, he shook his head.

"Nothing to worry over," he said. "She is simply reacting to the medicaments I gave her for her head sickness. She is very sensitive to something I gave her, though I am not sure what."

Sean let out a sigh as if his entire body was deflating of air. "Then she will wake from this without incident?"

"She will. But better to watch her to make sure that she remembers to breathe. The potion's property is strong and can, in fact, put one to sleep forever if one isn't careful."

Sean lifted an eyebrow. "If it is so strong, why did you give it to her to cure her head sickness?"

"I didn't give it to her to cure her head sickness. I gave it to her so that she would sleep until it passed."

Sean couldn't decide where he was more angry or more relieved. He settled for relieved. "You could have at least told us so that we wouldn't panic when we could not wake her."

Gilby grunted. He packed up his leather satchel and headed for the door. "I shall be by in a few hours to see how she fares," he said. "Until then, someone should stay away with her. If she stops breathing, pinch her. She'll resume quickly enough."

The physic wandered out into the antechamber, pulling his cloak tightly about him in anticipation of the chill of the corridor. Leaving a relieved Alys to watch over Sheridan, Sean followed.

"I'll send a guard to escort you back," he said.

Gilby shook his head. "No need," he said. "I welcome the solitude."

"Very well. We shall see you tomorrow, then."

The old man glanced at him, something of curiosity and disapproval in his eyes. "Do you plan on staying here? I would advise against it."

"So noted."

Gilby moved close to him. "The Chapel of St. Peter. One hour."

"That is sooner than expected."

"There is much to discuss."

Sean simply nodded and the old physician shuffled out of the antechamber, closing the door softly behind him.

The time was upon them. He could feel it.

ଓ

"SHE HAS BEEN cavorting with de Lara since nearly the day we arrived," Neely was obviously drunk. "We have all tried to explain to her the evils of the man, but she will not listen."

Jocelin sat across the table from the captain of the St. James guard. He had known the man for twenty years. Henry St. James treated him like a son, but that was never what Neely wanted. He wanted to be the son-in-law. It was not because of the wealth and power of the St. James clan; that much was certain. It was because of a deep and abiding affection he held for Sheridan. He'd become quite adept at controlling himself where she was concerned. Now, with disappointment, jealousy and liquor, the dam of control he had worked so hard to maintain had finally sprung a leak.

"Infatuated women are irrational creatures," Jocelin said quietly.

"They are indeed," Neely took another large swallow of the ale. He wiped his mouth on the back of his hand. "De Lara knows who she is. And there is little doubt that the king sent him to charm her to see what he could draw out of her. There is no telling what she is divulged to him, and in turn, to John's cause."

"Are you telling me that she is untrustworthy?"

Neely's dark eyes clouded with uncertainty. "I am not. I am merely… speculating."

"Are you sure that it is not your jealousy talking?"

Neely pursed his lips as if to bitterly retort, but he took another drink instead. When it became clear that he would not answer, Jocelin took the bottle of ale away and stood up. He set the jug upon the nearest shelf of his small, modest accommodations near the chapel.

"Why do you come to me with this, de Moreville?" he asked. "What would you have me do?"

"Stop her. Tell her that de Lara only means her harm."

Jocelin wriggled his eyebrows. "Were it only that simple. Do you not know of women, Neely? The more you try to discourage them, the more they will do whatever it is that you are attempting to discourage them from."

Neely nodded or swayed; Jocelin could not be sure. He had been drinking long before he had ever sought out the bishop. Now he was down to the bare bones of emotions and shame.

"I tried to tell her," Neely muttered. "She would not listen."

Jocelin scratched his chin, thinking on the all of the implications that clandestine communication with Sean de Lara could have. The long-term results, for both sides, could be immeasurable. He didn't like it at all.

"Sheridan may as well have taken up games with a viper," he said. "And this viper will kill her more swiftly than any reptilian creature. This viper has a brain and a heart, courage unparalleled and a skill beyond compare. To keep her away from him, we must be more cunning and more skillful than he is."

"Do you really think he is trying to draw information out of her about the resistance?" Neely was close to falling out his chair by now. It would not be long before he was passed out completely. "I cannot imagine what other purpose he may have. Surely he would not attempt to court her."

Jocelin frowned at him. "Court her? Of course not. Men like Sean de Lara do not court women. Their life and their loves are war and politics."

Neely tried to stand up, making a bad attempt of it. "Then you must speak to Lady Sheridan before she does something she regrets. Tell her… tell her to stay away from de Lara. Tell her that he only means her harm"

Jocelin steadied him and forced him to sit back down in the chair. "We may not have to worry over it much longer."

"Why?"

"Because the allies are leaving the Tower tonight. War is looming, Neely. Once Sheridan is gone, the threat of de Lara will be abolished."

Neely's reaction was slow. "So it is tonight. Pity I did not know it. 'Twill be difficult to command in my current state."

"You know it now," Jocelin replied. "There is still time for you to regain your senses before we depart."

Neely blinked his eyes, struggling to focus. "Indeed. But what if Lady Sheridan will not leave? You should have heard her defend de Lara. He was kind and considerate, she said. I fear that she will not want to go."

Jocelin lifted an eyebrow at him, a variety of schemes rolling through his mind. "I have," he said deliberately, "an interesting thought. Would you hear it without concern?"

"I would."

"Certainly, a husband would make her go. And a husband would do far better at keeping de Lara away from her permanently."

Neely wasn't so drunk that he did not understand the statement. "You will marry her off in order to keep de Lara away?"

"It seems logical."

Neely suddenly stood up again, his manner self-righteous and strong. "Then allow me to wed her," he half-demanded, half-pleaded. "I will kill de Lara if he comes anywhere near her. Bless me with that privilege, my lord, and I'll not ask for God's favor ever again."

Jocelin had been expecting that statement for years. He put a consoling hand on Neely's shoulder and shoved him, again, down into the chair. "Women like Lady Sheridan are not meant for men like you or me, my friend," he said softly. "She needs a man of station, with power.

De Lara wouldn't dare tangle with a man of rank."

It was not what Neely wanted to hear. But he had resigned himself to the inevitable long ago, as much as he told himself otherwise. "Who, then?"

Jocelin moved away from him, his weather-worn face lined with the glimmer of possibilities.

"Someone who had been vying for her hand for quite some time," he murmured.

"There have been many. Who in particular do you mean?"

Jocelin turned to look at him, his profile illuminated by the dim light from the lancet windows. It was an eerie portrait of a man forced into a game of deadly chance, of life and death. It was time to take the leap. Jocelin, more than anyone, knew what was at stake.

"The most powerful man on the Marches," he said quietly. "Guy de Braose."

☙

SEAN HAD BEEN waiting longer than he would have liked in the confession booth at the Chapel of St. Peter. It was a dark, musty, eerie place to be at any given time of the day. On the other end of the screen, he suddenly heard the door open and softly close. Heavy breathing, as if the person on the other side had just run the entire length of London, filled the small vestibule.

"Bless me, Father, for I have sinned," Sean began. "It has been a day since my last confession."

"What is it you wish to confess, my son?"

"Rumors of war abound, Father. It is said that I am to be sent to war on the Marches."

The breathing slowed, steadied. "When?"

"I am not sure. I have not been directly ordered yet. 'Tis only a rumor at this point."

"Why would you go?"

"De Braose is laying siege to Kington. Clifford has asked for help."

"I see."

"There is more."

"What?"

"It is also rumored that part of my directive will be to raze Lansdown Castle."

There was a long pause. "Why would you be ordered to do this?"

Sean sighed harshly, disgusted with the turn of events, though strangely he did not regret the actions that led up to it. "Because I stopped the king from raping Alys St. James. The king suspects my loyalties now and will ask me to raze Lansdown to prove that my fealty is to him and not to the House of St. James. All plans of the attack on London aside, this is a very real problem in addition to so many others."

"What will you do?"

"I am not sure. Much depends on the move against London."

"It is imminent."

"How soon?"

"Two days at the most. The majority of nobles are clearing out tonight."

"This is fact?"

"I just left a meeting with Jocelin, Rochester and Coventry. Arundel and de Warenne are already gone and gathering with their troops outside the city limits. The rest will move out by dawn."

Sean's thoughts immediately moved to Sheridan. "If the king intends on sending me to the Marches, it will take a few days to prepare the army. The siege of London will prevent me from leaving."

"Then the king must not know the nobles are leaving to join their troops. Their flight will spook him."

"Agreed."

"And you must do what you can to make sure the Tower is vulnerable once the siege has begun."

"I will undoubtedly lead the battle against the allies. 'Tis a pity that I will be seen as the loser in all of this."

"The truth will be told when this is all over. Just make sure you live to see it."

"I'll live to see it," Sean assured him. "And I will live to claim my prize."

The voice on the other side was silent. "Lady Sheridan?"

"Of course."

The voice grunted, as if in pain. "Sean," he spoke haltingly. "There is something you should know."

"I fear to ask."

"You should. Jocelin intends to marry Lady Sheridan to Guy de Braose before the week is out."

He wasn't surprised. He realized that he had almost been expecting it. But it took all of Sean's self-control not to burst through the panel and grab the voice around the neck. As it was, his big hands worked furiously and sweat popped out on his forehead, indicative of his level of emotion.

"Did he tell you this?" he asked through clenched teeth.

"Aye," the voice said. "He feels that you are a danger to her."

"He mentioned me by name?"

"He did. It seems that Neely de Moreville is aware that you and Sheridan have been, shall we say, meeting surreptitiously. Jocelin fears for Lady Sheridan's life."

Sean stood up; he couldn't help it. He braced his hands on either side of the confession window, a gesture that was as powerful as it was pitiful. His fingers dug into the walls, angst in every move, every gesture.

"Tell him who I am," his voice was a harsh whisper. "Tell him who I am and what I want. I'll not allow her to marry another. She is meant for me and only me."

The voice was laced with sorrow. He could feel the man's pain. "I cannot."

"You must or I will."

"We swore when we started that only a select few would know your worth. 'Tis safer for you, Sean."

"To hell with safety. Tell him. I beg of you."

The voice sighed heavily. There was no fighting him, no reasoning with him. As always, men in love were irrational creatures. What made it worse was that Sean deserved everything he asked for, and so much more. To deny him anything at this stage of the game was inherently wrong.

"I will do what I can," he finally said. "I cannot promise results. Jocelin's mind is set."

"Go, then." It was not a request. "Go and tell him now. Lady Sheridan belongs to me."

"He may have already told de Braose."

Sean didn't reply. He quit the vestibule before he was dismissed, storming blindly from the chapel. The contact waited a nominal amount of time before slowly opening the door.

Father Simon's gaze was laced with regret.

CHAPTER EIGHT

".... My entire life had been mapped, carefully controlled. I was infallible, omnipotent, the Fear of all. I believed myself beyond defeat. That would soon be put to the test as my angel was pulled into the bowels of Hell... the gates opened and I leapt wholeheartedly into the maelstrom to save her...."

The Chronicles of Sir Sean de Lara

1206 – 1215 A.D.

THERE WAS A corporeal sense of anxiety in the air of the halls near the Flint Tower. Everything in the St. James apartment was packed and ready to go less than two hours after the command to move out came down. Jocelin himself had given the order to the St. James men, who immediately started packing their gear and summoning the horses. Neely had faithfully joined his troops for the detail although he was still muddled by the alcohol that flowed through his veins.

Inside the apartment, the little maid had summoned the help of a few household servants to help pack her mistresses' items, which they had done so with efficiency. Capcases and trunks were stacked neatly in the antechamber. The women were ready to go before the army was.

Unable to sleep through the commotion and excitement, Alys had also helped pack with her one good arm. Sheridan had slept like the dead through all of it. Even now, when everything was bundled and being taken from the Flint Tower down to the waiting wagons, Sheridan was unable to awaken. The medicaments that Gilby had given her continued to render her incapable of responding, so everyone simply worked around her.

When their apartment was empty and most of the men had gone,

Alys and the maid struggled to dress Sheridan in traveling clothes. Ill or not, she had to be moved and it could not be done in her shift. The act of dressing her became even more complicated with Alys' bandaged arm, but they somehow managed to get a heavy wool shift and tunic on her. Even though she weighed next to nothing, it was like trying to dress a rag doll. They'd lift one arm and the other would fall. When they turned her over to fasten the dress, she nearly slid off the mattress. The entire event never gave them a moment's peace.

By the time the ladies were finished dressing her, they were exhausted. Sheridan was neatly bundled up, however, and prepared to depart. Alys went into the antechamber to notify the one remaining guard, but found it eerily empty. She found him in the hall, dutifully guarding the door. He proceeded to inform Alys that he was at his post pending the return of Neely and the bishop. Alys went back inside to wait.

The hustle of the past two hours had faded, leaving the apartments strangely still. There was a fire burning low in the hearth, the precious glass that lined the windows on this level frosted from the moisture inside the room. Alys wandered back into the bedchamber where the maid sat next to Sheridan, making sure her sister remembered to breathe. Sitting on the opposite side of the bed, she waited for the men to return.

Her arm throbbed and itched beneath the bandages. In truth, Alys wasn't particularly happy to be returning home. She rather liked it here at the Tower with a variety of men to look at. Glancing at Sheridan, she felt a stab of envy; her sister cared not for men in the least, yet she had de Lara and de Braose's attentions. It wasn't fair. But her bitterness fled as Sheridan coughed in her sleep. Alys reached out with her good hand to touch her sister's cheek. *Poor Dani.*

A knock on the antechamber door roused her from her thoughts. Alys rushed to the door to find Guy standing in the archway. His handsome, youthful face was grim.

"Where is Lady Sheridan?" he asked.

Alys pointed to the bedroom, disappointed that he had not asked for her. "She is ill."

He didn't say anything as he pushed past her. Alys trotted after him. Guy barged into the bedchamber, his gaze falling upon Sheridan's sleeping face. After a split-second of allowing himself the luxury of looking upon her beauty, absorbing it, he moved swiftly into action.

"We must get her out." He went to the side of the bed and scooped her carefully into his arms. "Get a blanket to cover her. I am taking her to the carriage."

The little maid hurried to do his bidding. A wool traveling blanket was produced. Alys was anxious at de Braose's clipped, rushed manner.

"What carriage?" she asked. "We came astride palfreys. Where are you…?"

"I have confiscated a carriage for her," Guy cut her off. "She obviously cannot ride in this condition. You will ride with her in the carriage to ensure her good health."

Alys couldn't argue. As the maid gathered up the last of their items, including the puppy, they followed de Braose from the apartment and into the long, dark corridor. He seemed almost in a panic to get out of the tower. Alys has to literally run to keep up with him.

"Why so hurried?" she asked him.

Guy didn't reply. He was absorbed by the urgency that filled every part of his body. His meeting with Jocelin just moments before had been brief. Guy came out of the meeting with a future wife. It had been everything he had been hoping for. But Jocelin also told him about de Lara. Guy understood the need for urgency in getting Sheridan out of the Tower better than most. Too much hinged on it.

"Sir Guy?" Alys would not be ignored. "Please tell me why you are so hurried. You are frightening me."

He hadn't meant to be cruel. Sometimes his dedication to a task caused him to lose sight of things around him and he realized that he was being selfish. "I do not mean to frighten you, my lady," he said quietly. "'Tis simply that the guard is ready and waiting to leave. I do not wish to leave them standing vulnerable."

It was a half-truth. Guy's own personal guard was mingled with the St. James men, all of them waiting to escort their lords and ladies out of the city. A siege was hours away and they had to get clear.

He was at the base of the steps, close to the doorway that lead to the yard and the Lanthorn gate beyond. He could almost smell the freedom and sent the maid on ahead to notify the troops of their impending arrival.

As he neared the open panel, a massive form stepped from the shadows. Guy knew who it was before he ever saw the face, simply by the size. He should have known the Lord of the Shadows would know his every move.

Guy came to a slow, unsteady halt. Alys yelped with fear, with surprise, as de Lara stepped into the soft gray light. Guy's forward momentum may have been arrested, but he stood his ground. He would not back down and he would not run. He could not believe that de Lara would attack him with Sheridan in his arms.

"Move aside, de Lara," he said calmly.

Sean was clad from head to toe in full battle gear. When he moved, metal brushed against metal and gave him a horrible, death-like resonance.

"Where are you going?" Sean sounded like the Devil.

Guy paused, fear and anger hand in hand. As long as he held Sheridan, he was certain that de Lara would do him no harm.

"I am escorting the ladies home, at the request of the Bishop of Bath and Glastonbury," he said. "If you would kindly step aside, we can be on our way."

"You are not leaving the Tower with Lady Sheridan."

"The ladies wish to return home."

Sean's hand went to rest on the hilt of his sword; the thing was so massive that it weighed as much as a small child. It was a gesture that did not go unnoticed by Guy, and the ripples of fear began to spread through his chest.

"Nay, they do not," Sean said steadily. "Give Lady Sheridan to me and be on your way."

The air grew tense. "I will not," Guy replied. "She goes home."

Sean shifted on his enormous legs. It was almost a thoughtful gesture. "De Braose, I have no quarrel with you. But you do not seem to understand the way of things. When I told you to give me the lady, that is exactly what I meant. To refuse my request is not in your best interest."

"You cannot use your sword against me without risking the lady." Guy's anger overshadowed his fear. "If your goal is truly to keep Lady Sheridan for yourself, what kind of man would risk her life simply to gain his wants?"

"That is not your concern. You are caught up in something you know nothing about. I would suggest you simply turn her over to me and be on your way."

"I will not."

"She does not belong to you."

"She is my betrothed."

"She is *my* betrothed."

The rapid-fire exchange came to a strange, unsteady pause. Guy finally shook his head. "The Bishop of Bath has consecrated our betrothal," he said. "I do not know whereby you make your claim."

"My claim is directly between the lady and me. I asked for her hand and she accepted."

Guy wasn't sure how to respond. There were apparently details that he knew nothing about. But, then again, de Lara could easily be lying. He gazed at Sheridan, collapsed against him, his thoughts and wants torn.

"I am sure that Jocelin would say that she has no right," he said softly. "'Tis not for the lady to dictate terms of marriage."

Sean watched Guy, the way he held Sheridan, and fought off the pangs of jealousy. "As heiress to Bath and Glastonbury, she can indeed express her desire. Jocelin has no formal control over her, other than by verbal agreement with her father." He took a step forward, his focus moving between Sheridan and Guy. "I can promise you that Jocelin will surrender to her will. And her will is to marry me."

In his heart, Guy suspected that was true. He could imagine no man denying Lady Sheridan. After a moment, he smiled wryly. "I would assume that Jocelin knows nothing of the agreement between you."

"He does not."

Sheridan picked that moment to awaken. Much to everyone's surprise, she suddenly raised an arm and slapped Guy across the face. Startled, he lost his grip and she almost tumbled to the floor. Only his quick reflexes prevented her head from striking the stone. Sean, as fast and agile as a cat, was on his knees beside her just as another hand came up. He grabbed it before it could strike Guy again.

"Bastards," she was half-awake, spouting obscenities. "I'll kill you both. Let me go. Let me go, I say!"

Sean knew her mind was not clear. Before he could speak, Alys leaned over her.

"Dani," she said softly. "'Tis all right. I am here."

Sheridan's luminous blue eyes lolled open. They kept rolling back into her head. "Alys?" she whispered. She blinked several times. "Where am I? What is happening?"

"We must leave the Tower," Alys told her. "Sir Guy… well, he is helping us…."

Sheridan was dreadfully groggy. She looked at Guy, then turned to Sean. Her eyes widened. "Sean," she whispered. "You are here, too?"

"I am here."

Guy could see in that moment, by the expression upon her face, that the feelings Sean de Lara had expressed for Sheridan were very mutual. It was a disheartening awareness. But Guy wasn't accustomed to surrender; it did not come easily to him. His father had taught him that. He knew that he would not relinquish Sheridan without a fight.

Sean still held her hand. Before Guy could stop him, he tugged gently on her arm and pulled her right up into his cradling grasp. They were smiling at each other, very glad to see one another. Guy's momentary surprise turned to resentment.

"No, de Lara," he said firmly. "She must go with me. I must remove her from the Tower at once."

Sean tore his gaze away from Sheridan long enough to cast de Braose a malignant glare. Strangely enough, he did not speak the multitude of threats that were on his mind. He saw no need now that Sheridan was in his arms.

"She will be removed," he said quietly. "But it will be under my protection."

Guy was normally a very calm man. What he did in the next moment was uncharacteristic. He unsheathed his weapon, a blade used in many battles by his forefathers, and leveled it at Sean. He ceased to become the calm, pleasant man he had established a reputation as. He became what his family had built their foundation on – a warring, confrontational de Braose.

"She is not yours, not by rights or by law," he said, as sternly as his mild-manner would allow. "Release her to me and I will forgive everything. Refuse and I shall be forced to defend what is rightfully mine."

The smell of battle was in the air. Sean had inhaled the heady scent too many times not to know it, not to feel it. He carefully put Sheridan down, holding her steady as she wobbled on weak legs.

"Go with Alys," he told her. "Alys, take your sister away from here. Go back to your apartment until I come for you."

"Nay," Sheridan shook her head, unsteadying herself to the point of nearly falling. "I'll not leave you. What is happening here?"

As Sean thought of a simple explanation for the events of the past few moments, Guy spoke.

"Jocelin has offered a betrothal between you and I," he said. "I have accepted."

Sheridan wasn't overly stunned. Her father had been trying to marry her off since she had been fourteen years of age. Five years later,

Jocelin had taken the mantle of matchmaker. She knew her worth as an heiress, and Guy seemed like a kind young man. Certainly he was well connected and an alliance between St. James and de Braose would be a smart one. But the fact remained that she did not want to marry him.

"Sir Sean and I have an understanding of betrothal," she said as considerately as she could. "Jocelin was not aware of this when he spoke to you. He did not speak with my permission."

"But he spoke on behalf of your father, who has asked this of him," Guy said. "My lady, I mean no disrespect, but surely you are aware of Sir Sean's… loyalties."

"I am."

"And yet you would still marry him?"

"I would marry the man, not his politics."

"But they are one in the same. You are heiress to the House of St. James, one of the king's strongest opponents. To marry the king's personal protector would be to forever ostracize your family from her allies. You would be alone, ruined. It would be political suicide."

She knew that. Seeds of doubt began to take root. Perhaps she was being too selfish in only thinking of herself. But looking at Sean, the way the man made her feel, she could not imagine living without him for the rest of her life. Still, she could not shake the feeling that all of this might only be a passing infatuation. She'd only known Sean a matter of days and already she was willing to risk her family's future because of her own selfish wants. Confusion and distress, coupled by the residual effects of the drugs that Gilby had given her, weakened her normally strong resolve.

Sheridan took a few steps back, grasping Sean gently by the arm. She pulled him back, almost to the door, so that they could speak privately. Her lovely face turned to him, the light from the fading moon casting shadows on her features. From her expression, it was obvious that there was much on her mind.

"When I look at you," she murmured, "all I see is what I want, not necessarily what is right."

He understood what she meant. He had been wrestling with the same thing for days. "And when I look at you, I am willing to forget everything I have worked for, everything that I am, just for the chance to spend the rest of my life with you."

She smiled ironically. "What a pair we make."

"Indeed."

"But is it right? I mean, is what we desire the right thing to do? We both risk so very much."

"I would risk my life for a chance to be with you, however small."

She put her hand to his cheek and he clapped a massive hand over hers, holding her warm flesh against his. There was tremendous sense of longing in that sweet, brief touch.

"As sudden and irrational as it seems, I would as well," she murmured. "But I have so much more to consider than just myself. There's Alys. There are my family's holdings. When you demanded marriage of me, I…"

"Demand? Did you say demand?"

"Aye, demand," she lifted an insistent eyebrow at him. He grinned, and so did she. "I did not think of anything other than myself. Now I am forced to think of everything other than myself."

"Are you saying that you would rather marry de Braose?"

"Nay," she shook her head. "I would rather marry you. But I am not sure if it is the right thing to do."

He sighed, his gaze moving across the doorway, out into the yard, back into the corridor, finally falling on Guy and Alys. After a moment, he refocused on Sheridan.

"I have only known you days," he said quietly. "But in order to answer your question, I must trust you. Trust is not easily given, not in my profession. What I tell you must never leave your lips. If it does, I will die. Is this understood?"

He was serious. She nodded her head. "Aye."

He took a deep breath. It was difficult for him. "I am not what you think."

"What do you mean?"

"Allied to the king, part and parcel to his madness. My position with him is well calculated."

She still didn't understand. "I am not sure…."

"I am a spy, Sheridan."

It took a moment for the implication to sink in. Her eyes widened. "You… you spy for…?"

"For William Marshall. I have for almost thirteen years."

Her hand flew to her mouth, covering the big "O" that had formed. "Sean," the hand came down so she could speak. "What are you telling me?"

He grabbed her by both arms, his grip firm and warm and powerful. "I am telling you that my true title is Viscount Trestylan. I have lands and holdings in the Welsh Marches that my family has held before the Norman conquest. But my devotion to my country is so great that I would risk everything to help the resistance against the tyrannical king, as my father did before me. I chose to become a hated man because it is better to be at the right hand of the Devil than in his path. Most of the information you and your allies have been fed has come directly from me. I know all, see all. But in order to maintain the illusion, I have been forced into some unsavory choices and actions. I am, therefore, very much an ally to the House of St. James. When you marry me, you will indeed marry a collaborator. Only no one can know about my true loyalties until John is unseated and we have a new king upon the throne."

Her mouth was back to forming the astonished "O". The expression on her face was something he would remember for the rest of his life.

"My God," she breathed. "Is it true?"

"I swear upon my honor."

"That explains why you lied to the king about the assembly of nobles you saw in my apartment that night. And it also explains why you saved Alys from his lust."

"I saved Alys from him because I did not want you to be hurt. Had

Alys been any one of the hundreds of other women passing through the king's bed, I would have let him have his way with her. I would not have risked myself."

Her hands threaded themselves around his fingers, tightening. "It… it is so difficult to believe all of this."

"As it should be. I have worked hard to establish my reputation."

"Who else knows of your true loyalties?"

"A select few, no more than I can count on one hand."

Several feet away, Guy shifted, noise from his armor echoing against the walls. It reminded them that they were not alone and that time was very short. As much as Sheridan wanted to linger on Sean's revelations, she knew their time together was quickly coming to an end. She began to feel a sense of panic.

"What do we do now?" she asked. "I do not want to marry Guy."

Sean could not leave with her. He could not marry her now. There were too many ingredients mixing into the great pot of chaos at the moment, creating a maelstrom of choices from which to pick. He had to choose the right course of action or all would be lost.

"I know you are unaware of the events of the past several hours, but suffice to say that an attack on London is imminent," he explained softly, quickly. "De Braose is taking you out of the city, as most of the allies have already fled. You and Alys must go home."

"But what of you?" she wanted to know. "What are you going to do?"

He would not tell her of his potential orders to march on Kington, to engage the de Braose army even as he now faced off against one of their kin. Nor would he tell her of the rumors that he was to march on Lansdown. He knew, no matter what his orders, that he would not do that. Now was not the time to rattle her brain with more information than she could rationally absorb.

"I shall stay here to ensure that London falls to the allies," he said. "Then I shall go to Lansdown. And you."

There was great fear in her eyes, not for the siege, but for Sean. "I do not want to leave you."

He smiled, kissing both her hands. "Nor I, you. But for your own safety, you must go."

Sheridan's gaze moved to Guy, standing silent several feet away. His sword was still drawn. "I swear that I will not marry him. I will commit myself to a convent first."

Sean's jaw ticked, feeling helpless to prevent anything from happening until his own tasks were completed. "I trust that you will hold both him and Jocelin off until I can come for you," he said. "I am sorry I cannot be of more help than that. It would seem that I have my own problems to take care of before you and I can be together."

She nodded, resigned and renewed. "I shall be strong, have no doubt. I shall look for you to return to me every day."

He touched her face. He didn't care if de Braose was looking or not; he kissed her so deeply that he lifted her off the ground. All he cared about at the moment was the taste, the feel, the smell of her. He was enraptured.

"My thoughts and affections go with you," he murmured in her ear. "Not a day will pass that I will not hold you dear in my heart and mind."

She was close to tears but held herself in check. "I am yours and only yours, for always."

"Swear it."

"I do. Oh, I do."

He kissed her again, his thumbs on her cheeks. He drew in the sight of her, something to keep safe in his memory for the long separation ahead. With a final wink, he took her arm and led her back to de Braose.

"Take her back to Lansdown," his request sounded suspiciously like a command. "Make sure that she is well and safe."

Guy still held the sword. He had witnessed the exchange between the lady and de Lara, though he'd not heard their words. But the affection between the two was readily apparent. He had not expected this outcome but he did not question it. As he went to take her arm, somewhat hesitantly, he was shocked to witness de Lara suddenly unsheathing his sword. It was like watching a bolt of lightning strike; flashy, loud, and nearly faster than the eye could track.

Men were rushing in from the courtyard, charging through the open door. It was dark and difficult to see the cluster of bodies filling the small stair well. But one thing was for certain; they were armed to the teeth and heading straight for de Braose. Sean had his sword leveled defensively, swiftly striking down the first two men who came within close proximity of him.

His primary concern was to protect Sheridan. In the darkness, it took him a moment to recognize the Royal guards and Gerard's shaggy head somewhere in the middle of them. He bellowed above the mob.

"Halt!" he boomed. "Lower your weapons!"

The guards haltingly slowed, obviously prepared for a row. They took their orders directly from Sean, rarely from Gerard, who had given the initial command. They looked around in confusion as Gerard pushed forward through the group.

"What goes on here?" Gerard asked. "Where are the de Braose men?"

Sean shook his head. "Who told you that?"

Gerard looked around, seeing Alys, terrified, followed by Guy and finally Sheridan. His gaze lingered on Sheridan.

"Who's that?" he pointed, ignoring Sean's question completely.

"Answer me," Sean said in a voice that would tolerate no disobedience. "Who told you de Braose men were here?"

Gerard looked at him. "Sentries saw young de Braose leaving with the St. James women. We came to stop him."

"Why?"

"All of the allied nobles are leaving, Sean," Gerard looked at him as if he should have rightly known this. "The king wants answers. De Braose will have them."

Sean didn't flinch, but already, he could see the far-reaching implications of what was about to happen. He knew, deep down, that news of the flight would reach the king. There was no way he could have prevented it with all of the eyes in the Tower. He moved to where Gerard stood; a half-head taller than the man, he hissed at him through clenched teeth.

"What do you think I was trying to do, you idiot?" he snarled. "You come rushing in here like a stampede of cattle and destroy all that I have been attempting to accomplish."

Gerard widened with understanding. "You intercepted him?"

"Of course I did, fool. Were it not for your intrusion, I would have answers by now."

Gerard began to realize that he had apparently ruined what Sean had been attempting to achieve. He put his hands up, his expression lined with doubt. "My apologies," his gaze moved between Sean and the three allies. "I should have known."

"Aye, you should have."

"The king wants to talk to de Braose himself."

Sean couldn't head him off with all of the men around them as witnesses. His clever try at redeeming the situation had been thwarted. He was cornered and he had no choice.

"Then take him," he said. "I will take the women."

Gerard glanced back over at Alys, sobbing softly with fear, and Sheridan, looking ethereal and angel-like in the soft, misty gray garment she wore.

"Who is the blond?" his voice was low. "I have not seen her around."

Sean could literally smell the man's lust and it inflamed him like nothing he had ever experienced in his life. But he held himself in check. He could not lose control, not now. The situation was going awry and he had to focus.

"Sheridan St. James," he replied. "Henry's eldest."

Gerard's face lit up. He flicked a hand at the guard, indicating for them to grab de Braose. "The king will want to meet her, don't you think?" he winked at Sean as he turned away.

Sean actually considered killing him. He put the hand on the hilt of his sword and was fully prepared to do just that. But there were too many men around, too many witnesses, and he realized that he had spent far too much time in the king's service where morals and conscience were not required. He had killed on behalf of the king, too many times, because it had been required of him in order to maintain his post. He was not, by nature, a murderer. But he had been forced to do what was necessary in order to accomplish his mission. He began to wonder if, after all these years, he was actually becoming what he pretended to be. A cold-blooded killer.

Guy was overwhelmed by the guards, who stripped him of his sword and knocked him around for good measure. Sheridan and Alys clung together, watching in horror. Sean moved in, like a phantom, and put one arm around each lady. As Guy was still struggling with Gerard and the Royal guards, he swept them away.

As they fled for the Lanthorn Gate, they were ambushed.

CHAPTER NINE

"... and it never occurred to me to be frightened for myself. In a matter of days, my life had changed so dramatically that I hardly recognized myself. My sun, my moon and my stars were Sheridan."

The Chronicles of Sir Sean de Lara

1206 – 1215 A.D.

HE WAS VAGUELY aware of a cloth on his head. The sounds of the world faded in and out for an indeterminate amount of time, distant echoes of things he did not recognize. Finally, he managed to open an eye. The room was small, dark, and smelled of old rushes. It was a damp place even though a fire burned somewhere. He could see the reflection of the flames upon the walls and smelled the smoke from the malfunctioning chimney.

Turning his head slightly, he saw Father Simon sitting at his head.

"So you are awake," Father Simon said. "We were coming to think that you would never awaken."

Sean stirred, the inherent sense of self-preservations influencing his movements. It was imperative that he rise and gain his senses. "Where am I?" he grunted.

Father Simon put his hands on him to still him. "Quiet, Sean," he said. "You have had a bad injury. Gilby has stitched you up, but you are still fragile."

Sean lay there, staring up at the priest, feeling an indefinable ache thundering through his body. His big hands move to his head, clasped to his forehead as if to hold his brains in. "What happened?"

"An attack," Father Simon pulled the cloth off his head and wrung it out in a basin nearby. "You were caught from behind as far as we could tell. We heard the noise of the scuffle. By the time I got there, I found you lying on the ground. Do you recall anything at all?"

He lay there, staring up the ceiling, struggling to clear the cobwebs from his mind. "I am not sure," he muttered. "I remember de Braose and Gerard. I remember nearing the Lanthorn Gate and…."

"That is where I found you with your brains nearly bashed out," Father Simon put the rag back on his head. "Someone had laid a heavy blow against you, Sean. It looked to me that you were clubbed from behind. Your scalp is split down the back of your head cleanly. Whoever did it must have left you for dead."

Sean blinked, pieces of memory coming back to him. "Sheridan," he suddenly struggled to sit up again. "Where is she?"

Father Simon put his hands on his wide shoulders, shoving him back. "Rest or you will not recover. Gilby will be back soon and…."

"Where is Sheridan? Is she here?"

Father Simon was standing over him, his small body trying valiantly to control the mountain of a man. "She is not," he dreaded those words. "Was she with you when this happened?"

"Aye," Sean felt cold fear grip his heart. "She and her sister. I was taking them back to their guard. Did you see any sign of her, then?"

Father Simon shook his head. "Nay," he said with regret. "No sign at all. When I found you, you were alone."

Sean pushed forward, dislodging the priest's hands. Father Simon stumbled back as Sean sat upright, struggling to orient himself against the spinning room.

"I must find her," he said.

"It has been days, Sean. You have no idea where she would be."

"Did you see any blood around me, as if someone had been injured or killed in the fight?"

"Only yours."

The room was gradually righting itself. Sean looked at the priest. "The let us pray that she had not been hurt," he muttered. "How many days have I been out?"

"Two. The siege has begun. The north and west border of the city has been taken, with more troops moving into the city towards the Tower of London."

"What else?"

"Nothing else that I know of," Father Simon held a cup for him to drink. Sean took a sip and pushed it away. "I have not seen the king at all, though his troops line the parapets."

"Who is directing the defense of the Tower?"

"I do not know."

Sean stood up, swaying. His entire body felt boneless and weak but he fought it. He had to locate Sheridan.

"I must find her," he said, staggering towards the door.

"But you have duties here, Sean," Father Simon lowered his voice. "Whatever has happened to Lady Sheridan happened two days ago. You cannot change that or save her if she needs to be saved. What is done is done. What is important now is your mission. The Tower must not hold. You must see to it."

"De Braose," Sean muttered. He put his hand on the priest's shoulder, mostly to steady himself. "Gerard took young de Braose. I must find out where he has taken him."

Father Simon tried to argue with Sean, all the way out of the small quarters attached to the Chapel of St. Peter. But the man had his own agenda and would not be swayed.

Father Simon seriously worried for him.

ଓ

"SOMEONE HIT ME on the back of the head," Sean said. "I have lain for two days unconscious. Surely you know that I would have been here sooner had I not been incapacitated."

"I thought you were dead," the king said. "No one could find you, not even Gerard. Where were you?"

Sean lifted a hand in the general direction of the chapel. "One of the priests found me. Gilby sewed my scalp. I have only regained my senses within the past hour. I still feel as if I should take to my bed, but it is of no matter. What matters is that I am here now to assist you as needed."

John had walked a circle around Sean, three times. Twice he had inspected the massive gash across the back of his head as if making sure that Sean was not lying. With the final inspection, he went back over to the chair that sat near the massive hearth of his warm, smelly, dirty bedchamber.

"Thank God," the king muttered as he sat. "I have been in a panic for two days wondering what to do. My enemies have fled, only to rouse armies to attack London and my supporters are spread too thin. We should have known about this, de Lara. We should have seen it coming."

"We did, sire." Sean gingerly touched the back of his head. "We saw it and we told you it was coming. We just did not know the exact time."

"With all of the spies I employ, surely someone would have known something."

"What about de Braose?" Sean wanted to know. "Before I had my brains bashed in, we had captured young de Braose. Have you not discovered anything from him?"

The king shook his head. "Gerard does not have your touch in such matters. De Braose is useless now."

"Why?

"Because Gerard beat him so badly that the man has been unconscious for days."

Sean cast a long glance at Gerard, hovering back in the shadows as the two of them usually did. He lifted an eyebrow. "That," he said, "was not necessary. I have taught you better than that."

Gerard smiled at him, an admission of wrong-doing without truly admitting it. Sean shook his head, sighing heavily as he did so. "And I had the St. James sisters as captives. Whoever did this to me must have taken them."

"Pity," the king said. "Gerard told me that the elder daughter was a beauty."

It was Sean's way of discovering if Sheridan' was in the king's possession. Sean didn't know if he felt better or worse to realize that she wasn't. Even though she wasn't here, he still did not know where she was.

Now he faced a desperate internal struggle; to go after Sheridan or to complete his mission. He went back and forth until his head was ready to explode. His thoughts were misty, chaotic, but he was able to discern one prevalent concept; he did not want to ruin what he'd worked so hard to achieve. He was so close to victory that he could almost taste it. Sean had never been a quitter. He had to finish what he started and go after Sheridan with a clear mind.

"Where are the commanders of the army?" he asked. "I must be updated immediately. If there is even a chance that the Tower will be breached, then we must act now to get the king to safety."

"It is under control, Sean," Gerard spoke up. "Michael de Vere has the command of the Tower. He assures me that it will not fall."

Sean lifted an eyebrow. "De Vere is not the most capable. His family connections, not his knowledge, got him this post. Has he assessed the enemy's strength? Does he know what other strengths they bring with them?"

Only Sean could speak so frankly in the presence of the king and get away with it. John put his hand up, calming any storm of conflict that might be arising.

"I will call a meeting with de Vere," he said. "He can brief you on what has been done. Gerard, send out the word to my supporters. De Lara is back with us and we meet in one hour."

Gerard fled, leaving Sean standing with the king. Sean's head was killing him and his mind was racing like the wind, but he could feel the king's gaze upon him. He knew it was mistrust, as Gerard had told him. Given the fact that he had been missing for two days, however justified, he could not blame him. John had been surrounded by intrigue all of his life. Suspicion was second nature. He turned to the man.

"Is there anything further you wish from me at this time, sire?" he asked.

John seemed inordinately calm in the face of London being attacked. He shook his head. "Why would you ask?"

"Because I thought there might be something more on your mind. My loyalties, perhaps?"

The king grinned, a lazy, ugly gesture. He knew what the man was referring to, with hardly a word of explanation.

"Sean," he clucked softly. "Gerard should not have told you. Yet I should have expected it. There are no secrets between you two."

"Do you wish to ask me anything?"

"Of course not."

Sean didn't believe him for one minute. The king was, if nothing else, perpetually wary of everyone around him.

"Very well," Sean replied. "If there is nothing else, sire, then I will go clean myself up and return for the conference."

Sean was almost to the door when the king spoke again. "I am told the allies will not reach the Tower for at least another day or two, enough time for you to raise an army and depart the city."

Sean had a sickening feeling that he knew what was coming. It was inevitable, given the cloud of doubt lingering over the past few days. He stopped and faced the king.

"My lord?"

John rose from his silken sling-back chair. He was a short, weak, twisted man, hardly enough of a male to be in the same category as men like Sean. The only strength he had was his royal name and the power it wielded. He was very good at wielding it.

"I wish for you to ride for the Welsh Marches," he said. "Surely Gerard told you that, too."

"He did," Sean said steadily. "But I would question why you would want me to go now, of all times. We are facing a serious siege and need all of our manpower here."

"I must not lose the Marches," the king said. "Clifford's castles are key. They must be held. And when you are finished securing them, you will ride on Abergavenny and raze her."

Abergavenny Castle was the de Braose stronghold. Sean knew this directive for what it was; a test. The king was demanding he prove his loyalty, no matter what was happening to London. John seemed oddly certain that London would hold, as would the Tower. He appeared more focused on insisting Sean prove his allegiance. His priorities were twisted just as the man himself was.

Even though Sean knew exactly what was happening, it made a serious issue far more complex; were he to march to Wales, he could not ensure the fall of the Tower. If the Tower did not fall, then the siege would break down and prove futile. Years of planning would be waste. The allies were counting on him.

"I would strongly advise against dividing your forces, sire," he said. "You will need your strength here to protect the Tower."

"Go to the Marches. And burn Lansdown along your way. While most of her troops are here trying to breach the Tower, we will attack her compromised castle. We will show both de Braose and St. James in one stroke that their treachery against the king shall not go unpunished."

So there it was. Everything Gerard had warned him about. Sean did the only thing he could at the moment; he agreed.

"By your command, sire."

ꟽ

THE SMELL OF the food made her nauseous. She pushed it away, not even wanting to look at it. It was a lovely tray of squab and boiled vegetables, but she couldn't muster the appetite. Alys, seeing that her sister wasn't eating yet again, took the food for herself.

"You really should eat something," Alys said, her mouth full. "The food is wonderful."

Sheridan didn't reply. Seated in the impressive solar of Watford House in the town of Eastbury, a holding of the Earl of Warenne through his wife's family, she hadn't eaten or slept in three days. Three long, hellish days as the battle for London commenced. News was coming fast and furious, sometimes hourly. Though she should have been concerned with the outcome of the battle, all she could think about was the enemy. Sean was, after all, still her enemy.

The strong walls of Watford House had turned into a command post. Most of the allied nobles were gathered in the fortified manor house to discuss their strategies. The rooms reeked of stale rushes and old ale, and the house in general had a bad mood to it. Jocelin was there and Sheridan had singled him out for a particular hatred. When she found out what he had done, there was nothing on earth that would convince her to forgive him.

"Eat something, Sheridan."

Jocelin's command came as he entered the chamber with Arundel and Fitz Herbert. They had a map between them and headed straight for the large, heavily-constructed table near a set of nine very long, very thin lancet windows built into the northern wall of the room. It allowed for light and air in the massive chamber. While some of the nobles chose to attend the battle themselves, many of them maintained a distance while their men handled the task.

The bishops of London, Lincoln, Worcester, Rochester and Coventry had all returned to their homes, while de Warenne, Arundel, Salisbury and the Bishop of Bath and Glastonbury moved to Watford House to be near the siege. De Neville and de Burgh had moved to a location in Kent to ride out the storm, while Fitz Gerold and Fitz Hugh remained with the nearly twenty thousand men now storming the city of London.

The atmosphere was tense even at the best of times. War was never easy, and this war was the culmination of years of strategy. Now, as Jocelin and the others were reviewing the latest reports from London, Sheridan could only think about returning to the city and to Sean. It consumed every second, every moment of her day and night.

"Let us go walk in the garden," Alys said, trying to get her sister's mind off her troubles. "The weather isn't so bad."

Sheridan stood up without a word. She was a bitter, sullen woman these days. She didn't acknowledge Alys' kindness as her sister placed a heavy cloak on her shoulders to protect against the chill outside. Jocelin caught the movement out of the corner of his eye and excused himself from the gathering. He caught up to the pair just as they were leaving the room.

"Dani," he said softly. "Have you eaten today?"

"Nay." She would not look at him.

"I know you are upset, but you cannot go on like this."

"Upset?" she growled. "Nay, I am not upset. I am destroyed and you are personally responsible."

Jocelin had been drawn into this conversation with her too many times in the past three days. He'd tried to be logical, reasonable and kind, but she would not return the favor. It took all of his abilities to remain calm. These were the times when he thanked God for his celibacy and the fact that he had no daughters.

"Neely did what he had to do, what I told him to do," he said steadily. "De Lara was abducting you and Alys to take you to the king."

"He was not," Sheridan seethed. "How many times do I have to tell you that Sean was taking Alys and me to safety? If he had been trying to abduct us, why was he taking us toward the Lanthorn tower?"

"Neely intercepted you *near* the Lanthorn," Jocelin replied quietly. "That does not mean de Lara was about to enter it. From where we found you, he could have taken you to any number of areas in the Tower."

"He was saving us."

"Neely saved you. Understand that, girl, and you'll live longer."

Sheridan was as close to striking someone as she had ever been in her life. "Neely did nothing of the kind," she hissed. "Neely's jealousy is raging so that he would do or say anything to gain favor with me right now. And God only knows what he has you convinced of."

"What do you mean?"

"Exactly that. Surely he has you convinced that I am stark raving mad because of my association with Sean."

"We have been through this, Sheridan. I do not believe you are thinking clearly. It was good that we removed you from the Tower when we did to get you away from de Lara's influence."

Flustered and furious, she turned away from him, wishing she could tell him what Sean had told her about his loyalties. But she would remain steadfast to her promise and not reveal Sean's true self. All her life she had admired and loved Jocelin. Now all she could see was a suspicious, foolish old man. She walked away from him without another word.

With a heavy heart, Jocelin let her go. Though they were at odds, still, he was sorry. He knew that she was stubborn like her father, sometimes to the point of blindness, and this was simply one of those times. Once married to de Braose, providing the young man survived his adventure in the Tower, she would return to her senses. He was sure of it.

Outside of the manor, it was cool and clear for January. Fat puffy clouds danced overhead as Alys led Sheridan into the elegant formal garden. Lady de Warenne was an avid gardener and all manner of flowering shrub covered the grounds. Though most were dormant at this time of year, some still held their bloom. Alys fussed over the one and only blossom in the entire garden, inhaling its non-existent scent until she sneezed.

But Sheridan had no interest in the garden. Her thoughts were elsewhere. Though they'd spent much time walking the pebbled path, she'd paid little attention to the surroundings. She could have been in a blighted desert for all of the attention she was paying it.

Finding the small lover's bench lodged under a silver birch, she sat on the cold stone and brooded. She could still feel the delicious sensations of Sean's lips against hers and the extraordinary power of his embrace that made her feel as if nothing else in the world mattered. She would give anything to feel that again, but the more time passed, the more impossible that chance seemed.

She was terrified that Neely had killed Sean in his jealousy; all she knew was that Neely had struck Sean across the back of the head with the hilt of his sword, sending Sean to the ground in an unconscious heap. She had seen all of it. She had fought with Neely even as he had picked her up and carried her from the Tower grounds, so much so that she had ripped several gashes with her fingernails into his neck. Neely hadn't so much as uttered a sound as the pain tore through him; he held her tightly and carried her off on horseback. The last Sheridan had seen of Sean was several Glastonbury men kicking his limp body in the moonlight, pounding the man they had all grown to fear. It had been a horrible sight, one she tried desperately to forget.

But she couldn't forget, no matter how hard she tried. She and Neely had ridden for an hour before reaching Watford House. Sheridan had been exhausted and nearly incoherent by the time they arrived at the fortified manor. Neely had left right away to return to London but not before making all attempts to apologize to Sheridan; he didn't want her hating him. Her response had been to spit on him. He had his answer and, bitterly, returned to the brewing battle.

So Sheridan found herself still at Watford House, feeling no differently than she had three days ago. Her anger had turned bitter, her hurt to anguish. She was learning to hate those around her, including Alys. It was wrong and she knew it, yet her reason was unsteady these days. She was desperate to find Sean, desperate to know if he had survived the ambush. Dead or alive, something inside of her had to know.

As she sat on the small lover's bench beneath the barren tree, she began to realize that her only course of action, her only hope, was to escape back to London. Foolish as it was, she could think on nothing else.

Alys was still studying the shrubs and ended up chasing a lizard across the pebbled path. Sheridan watched her younger sister, knowing she could easily manipulate the girl into obeying her wishes. If she was to escape this place, then she had to remove herself from Alys' presence.

The plan in her mind began to grow.

"Alys," she said softly. "Would you do something if I asked you?"

Alys perked up. "Of course, Dani. What would you have me do?"

Sheridan averted her gaze to her hands, resting in her lap. She found that she couldn't look her sister in the eye. "I find that I am rather hungry. Would you go to the kitchens and prepare a meal for me?"

Alys's features lifted joyfully. "Of course I will. What would you like?"

Sheridan shrugged. "I have a craving for an almond pudding. But that would take much effort, wouldn't it?"

"Not at all," Alys said, thrilled that her sister was actually interested in food. "I'll tell the cook to prepare it right away. Is there anything else you would like?"

Sheridan pretended to think. "I would like fresh bread. White bread, without a hint of brown in it. And lots of butter."

Alys nodded swiftly, making mental notes of her sister's wishes. "Almond pudding and fresh bread. I will tell the cook right away."

As Alys sprinted for the entry into the manor, Sheridan stopped her. "Alys, you will stay and make sure they prepare everything fresh, will you not? I cannot stomach anything that is not freshly prepared. And I trust you to see that it is done correctly."

Alys nodded eagerly and dashed inside without another word. Sheridan waited until she was sure Alys wouldn't return before bolting from the bench. She remembered where the stables were from the day they had arrived. Wrapping the deep green cloak about her tightly, she made haste for the livery and prayed with every step that her deceptive request to Alys would give her enough time to do as she must. She didn't care who she lied to or who she coerced, just so long as she could get away from Watford House.

She had to find Sean.

CHAPTER TEN

"...the days, as they passed, introduced me to a fresh, new hell...."

The Chronicles of Sir Sean de Lara

1206 – 1215 A.D.

GERARD HAD PUT Guy in the deepest depths of the Tower vault, down into the rooms that seeped of water and rot that permeated the ground from the Thames. It was a hellish place and the lower levels were a maze of horror and darkness. These paths of despair were used only for the very lowliest offenders, those to be locked away and forgotten by time. Men came down here to be swallowed up as if they had never existed.

Sean had some difficulty maneuvering his massive body down the narrow, slippery stone steps of the lower level, made more difficult by the fact that his head was still swimming slightly from the blow to his head. By the time he reached the bottom level, it was nearly pitch black and smelling heavily of decay. He knew from memory there were four cells in this block, small rooms with no ventilation. He lit a larger torch on the wall from the small one he was carrying, giving him just enough light to locate de Braose's compartment. Lifting the splintering plank that slid across the door to lock it, he pushed it aside and shoved open the panel. The oak and iron door jammed and he was forced to thrust hard, twice, to unstick it.

The chamber smelled of death. It was a horrible scent. Sean didn't see Guy right away until he looked over into the corner and saw a body half collapsed, half propped against the stone. He was frankly surprised to see de Braose's dark eyes gazing back at him, wincing with the introduction of the light. He took a step into the cell, lifting the torch for a better look.

"How badly are you injured?" he asked.

Guy blinked rapidly in the weak light. He could see de Lara, larger than life, dressed in full armor. "If you have come to finish what your comrade started, then know that I am no match for you. You can kill me if you have a mind to."

"I have no mind to. How badly are you hurt?"

Guy wasn't sure how to answer. He could barely move, but that wasn't what de Lara was asking. "My right arm is useless."

"Broken?"

"Aye."

"Can you stand?"

"I have not tried."

Sean reached down and pulled de Braose to his feet as if the man weighed no more than a child. But Guy was gravely injured and groaned at the movement. Sean could see that Gerard had done his work very well, for Guy was a mess. His face was battered, his right arm broken, and there was no telling what other injuries lay beneath the torn and stained clothing.

"What are you doing?" Guy demanded, pain in his voice. "Put me down, de Lara."

Sean didn't reply. He hoisted Guy from the cell, listening to his grunts of pain. When they hit the slippery steps, Guy began to weakly struggle.

"Put me down," he groaned. "Where are you taking me? If you are thinking to…."

Sean cut him off then. "Keep silent," he snapped lowly. "If you value your life, you'll do as I say. You must play dead."

"What in the hell are you talking about?"

"I said play dead," Sean's clear blue eyes blazed into Guy's youthful features. "And shut your mouth. If you want to live, you'll keep it shut."

"I still do not understand."

"You do not have to. But I ask that you trust me."

Guy's eyebrows flew up. "Trust *you*?" he repeated, outraged. "After everything that has happened, you are asking me to trust you? You must be mad."

"Indeed, I very well may be. But your only other choice is to rot away in that cell. Is that what you wish?"

Guy opened his mouth to speak, but thought better of it. He was cornered. "What are you going to do?"

"You must play dead, no matter what you hear and no matter what happens. You must play the lifeless, limp corpse. Your life depends on convincing others that you have met your end. Can you do this?"

Guy lifted his one good shoulder, a weak gesture. "It appears that I have no choice." His dark eyes cooled, grew shaded. His mind was thinking many things, not merely of de Lara's strange request. He was especially thinking on the last time he and the Shadow Lord had met. "Where is Lady Sheridan? Is she all right?"

Sean had been collected and professional up until that moment. But hearing her name was like a dagger through his heart. He dare not allow himself to falter in front of de Braose. Yet knowing that the young knight felt for the lady as he did, knowing that somehow he may have a kindred spirit in the man in their mutual concern for the lady's welfare, he told the truth. Besides, it was the very reason he was releasing Guy from his imprisonment.

"She is missing," he said frankly.

Guy's eyes widened. "But… the last I saw, she was under your escort. You had her, de Lara. What happened?"

Sean's emotions had the better of him and he struggled against the anguish that threatened. "I was ambushed after I left you," he said truthfully. "I was rendered unconscious and the lady was taken."

Guy's big brown eyes widened with dismay. "Why are you not out looking for her? Why are you here wasting time with me?"

Sean's jaw ticked dangerously. "I tell you this because I require your help," he rumbled. "In spite of my reputation, I cannot be everywhere at once. The lady is missing, presumably in danger, and as much as I loathe the idea I require your assistance. I will get you out of this place, but in return you must do everything in your power to help me find the lady. You are allied with her. You have many mutual friends and acquaintances. Perhaps one of them will know where she is. They will speak to you far more easily than they will speak to me."

It suddenly all came clear to Guy. De Lara was taking him from the vault because he needed Guy's help to find Lady Sheridan. He began to feel his sense of worth where a moment ago, he had none. Now, the mighty de Lara needed him.

"In spite of the fact that we both lay claim to her, you would ask this of me?" Guy repeated, somewhat guardedly. "Are you so desperate, then?"

"Nay," Sean shook his head slowly. "I am only concerned with her welfare. I care not for our petty contention at this point, de Braose. All I care about is finding the lady safe and whole. I believe you are the one man who can help me accomplish this."

"And if I find her and marry her? What then?"

Sean lifted an eyebrow. "I would ask that you not, but I cannot order or demand it. I will leave it to your conscience to do the right thing. All I care about is that she is found. Will you do this?"

Guy was seriously attempting to ascertain Sean's motives in all of this. Either he was up to something, or Sean was the most selfless man he'd ever met. He wasn't sure which but he was impressed with the man's altruism nonetheless. Slowly, he nodded his head.

"I will."

There was nothing more to say. The two enemies would, for the moment, work together for the common cause of Lady Sheridan. Guy was easily half Sean's size, so it was little effort for Sean to literally throw him over his shoulder and carry him up the stairs to the next level. This floor of the vault was busier, however, and the master jailer focused his attention on the pair as Sean carted Guy through the area. He went to them.

"You found him, I see," the burly, one-eyed man spoke to Sean. "Is he dead?"

"He is. I am sending the body back to his father as a message against all those who would oppose the king."

Thankfully, the jailer didn't check. He took the Shadow Lord's word for it. Sean continued to lug Guy through the vault, up the next set of stairs, and up into the gatehouse. There were soldiers everywhere and smoke from the battle filled the air as Sean passed into the ward beyond. Even though it was the north and east sections of London that were burning under attack, the wind had carried the smoke and ash to the Tower. It was an eerie sight as the late afternoon sun turned red behind the clouds of burnt orange and black.

Guy peeped an eye open, noting the tense mood of the courtyard and the soldiers in battle mode going about their business. He could smell the smoke and knew, without being told, what was happening. The siege was well underway.

Sean pulled Guy into a shadowed corner against the wall. It was apparent that he was searching for something, or someone. Guy winced as his broken ribs brushed against each other, his torso wedged up against Sean's massive shoulder. After several moments of hovering in the shadows, the pair rounded the corner of the gatehouse and headed straight for a small, enrobed man pulling a donkey cart along the edge of the western wall.

Without a word, Sean lifted Guy over the side of the cart, burying him beneath the mounds of hay that filled it. Guy sputtered as dried grass hit him in the mouth, but for lack of a better response, lay there as Sean and the tiny old man threw great piles of hay over him. When they were finished satisfactorily burying Guy, Gilby peered out at Sean from beneath his hood.

"He is badly hurt," Sean said quietly. "Take him somewhere safe where you can tend his wounds. Then send him back to his men. I don't care how you do it, but get him there."

"It will not be a simple thing," Gilby said. "The gates are sealed."

Sean lifted an eyebrow. "The gates are not the only way in and out of the Tower."

"And if I need your help?"

Sean shook his head. "I am riding for the Marches in two hours. If you need help, you'll have to seek it elsewhere. I cannot help you."

Gilby's brow furrowed. "Why are you riding to the Marches, man? London is under siege."

Sean's normally emotionless face rippled with disgust. "Be that as it may, our king has ordered me to the Marches." He lowered his voice dramatically. "And I need you to deliver a message."

"As you wish."

"The Chapel, one hour."

As Gilby watched the enormous knight slip off into the darkness of the Tower yard, he couldn't help wonder what de Lara was doing. For the king to order him away from London in the face of a siege was most unusual. It was a curious move on the monarch's part. Behind him, Gilby could hear the straw rustling about. He turned in time to see Guy's dark head pop up amongst the hay.

"He is going to the Marches?" Guy repeated what he'd heard. "Why is he going there? And who are you?"

Gilby cocked a bushy eyebrow. "Which question would you have me answer first?"

"All of them."

"It would appear so, because the king has ordered him to, and my name is Gilby."

Guy processed the answers slowly. In fact, he was processing the entire circumstance rather slowly. His mind was muddled with pain and lack of food, and now that he was out of the vault, it was also muddled with relief. As Gilby collected the lead rope and smacked the mule on the buttocks to get it moving, Guy lay back down in the hay. He had the presence of mind to cover himself back up. His body was killing him and his head was swimming, but above everything, he felt a new resolve to do as he must. Lady Sheridan was out there, somewhere, and he had to find her.

When he did, he would marry her. To the Devil with de Lara.

ᴄᴙ

SHERIDAN KNEW THE locale of Watford House in relation to London simply because she'd heard enough talk over the past few days to give her a very good indication. She therefore knew that she must travel southeast to the main highway leading from London to Gloucester. It had taken her and Neely an hour to reach Watford House and that had been at a moderately slow pace, so she assumed it would be even less if the horse was swift.

She had selected a high-bred bay steed that she thought might have belonged to Salisbury. The animal's blanket bore Salisbury's colors of yellow and light blue. In any case, it was a cooperative animal and she was able to saddle the horse and remove it past a dumbstruck stable boy without much trouble. Though she had no food or money, she did not want to take the time to procure those items lest her plan be discovered. She would simply have to worry about those things when the time came.

The big bay gelding had a smooth gait, making it an easy canter as she stole away from Watford House. She kept to the fields to shield herself from the view of the fortified manor, but soon enough was able to travel the road. The day remained cool, bright, and unusually quiet. As she loped down the road, the entire adventure began to take on the feel of a leisurely ride. Sheridan felt a tremendous amount of relief now that she had left Watford House, as if she was finally on her way to accomplishing her task. She struggled not to entertain the thought that Sean was dead. She had to have faith that he had survived.

Determination fed her actions where common sense did not. She knew very well how dangerous her actions were, but it didn't matter. She further knew that she was riding into a city under siege, but that didn't matter either. As the horse galloped south and midday turned to afternoon, she decided the best course of action upon reaching the

Tower would be to go to the Chapel of St. Peter ad Vincula and speak with the priest who had said mass for her father. Perhaps the priest would know of de Lara's whereabouts; truthfully, other than asking the king himself, she did not know where to start. Priests usually knew most of what was going on around them. Maybe the man could help her find some answers.

Since the topography was fairly flat as it neared the Thames, a few miles in the distance, the main road from Gloucester to London came upon her like a flat gold ribbon along the deep green of the land. Sheridan paused at the crossroads, noting a carriage off in the distance to the east, but little else. The road, for the most part, was vacant. Spurring the bay horse, she took off to the southwest, following the path that would take her right into the heart of London. From there, it would be straight to the Tower and straight to the chapel. Beyond that, she would take it from moment to moment. She did not want to think more than two steps ahead. She hoped the priest would be kind enough to help her. She hoped she wasn't being completely foolish. She further hoped that she would survive all of this.

In the distance, she could see the smoke from the battle for London. Unnerved but no less determined, she spurred the horse faster.

☙

"SHE IS AT Watford House, Sean."

This time, they met in the confessional at the Chapel of St. Peter ad Vincula. Sean felt his heart leap into his throat at those five simple words. It was as if his entire life hinged on that straightforward little statement and the relief he felt brought unexpected tears to his eyes. It was an indescribable moment of joy, relief, and odd desperation. His hands, against the wall of the confessional, now formed claws as his fingers, subconsciously, dug into the wood in a release of tension.

"You know this for certain?" he managed to ask.

"I do. The allies have reported this to me."

"Is she well?"

"As far as I know," the voice responded. "Jocelin has charge of her."

Sean's relief was tempered by the attack at the Lanthorn Tower. "So it was Jocelin who set upon me."

"It was."

Sean sighed heavily. "Then you did not tell him of me."

There was a long pause. "I told him. But he does not want you for the lady. He feels that her life would be filled with hatred, political intrigue, and strife. He feels you court nothing but danger."

"And he is correct," Sean snorted. "But that does not change the fact that I will marry her. If Jocelin stands in my way, I will kill him. Mark my words."

Passion in men did strange things to their common sense. The voice on the other side of the panel remained calm. "Is that how you would wish to begin your marriage? With a murder? I wonder how the lady would react."

Sean slumped back against the side of the booth. He drew a weary hand over his face. "Probably not too well," he admitted. "Then what would you suggest I do?"

"You will do your duty," the voice grew oddly hard. "We are at the crest of our plans, Sean. I cannot have you running amuck with wild emotion. I must have you stable and focused. The Tower must fall."

"Then it will fall without me, for I have been ordered to tend The Marches."

The voice was clearly startled. "The Marches? *Now*?"

Sean wiped another hand over his face; his head was killing him and he wanted nothing more than to forget this day had ever happened. "I am ordered to reclaim Clifford's castles from de Braose, raze Abergavenny and Lansdown Castles, and secure the Marches for John. While London is burning around his ears, he is more concerned for the Marches." He sat forward, elbows resting on his knees and the clear blue eyes weary and unfocused. "Nay, 'tis more than that. It is a test. Our king is testing me."

"A test? Why would he do that?"

"Because I stopped him from ravaging Alys St. John. In his twisted mind, he is now demanding a show of loyalty from me."

The voice was silent a long while. "This cannot be good, Sean. If seeds of doubt have begun to sprout...."

"I know," Sean wouldn't let him finish. "The seeds are there. With John, they are always there. But I think I can kill whatever suspicion grows. He needs me too much to so easily dismiss me."

"What are you going to do? We cannot see nine careful years lain to waste."

Sean drew in a long, deep breath. "I am going to do as ordered with the exception of razing Lansdown. And I am going to Watford House to claim Sheridan."

"It will be an ugly fight, Sean. Moreover, since Jocelin is aware of your position, it is quite possible he will reveal your cover in a fit of emotion. This must not happen."

Sean's jaw ticked as he hung his head, staring at the floor, his hands. "The north and east borders of London are falling," he said quietly. "With the size of the army that approaches the Tower, I have little doubt that it will fall with or without my help. Is my presence really necessary here any longer? Is this cover I have held all this time still an essential one? Our plan is coming to action. There is nothing more I can do. Why can I not reveal my true self now and fight against John in the open as the others do?"

The door to the confessional suddenly flew open. William Marshall stood in the entry, his weathered face taut with rage.

"Get ahold of yourself, de Lara," he snapped. "Of all the men in my employ, you are the last person I would expect this nonsense from. I told you once that I would whisk Lady Sheridan away from you if she is too much of a distraction until this is all over. Do not force my hand, boy."

Sean stood up, facing his liege. He was half a head taller and far more muscular. "And I told you that I would kill you if you tried."

The Marshall had a temper, but it was one that he controlled admirably. It would not do for him to fly in Sean's face; the Lord of the Shadows could not be intimidated. William had known Sean long enough to know that. But he could see something in Sean's eyes that he had never seen before. He wasn't quite sure what it was, but he knew he didn't like it.

He put a hand on Sean's shoulder, in apology and acquiescence. "You probably would," he muttered. "But I am serious, Sean. I need your focus, now more than ever. It concerns me to hear you speak of deviating from our plans."

Sean backed down somewhat, but he was still unsteady. "I was simply asking a question," he offered weakly, though they both knew it was not the truth. "Nothing will deter me in my quest to marry Sheridan. You may as well know that I would give up my mission if it meant not having her."

It was a blow to William to hear that. He knew it would do no good to rage. All he could do was bargain. The Marshall had made a life out of bargaining and he was very successful at it. But this bargain would prove to be particularly critical.

"Then I will strike a deal with you," William said. "Will you hear me?"

"I always do."

"I need for you to stay where you are for the time being. You are far too valuable to our cause to give this up so easily. We cannot know how this battle will go or even how the next few days will go. I need you on the inside to observe and report. If John says you will go to the Marches, then go you will. It is vital that you remain loyal to him until the tides turn in our favor. For this continued service, I will make you a promise."

"What is that?"

The Marshall's dark eyes glittered. "You will have Sheridan St. James upon your return from the Marches. I swear to you that she will be yours but only if you see this task through. I cannot promise anything to a man who would turn from his duty."

Sean had never known William Marshall to make a vow he could not keep. There were many years of trust between them. "And just how will you accomplish this if Jocelin is so opposed to the idea?"

"You must trust me."

Sean could not doubt him. He nodded, his jaw ticking with the reservation he could not voice. Suddenly, a small figure entered the doorway, casting a shadow against the dying sunlight. Startled, Sean and William turned to see Gilby entering the chapel. He had a queer look on his face.

"Sean?" Gilby paused just inside the door. "I have been looking everywhere for you."

"And so you have found me," Sean replied. "Is something wrong? Where is de Braose?"

Gilby jabbed a thumb in the general direction of the Tower grounds. "In my bed," he said. "He is very broken up inside."

Sean nodded. "I assumed as much. Gerard is, if nothing else, thorough in his brutality."

Gilby shook his head. "But de Braose is not why I was looking for you."

"What is it, then?"

The old man lifted his shoulders, unsure where to begin. "I was on the wall near the Bell Tower, you see, searching for the best avenue in which to remove young de Braose. There is the tunnel near the Bell and Middle Towers, and there is the Traitor's Gate that leads to the river, and...."

Sean put up his hand to silence him. It was the first time he'd ever seen Gilby rattled. "What has you so stricken, old man?"

"I just wanted you to know where I was when I spied it, clear as day, jaunting along the road to the Tower gate."

"Spied what?"

"If I had not bribed the guard to open the Middle Tower gate, I fear something horrible might have happened."

"Gilby, you are not making any sense. What are you talking about?"

Gilby crooked his finger at Sean. The massive knight did as he was asked and made his way over to the old man. Gilby pointed out into the yard. Puzzled, Sean looked into the dusk only to see a small figure standing several feet away by the massive tree that stood between the chapel and the White Tower.

"Who is that?" he asked.

Gilby's old eyes twinkled. "A very foolish young lady."

It took several long moments but the color eventually drained from Sean's face as he stared at the lone figure. The old man took pity on him and called out softly.

"Lady Sheridan?"

Sheridan's head snapped in his direction, so sharply that the hood of her cloak came off. Her glorious hair spilled free, covering a shoulder and draping across her mouth. Expecting to see only the priest, it took her a moment to realize that she was gazing at Sean.

Sheridan began running towards Sean and he towards her. Suddenly, she was in his powerful arms and he lifted her up, holding her so tightly that his embrace threatened to crush her. The soft sounds of joyful weeping filled the air as Sean kissed every inch of flesh he could manage to come into contact with; her eyes, forehead, cheeks, ears and mouth were open territory for his passionate, and surprised, delight.

"My God," Sheridan sobbed softly, trying to catch her breath between heated kisses. "You are alive. I hardly dared to hope."

He held her as if to never let her go. "And you...," he could hardly form a coherent thought. "I was told you were at Watford House. How is it that you are here?"

She pulled back then, gazing into his clear blue eyes and feeling more emotion than she could sufficiently express. Her hands gripped him tightly, even as he set her on her feet.

"I ran away," she told him breathlessly. "They could not keep me from you, Sean. They tried but I would not let them. I had to find you."

He touched her face, not understanding what she apparently meant. "Who brought you?"

"No one."

Then it began to register. "Are you telling me that you rode all the way from Eastbury alone?"

She sniffled, wiping at her nose. "Aye."

He just looked at her. So that was what Gilby meant when he called her a very foolish young lady. His joy was tempered with horror for all of the things that could have befallen her on her determined quest and he pulled her into his arms once again, holding her closer. Momentary anger gave way to extremely relief.

"Sweet Jesus," he breathed. "You would risk yourself like that for me?"

She clung to him, a mountain of strength. "I would do anything for you," she murmured. "I love you."

It was difficult for him to keep his balance. Sean bobbled, ending up on one knee. On the ground, he was almost eye to eye with her, his clear blue eyes piercing deep into her soul.

"Are you all right?" she asked softly. "What is wrong?"

He snorted with the irony of the question. His mailed gloves came up, clasping her sweet face between them. "Tell me again."

"Tell you what?"

"That you love me."

Her tears were nearly gone, replaced by a delicious smile that spread across her face. "I love you."

His expression took on the most amazing glow. "Do you really?"

"Aye."

He took her in his arms, then, still on one knee, his face buried in the valley between her breasts. She held him tightly. "Does this displease you?"

His face suddenly came up, looking at her. The clear blue eyes were wet with unshed tears. "Of course not," he whispered. "For I, quite clearly, am deeply in love with you."

Her grin broadened. "Marry me now, Sean. Marry me and let us grow old together."

"Would that I could, sweetling."

"Why not?"

"Because there is too much looming in the near future. You and I have much to discuss."

She thought on that a moment. "Will these events in the future affect us?"

"Aye."

"Is it possible that they will affect us so that we will never marry?"

"We will marry, have no doubt. But these events…."

"Then if we will marry, I would do it now. Please, Sean. That way, no one can ever rightfully keep us apart."

He hadn't the will or the heart to refuse her. He wanted it as badly as she did, probably more. William Marshall, therefore, had to amend his promise; it was difficult to say no to such a beautiful lady. Sean received his bride before finishing his task, leaving the task of breaking the news to Jocelin to the Marshall. Though William didn't mind that he was to be the bearer of unwelcome information, he minded the fact that his bargain was somehow twisted in Sean's favor.

Even as Father Simon married Sean and Sheridan with Gilby and the Marshall as witness, still, William could only hope that Sean would follow through and keep his part of the bargain. Once, William had asked Sean to trust him. Now William would have to do the same.

But those thoughts were violently dashed as they quit the chapel and ran head-long into the king, preparing to take Vespers with his retainers. John took one look at Sheridan and Sean knew they were in for a world of trouble.

CHAPTER ELEVEN

"... the game was afoot. I had stepped into a new world of deception and subversion that I could hardly begin to comprehend. Everything I had worked for was in danger of shattering but, strangely enough, I did not care. I had my wife and that was all that mattered...."

The Chronicles of Sir Sean de Lara

1206 – 1215 A.D.

SEAN HAD ALWAYS thought fast on his feet. In his vocation, it was an essential and practiced skill. As he looked at the king's sagging face, his senses rapidly calculated the situation, the odds, and the path of most convincing progress. Never in his life had he faced something so critical; now it wasn't only his life at stake, but his wife's. He fought down his shock for the sake of thinking clearly.

The Marshall had not followed them from the chapel. He and Father Simon were still inside, aware that the king and his entourage were at the threshold. With the focus on Sean, they were able to slip away unseen. Realizing this, Sean's peripheral senses reached out to Gilby and Sheridan, standing just to his right. The old man would be inconsequential to the king; he was one of the Tower physics, an old man that hardly presented a threat.

As Sean faced the king, many thoughts ran though his mind and it was a matter of selecting the most plausible one. He fixed John straight in the eye.

"Sire," he said smoothly. "I was on my way to seek your audience."

John wasn't looking at Sean; he was looking at Sheridan. "You are supposed to be riding to the Marches," he commented casually. "Why are you still here? And who is this?"

Sean kept his composure. "The army is mobilized, sire, though getting out of the city now under siege will take some difficulty," he reminded him yet again what a folly it was to be sending an army to the Marches while London was under attack. "I was distracted from my departure by this lady I now hold captive."

A leering smile spread across John's lips, full of indelicate suggestions of lustful thoughts. "And does your captive have a name?"

Sean's expression didn't change. "Good news, sire," he answered. "I have within my control an excellent investment for the future of your reign. Be presented to the Lady Sheridan St. James."

John's eyes widened. He clapped his hands together as an excited child would have. "Sheridan St. James," he reached out, fingering a tendril of blond hair. "By God's Rood, d'Athée was correct. She is exquisite. But what is she doing here? D'Athée told me the last he saw of you and Lady Sheridan, you were both fleeing towards the Lanthorn Tower."

It took all of Sean's self-control not to break the man's neck as he toyed with Sheridan's hair. If he was going to pull this off and save both their lives, then he had to be convincing. He had to remain in control. But it was growing more difficult with each passing moment.

"We were, sire, until I was ambushed and the lady escaped," he said evenly. "Be that as it may, she has been recaptured. And she is now my wife."

John stopped toying. He looked at Sean as if the man had lost his mind. "She is *what*?"

"My wife. I have just married her."

"De Lara, if this is a joke...."

Sean shook his head, moving to grab Sheridan by the arm in a less-gentle and more-controlling gesture. It was meant to be a dominating action. But Sean managed to very discreetly pull her to his other side, putting himself between John and Sheridan.

"No joke, I assure you," his voice lowered. "I caught the woman hiding in the church. Were we to simply hold her hostage against the rebels, it would be a sentimental prisoner and nothing more. The allies would not surrender simply for the sake of Sheridan St. James. However, to marry her means that I, as her husband, inherit control of Lansdown, her wealth and her men. Men that are currently laying siege outside of the city. One command from me and fifteen hundred men will return to Lansdown."

The gleam of lust in John's eye flared, dimmed, and then turned into something else. Sean watched the king's expression with such inward scrutiny that, for a few moments, he forgot to breathe. He could only pray the man believed him. The seconds ticked by with agonizing slowness as the king digested the statement.

But it was thankfully not for long. John's expression gradually slackened. Though naturally suspicious, he could not deny the Shadow Lord's train of thought nor his sacrifice for the king's cause. His features began to bloom with the light of understanding.

"Amazing," he breathed, his gaze moving from Sean back to Sheridan. "So you have married Henry St. James' daughter and heiress."

"The St. James army is now my army and will do as I command."

It was apparent that the king was thrilled with the prospect. He clapped his hands again, a disturbingly gleeful gesture in the face of an impending siege. But Sean was determined to keep control of the conversation before the king could do or suggest anything that would cause him to snap and give himself away. He stepped away from the king, respectfully, still gripping Sheridan by the arm. He tried not to appear as if he was hurried, merely going about a duty.

"I will take her for safekeeping now, sire," he said as he walked. "I will send word to the St. James captain to return to Lansdown and then I shall meet up with my army preparing to leave for the Marches."

Sean's departure was swift but the king didn't notice. All he could see was that a prize was escaping him and he would not let such a trophy go so swiftly. He took a few steps after Sean, calling out as the distance between them grew.

"I should like to become better acquainted with your wife," he said in a tone that suggested it was a command. "Perhaps over a meal after Vespers. And I should like for you to attend me before you leave for the Marches."

Sean knew exactly what he meant. Nine years had given him that gift of insight. He was marginally thankful the man hadn't made demands for her at that very moment, but still, it would be a turbulent evening ahead. Though his body tensed, he remained controlled on the outside; he had to.

"As you wish, sire," he answered.

He whisked Sheridan down the long axis of the chapel, turning the corner and realizing they were far from where he wanted to take her. The Flint Tower was in front of them, looming against the dusk. Sean took her into the Tower with Gilby on their heels. He had to get away from the king, anywhere.

The Tower was cold and damp. Sean took Sheridan up to the second floor, pausing once they reached the adjoining building where the nobles were sometimes housed. It was dark but for a few torches smoking lazily. Pausing to catch his breath, he turned to look at her.

Sheridan, thankfully, was composed in spite of what could have been a horrible happenstance. She smiled timidly as their eyes met.

"Now what?" she asked, trying to make light of the situation. "Do you plan to take me somewhere and ravage me?"

He almost frowned at her but she was smiling so charmingly at him that he cracked a smile. She knew how serious the situation was, or at least she sensed it. His smile softened as he gazed down at her. A hand came up to stroke the same hair that the king had touched.

"You will have to wash your hair," his voice was husky. "I cannot stomach the man's scent on you."

She could see how anxious he was, which was unusual given the fact that the man was perpetually in control of himself. She pressed against him, curling against his massive body. Sean wrapped his arms around her, gazing down into her lovely face.

"All in good time," she murmured. "What do we do now?"

He lifted an eyebrow. "This is not how I had planned our wedding night but I am afraid I will have to turn you over to Gilby's care while I tend to the king."

She nodded, masking her disappointment. "He wants to have supper with me."

Sean's face hardened. "He will be sorely disappointed. The man will never be near you again."

"But… what are you going to tell him?"

"That you are ill, or asleep, or that you have run off in terror. I do not know at the moment. Anything I can think of."

She could see how much the very idea distressed him. She could not know that he had been dreading this moment since almost the very moment he laid eyes upon her in the ward those days ago. Now it was coming to pass, that which he feared most. The king was on to Sheridan's scent. Though she sensed Sean's distress, she could not truly know how badly it was affecting him.

"I am sure that Gilby shall take good care of me while you are doing your duty," she assured him quietly. "You must return to the king quickly or he might become suspicious."

He almost snorted; *he is always suspicious.* But he would not say what he was thinking, what she could not grasp at the moment. One had to be in the trenches for as long as he had been in order to know just how serious this situation was.

"Not before I get you settled," he said, taking her hand and leading her down the hall. "I would make sure you are safe and cared for before I return to the king."

Orienting himself, he knew exactly where he was and what chambers, or apartments, were in close proximity. The length of the structure, moving north to south, was several hundred yards long. It was a massive structure of apartments and rooms. Most of the upstairs chambers were for visiting nobles, not assigned to any one particular house. Sean chose a random apartment that was small but functional.

They were away from the bustle of most of the Tower so that Sheridan could easily remain out of the public eye.

The little antechamber was small and chilly, with very little furnishings. In fact, it looked as if it had been unlived in for some time. The sun had almost completely set, giving the room an eerie feel. Sean let go of Sheridan's hand as Gilby shut the door and threw the bolt. As Sean made a fire in the dark, cold hearth, Gilby took the lady's arm gently and guided her to the only chair.

Sheridan sat in the darkness, watching Sean's broad back as he worked the fireplace. Gilby drifted into the bedchamber and emerged a few moments later to declare that there was a serviceable mattress but no linens. Then he announced he would go in search of some food for the lady and left the apartments entirely. Sean remained silent as he sparked the flint that eventually gave birth to a small flame. Sheridan left her chair and went to kneel beside Sean, her arms going around his neck and her head against his massive bicep. It was a comforting, consoling gesture.

He patted her arm with his free hand, stoking the little flame until it picked up into a friendly blaze. She leaned against him, feeling his massive strength beneath her arms, acquainting herself with the scent and feel of him. It was wonderful.

"What did you mean about sending my army back to Lansdown?" she asked one of many questions on her mind. "Are you really?"

He sighed heavily; she could feel it as well as hear it. "Things are by far more complicated than they were an hour ago," he replied. "The Marshall will be sending word to Jocelin of our marriage, but I must have your declaration on a document to de Moreville verifying our marriage and the fact that I now have control of the St. James army."

She lifted her head from his arm, looking at him. "Neely will not take the news well."

"As I would not expect him to, which is why I require your verification."

"Are you going to send the army home?"

He looked at her, then. "No."

"But you told the king...."

"I told him many things to save both our lives," he interrupted her softly. "You know the truth, Sheridan. The king knows only what I tell him."

She gazed into the clear blue eyes, seeing his vulnerability for the very first time. She'd never seen that before, ever. It was at that moment the seriousness of the situation began to sink in.

"Why are you going to the Marches?" she asked, almost a whisper.

The fire was picking up steam. Sean stood up and led Sheridan back over to the chair. He took it, seating her on his lap. She curled up against him, a deliciously wonderful moment between them. He had never held her on his lap before. He knew the moment her rounded buttocks settled on his thighs that he liked it tremendously. He held her close.

"I have orders to ride for the Marches," he murmured, his lips against her forehead. "The king seems to think that I am needed more on the Welsh border than at a city under siege."

"But why?" she was enjoying the warmth, the strength, from him tremendously. "I do not understand why he would send his bodyguard to battle."

"More than a bodyguard, I am a knight. I have been swinging a sword longer than most."

"I know that, but I would think that he would rather have you here."

He debated how much to tell her. Though she understood politics by virtue of her father's teaching, still, he did not want to frighten her. But he felt he had to be honest with her. He'd lied a great deal in his life, to a great many people, but he made a firm vow at that moment that he would never lie to Sheridan, no matter what.

"'Tis a test, Sheridan," he said quietly. "The king has doubts about my loyalty stemming from the time when I prevented him from raping your sister. He is a suspicious man by nature and my actions fueled some doubt in his mind. He has asked me to ride to the Marches to assist Clifford in fending off de Braose's attack against disputed holdings. He has also asked me to raze Lansdown to prove that I am more loyal to him than to the House of St. James, which presents something of a problem considering I married the heiress. Lansdown belongs to me now."

Her head came up and her eyes were huge on him. "Raze it?" she repeated. "Oh, Sean, you do not mean to…?"

He put a finger on her lips, quieting her. "I will not raze my own castle," he was more aware of his finger on her soft lips than the subject at hand. "When I go to the king this night, it will be to discuss an entirely new set of orders."

"But why must you go at all? Now that we have married, surely it changes things."

He looked at her, his clear blue eyes soft yet resigned at the same time. "I made a promise that I must keep," he said after a moment. "Long before I met you, I made a promise to William Marshall that I would do all in my power to see John fall. I must keep that promise."

She didn't look entirely accepting. "But… but riding to the Marches, to battle, is part of that promise?"

He nodded slowly. "Absolutely," he shifted her on his lap, his hands searching out new places on her torso he'd not yet touched. "You see, before you and I found each other at the chapel, I had made the Marshall a promise that I would fulfill my mission if he would ensure that, in the end, you became mine. But your happenstance arrival changed things. Now that I have you, I still promised the Marshall that I would complete my task. And I intend to do so."

"So you must ride to battle?"

"I must keep up the illusion that I am still loyal to the king. And that means that I continue to follow his orders. If the man wants me to go to the Marches, then go I must."

She looked at him, scrutinizing every angle, every feature. He had explained himself and she would not argue his sense of honor.

"I have made a mess of things, haven't I?"

He grinned. "Not at all. 'Tis I who have made the mess. But we shall get through this, have no doubt."

She wrapped her arms around his neck, pulling herself closer to him. She could feel his breath on her face. "Will you promise me something, then?"

"If I can."

She wriggled her nose as she thought of what she would say. She was sure he would refuse but she would ask nonetheless. "I am afraid to stay here," she whispered. "When you ride for the Marches, please do not leave me behind. I want to go with you."

He didn't outright refuse her. In fact, he lowered his gaze, perhaps contemplating her words, perhaps contemplating something else. Finally he spoke.

"I will not leave you here, but you cannot ride to battle with me."

"Then where will I go?"

"Back to Watford House. It will be the safest place for you until this madness is finished." His eyes took on a distant look. "In fact, I think I shall ask the Marshall to escort you. He must inform Jocelin of our marriage and it would be good to have him as moral support for you should Jocelin rage."

"He will rage," she agreed, somewhat sadly. "But I do not need the Marshall's support. I can face him alone."

"You will not face him alone. The Marshall will be there."

She opened her mouth to protest but thought better of it when she saw the look on his face. She studied his expression for several long moments before pressing her face into the crook of his neck. Her arms around him tightened.

"Your decision is made?" she asked softly.

"It is."

"Then do you think we could forget all of our troubles for five minutes this night and simply enjoy the happiness of our marriage?" She lifted her head to look at him. "Since the moment we've met, politics and war and the king have dominated our relationship. Can we not think of anything but ourselves for the next five minutes and feel the joy of this union?"

He grasped her by the chin, his sharp gaze studying every line, every contour of her face. With a seductive smile on his lips, his mouth closed down gently over hers, taking several long tastes of her honeyed lips. It wasn't long before his tongue plunged deep into her mouth and his hands moved to her head, holding it fast and still against him. As his lips ravaged her, Sheridan managed to speak through his fevered attention.

"Take me as your wife this night, Sean," she whispered. "I do not want to wait. If we are to be separated, then give me the memory of this night to hold deep in my heart until you return to me. Please."

He stopped kissing her long enough to gaze into her luminous eyes. "We have no time, sweetling," he murmured. "Even now, I must return to the king. Every moment I delay invites more suspicion."

Tears welled in her eyes. "Give me five minutes," she begged softly. "You are riding to battle, Sean. What if you do not return? What if…?"

She couldn't finish and he pulled her close to him, holding her tightly as he rose from the chair and carried her into the bed chamber.

It was cold and dark but for the weak moonlight streaming in through the thin lancet window. Sean lay her carefully down on the mattress, rough though it was, and resumed his gentle kisses. He could give her five minutes, though he very much wanted to give her more. She deserved far more.

Sheridan was partially covered by his massive body, feeling his weight atop her. It was a new, exhilarating feeling. His mouth was on hers, his hands in her hair, on her neck, moving down her arm. Boldly, she took a hand and placed it on her breast, their eyes meeting as she did so. Sean's gaze was powerful, consuming, as his hand gently tightened over the delicious fleshy mound. Then his lips descended on her again, with such passion that she sucked in her breath at his lustful attack. The hand on her breast began to massage it, rubbing at the peaked nipple through the fabric. Though she was a maiden, Sheridan knew she must have more of him. She must have all of him. The man was her husband and she would know him.

The surcoat she wore fastened on the side and she reached a hand down to unhook the stays. Without a word, she unleashed the entire garment and began to pull it off. Sean saw what she was doing; too weak to stop her, for he very badly wanted the same thing she did, he helped her. The surcoat ended up on the floor followed very quickly by her shift. His lips against her mouth, her face, he gently removed her pantalets and unfastened the ribbons that held her hose. As he pulled them off, he stroked her silky legs, acquainting himself with something he never thought to have.

It was an empowering feeling, more overwhelming than he could have imagined. Never had he had anyone that belonged only to him. He paused a moment in his tender assault to remove his tunic. His breathing was coming in heavy gasps as he yanked off his boots, followed by his breeches. He could feel Sheridan's hands timidly, gently, touching his flesh as he removed his clothing, inspecting his body for the very first time. By the time his hose were off, he collapsed on her warm, tender body, gathering her up in his arms and feeling her naked flesh against his. It was almost more than he could bear, for she was warm and soft. His lips found hers once again and he growled as his tongue plunged into her mouth.

He wanted to take his time with her; God knows he did. But there was no time left. His mouth left hers, his lips moving down her neck to her full breasts to find a taut nipple. Suckling gently, he carefully wedged his enormous body between her legs, his hands on her thighs to gently part them. He could feel her panting beneath him, small cries as he suckled harder. He could feel her hands in his hair. It was the most wonderful thing he had ever experienced.

One hand moved to the sensual core between her legs. He fingered her delicately, feeling her flinch beneath him. After a few brief moments of acquainting her with the feel of his touch, he began to stroke her more boldly. Sheridan started but kept her calm; he proceeded to insert a gentle finger into her. She gasped at the intrusion but he could not wait to soothe her or talk her through the act; she was wet from his attentions, her virgin body preparing itself for his entry. And enter he did; removing his hand, he held her tightly and carefully, firmly, thrust into her.

Sheridan yelped at the passionate invasion but quickly bit her lip to stay silent; as Sean thrust again and still again to seat himself, she bit her lip harder and buried her face in his chest. Holding him tightly, she worked through the pressure, the slight pain, feeling him move within her as a husband moves within a wife. This was what she had wanted; all of the man. Now she had him. As the slight pain faded and Sean began to move, a most remarkable sensation began to blossom.

His thrusts were tender, firm and measured. One hand gently fingered her breast, causing wicked sensations throughout her body. The more he moved, the more heated her loins became until she gasped his name. Sean's mouth covered her lips, somewhat to silence her but mostly to taste her. He couldn't get enough of the woman, body and soul, and gorged himself while he had the chance. She was more than he could have imagined and far more than he had hoped for.

But he knew he could not take his time with her, drawing out their passion until they were both weak with it. This night was a duty, a pleasure, a necessity and a foretaste of what was to come. As much as he would have wanted it to last, he knew it could not. His hand moved from her breast to her Venus Mound and he rubbed at the throbbing nub where their bodies joined. Within the first two strokes, her body stiffened and he felt her tender walls pulling at him in climax. Sean answered immediately, finding his release, feeling every throb with the greatest pleasure he had ever known. Even after he was spent, he continued to move. He did not want the moment to end; it made him heartsick to think about it.

But end it must. It had been more than five minutes, but not much more. As his senses and even breathing returned, he opened his eyes to gaze into the most beautiful face he had ever seen. Sheridan was looking at him, her cheeks flushed and her expression delightfully sated. When their eyes met, she smiled.

"It was a remarkable five minutes, husband," she murmured, watching him grin. "You would have denied me that?"

He propped himself up on one elbow, gazing down into her exquisite features and brushing a stray bit of hair from her cheek. "What a fool I was to resist," he kissed her tenderly. "How I wish I could have taken all the time in the world. Are you all right?"

"I am all right," she whispered, her smile fading. "Thank you, Sean."

"For what?"

"For giving me a part of you."

The corner of his mouth twitched. "You have more than a part of me, Lady de Lara. You have all of me. You are the most important thing in the world to me."

Unable to reply, feeling increasingly saddened as the pangs of separation threatened, she lifted herself up to his lips, attaching herself to his mouth and kissing him with passion that defied explanation. Sean enfolded her in his arms, taking a last few moments to experience the taste and feel of her. He would need the memory to sustain him in the dark days to come.

"I love you," he murmured against her mouth.

"And I love you," was her whispered reply.

A few minutes later, they were dressed. It had been done silently, swiftly. Sean took her hand and led her back into the antechamber, sitting her carefully in the chair and patting her shoulder affectionately as he moved for the lancet window to view the grounds below.

Fortunate for them that they had possessed a keen sense of timing; no sooner had Sean reached the window than Gilby was rapping at the door. Sheridan leapt up and unbolted the panel, allowing the little man entry and locking the door behind him.

"You had better go, Sean," he blustered inside. "There are men looking for you; I could hear them speaking your name across the grounds."

Sean swore softly under his breath, knowing that he had delayed too long, and moved swiftly for the door. He was about to leave when he suddenly stopped as if a thought had just occurred to him. Retracing his steps, he took Sheridan in his arms and kissed her deeply. It was enough to weaken her knees and he had to steady her when he released her. She grinned and he winked boldly.

"Gilby, take care of her," he instructed the old man, his soft gaze lingering on his wife's lovely face. "She is all to me."

"I must remove her from the Tower," Gilby replied, witnessing the tender looks between Sean and his wife. "She cannot stay here, Sean. You know that."

"I am going to ask the Marshall to take her back to Watford House."

Gilby went to Sean and yanked on his sleeve. "She cannot wait for the Marshall to come for her. I must remove her, and young de Braose, immediately. I shall take them both to Watford House if that is your wish."

Sean tore his gaze away from Sheridan long enough to look at the little old man. "She needs a full escort. There are twenty thousand men attacking London as we speak. You'll never get her through their lines without protection."

Gilby raised an eyebrow. "She made it through their lines by herself."

"It was a stroke of luck."

"Be that as it may, I will take her and de Braose out of London myself, this very night. No one would dare bother a physic on his duties."

"What duties would that be? You are pulling a cart laden with hay like a farmer."

"I shall tell them that I have been ordered to attend the king's troops outside the walls. The hay is for their animals."

It was a plausible scenario; moreover, most of the king's men knew Gilby. He'd been at the Tower forever. It was a rare moment of indecision in Sean' eyes; both Gilby and Sheridan saw it. When the old man looked at Sheridan as if silently beseeching her to support his statement, she went to her husband and wrapped her soft hands around one of his enormous mitts. When Sean looked down at her, she smiled sweetly.

"He is right," she said quietly. "You must return to the king and you must allow Gilby to remove me from the Tower. Have no fear; I will be waiting for you at Watford House."

His indecisive expression was replaced by one of raw longing. "It may be quite some time before I see you again," he squeezed her hands gently. "I have no way of knowing when I shall come for you."

It was like a stab to her heart but she fought it. Tears would do no good at the moment; she had what she wanted. She had married him. Now they both knew what needed to be done. Sean had a destiny he needed to fulfill; she could do nothing more than wait for him to fulfill it.

"I understand," she said as bravely as she could. "However, I may move from Watford House at some point and return home. If I am not at Watford, then I will be at Lansdown. There is nowhere else I will be."

"Go, Sean," Gilby urged quietly. "You must not linger here."

Sean nodded sharply, put both hands around Sheridan's face, and kissed her strongly. When he pulled back, his eyes were glimmering with emotion.

"If I never see you again, then know that this brief moment in time has made my entire life worth living," he murmured. "Nothing else on earth, nothing else I have ever done, can compare. You are my angel and I will love you, and no other, in this life and beyond."

With that, he was gone. Sheridan didn't even have the time to reply. She stood there a moment, in shock, digesting his words and unaware of Gilby's sympathetic gaze upon her. It didn't matter. Nothing mattered but Sean. She continued to stand for the longest time, gazing at the closed door, feeling hollow. She wasn't sure that she would ever see him again and the thought nearly killed her.

Gilby finally encouraged her to gather her cloak so they could leave. She had to go back into the bedroom to retrieve it, but one look at the raw stuffed mattress where she had experienced her first intimate taste of her husband brought floods of tears. When Gilby came back into the room to see what was keeping her, he found her curled up on the old mattress sobbing as if her heart was broken.

The old man wished he had a potion to heal such a thing.

CHAPTER TWELVE

".... in reflection, I should have known what the outcome would be. As opposing armies clash with a mighty cheer, so it seemed that I should also clash with those I had once served ...."

The Chronicles of Sir Sean de Lara

1206 – 1215 A.D.

"WHERE HAVE YOU been?"

It was the first question out of John's mouth when Sean appeared in the king's private dining room adjacent to his bedchamber. There were a few retainers present but, for the most part, the king was supping alone. Sean realized it was because of the anticipation of Lady Sheridan; John had not wanted to share her so he had dismissed most of his entourage. But Sean was entering the room alone and instantly, the king's fury, and distrust, was peaked.

"I was seeking safety for Lady Sheridan, sire," Sean replied steadily, his clear blue eyes locked with the king's black orbs. "She is too valuable to the cause not to amply protect. I apologize if I was gone overlong."

D'Athée stood several feet behind the king, watching Sean with a mixture of amusement and suspicion. Truth be told, he was enjoying this; Sean de Lara had been the perfect son for nine long years. Too long to serve in someone's shadow. D'Athée could see that perhaps now there was a chance for him to be the favored retainer of the king. He was pleased with the fact that de Lara's reputation was fading before his eyes.

John's gaze lingered on Sean for several long moments; it was clear that his distrust of the man was growing. No matter what he had told him about marriage to the St. James woman, there was more to it. John could feel it. Others had even suggested it and, being a pliable man, John would readily agree. It was sickening to think his Shadow Lord was turning on him, turned by the head of a woman no less. After a properly suspicious pause, he returned to his food.

"I told you to bring her to sup with me," he said casually. "Why did you disobey?"

"She has fallen ill," Sean replied. "This day has been too much for her. Rather than tax her further, I have locked her away where she can rest. She will be well enough to entertain you another day."

John lifted a dark eyebrow at him. "I do not want her another day. I wish to see her today. Go and get her."

Sean could feel the test of wills coming. It was faster than he had anticipated. How he handled the king's demands could very easily dictate the course of his future and the decisive end of nine horrible years. He could not destroy it now, not when all eyes were upon him. But he was facing a situation that he had never before faced; that as a husband protecting his wife. A man protecting the woman he loved. There was something overwhelming about that realization, fierce and crazed yet controlled and deadly. As much as he wanted to snap the man's neck, he knew that he could not.

"It must be another day, sire," Sean replied. "She is in no condition for socializing. If you push her, she will fail, and her health is very weak. She will be no good to us dead."

John's black eyes flared. He stood up, knocking over his chair in the process and placing himself up against Sean as if to forcibly intimidate him. But there was a tremendous difference in size and height, and the king merely looked like an angry child standing before a man of Sean's stature. Sean didn't flinch as the king thumped him on the chest.

"Since when do you deny my orders?" he snarled.

Sean met him steadily. "I have explained to you my reasons, sire. They are beyond our control and I would ask that you trust me in this matter."

The king's cheeks flushed and his mouth began to work; Sean,

Gerard and the few other retainers in the room could see that he was working himself up to a fit. It was a fast rise. When his fists began to clench and unclench and the veins on his neck throbbed, they knew the worst was coming.

"I do not believe you," he hissed. "You have married this woman to keep her all to yourself. I have seen her; she is a beauty. You want her all for yourself!"

"I married her to better serve you, sire," Sean answered steadily.

"Liar!" John screamed, spittle flying from his lips. Reaching out, he slapped Sean across the face, hard. "You are keeping her from me and I shall not have it. Do you hear me? I shall not have it! Bring her here if you value your life, de Lara. You will not disobey me!"

The slap hadn't hurt in the least but Sean was beginning to sweat. He was starting to lose his patience against a madman and that was not a good sign.

"A dead heiress will do you no good," he repeated as evenly as he could manage. "Bear in mind that I have lied, killed and absconded for you for over nine years. I know for what purpose you wish to see Lady Sheridan and it is not simply to talk to her. I know you well, sire, and I tell you now that whatever you have planned for her will kill her. She will not be able to handle it in her present state. Is that what you want? To kill her?"

The king lashed out again and hit Sean with a balled fist, once on the arm and once on the jaw. It was hardly enough to take notice and Sean watched as the king began to foam at the mouth.

"You are sworn to me, de Lara," he sputtered, backing away from the mountain of a man. He jabbed a crooked finger at him. "You are sworn to me and must do what I command. And I command you to bring the woman!"

Sean's face did not change expression. "I regret that I must deny you, sire."

John emitted something that sounded like a strangled scream as he whirled to d'Athée, a few feet away. He gestured at the man with claw-like hands.

"Go and get her, Gerard," he commanded in a strangled voice. "Get her and bring her to me."

"Do this and I will kill you," Sean said to Gerard from across the room. "Do you understand?"

Gerard's amusement from the beginning of the conversation had faded. Now he was in the middle of it, confused and edgy. He immediately unsheathed his sword at Sean.

"Make no threats to me, Sean," he growled. "I am armed. You are not."

Sean lifted an eyebrow at him. "I have no reason to arm myself unless you do not do as I ask. If I arm myself, you will die."

John screamed again, this time in pure frustration. His body was beginning to contort. "Will no one do as they are told? I said get the St. James woman. I meant it. Gerard, go this instant if you value your life!"

Gerard was cornered but he was also stupid; he did not think for himself and was only able to do as directed. As much as he feared Sean, he was sworn to the king. If the king ordered him to do something, then he would do it. He swung the sword in a deadly series of arcs to prove to Sean that he meant business.

"Where is she, de Lara?" he asked in a low voice. "If you do not tell me, then I will tear this place apart looking for her and when I find her, it will not be pleasant."

Sean didn't react at first; he simply stared at the man. He could see where this was leading. After a moment, he turned his back on both men and walked to the entry to the room; two guards waited there, watching the happenings of the room with wide-eyes. Sean reached out and unsheathed the sword strapped to the side of one of the men; it was a smaller sword, more ceremonial than functional, but it was sharp and strong. It would have to do. Sword in hand, Sean turned in d'Athée's direction.

"Now," he said in a tone that caused most men to run in terror. "If anyone is to experience unpleasantness, it will be you. You will not go anywhere near Lady Sheridan. She is out of your reach."

"You see?" John screeched. "He is trying to keep her from me!"

Gerard's lip twitched menacingly. "Once the king is done with her, I will take my fill and there isn't a damn thing you can do to stop me."

Gerard had just signed his death warrant; Sean knew that he meant his threat. Only death would stop him and Sean fully intended to kill him to protect his wife. Any control over the situation had fled and now it was deadly. Sean intended that he and Sheridan would survive it.

"Aye, there is," he rumbled. "I will end your miserable life before you leave this room."

"You can try."

Sean's sword went up.

ꝏ

GUY WAS VERY surprised to see Sheridan. When she and Gilby entered the old man's tiny rooms that were inconspicuously lodged in a corner of the barracks, Guy nearly leapt out of the bed with joy. But his broken ribs and cracked collar bone prevented it. He lay there with an amazed smile on his face as she came near the bed and greeted him warmly. When he reached out to take her hand, she let him. He was obviously very glad to see her and she was genuinely touched by his concern.

But there was no time for the polite reunion. Gilby needed Sheridan's help to move Guy and the old man hustled around the room, gathering things they would need and rattling instructions.

"My lady, I need for you to assist young de Braose," he said as he threw items into a satchel and collected an old black bag shoved under a table. "He cannot walk without assistance."

Sheridan took a closer look at Guy; she had a suspicion why he was lying in bed looking as if he had been run over by a stampede. The last time she had seen him, he was being taken away by the king's guard. She bent over him, inspecting the enormous bruise on the right side of his head.

"Oh… Guy," she breathed, stopping short of actually touching the wound. "What did they do to you?"

Guy smiled, lop-sided from the swelling on his face. "Beat me within an inch of my life," he said, almost proudly. "But they could not make me tell them anything."

"What did they want to know?"

Guy tried to shrug. "Everything. Our strength and strategy, mostly. I seem to remember Walter Clifford doing some of the interrogating, I am sure, to seek revenge against my father. They are old enemies, you know. My father will be furious when he finds out."

"But you told them nothing? Not even Clifford?"

Guy shook his head. "Not a word. No matter how hard they beat me, which was quite hard at times."

He seemed rather casual about the entire thing but Sheridan was horrified. "I am so sorry," she whispered sincerely. "Can you at least stand? You may lean on me."

He nodded, moving extremely slowly as he swung his legs over the side of the bed and grunting with pain as his ribs moved around. Sheridan had him by the arm, struggling to help him to stand, as Gilby finished collecting his tools and medicaments. He seemed indecisive with a few things, putting some things aside while collecting others. But when he saw that the lady was having difficulty with the patient, he stopped his collecting and helped the man finally rise to his feet.

"There is a cart off to the side of the barracks, near the alley," he said. "We must go to it."

Sheridan had a good grip on Guy as they moved from the room, cloaked by the darkness as they moved into the corridor. Guy moved like a crippled old man and it seemed to take forever simply to move across the floor.

The door leading to the grounds was a few feet away and they were able to make it clear of the barracks in relative stealth. When it was clear that Guy could go no further, Gilby bade him stop when they were just a few feet clear of the barracks. As Sheridan practically held Guy on his two feet, Gilby scurried around the corner to his cart and grabbed hold of the small mule strapped to the guides. Leading the animal forward, he directed both Sheridan and Guy onto the back of the cart.

It was the same wagon that had been waiting for Sean when he had brought Guy from the dungeons. It was piled high with dried grass and dead weeds. With Sheridan's help, Guy was able to burrow under the pile. Gilby waited until they were both settled before piling hay over them. He took his time in making sure they were adequately covered. It wasn't the most comfortable way to travel, but it was essential in order to get them clear of the Tower. Covering the cart with an oiled tarp and piling his bags onto the back, he led the mule towards the gatehouse.

Truth be told, the old man was nervous. He hadn't been nervous in years and it was a strangely exhilarating feeling. He would have been worried about himself if he hadn't been nervous, for the gravity of the situation was wearing heavily on him. He knew how important it was. He had to get them to Watford House.

☙

SEAN TOSSED THE sword aside, ignoring the trail of blood he left splattered across the floor. With a lingering glance at d'Athée in a wounded heap, he turned to the king.

John gazed back at him with more fear than he had ever exhibited. He had just witnessed a brutal swordfight ending in the goring of Gerard, who lay groaning on the ground. Sean had hardly raised a sweat. The king raised his hands.

"You are still my chosen one, de Lara," he insisted, a far different attitude from the screaming man just moments before. "I did not mean it when I called you a liar. You have never lied to me. It was Gerard who thought so. He is the one who poisoned me against you."

Sean was quite calm; he did not believe the king for a moment. "It is of no matter," he said evenly. "If you have no more directives, then I must gather what is left of your army remaining at the Tower and head for the Marches. De Vere will not be happy that I must confiscate a good deal of the forces he commands."

The king was like an eager dog; he couldn't seem to apologize enough or be supportive enough. He was terrified and it showed. "You do not need to go to the Marches," he told him. "I would have you here in charge of the Tower defenses."

Sean looked at him, lifting a slow eyebrow. "What of your holdings on the Marches that were so important to you, sire?"

"It is more important to protect me at this moment. London is under siege."

"What of Abergavenny and Lansdown?"

"Leave them. There will be another time. Moreover, Lansdown is now your holding and I suspect that you do not wish to raze your own property."

Sean almost sighed with relief but he held himself in check. Still, there were unanswered questions lingering in his mind. "And my loyalties, sire? Do I still need to prove them?"

John shook his head until his dirty, shaggy hair slapped back and forth. "You are my most loyal servant, de Lara. I am sorry for the things I said. I will not let a woman destroy the trust that you and I have for one another."

Sean knew he meant what he said. But in a minute, he could mean the exact opposite. That was the trouble with the king; he was indecisive, pliable, and underhanded. Sean knew better than to trust him.

"We have more things to worry about than a woman, sire," he tried to turn the subject from Sheridan. "I must go now and see to the city. If I feel you are in too great a danger, then I will facilitate removing you from the Tower to a safer location."

John nodded eagerly. "I will trust you, de Lara. You have kept me alive for nine years and I will not doubt you."

Sean's gaze lingered on him a moment before begging his leave. There was nothing more to say, at least not outwardly. Actions, at this point, spoke far more than mere words and Sean was eager to regain whatever was left of the tattered situation. More than that, he was vastly relieved that he would not be going to the Marches. Now he could do what he had planned all of these years in spite of the last-moment complications. Silently, he slipped from the room, leaving John to breathe a heavy sigh of relief when he was finally gone.

The king wiped the sweat from his brow, his heart pounding in his chest and grateful that de Lara had not turned the sword against him. Looking to Gerard on the ground, now pressing his hands against the wound in his side, he knew at once what he needed to do. De Lara was no longer controllable; he feared that one day soon the man would turn against him. Though Sean still seemed to be the same man on the surface, John could tell that something had changed. Everything had changed. Whether it was because of Lady Sheridan or not was no longer the issue. The fact remained that John believed Sean to be a threat to his life. Someday, the man would kill him. He knew it.

He had to do away with the threat. And there was only one way to do that.

CHAPTER THIRTEEN

".... chaos, it seems, is contagious...."

The Chronicles of Sir Sean de Lara

1206 – 1215 A.D.

NEELY COULDN'T BELIEVE his ears. He had to make a conscious effort to keep his mouth from hanging open.

"How long has she been gone?" he demanded.

The messenger from Watford House was a stable boy, nervous and exhausted from his ride. He cowered. "Two hours at the most, my lord."

"And no one saw her leave?"

The boy swallowed hard. "I did, my lord. I saw her leave on a Salisbury steed but I did not know she was running away." He paused as he watched Neely twitch and pace. "But there is more, my lord; her sister, the Lady Alys, was so guilt stricken over her sister's departure that she ran off as well. Jocelin thinks she has gone to find her sister."

At the northwest edge of London where two thousand men were gaining headway into the city, Neely was on the receiving end with a frantic message from Jocelin. The messenger had ridden hard from Watford House to inform him that the Lady Sheridan had run off and then the Lady Alys right after her. The boy could tell him no more than he already had; no one seemed to know where, exactly, Sheridan had gone, but they could certainly all guess. She had gone to find de Lara and Alys had run after her.

Neely hissed and cursed and threw the cup in his hand, listening to it clatter off in the darkness. It was a hellish night, full of death and fire and destruction, and he personally had fifteen hundred men under his command. But all that was put aside with the latest message from Jocelin.

Neely had two men second in command to him, one he had brought from Lansdown and the other as the head of the bishop's men. Sir Roget Henley was born and bred at Lansdown; his father had served Henry St. James for many years. He was young, flashy and brave but was molding into a calm and collected knight quite nicely. The other knight, an older man by the name of Sir Wyat de Tobins, had been with Jocelin for years and tended to be far more cautious than Neely liked. In spite of this, however, he was a capable commander.

It was to these men that Neely turned upon sending the nervous messenger back to Watford House. Since Roget knew the Lady Sheridan and the Lady Alys, the news meant more to him than it did to Wyat. The young knight had heard the information and was concerned at Neely's reaction.

"Why have they done this, my lord?" he asked. "Where would they go?"

Neely would not tell him all of it; partly because it was none of his affair and partly because he was ashamed on the lady's behalf. Why such a level-headed woman would suddenly lose her mind over a killer was beyond him. Alys, he could understand, but not Sheridan. Even without the mind-bending jealousy it provoked, he was still at a loss to explain her actions. He turned away from Roget and headed for the rear of the battle lines where the fresh supplies, wounded and horses were kept.

"I must go and see if I can find the ladies before something horrible befalls them," he said. "You and Wyat have command of the men for now. Continue along this path until I return."

"But you are needed here, my lord," Roget insisted. "Allow me to look for the ladies. I can find…."

Neely cut him off. "You do not know how they think. I believe I may know where Sheridan has gone and hopefully Alys with her." He moved between some tarps sheltering the wounded and past a large fire that had a giant pot of steaming water hovering atop it. "I need you here, Roget. You are capable of commanding. Just remember what you have been taught."

Roget didn't argue with him; they all knew that Neely had been in love with Lady Sheridan for as long as any of them could recall. They also knew she did not return the feelings. But it did not stop Neely from acting like an angry lover. So Roget kept his mouth shut and let his commander go, and returned to the battle that was making slow headway into the suburbs of London.

Neely was glad the man hadn't pestered him further. Given his current mood, he would have more than likely taken his head off. He knew that Sheridan must have returned to London and must surely be attempting to gain entrance to the Tower. Even without a battle threatening the city, the adventure would have been foolish enough. But with the added element of warfare, it was positively deadly. And Alys was more than likely right on her heels, guilt-ridden over her sister's departure. He alternately cursed Sheridan and prayed for her safety. He also prayed that, come what may, he would be in time.

As Neely rode into the night, the angrier he became; angry at Sheridan for overlooking him, angry at de Lara for interfering, and angry at Jocelin for denying him. In fact, he was furious. Then he thought of young de Braose stepping into the picture and Jocelin handing Sheridan to the man on a silver platter. Sure, he was a de Braose and the match was a brilliant one. But there were much more to Neely's feelings for Sheridan than bloodlines or money could accomplish. He loved her, pure and simple, and would do anything in the world for her. Even save her from herself.

He pushed the charger harder, his mind racing through the past several days, feeling his emotions morph into something more forgiving. He couldn't blame anyone except de Lara and the man had been dying last he saw him. Or at least, that was what his men told him. They'd beat him within an inch of his life and left him for dead. And Sheridan had hated him for it.

He rode deep into the night, pushing his charger more than he should have in order to reach London. He could see fires in the distance, set by his allies in an attempt to drive out the king's forces. The closer he drew, the more anxious he became. He needed to find Sheridan before something horrible happened to her. He couldn't even entertain the thought that something already had. And when he found her, he would give her a tongue lashing that she would not soon forget.

☙

"I HAVE COME to see the king," Alys stood at the Middle Tower entry, yelling up to the sentries upon the walls. "Please let me in."

The men were armed for battle. The city was burning to the north and the streets were eerily still. This had allowed Alys to ride all the way to the Tower with very little trouble. But the horse was exhausted and so was Alys, so she stood at the gatehouse begging for entry. The men on the battlements merely stared at her.

"Will you please let me in and tell the king I am here?" she demanded. "I am the Lady Alys St. James. He will want to see me."

The men on the wall looked at each other. There was a sergeant with them who suddenly found himself paying more attention to her. He hung over the top of the wall, peering down at her.

"St. James?" he repeated. "Henry St. James?"

Alys nodded. "He was my father. Will you let me in now?"

There was increased motion up on the walls as a great deal of discussion floated around. Alys could see the men moving, shifting, finally someone rushing to the ladders that led from the wall walk to the yard. Alys could hear shouts behind the massive gate and, slowly, it began to crank open. When the opening was large enough for the horse to pass through, she entered the gates only to listen to them shut ominously behind her.

Several soldiers grouped around her, a few with torches. The glow of the flames against the darkness of the Tower yard was eerie and disturbing. Alys began to feel very unsettled as a host of serious faces gazed back at her.

"The king," she said timidly to the collective group. "Will someone please take me to him?"

"What is your business with him?" an older soldier asked.

Alys looked at the man. "I must speak to him. I am sure he will want to see me."

"Do you come to discuss a truce?" another soldier sneered. "Your father's troops are burning the city."

Alys swallowed, seeing that this was not going in her favor. "I do not know anything about that. I came to find my sister."

"Your sister?" the same soldier echoed. "Who is that?"

"The Lady Sheridan St. James."

"Never heard of her. What would she be doing here?"

"She would be looking for…," Alys didn't want to divulge too much. She tried again. "Have you seen a woman arrive here in the past hour? She would be a lovely woman, blond. That is my sister."

The soldiers looked at each other before shaking their heads. "No woman has come here in the past hour," the older soldier said. He jabbed a finger at the men on the walls. "In case you haven't realized it, we're anticipating a battle. If you came by yourself, then you are a stupid girl. And if not, your escort had better be prepared to pay a high price to have you returned. You are here to stay, missy."

Alys was becoming increasingly afraid. She did not like the sense that she was getting from these men.

"Perhaps… perhaps I could go and find the king myself," she stammered. "I know where his apartments are."

She didn't wait to be escorted; leaving the horse standing where she left it, she scuttled off into the darkened yard, putting distance between herself and the leering soldiers. But a couple of men ran after her and she bolted, darting across the barren yard and into the shadows.

Since Alys knew where the king's apartments were, she was confident that she could find him and perhaps her sister also. She didn't even know what had become of de Lara after Neely and his men had beaten him unconscious; perhaps he was dead. Perhaps Sheridan had already found that out. If that was the case, then she would have no way of knowing where Sheridan would go next. There was no telling what she would do in her grief.

Alys' could hear the soldiers behind her as she approached the entry to the royal apartments. She was having second thoughts about presenting herself to the king. Sean had warned her off too many times and the last time she had come into contact with John, he had almost stolen her innocence. That sickening reminder made her come to a halt and duck deep into the recesses of the dark shadows. Alys may have been a foolish young girl, but she wasn't entirely stupid. She needed help, but to put herself in contact with the king again was perhaps not the best way. There was no Sean to save her tonight.

Off to her left, almost hidden by the darkness of the night, lay the chapel. Alys stared at the mortar and wood building a moment, inspecting the lancet windows that opened into the blackness, thinking that perhaps she should speak with a priest before she proceeded. Perhaps a man of God would help her think more clearly. It seemed like a safer choice that visiting the king. In the light of the half-moon, she veered off course and made her way towards the chapel.

Father Simon was very surprised to see Alys St. James.

☙

FOR SOME REASON, the cart had come to a halt and they could hear muffled voices through the barrier of straw and canvas. It was pitch black inside their hiding place and Sheridan couldn't see Guy's face, but she knew his features were as anxious as hers. She wondered who Gilby was speaking to, for she could hear the old physic's voice, low at times and then louder at others. The longer they sat idle, the more she worried.

The voices outside were growing closer. Someone shook the wagon and began moving things around. The words became discernable and someone was questioning what Gilby had in the cart. They clearly knew the old man for they called him by name and they doubted that all he was carrying was hay since the cart seemed so heavy. Gilby insisted it was only hay and told the man to search the cart if he didn't believe him. Unknown to Sheridan and Guy, the soldier at the gatehouse would take Gilby up on his offer. Withdrawing his sword, he plunged it into the straw before the old man could stop him. The blade sliced into Sheridan's right thigh.

She screamed at the top of her lungs and the sword was abruptly removed. Suddenly, the tarp was being pulled away and the hay was being hastily removed. She could hear someone calling Gilby a liar and the old man swearing in return. Soldiers jumped up on the wagon, throwing off the dried grass until they revealed two figures buried in the pile. De Braose was already injured, his state obvious. But a beautiful blond woman lay in the straw with tears on her face and her bloodied hands over a bloodied leg. It was a puzzling sight.

Gilby leapt up on the cart with more energy than anyone had ever seen from him. He descended on Sheridan, removing her hands so he could gain a better look at the wound.

"Allow me to see what has happened, my lady," he said in a surprisingly gentle voice. "Let me see the damage."

It hurt terribly and Sheridan wasn't very brave. She sobbed and looked away as Gilby tried to assess the wound through the torn material and blood. Sheridan's screams had brought several men from the top of the wall walk, the king's soldiers armed for battle and curious about the cries. Gilby was able to gain a moderate look at the injury and began looking around for his bag.

"My bag," he snapped to the soldiers around the cart. "Where is my bag? And for God's sake, somebody find de Lara."

The sergeant who had gored Sheridan stood next to the cart, directing his men with mild disinterest to find the physic's bag. But at the mention of Sean's name, he peered more closely at the old man.

"De Lara?" he repeated. "What in the hell do you want him for?"

Gilby didn't look at him as someone set the black bag beside him.

"Is he still at the Tower?"

"He is up on the walls."

"Get him."

"What for?"

Gilby's head snapped up to the man, his white hair undulating with the motion. "Because you just stabbed his wife. He will want to know."

The sergeant stared at him a moment. Then his eyes widened. "You lie."

"Call him and see."

"De Lara isn't married. What kind of a fool do you take me for?"

"The only way to find out whether or not I tell the truth is to summon him. If I am lying, what are you afraid of?"

The man's shock was obvious as he struggled with conflicting thoughts. "But… but if she is his wife, what is she doing in here? Why are you hiding her? And who is the man with her?"

"Go find de Lara and he will answer your questions if he allows you to live."

The sergeant swallowed hard, his face pale in the soft moonlight. There was suddenly a sense of panic among the men; they were scrambling, racing back up the ladders to the wall walk, shouting de Lara's name. The sergeant took several steps back, knowing he should probably run for his life if what the old man said was true. De Lara would strike first and ask questions later. But a twenty year career forced him to take a stand and face de Lara even if it meant his life. At least he wouldn't be considered a coward for running. An idiot for staying, perhaps, but certainly not a coward.

As the call for Sean went up among the men at the Tower, Gilby concentrated on Sheridan's leg. It was a sizable gash that would require stitches but it wasn't too serious. He was more concerned at the moment with stopping the bleeding. As he fumbled with his bag, Guy summoned his strength to sit up and help. He opened the bag for the old man.

"It is not serious," Guy comforted Sheridan. "I have seen much worse. You will be whole and sound in no time."

Sheridan wasn't dealing well with the pain or the blood. She knew she should be of stronger constitution, but she had never done very well with that sort of thing. Lying back against the hay, she kept her head averted from the mess.

"It… it does not hurt much," she lied, still sniffling. "Does it look bad?"

Guy smiled at her, trying to be positive. "Not bad at all. 'Tis hardly more than a scratch."

That statement slowed her tears. "Really?" she hiccupped. "It feels awful."

"That's because you are not used to battle wounds," Guy was deliberately trying to distract her. "Once, my father was in battle on the Marches and he received three horrible wounds; one to the arm, one to the neck, and one to the foot. His foot was almost hanging off, but the physicians were able to fix it. He is as good as new. He considers each new battle scar a badge of honor."

Sheridan's tears had stopped although her face was wet. She gazed up at Guy with her luminous blue eyes. "I do not want a badge of honor."

She flinched when Gilby pressed a square of linen against the wound to stop the bleeding. Guy reached down and grasped her hand, squeezing it encouragingly.

"It will be over in a moment," he said quietly. "You are very brave, my lady."

Sheridan didn't reply; she closed her eyes to the intense pain as Gilby put pressure on the wound. It didn't even occur to her that she was being comforted by a man who was wounded far worse than she was; it would only occur to her later how selfless Guy had been.

There were still several soldiers standing about, watching the event unfold. They were so involved in the scene that no one saw Sean descend the wall until it was too late. In full armor and mail, loaded down with a full complement of weapons, he suddenly appeared beside the wagon.

The truth was that from his post on the north side of the wall, Sean had seen Gilby's wagon stopped at the gatehouse. He had been too far away at the time to be of any assistance but he was already making haste for the gate when the events unfolded. He had seen the sergeant jab his sword into the hay and he had heard the distant cries. Realizing it was a female scream, he had nearly buckled in horror. But he kept his wits about him, making his way to the gatehouse with de Vere on his tail.

He had therefore tried to steel himself. Sean's expression was neutral when he happed upon the cart but the color drained from his face when he saw his wife lying there with a massive blood stain on her gown. God help him, he couldn't stop his reaction.

"Sweet Jesus," he hissed, shoving a soldier aside that was partially in his way. "What in the hell happened?"

Gilby looked up. "One of your sergeants was very thorough in his search of my cart."

At the sound of Sean's voice, Sheridan's eyes flew open and she fixed her gaze on his serious, handsome face. The tears, so recently fled, returned with a vengeance.

Sean watched her face crumple and his heart leapt into his throat. "Is it serious?" he demanded of Gilby, moving around the cart so he could be closer to Sheridan. "Will she survive?"

"She will survive," Gilby said steadily. "Sean, I need to take her someplace warm and safe. I need to stitch this wound."

Sean reached over the old man and lifted Sheridan into his arms. Sobbing, she threw her arms around his neck and held on tightly. He cradled her, thinking that his best laid plans had failed to remove her from the Tower. She was still here and so was the king. More than that, the opposing armies were fast approaching. The situation was going from bad to worse, but all he could think of at the moment was tending to his wife. The need seemed to block out all else.

"That man," he snapped to the soldiers around him, indicating de Braose. "Someone bring him. And be mindful of his injuries."

Leaving de Vere standing next to the cart scratching his head, Sean carried Sheridan across the darkened yard toward the apartments they had so recently vacated. Gilby was shuffling behind him and even further back, two soldiers carried de Braose between them. They made a strange procession across the dark and eerie courtyard with the smell of smoke in the air from the approaching battle.

The quarters were just the same as they had left them and the fire had long since died in the hearth. Sean ordered one of the soldiers to relight the flame as he carried Sheridan into the bedchamber. As de Braose was deposited into one of the chairs, Gilby followed Sean into the room.

"Lay her down," the old man instructed. "I must sew the gash before it begins sealing itself too much."

Sean tried to lay Sheridan down but she clung to him. She was scared and hurt, finding comfort in the arms of the husband she was so glad to see. When he realized she wasn't about to let him go, he squeezed her gently.

"Release me, sweetling," he said softly. "Gilby needs to see to your leg."

She shook her head, still buried against his neck. "No," she wept. "I want to stay with you."

Sean and the physic passed glances. "I will not leave you," Sean promised. "I shall stay right here until he is done."

After a few encouraging kisses to her forehead and more words of reassurance, Sheridan eventually let him go and he laid her upon the bare mattress. He could see how terrified she was just by looking at her; the luminous blue eyes were edgy. His heart ached for her.

So he sat down and held her hand as Gilby gave her a bitter potion to drink and put seven fast, small stitches into the soft white flesh of her right thigh. Sean remembered that thigh from his brief taste of her, remembering its texture against his hands and feeling warmth in his loins from the mere thought. So he distracted himself by stroking Sheridan's head, comforting her as Gilby finished the last of the stitches. She had, remarkably, kept quiet the entire time, mostly due to the potion Gilby had given her. It had calmed her sufficiently to the point of putting her to sleep.

When it was finally over, Sean watched her sleep for a few moments before casting a long glance at Gilby.

"Remember the last time you gave her a potion?" he asked pointed. "We could not wake her for hours."

Gilby glanced at the lady as he put his things away. "This is not the same stuff. She will sleep through the night, no doubt, but it should not have the same effect on her."

Sean returned his gaze to his wife, sighing heavily at the sight of her pale, sleeping face. He was relieved that the crisis, for the moment, was over. "Sweet Jesus," he muttered. "It has already been an eventful evening and it is not even half over with."

Gilby tied up his bag. "What are you doing upon the walls? I thought you were going to the Marches."

Sean stroked her soft cheek with a big finger. "The king has changed his mind. He wants me here, at the Tower, leading her defenses."

Gilby nodded casually, putting his bag to the floor. "The Marshall should be pleased."

Sean looked at him. "Do you know where he has gone?"

The old man shook his head. "I have been with young de Braose and your wife. I have no knowledge. You'd best check with the priest."

Sean returned his gaze to Sheridan, breathing heavily as her sleep deepened. "I had to kill Gerard," he muttered.

Gilby looked up at him, watching emotions play across the usually emotionless face. He thought of the ghastly bear of a man who was always at Sean's side.

"Is that so?" he lifted his eyebrows. "It must have been an excellent fight."

Sean sighed again, his gaze on his wife as he spoke. "The king demanded I bring him Sheridan. When I refused, he ordered Gerard to do it. So I killed him."

Gilby shook his head. "Feel no remorse, de Lara. The man was a beast."

"I do not feel guilty. But I have signed my death warrant."

"Why?"

Sean suddenly seemed weary; some of the strength went out of his voice as he spoke. "Because the king's trust in me was already dangerously brittle," he let out a blustery sigh and wiped his hands over his face. "In killing Gerard, I killed the only other bodyguard that the king permits such close access to him. Now it is only me and the king has already seen me disobey him this night. If I know the man, and I believe that I do, he now fears me as well as distrusts me. Although he can live with distrust, he cannot live with fear and, like any creature, will do what is necessary to alleviate the threat."

"So he will have you killed?"

"More than likely, he will try."

"But he loves you, de Lara. He has taken great pride in your horrific reputation. Are you so sure he will turn on you?"

Sean nodded, slowly. "I would be surprised if he did not. I have shown him that I no longer mindlessly obey and that I will kill in order to refuse him his wishes. I have revealed my true self." He shook his head, hanging it in a rare display of emotion. "Nine years, Gilby. I have ruined nine years of hard work, blood, sweat and pain."

Gilby was listening seriously. "Then if that is the case, you must flee. Do what you must to sabotage the Tower defenses, but leave this place and take your wife with you. You are much more valuable to us alive than a dead martyr."

Truth be told, Sean already had a plan in place to sabotage the Tower's defenses. It had been decided long ago between him and The Marshall; as far as Sean still knew, as he had not been told differently, the allied army had orders to approach and attack from downriver; the fires to the north were only a diversion. Sean's plan focused the Tower's army on the north wall and well away from the river.

Sean scratched his head, feeling some need to confirm that the plan, as it was intended, still held. "That is why I need to find out where the Marshall has gone," he told the old man. "Though I am still at the Tower, things are not as they once were. The situation has changed."

Gilby moved for the door. "Let me find Father Simon. Perhaps he knows something. I will return."

Sean put his hand on him. "Nay," he said. "I will go. I move faster and more undetected than you. Stay with your patients until I return."

"Are you sure?"

Sean did nothing more than nod his head, his gaze moving to Sheridan's pale, sleeping face. Gilby watched the emotions play on the man's face.

"You cannot blame her, you know," the physic said quietly.

Sean looked at him. "Blame her? For what?"

"For ruining all that you have worked for."

Sean's brow rippled with confusion. "Is that what you think? That I blame her?" he shook his head with more emotion than Gilby had seen from him in a long time. "Good Christ, Gilby, that woman has saved me. She has saved me from myself and if I die tonight, I die the most fulfilled man who has ever lived."

Gilby didn't say another word; he didn't have to. With a lingering glance at his wife's slumbering form, Sean quit the room in swift silence.

Guy was still sitting in the antechamber near the warming hearth. Given the fact that the man was worse off than Sheridan, he had done a remarkable job of not complaining. He sat quietly, listing to one side to favor his injured ribs, and watched de Lara blow from the room. When the door slammed, he turned to see Gilby standing in the bedchamber doorway. Their eyes met.

"Where is he going?" Guy asked.

Gilby knew he had heard the conversation in the bedchamber. There was no use denying what the young man had heard; besides, events were already happening. Even if de Braose knew Sean's true identity, it was of no matter. No more harm could be done.

"To secure a safe and peaceful England," the physic said, moving towards Guy. "You have been jostled a bit this night, young de Braose. Let me take a look at those ribs. Careful one does not break free and impale a lung."

Guy lifted an eyebrow at the encouraging thought but dutifully sat back in the chair and allowed the old man room to work. He watched the physic closely as the man began to poke at him.

"I heard what you said," he muttered.

Gilby was busy examining him. "What did I say?

"You called Lady Sheridan de Lara's wife. Was that just a scare tactic for those soldiers so they would not harm us?"

Gilby did look at him, then. "It was the truth. I was witness to the marriage."

Guy stared at him a moment before looking away, barely flinching when Gilby caused him pain. At the moment, his disappointment and shock had him quite distracted.

"When?" he managed to ask.

"Tonight."

Guy pursed his lips and looked away. "So de Lara is the victor," he grunted when Gilby tightened the bindings on his ribs. "I should have removed her from the Tower when I had the chance. I should have taken her out of this place when Jocelin agreed to the contract and never looked back."

Gilby secured the binding. "It was not meant to be." He cast a long glance at Guy. "Sean was always to be the victor, young de Braose. You could have taken Sheridan to the ends of the earth and Sean would always be first in her heart. Never you. 'Tis time to accept the truth."

Guy was in pain, disappointed and exhausted. He'd spent far too much energy on the struggle to survive over the past few days and this latest blow had his strength finally crumbling. So the lovely Lady Sheridan was not to be his; the discouragement was tangible. He should have been extremely bitter but he found he was just heartsick. He had fallen in love with the lady more than he'd realized. She wasn't a possession to be had. It was more than that.

Gilby watched Guy slump against the back of the chair, closing his dark eyes. The old physic's gaze lingered on the man, inordinately strong for one so slender and seemingly weak-looking. But the loss of the lady had taken his toll on his constitution; Gilby could see it draining before his eyes.

He wondered if that was all he would see drained before this night was out.

CHAPTER FOURTEEN

"... even if I had known my own death was approaching, I would not have changed my actions for better or for worse. For a bright, shining moment, I saw my fate and I welcomed it...."

The Chronicles of Sir Sean de Lara

1206 – 1215 A.D.

"BUT WHY DO you wish to see the king?"

Father Simon asked the question gently. He was still trying to figure out why this foolish young girl had returned to the Tower on the eve of a siege. All was smoky and apprehensive in London at this time, but Alys seemed oblivious to it. In fact, she seemed almost defiant.

"Because my sister is here," she insisted. "I must find her. Perhaps the king will know where she is."

An odd gleam came to Father Simon's eye. "Is that why you have come? To find your sister?"

Alys nodded firmly. "She... well, she was quite upset over... well, it does not matter what she was upset over. She has come back to the Tower to find Sean de Lara."

"How do you know?"

"Because there is nowhere else she would go."

Father Simon gazed at her a moment; she was a pretty girl, not nearly the beauty her sister was, but pretty nonetheless. He was still having trouble with the concept that she had come back to the Tower in the midst of a building battle to look for her sister. But, then again, her sister had done the exact same thing so the priest should not have been surprised. It seemed that all the St. James women had somewhat of a foolish streak in them.

After a long pause, the priest puffed out his cheeks and sat heavily next to her on the narrow pew. Alys watched him anxiously.

"It is not necessary to see the king," he said quietly.

"But…!"

He cut her off. "Your sister is here. I saw her myself not two hours ago."

Alys' eyebrows flew up. "Where is she?"

Father Simon debated how much to tell her. He opted for all of it; she would find out that her sister had married de Lara soon enough.

"I am not sure at the moment," he said in a low voice. "But she married Sean de Lara two hours ago and he took her away. I do not know where he has taken her."

Alys' mouth popped open with astonishment. "She *married* Sean?"

"I officiated myself."

Alys suddenly leapt up and began jumping up and down. "You must find her. You must find them both!"

Father Simon rose and put out his hands in an attempt to soothe her; she was certainly an excitable girl. Noisy, too. He shushed her.

"I will do what I can," he assured her. "But you must remain here and not leave this place. It is not safe for you on the grounds. Do you understand me?"

Alys was still jumping around, though trying to contain herself. She was exhausted and agitated, now with the added excitement of her sister's marriage. She could hardly stand still.

"Aye," she insisted hurried. "But you must find Sean."

Father Simon nodded and put his hands out to her again as if to wordlessly caution her. His expression told her much. Alys stopped jumping and watched, wide eyed, as he made his way to the chapel door.

The priest opened the door carefully, peering outside into the darkened courtyard. It was dark and relatively vacant. Seeing that the soldiers were upon the battlements and focused on the city beyond the walls, he slipped from the door and shut it softly behind him.

He stayed to the shadows mostly, making his way towards the east side of the fortress. He wasn't sure where Sean would be with his new wife but he suspected as far away as possible from the king, which meant he would not be in the Tower. The priest wasn't really sure where he was going as he moved across the mud of the ward. He was almost moving aimlessly, pondering which direction to take. But soon he had his answer.

The Shadow Lord was unmistakable as he crossed the compound. He did so without his usual stealth, as he had no reason to skulk in the shadows as he normally did. Tonight, he was allowed to move in the open as a major battle loomed outside of the walls. Father Simon recognized Sean right away and headed towards him, picking up his pace as he crossed the gently sloping bailey. They were to the north of the White Tower, the half-moon glow hidden behind the great turreted top. All was silent and still for the moment and Father Simon was trying to decide how to tell Sean of Alys' appearance; surely the man would be enraged by the foolish behavior and Father Simon didn't want a brotherly beating on his hands. But just as Sean passed the mid-way point of the Tower heading towards him, all hell broke loose.

It started as a loud crash when the door leading from the Tower suddenly slammed back on its hinges. As Father Simon watched in horror, soldiers poured from the door and leapt down the steps, rushing in Sean's direction. Sean didn't seem overly surprised by the sight; in fact, he was rather calm as he unsheathed his sword and the tide of men rushed at him. But the men pouring from the Tower were too great in number and in a matter of seconds, Sean was overwhelmed. It was as if he was literally swallowed alive. His body vanished in a sea of mail and men.

Father Simon scattered, not wanting to become upswept in the ambush overtaking de Lara. He threw himself against the outbuilding lodged against the north side of the wall, hiding like a coward as he watched Sean battle for his life. Whoever had arranged the ambush had not taken anything for chance; they knew the Shadow Lord well. De

Lara could have handled a dozen men quite easily, but there was at least triple that number descending on him. Father Simon could no longer see him in the dark, jumbled mass of men but he could hear sword against sword. There was still a fight going on somewhere in the middle of the throng. But the priest was positive that de Lara did not have a chance of survival.

He was sure that he had just witnessed the Shadow Lord's demise. Shaken, Father Simon fell back into the shadows and rushed away from the fighting. The chapel was his only safe haven and he raced for it, hoping he would not be followed by the blood thirsty soldiers who had de Lara in their grasp. By the time he reached the chapel, he burst into the warm hall as if the Devil himself was chasing him.

Alys both heard and saw him charge in. The panting had been a dead giveaway that something terrible was amiss. She further watched as the man hurriedly retrieved a large wooden bolt from the corner and threw it across the door to secure it. He was breathing heavily to the point of gasping and Alys approached him timidly.

"What is wrong?" she wasn't entirely sure she wanted to know. "Why did you come back so soon?"

Father Simon's hand was over his mouth in horror as he leaned against the door, beads of sweat upon his pale forehead. But his gaze found Alys and, still horrified, he went to her and grabbed her firmly by the arms.

"We must find your sister immediately," he hissed, taking her by the hand and dragging her towards the altar. "She is in great danger."

"Why?" Alys demanded, half terrified and half outraged. "What has happened?"

Father Simon did not want to tell her. He did not want her to panic. He already had far more panic than he could handle.

"Ask no more questions," he told her, throwing open a small door that was in the vestibule behind the chapel. "Keep your mouth shut if you want to live."

Wide-eyed with fear, Alys wisely did as she was told. The small door led to a narrow staircase that sloped slightly before ending in another small door. This opening led to the cloister behind the chapel where the priests lived. Father Simon yanked Alys through the darkened corridor and into a building smelling of stale air and body odor.

But they did not stop there. They continued through the building and exited the other side where they found themselves on the north side of the inner courtyard. Father Simon was heading for the buildings where the nobles were usually housed, buildings he suspected where Lady de Lara would be. A wall separated him and Alys from Sean's battle and he kept his ears peaked, listening for any sounds of a struggle. But he could not hear any. Everything was strangely silent.

His attention refocused to the lady in his grasp, knowing he had to find her sister and get them both out of the Tower. He could not wait for direction from the Marshall; as far as he knew, the man was conferring with the allies laying siege to London and out of reach. He would therefore have to depend on his own instincts in handling the fall of the Shadow Lord. Their network of intrigue was crumbling. God help him, he could still scarcely believe it. He had to get to Lady de Lara before the king did.

Yanking Alys behind him, he tried to stay to the shadows as he made his way to the east side of the Tower. The Flint Tower was closest and he headed towards it; a safe, dark haven in the midst of the hell going on around him. Next to the Tower were the buildings that housed the visiting nobles. He could only guess that was where Lady de Lara was located; if she wasn't, then he was at a loss to know where she would be. He began to pray very hard that his assumptions were correct. There was little time to go hunting for her. Behind him, he could hear Alys panting with fear.

A corridor led from the Flint Tower into the upper floor of the two level building. It was dark and eerily still as he and Alys slowed their pace, traversing the black corridor by clinging to the walls. These old corridors smelled like dust and smoke, adding to the ambience of uncertainty and fear. Father Simon had no way of knowing who might lay in wait for them; with the chaos of the Tower at the moment, every shadow and every door could be deadly. Their pace was very slow.

They had traveled about halfway down the length of building when Father Simon saw a sliver of light coming from one of the closed doors. Leaving Alys in the shadows, he made his way silently to the door and leaned into it, listening carefully. All was silent for several long moments and he almost pulled his ear from the door. But then, he thought he heard humming. It was faint, but the sound was unmistakable. Puzzled, he continued to listen, wondering who would be shuffling about the room humming until he heard something clatter to the floor and a softly uttered curse. The light of recognition came to Father Simon's eyes; he knew that voice. God be praised, he knew it. Softly, he knocked.

The humming stopped immediately and he heard more shuffling going on. Father Simon knocked again.

"Gilby?" he called softly. "Gilby, open the door. Let me in."

Another long pause and then the door flew open. Gilby stood in the doorway but so did Guy, the knight with a broadsword in his hand. Gilby yanked the priest into the room. Alys bolted in after him and they locked the door.

Inside the room with a faint fire flickering in the hearth, the four of them faced one another with trepidation. Each was waiting for the other to say something. Finally, Gilby was the first to speak.

"What are you doing here?" he asked the priest.

"Looking for you," Father Simon told him. "Is Lady de Lara with you?"

"She is," Gilby nodded. "Why? Did de Lara send you?"

Father Simon wasn't sure where to start but he had to speak and he had to do it quickly. The situation was spiraling and he felt a panicked sense of urgency.

"We must remove Lady de Lara immediately," he said. "Something… something dreadful has happened."

Gilby's eyebrows rose. "What?"

Father Simon swallowed, eyeing Alys as he did so; she did not know why they had fled the chapel and he hoped she would not fly into hysterics as he told the sordid tale.

"De Lara was ambushed by the White Tower," he lowered his voice. "I saw it with my own eyes. It will only be a matter of time before the king comes looking for Lady de Lara. We must remove her immediately."

Gilby didn't change expressions but Alys grabbed the priest by the arm; she had a wild look to her eye. "He was ambushed?" she screeched.

Father Simon pried her fingers off his flesh. "He was set upon by dozens of the king's soldiers," he said. "Even a warrior as strong as de Lara would have difficulty surviving such a thing. I can only assume that... that he is...."

"Did you see him fall?" Guy entered the conversation, sounding stronger than he looked. His dark eyes glittered in his pale face. "Did you see his death?"

Father Simon shook his head. "Nay," he said. "But there were dozens of soldiers, my lord. There is no way for him to survive such a thing."

"I would not be too sure," Guy replied. "You speak of the Shadow Lord, after all. If anyone could survive such a thing, he could."

"I did not wait around to find out," the priest lifted an eyebrow. "I came to take Lady de Lara from this place. She cannot remain."

"Why not?" a very weary, very intense female voice came from the doorway leading to the bower; with all of their chattering they had awoken the sleeping patient. Sheridan stood there in her blood stained dress, looking pale and exhausted. "Moreover, I am not leaving without my husband. Where is he?"

The four of them stared at her, unsure how to tell her what had just been reported. They felt guilty that they had been caught in conversation, guilty that they did not want to tell her the truth. But she had overheard some of it. They had to tell her the rest. Alys finally broke the silence.

"He has been ambushed, Dani," she tried to be gentle. "We must leave this place before they get you, too."

"Ambushed?" Sheridan gasped, taking halting steps into the room and trying to shake off Gilby's sleeping potion. "Who has told you this?"

"I did, my lady," Father Simon was trying to be gentle, but in truth, he was heartbroken. He knew what Sean and Sheridan meant to each other. He had seen their expressions of love at the marriage earlier that evening. "He was ambushed by the White Tower several minutes ago. I came to find you so that we could leave immediately for your safety."

Sheridan's eyes were wide but, to her credit, she did not dissolve into tears. She simply looked shocked.

"Is he dead?" she asked, her tone dull.

Father Simon shook his head. "I did not see him fall. I came to find you. It is what Sean would want."

Sheridan's breathing grew faster. She simply stared at the priest in disbelief. Then, quite calmly, she turned to Guy and pulled the broadsword out of his hand, an old thing that had been left in the room by some previous visitor who had probably grown tired of it. It was a pathetic weapon, old and dented, but a weapon nonetheless. She wielded it with both hands.

"I am going to find him," she said steadily. "He needs help."

Guy grabbed her before she could move away. "You cannot go," he told her. "The priest said dozens of men set upon him. If you walk into their midst, they will take you straight to the king."

She yanked herself from his grip, taking a swing at him when he grabbed her more firmly the second time. She was beginning to lose her composure.

"He needs help," Sheridan repeated loudly. "I must help my husband. I must go to him."

Guy had a good grip on her but he could see she was growing hysterical. "Sheridan, think about what you are doing," he wrestled with her to the point of pinning her against the wall. Her eyes were wild with fright as he gazed steadily at her. "Listen to me; this is a battle you cannot win. You will end up dead or worse. Do you think that will save Sean? Do you think it is what he would want?"

She lost the battle against her fear and began to crumble. She tried to chop at him with the broadsword but he took it away from her easily. "I cannot lose him," she wept. "I must go to him and I will kill you if you try to stop me, do you hear? I will kill you."

Guy had the sword, gazing into her lovely face and feeling her pain. Part of him was jealous that she was so passionate about another man when he himself still wanted her so badly. But most of him felt a good deal of pity. He let go of her and shifted the sword to his left hand, opposite his broken collar bone.

"Then I will go to him and see if I can be of assistance," he told her quietly. "You go with the priest. Let him take you from this place."

"You cannot go," she sobbed. "You are injured."

He lifted his eyebrows in agreement; still badly injured, he was at least able to move about better than he had been earlier. "Maybe so, but I am still stronger than you are."

Tears coursed down her face as she gazed back at him, realizing that he was serious. With all the man had been through over the past few days, he was deadly serious about aiding Sean. It was difficult to believe.

"You would do this for him?" she asked with incredulity.

"I would do it for you." He stared at her intently for a moment before lowering his gaze, patting her on the arm as he did so. "Go with the priest, I say. I will do what I can for de Lara."

Sheridan sniffled, wiping at her cheeks as Guy moved towards the door. She could hardly believe he would aid Sean, but she was nonetheless deeply thankful. Guy de Braose had proven himself more of a man than most and her respect for him grew a little bit more. She wasn't sure how she could ever repay him for such loyalty. But she was no fool; she knew he did it because of his feelings for her. It wasn't out of some misplaced desire for heroism. But she was selfish in that she didn't care what his reasons were, so long as he went.

"Thank you, Guy," she went to him before he quit the room and very gently kissed him on the cheek. "For your loyalty and your chivalry, I will always be in your debt."

Guy glanced at her but it was too much for him to take; he was in love with the woman. He knew it. He realized he would have done anything for her to keep her happy, even defend the man who stole her away.

"Go with the priest," he insisted weakly.

Gilby suddenly provided a distraction from their awkward parting as he picked up his medicament bag.

"I will go with you, young de Braose," he said firmly. "Sean may need my help as well."

Guy looked dubious. "A battle is no place for you."

Gilby gave him a shove towards the door. "Nor you. Get going."

There was no point in arguing. The door shut behind them and Sheridan stood there, staring at the door and wondering if Guy would survive. She wondered if he would be in time to help Sean. The tears came again and she rested her forehead against the door, fears and prayers filling her heart.

CHAPTER FIFTEEN

"... suffice it to say that the End had revealed itself. There was nothing I could do but stand fast and face it."

The Chronicles of Sean de Lara

1206 – 1215 A.D.

THEY HAD NOT come to take him alive. Sean had already decided that the moment he realized that his fears had come to fruition; the king had sent his personal guard to assassinate de Lara and Sean knew, even as he saw the hordes of soldiers dropping down on him, that this was not meant as a threat or an abduction. This was meant for death and he was prepared.

So Sean gave them death. He used his sword as both axe and spear, goring men, chopping them, trying to keep their weapons away from his body. He was clad in full armor and well protected, but even armor had points of weakness. There was no denying that he was vulnerable to a certain extent. But he vowed to do all in his power to get away from them alive so that he could get back to his wife. Above all else, he had to return to Sheridan and get her away from the Tower. If they were after him, then soon they would be after her and he could not stand the thought. He had to protect her.

So he fought valiantly, trying to move away from the group even as they swarmed him. Though the king's guard was well trained, Sean knew their tactics and he knew each man individually. He knew their strengths and weaknesses and tried to exploit them. Two men fell, then four, then seven as he continued his battle. But he could not kill all of them; even he knew that. So he tried to move away from the flashing blades and back towards the Tower so he could make an attempt to flee.

He had to lose them somehow. But that was his last coherent thought before someone plunged a blade deep into his groin.

It was a bad wound; he knew that right away. It cut into the tender portion of his upper leg, slicing through mail and linen. Sean grunted with pain but did not falter; as he dispatched the man who had cut his groin, someone else managed to jam a blade into his right side. When he brought his weapon around to address the assailant, someone else thrust a cold sword into the right side of his chest, just below the arm pit. Sean stumbled back and went down on his knees.

But he was still fighting. Oddly enough, however, his attackers suddenly seemed to stop. Bleeding heavily, Sean managed to get to his feet to prepare for another onslaught but none was forthcoming. The men seemed to back off, standing around to watch him bleed to death. At least that was what Sean thought until he saw the reason for their pause.

It was moving through the shadows like a dark specter; he could see a shaggy head making its way through the crowd. Gerard's face was suddenly illuminated by the ghostly moonlight, his black eyes full of death and fury. Sean's brow furrowed slightly, remembering the man he had gored and left to die on the floor of the king's chamber. But he had apparently not done a good enough job of it because Gerard was indeed walking. He was listing heavily to one side and appeared ghostly pale, but he was moving nonetheless. And he was moving for Sean.

"I told you I would kill you," Gerard rasped, his sword in his right hand although not yet raised. "You will die this night, de Lara, make no mistake. Your time is finished."

Sean was shocked though he tried not to let it show. He was having enough trouble dealing with excruciating pain and tremendous blood loss. But he tried to stand straight to accept Gerard's onslaught, wondering if he would be able to kill the man this time and make it back to Sheridan before he himself collapsed. He could feel his strength draining away by the second. If he was going to die, then he wanted it to be in her arms. He wanted her face to be the last thing he ever saw.

"It seems that both of our time is finished," he replied to Gerard. "You may kill me, but I intend to take you with me."

Gerard wasn't as healthy as he wanted Sean to believe; the man had a horrendous wound to his gut that was taking its toll. It was a testament to his brute strength that he was still standing. But he tried to put up a good front and lifted his weapon.

"We shall see."

The first blow was heavy but sloppy. Sean easily deflected it, but he was struggling with his breathing. He suspected a lung had been punctured and it made it extremely difficult to move around. He began unlatching his breastplate with his left hand, anything to help him breathe. Gerard charged at him again but it was more like a stumbling fall; Sean pushed him aside and the man fell on his arse. In the time it took Gerard to get to his feet, Sean had removed both his helm and his breastplate and cast them aside.

The crowd of the king's soldiers stood silent as the battle of two mortally wounded men continued. It was an odd assembly, like vultures waiting for the kill. Sean and Gerard were without a doubt the two most feared men in England and to see the clash between them was truly something to behold. It was like watching demons in battle.

The fight continued on. Sean seemed to be defending himself rather than launching any offensives against Gerard; Gerard, however, was sloppy and exhausted, throwing himself at Sean only to be shoved to the ground. This went on several times. Gerard finally bellowed at the king's soldiers, ordering them away. He didn't want anyone to witness what might be his shame. The men disbursed for the most part, though a few lingered out of range. They were watching, waiting for the final blow. Like the lure of blood lust, it was too good to pass up.

Their battle had also attracted the attention of the men on the parapets. Now an audience was watching from above, having no idea why de Lara was battling d'Athée. It was entrancing, harrowing. When they should have been watching the siege of London, the men guarding the Tower of London found themselves distracted by a life and death battle between two titans. It was distraction enough so that William Marshall was able to move two siege engines within range and decimate the gate of the Bell Tower in two enormous blows. The men guarding the Tower never saw it coming until it was too late.

Suddenly, the men on the wall were rushing to the west side of the Tower where two thousand men had now managed to sneak up on them. The shouting, the cursing, was evident all over the compound. Even the king's guards fled when they realized the castle was compromised. But Sean and Gerard stayed in battle mode, fighting each other to the death, oblivious to what was going on around them.

Sean had been ordered to sabotage the Tower's defenses; he could not have done a better job if he had tried. The distraction of his battle with Gerard had proved sabotage enough.

But his strength, and Gerard's strength, was fading quickly. Although they were still tangling, it was punctuated by long periods where they did nothing more but stand and glare at each other. Sean was leaving a bloody trail all over the ground as his groin wound poured blood down his leg. Worse than that, his vision was beginning to darken and he suspected he did not have much time left to swoop in for the kill. If he did not do it first, Gerard would.

As the gates at the Bell Tower burned brightly, Sean threw himself in Gerard's direction, intending to give the death blow. But he tripped in his weakness, falling to his knees as Gerard raised his sword in response. When the bear of a man saw Sean on his knees, he knew it was time to strike the final blow. Sean tried to roll out of the way but Gerard was nearly on top of him. As Gerard brought his arm down to deliver the deadly impact, he suddenly jerked to a halt and listed heavily to one side. The sword remained poised above Sean's head as if frozen there. As Sean watched in astonishment, Gerard fell to the ground and his sword clattered into the dirt.

Guy de Braose stood behind Gerard's collapsed body, a broadsword in his hand dripping dark with blood. The slender young lord with the dark eyes gazed steadily at Gerard on the ground before he, with a great amount of bitterness and an even larger amount of vengeance, rammed the blade once more into the man's back; he couldn't help himself. He delivered the death blow and this time, Gerard stilled for good.

Guy held the left side of his torso, supporting his cracked ribs as he pulled the sword from Gerard's body. He stood there a moment, gazing down at the man who had beaten him so badly, feeling tremendous satisfaction in his death. He considered it justice. But then he remembered that Sean was several feet away laying on the ground and, from what he had seen in the brief time he had witnessed the fight, he could tell that Sean was badly injured.

Guy made his way to Sean, going down on a knee beside the man. Their eyes met and a strange sense of unity filled the air. There was no longer a rivalry; for the moment, they were both on the same side.

"How badly are you hurt?" Guy asked.

"Badly enough," Sean rasped. "Why in God's name are you here?"

Guy was trying to assess Sean's wounds. "The priest said you were in trouble," he told him. "I came to help."

Sean's brow furrowed at the overload of information. "The priest? How did he know?"

Guy peered at the torso wound. "He said that he saw you being set upon by the king's soldiers. Your wife wanted to come and do battle on your behalf but I talked her out of it. I told her that I would help you."

Sean shook his head weakly. "Are you serious? Why would you do such a thing?"

"Because of your wife," Guy finally fixed him in the eye. "Make no mistake; what I did, I did for her."

Sean gazed steadily at the young man. "I would not assume otherwise."

Guy maintained his pointed gaze a moment longer before relenting. "Besides," he said, averting his eyes. "You saved me from the dungeons. I should return the favor."

Sean snorted softly. "A noble attitude. But you are not in much better shape than I am at the moment."

"At least I am not bleeding to death."

Sean sighed heavily, conceding the point. "Then I owe you a great deal of gratitude," he said. "Where is Sheridan?"

"The priest is taking her from this place."

"Where is he taking her?" Sean suddenly grew agitated. "Have they left already?"

Rapid, shuffling footfalls interrupted before Guy could answer. Gilby was abruptly beside Sean, his old face etched with a good deal of concern.

"Good God, de Lara," the old man muttered, pushing Guy back so that he could assess the damage. "I thought you said that Gerard was dead?"

Sean lay back on the ground, staring up at the starry night and thinking so many thoughts that it was difficult to grasp one. His most powerful thought was of Sheridan; he did not want to acknowledge that he was dying but he knew it was the truth. He had seen enough battle wounds to know. He reached out and grasped Gilby by the arm as the old man inspected the groin wound.

"Do not let Simon take Sheridan away, not now," his voice was hoarse. "I will not make it from this place, Gilby. You know this. I want to see my wife before… before I pass."

Gilby cast a long glance at Guy, who gazed back with a mixture of sorrow and resignation. They both knew how dire the situation was and neither one would refuse the request of a dying man.

"You will not pass if I can help it," Gilby said steadily. "But I will send young de Braose to find your wife. Perhaps they have not left yet."

Gilby nodded sharply at Guy, who struggled to his feet and took off as fast as his injured body would allow. When the young lord moved away, Gilby began attending to Sean's groin wound.

"Stay with me, Sean," he said evenly. "Do not go to sleep. Stay awake."

Off to the west, the sounds of a battle began to fill the air as the attackers broke through the gate. But Gilby ignored the sounds, concentrating on saving Sean's life.

"Gilby?" Sean muttered.

"What is it?"

"Do you remember I told you earlier that if I die this evening, I will die the most fulfilled man who has ever lived?"

"I do."

"I lied. I want to see my children."

Gilby glanced at the man, giving him a half-grin. "I know you were lying," he refocused on his task. "That is the problem with you, Sean; you are too noble. Now see what your sense of duty has cost you."

Sean nodded faintly. "It will cost my life. But we always knew that was a possibility."

The groin wound was bad; a main vessel had been nicked and Gilby was struggling to stop the bleeding. It had clotted somewhat but the flow was still heavy. Without any choice, he stuck his fingers deep into the wound to pinch the vessel closed, feeling Sean flinch with pain as he did so. But the man didn't utter a sound. With his other hand, Gilby took his needle and cat gut and tried to throw a stitch into the big vein. It was messy and excruciating. In the end, he wasn't sure if he did any good given the fact that he could hardly see what he was doing, but he had to do something. Sean was bleeding to death before his eyes.

"Stay awake," Gilby commanded softly, wrapping up the groin and going for the chest wound. "Do not go to sleep. Stay with me. Talk to me."

Sean was still staring up at the sky. "I am here."

"Tell me of Trelystan. I have never been to the Marches, you know."

"How did you know about Trelystan?"

"You would be surprised what I know about you," the old man snorted; the chest wound had nicked a lung and he moved to seal it. "I know that you have a brother."

"Everyone knows that. My younger brother serves the Marshall."

"When was the last time you saw him?"

"Years ago. Kevin and I do not speak much."

Gilby opened his mouth to reply when a scream startled him; looking over his shoulder, he could see Sheridan racing towards them across the dark bailey. For some reason, his heart suddenly felt very sad. He knew what Sean and Sheridan had gone through to be together and to see it end in this fashion was overwhelmingly depressing. He looked at Sean.

"Your wife is coming," he told him.

"I heard."

Sheridan came upon her husband in a rush; in her torn, stained gown, she moved as if her leg had not been stitched earlier that evening. She fell to her knees beside Sean, her upper torso collapsing on his neck and chest. Gilby wasn't done with the chest wound yet and had to fend through her hair in order to find his target again. On Sean's chest, Sheridan wept loudly.

"God, no," she sobbed. "Sean, you cannot die. Please do not leave me."

Now that Sheridan was with him, Sean felt a tremendous amount of peace, so much so that his entire body filled with an odd sort of warmth. He put his arms around her, his face in the top of her head, inhaling her scent and feeling it stoke his strength. His arms tightened as if to never let her go.

"I am sorry if I have frightened you, sweetling," he murmured into her hair. "This was certainly not part of my plan."

Sheridan was beside herself, terrified beyond reason that she was going to lose him. She raised her head to look at Gilby.

"Please," she begged, tears streaming down her face. "Please save him. Please do not let him die."

Gilby wouldn't look at her; he couldn't. It was becoming far too emotional for his liking. "I am doing all I can, Lady de Lara."

"How bad is it?"

He did look at her, then. His voice made her blood run cold. "Bad."

Sheridan's hysterics abruptly faded; she didn't know why, but suddenly, the anguish went beyond tears. It burrowed deep into her chest like a great broadsword, hacking her tender heart to pieces. She knew her tears would not help Sean. She wondered if anything could. Swallowing hard, she gazed into her husband's white face, stroking his cheek gently and struggling to calm.

"I love you," she murmured, kissing him tenderly on the lips. "If there is only one thing I can tell you at this moment, it is how much I love you."

His clear blue eyes glimmered weakly and his hand, cold and clammy, touched her face.

"Never did I think I would live long enough to gaze into the eyes of the woman I love and tell her what is in my heart," he murmured. "Now that this moment has come, I hardly know what to say. I do not think I can adequately describe what I feel for you. It goes beyond love, Sheridan. It is something timeless and immortal. I may die, but my love for you will live forever."

So much for her attempts to remain calm; she couldn't help the tears that sprang from her eyes, pelting his pallid cheek. She kissed his forehead, his cheek, rubbing her nose against his and feeling his hot breath on her face.

"You will live," she whispered. "You will live to raise our children and watch your sons grow into fine, strong men. The name de Lara will live on and we will grow old together, I swear it."

He kissed her cheek, her lips. His lips were cold and she struggled against the instinct to burst into tears again. He seemed so very cold.

"I will try," his voice was faint. "But if I should not be able to keep that vow, then you must promise me something."

Her lower lip began to tremble and the tears fell faster. "Anything," she whispered.

Sean suddenly jerked as if he had been struck. Then, he exhaled heavily, paused, and abruptly resumed breathing. Gilby looked concerned and Sheridan nearly came apart.

"Sean?" she asked, trembling. "What is happening?"

He closed his eyes, patting her arms gently. "I am all right," he took another deep, ragged breath and resumed. "If I do not make it out of here alive, then know that it is my wish for you to marry de Braose. He is an honorable man and will be good to you."

Sheridan lost her battle against tears and she began to sob softly. "Do not say such things. You are not going to die."

"But if I do, I want you to promise me. I will be comforted knowing you will be well taken care of."

She was struggling against explosive grief. "If that is your wish, I will promise you," she wept. "But you are going to get well. You are going to come with me to Lansdown and we are going to raise a dozen children."

He smiled faintly. "I could only be so blessed."

As Sheridan wept, she suddenly noticed a pair of boots standing on Sean's other side. She looked up to see Neely gazing down at her with a certain amount of distress. He was dressed in full battle armor, having broken through the Bell Tower gate along with a thousand other ally soldiers. He had come looking for Sheridan; now he found her.

"Oh, Neely," she sobbed. "He was trying to take me out of the Tower. Now see what has happened."

Neely removed his helm and crouched beside de Lara; the man was dying, that much was certain. He had suspected as much as he had come upon the group huddled near the east side of the Tower walls; a massive body supine on the ground with a little man and Sheridan hovering over it. In all, it had been a sobering sight and Neely suddenly forgot about all of the terrible things he was going to say to Sheridan, the anger and jealousy he had felt. For her sake, he had to reach deep inside to find compassion for a man he had long been taught to hate.

"De Lara," Neely said quietly. "We must get you out of here. We need to move you away from the fighting."

Sean looked at him. "You will have to discuss that with the physic. I am under his command at the moment."

Neely looked at Gilby, who was busily stitching up the deep gouge to Sean's right side. The old physic waited until he was finished before acknowledging the St. James knight.

"Let me finish with this and then we shall move him," he said quietly.

Neely nodded his head and stood up. There was nothing left for him to do so he wandered over to where Alys stood with Guy. There was a priest standing with them, muttering last rites for de Lara. Alys was sobbing heavily and Neely put a comforting hand on her shoulder. No matter what the politics or circumstances, for Sheridan's sake, the wounding of de Lara was still a brutal happening. Somehow they were all united in Sheridan's grief no matter their individual opinions.

Gilby finally put his things away and moved to Sean's other side, feeling the man's neck for his pulse. After a moment of assessing his current condition, he looked at Sheridan.

"If we are going to move him, let us do it now," he said, looking over at Neely. "Come lend a hand, knight."

Neely moved to Sean's left side, gently pushing Sheridan out of the way. Gilby was far too small of a man to effectively move Sean's bulk so Father Simon came to his aid, followed by Guy. Guy could hardly lift a fly given his ribs and other injuries, but he was bravely attempting to help. Even Sheridan and Alys jumped in. It took all five of them to get Sean into a sitting position. Neely, being the largest of the group, was doing the bulk of the work; he got in behind Sean and lifted him by the armpits. Just as he got Sean halfway to his feet, an armored figure suddenly materialized before them.

William Marshall's face was grim as he beheld his mighty Shadow Lord. It seemed that beyond his shock he looked rather ill, but he steeled himself admirably. He, too, had entered the breach in the Bell Tower and had, in fact, gone searching for de Lara to congratulate him on a task well done. The Tower had fallen just as they had planned. But he found sorrow instead. In truth, he was not surprised; disappointed, but not surprised. He shoved the old physic out of the way and took hold of Sean's right arm.

"We must get him out of here," the Marshall said gravely. "Where are you planning on taking him?"

Gilby gestured to the buildings off to his right. "Back to his apartments."

The Marshall shifted Sean's weight, putting Sean's enormous arm over his shoulders. "'Tis not safe, Gilby," he snapped softly. "We must get him out of the Tower."

Gilby looked at the Marshall, a man he had served for many years. "He'll not survive a drastic move," he told him plainly. "He has lost too much blood."

"He will die if he stays here."

"He will die if we transport him any lengthy distance."

By this time, Sheridan was sobbing softly. She was next to Guy, trying to help support her husband's weight, but the argument between Gilby and the Marshall was too much for her to take. Sean, scarcely conscious, tried to touch her with the big arm slung across Guy's shoulders.

"'Tis all right, sweetling," he mumbled thickly. "Do not weep."

Sheridan struggled to stop, wiping at her damp cheeks. The group of them managed to half-carry, half-drag Sean for several feet when Gilby suddenly came to a halt. This caused William to bash into him, an irritable snap on his lips. But it died in his throat when he saw the look on Gilby's face. The old man was looking up at the White Tower.

Several of the king's guards were pouring from the south entry on the second floor, descending the stairs with weapons drawn. Behind them, delineated in the moonlight, came the small, cloaked figure of the king. The man was surrounded by soldiers and a pair of knights; it was apparent that they had chosen this moment to remove the king from the Tower. The Marshall hissed at Father Simon.

"Get Lady de Lara out of here," he commanded quietly, authoritatively. "If he sees her he will take her. Guy, go with them. Remove the lady and her sister now!"

Guy didn't hesitate; he moved from Sean's side and grabbed Sheridan, who started to struggle. But one word from her husband stopped her.

"Sheridan," he voice suddenly sounded strong and controlled. "Go with the Guy, sweetling. Go wherever he takes you. I will come for you as soon as I am able."

She panicked. "But…!"

"Do this for my sake. Please, sweetling. Do it for me."

Sheridan could see the men coming down from the Tower and she realized that there was no time for her to plead. Not this time. Too many lives depended on her cooperation. The time for separation had come and she was anguished with the thought. Turning swiftly to Sean, she put her hands on his face, convinced that this was to be her last look of the man for all time. No one would have guessed by looking at her that her heart had just exploded into a million painful little pieces.

"I will go," she murmured. "Remember how much I love you."

"And I love you," he whispered.

"Promise we will be together again."

"You are my angel and I will be with you, and no other, in this life and beyond."

"Come on, Sheridan," Guy was tugging at her urgently. "We must go now."

She knew that. With a final look to sustain her, she kissed him again and was gone. Sean watched her fade into the shadows near the Flint Tower with her sister, de Braose and the priest.

This time, it was Sean who wept.

CHAPTER SIXTEEN

Lansdown Castle, Somerset
July, Year of our lord 1215

"Dani, where are you?" Jocelin's disembodied voice floated upon the warm summer air. "Dani?"

It was July in the lush green countryside of Somerset. The humidity was heavy, both from the River Avon and the not so distant sea, but it was nonetheless a lovely day infused with the scent of summer flowers.

Seated beside the lake just outside the walls of Lansdown, Sheridan lounged comfortably beneath a colorful umbrella with the water licking at her feet. Alys was sitting in the lake, for the weather was too hot for her liking, and the little pup, now grown into a little dog, leapt through the grass chasing imaginary rabbits. At the sound of Jocelin's voice, Sheridan turned to see him wandering in the tall grass on the rise above the lake.

"Here we are," she called back to him, waving her hand.

The bishop caught sight of her, partially hidden by a sapling, and made his way down the hill in her direction. Sheridan turned in her chair, facing the lake again and watching the bugs dance upon the waters. To her left was an easel with a half-finished painting of the lake; she wasn't very good at painting but she enjoyed it. She'd been able to do little else over the past few months as her pregnancy advanced. She was enormous at almost seven months and her mother's physic said she carried twins. With all of the tumbling and kicking in her belly, she was positive that he was correct.

At her feet, Alys rolled around in the water, playing with the grass at the lake's edge. Her little sister was still the same after all these months only she had grown up just a little; she seemed more mature somehow, more somber. She no longer believed herself in love with every man she met. Gone were the flighty tendencies and temper tantrums. She lived and breathed for her sister's comfort. Wars and tragedy had a way of maturing those they touched.

"Do you think Guy will come and visit soon?" she asked her sister as she picked at a blade. "The last time he was here, he said that he would return soon. Do you suppose that he will?"

Sheridan's thought of de Braose and his constant presence. "I am sure he will be back shortly."

"He always comes back."

"Indeed he does."

Alys cast her sister a sidelong glance as she toyed with the grass. "He loves you so, Dani," she said softly. "You really should marry him and put him out of his misery."

Sheridan ignored her sister, turning back to her painting. "You are going to turn into a prune if you stay in that water much longer."

Alys tossed the grass aside and sat up, splashing water on her arms. "'Tis too hot to get out just yet," she eyed her sister again. "Dani, do you not want the baby to have a father when it is born? Guy has been very kind to you and he would love this baby as his own. Moreover, you promised Sean that you would marry him. Do you intend to go back on your promise?"

Sheridan's jaw began to tick. "I do not wish to discuss this with you."

Alys suddenly stood up, water cascading off her white thighs. "And why not?" she sloshed through the water towards the shore. "You have avoided speaking with anyone about it for six months. You cannot put it off forever."

"I can put it off forever if I wish."

Alys reached the shore. "But this is not healthy for you," she pleaded. "I know that you do not want to make any decisions until you have confirmation of Sean's death, but it has been seven months now and no one has seen or heard from the man. Jocelin has sent missives to the Marshall that have gone unanswered. No one can find Gilby and not even Neely knows what became of Sean after he left him at the Tower. When are you going to come to terms with the fact that Sean is dead and you must move forward with your life?"

Sheridan threw her brush to the ground and stood up as swiftly as her swollen body would allow. Alys sighed heavily as her sister crossed her arms stubbornly. By this time, Jocelin had joined them and he instantly sensed the tension in the air. He eyed both girls.

"Dani?" he ventured. "Alys? What is the matter?"

Sheridan refused to look at him; unwinding her arms, she put her hands to the small of her back and wandered towards the lake. Alys watched her walk away with the little dog jumping happily at her feet.

"Nothing new is the matter," Alys told Jocelin. "We were simply speaking of Guy."

Jocelin wriggled his eyebrows at the very touchy subject matter.

"I see," he watched Sheridan as she stood at the edge of the water and threw a little stick to the dog. He wasn't sure he should even tell her what he had come to say but he could not keep it a secret. She would find out soon enough. "I came to tell you that the sentries have sighted riders about a mile out. I suspect that it is Guy returned."

Sheridan simply hung her head. Jocelin cast a long glace at Alys, silently ordering the girl away. Alys did so reluctantly, taking the dog with her as it raced up the hill. When the red-headed sister was gone, Jocelin went to stand next to Sheridan. His gaze moved over the lake, the gentle reeds and finally the distant horizon. He could feel Sheridan's sorrow; he had been feeling it for months. But her sorrow did not erase the facts.

"Perhaps…," he began, then cleared his throat. "Perhaps you should think on consenting to Guy's proposal. The man will not wait forever."

"Then let him move on," Sheridan snapped softly. "I did not ask him to wait for me."

"But you promised Sean that you would marry him. That is why he waits. And also because he loves you a great deal."

Sheridan turned away from him and began to walk the muddy shore. "Why must we speak on this every time he comes around?" she asked. "I have told you this time and time again; I have no intention of marrying Guy until I know for certain that Sean is dead."

Jocelin drew in a long, deep breath, shaking his head. "Dani…."

She whirled on him. "Show me his body and I shall believe," she said forcefully, "because until such time as I have proof, my husband is still alive and I will not marry anyone else."

Jocelin exhaled sharply. "I have sent missives to the Marshall asking for proof. The man has not responded because he is too busy with more important things. You know that the barons are on the march against the crown and the Marshall is with them. You must accept that…."

"Nay!" Sheridan roared, kicking at the water at her feet. "I will not accept. If you want me to believe that my husband perished, then I must have proof."

"It has been six months since you last saw him. I would say the fact that he has not come for you in all that time is proof enough."

Her raging came to an abrupt halt and she simply stood there, staring at her feet. She was between sorrow and anger so often these days. "Father Simon said that…."

"Father Simon is in London."

Her head came up and she fixed on him. "Father Simon said there is always hope. Sean is stronger than we know."

Jocelin pursed his lips sympathetically and went to her, putting his meaty hands on her arms.

"Father Simon was trying to give you comfort," he shook her gently. "I believe the time has come for you to accept that your husband did not survive. Now, when young de Braose comes today, I would suggest you reconsider his proposal. He is a good man, Dani. He will make a fine husband and father."

"I like Guy a great deal but I do not want to marry him."

"I know you do not. But you must consider what is right for the baby. And you promised Sean that you would."

He always threw that into the mix; Sheridan was coming to wish she had never told him that detail of her last conversation with Sean. As the months passed and her pregnancy advanced, so did her resolve against remarriage. She wasn't foolish; she knew that they were trying to force her into marriage with de Braose for her own good. Moreover, Guy loved her. Over the past several months he had proven himself wise, humorous and compassionate and Sheridan had come to like the man a great deal. But she did not love him. She probably never would. Her heart would always belong to de Lara.

Yet she could not deny that it was increasingly apparent that Sean was dead. She kept hope in her heart that he had survived, but the more time passed, the harder it was to keep that hope alive. One day it would break down completely. Every time she reflected on the last time she saw him, her heart shattered just a little more. Perhaps it was time to finally accept the obvious.

She chewed on her lip, staring at the ground. After a moment, her blond head came up and she struggled with the words that were forming.

"If it will make you happy, I will make Guy a counter proposal," she spoke so softly that he barely heard her. "If he can bring me proof that Sean is dead…."

Jocelin cut her off. "He has tried that. He has gone to London to find out what became of Sean but he was unable to discover anything except those journals he brought to you."

Sheridan's gaze moved across the water as she thought on the volumes that Guy had brought back to her from the Tower. A priest at the Tower had given them to Guy when he had come around asking about de Lara; no one was sure how the volumes of journals had ended up in the chapel, but they had. The priests had found them in a dark corner, covered with a cloth, and left them there because they were unsure what to do with them. But that changed when de Braose came to the Tower on a spring day in April. Guy had dutifully turned them over to

Sheridan, who, unable to read Latin, had asked Guy to read them to her.

It had been an eye-opening experience into the life and thoughts of a spy. The Chronicles of Sean de Lara had, if nothing else, fed false hope in Sheridan that the man was still alive. Surely one so strong could never die.

"Dani?" Jocelin gently shook her from her reflection. "Did you hear me?"

She sighed faintly, allowing thoughts of the chronicles to fade. "I heard you," she murmured. Then she looked at him. "I am only asking for something which I believe is my right. If Guy could find an eyewitness to Sean's death or even the location of his burial, I would no longer resist his marriage proposal. There would be no reason to."

Her statement was the first truly positive inkling she had issued towards a marriage to de Braose in six months and Jocelin squeezed her arms encouragingly.

"Very well," he said quietly. "If that is what it will take, then surely there is something more he can do to help you come to grips with Sean's death. I am sure if he knew you would agree to marry him right away, he would do everything possible to meet your terms. Shall I tell him?"

She paused a long moment before nodding. Jocelin kissed her on the top of the head and let her go.

"Then I shall go and tell him," he said as he began the long trek up the hill. "He will be pleased."

Sheridan turned back to the lake, standing alone as the gentle waters lapped at her feet. After a moment, the tears came, silently pouring down her cheeks as they had done so often these past six months. She wiped at her face, trying to stay ahead of the torrents that dripped onto her bosom. But it was of no use; the tears sprang from a well of grief that would never run dry.

She continued to stand there for quite some time, pondering her future. She did not want to return to the castle where Guy had arrived and was now undoubtedly asking where she was. It would take little time for him to find her. He was, if nothing else, predictable. She wanted to spend a few moments alone with her thoughts before he came hounding after her like an eager puppy.

Sheridan put her hands against the small of her back again and began to pace around the shore of the lake. Lost in reflection, she barely missed stepping on a harmless little snake as it drank from the water. She shrieked, first in surprise, followed by giggles when she realized what she had nearly done. She stood there a moment, watching the snake fade into the weeds.

"Sheridan?"

A familiar voice caught her attention and she turned abruptly to see Guy standing a few feet behind her. Her heart sank a little at the sight of him; he had found her sooner than she had hoped.

"Greetings, Guy," she said pleasantly. "How was London?"

He shrugged vaguely. "It was… eventful," he seemed rather unsteady in his manner. "I heard you scream. Are you all right?"

She grinned, pointing to the grass. "A little snake startled me," she said. "I am fine."

Guy nodded and it was then that Sheridan noticed he seemed tight and drawn about the face. She peered more closely at him.

"What is wrong?" she asked. "You look strange."

Guy seemed taken aback that she noticed his demeanor; he was hoping that it was not too noticeable. Then again, he had never been any good at hiding his feelings.

"Do I?" He tried to bluff his way out of it but found that he could not. "It… it is nothing, really. Well, perhaps something. Aye, it is something."

He was rambling and she lifted her eyebrows at him. "What is it?"

He wasn't sure where to start. Reaching out, he took her gently by the arm and began to walk her back over to the chair and umbrella spread beneath the sapling. It was cooler in the shade.

"I just want to say something," he began softly. "I have… well, I have loved you since nearly the moment we first met. You know that. And I have wanted to marry you for nearly as long."

She sighed faintly, pausing to look at him. She was hoping they could have avoided this subject for a little while but she was not surprised that it was the first thing out of his mouth.

"I know that," she said quietly. "And I am not trying to be cruel by refusing, but...."

He cut her off. "I realize that. Your heart is with Sean; I have always known. And I want you to know that I have finally accepted that. I have accepted the fact that you and I shall never wed."

Her brow furrowed faintly; his manner seemed rather abrupt and slightly nervous. "Why would you say such a thing?" she asked curiously.

He regarded her a moment before taking a deep breath. "You are aware that I went to London at the bequest of my father."

She nodded. "Of course. You were here at Lansdown when he sent a missive and asked you to go to London on an errand."

"Aye," Guy was having difficulty looking at her. "I did go to London. But it was not on an errand for my father. It was because my father had received a missive addressed to me at Abergavenny Castle."

"What missive?"

"A missive about Sean."

Fortunately they had reached her chair because Sheridan felt all of the blood rush from her head. Guy carefully lowered her into the chair. The tears were already pouring from her eyes as he sat beside her.

"My God," she breathed. "Is it true?"

"It is. It said...."

"Please," she wept softly. "I do not want to know what it said. Please do not tell me."

He knew she did not mean it; she was simply refusing the pain that she believed such a missive would bring. Guy put his hand on her shoulder comfortingly.

"I must tell you," he said quietly. "You must be strong and listen to every word. Please, Sheridan. It is important."

She looked at him, sobbing fearfully. Although she had wanted proof of his death, still, the reality of it was difficult to bear. But she eventually nodded and he continued.

"The reason that no one was able to discover anything about Sean is because the Marshall had him taken to Rossington House in north London," he said gently. "When the Marshall went on to fight the baron's wars, there was no way to know that Sean had ended up at Rossington. Only two people knew of his location; William and Gilby. The missive I received was from Gilby."

"Gilby?" She was sobbing into her hand. "What… what did he say?"

Guy stroked her head gently, trying to keep her calm. "He sent it to Abergavenny because he thought you would be there, with me," he told her gently. "You did, after all, promise Sean that you would marry me. He naturally assumed you would be there."

"Tell me what it said."

Guy sighed faintly. "It said that Sean survived his trip from the Tower to Rossington. God knows how, but he survived. Gilby did not expect him to live after that. He said that he waited daily for Sean to die."

Sheridan was sobbing so hard that she was almost incoherent. Guy shook her gently, forcing her to look at him. When he saw how distraught she was, he took her kerchief and dipped it in the lake, gently swabbing her cheeks so that she would calm. He did not know what else to do.

"Why…," she gasped. "Why did you go to London?"

"Because Sean was in London."

Sheridan was growing faint with grief. But she struggled through it, knowing it would do no good to weep for her husband dead these long months. Perhaps she really had known all along that he had perished but had refused to accept it. The confirmation was hard to face.

"Did… did you see him?" she whispered.

"I brought him with me."

She yelped, looking at Guy with such horror that the man put his hands on her to still her. Sheridan struggled to stand up.

"I must go to him," she sounded extremely unsteady. "I must go to him right away. Where is he?"

Guy was struggling to calm her, letting out a piercing whistled as he did so. It was evident that he was calling for someone, perhaps assistance for the hysterical lady. She was veering out of control and he needed help.

"Sheridan, you must calm yourself," he pleaded. "You do not need to go to him. He will come to you. But I wanted to prepare you."

"Prepare me for *what*?"

Guy blinked, realizing she did not understand. It was the most obvious thing in the world as he had explained it; or, at least, he thought so. But given her reaction, he realized that he had not been clear. Before he had a chance to clarify, a massive silhouette appeared on the crest of the hill above the lake. The sun was at such an angle that it was difficult to make out any features, but the size alone was explanation enough.

Sheridan caught a glimpse of the figure in her peripheral vision, turning when she realized someone was approaching. She inspected the body, watched the familiar gait, and an odd feeling swept her. She suddenly felt as if she was in a dream, for surely, things like this only happened in dreams. There was no other explanation. She began to feel faint as she realized that she was gazing at her husband.

As if by a miracle, her hysteria vanished. She stared at Sean as he walked towards her; there was no mistaking his proud stance or the soft expression on his face. He looked like he did when they had first met; dressed in a soft blue tunic, leather breeches and boots, he was more handsome than she had remembered. As she continued to stare at him, she noticed that he had lost some of his bulk. It was Sean, only leaner. Somehow, someway, the man had survived.

It was too much to take. With a whimper, she fell back in her chair. Guy tried to support her, looking at her astonished face and hoping she wasn't about to have a spell.

"He survived, Sheridan," he said gently. "Sean was in London with Gilby. He thought you would be at Abergavenny with me, which is why Gilby sent the missive there. The missive asked for me to bring you to London, yet I knew that I could not. Not with the baby. So I went to retrieve Sean to bring him back to you."

By this time, Sean was nearly upon them. Sheridan hardly heard any of Guy's words; she was focused on her husband's smiling face. Guy backed away as Sean knelt timidly beside his wife, his expression one of utter tenderness as he beheld her face for the first time in ages. For a small eternity, they simply stared at each other. Sheridan remained frozen until Sean finally spoke to Guy.

"You were supposed to prepare her, de Braose," he said. "I see that you did not do an adequate job. She thinks I am a ghost."

The sound of his voice was all Sheridan needed to snap her out of her trance; she suddenly threw her arms around his neck, squeezing him so hard that she threatened to strangle him. Sean laughed softly and enveloped her in his massive arms, feeling her life and softness. It was better than he had remembered; words could not adequately describe the elation of the moment. It was enough to bring tears to his eyes.

"Sweet Jesus," he muttered, his hands in her hair. "Are you all right, sweetling? Say something."

Sheridan was literally speechless. She refused to let go even when he tried to pull her away from him so he could get a good look at her.

"Nay," she gasped. "I shall not let go. If I do, I will wake up and this all will have been a dream. Let me dream a little longer."

Sean gave in to her request and held her tightly. For the first time in his life, he turned himself over completely to the weakness of emotion, closing his eyes and feeling the tears course down his cheeks. He'd never truly allowed himself such a lack of control. It was the most magnificent moment of his life.

"It is no dream, sweetling," he murmured into her hair. "I told you I would come for you no matter what. I am sorry it has taken me so long to live up to my promise."

Sheridan had a death grip on him. "You survived."

"I survived."

"I do not believe it."

He laughed softly. "Believe it. It is the truth."

She suddenly pulled her face from the crook of his neck, her luminous blue eyes glistening with tears of joy. She was weeping again, but this time from disbelief and jubilation. She ran her fingers across his wet cheeks, then his lips, and he kissed them tenderly. But it wasn't enough; he pushed past her fingers and latched on to her mouth. He kissed her with something more powerful than joy or passion; it was love in its purest form.

"My God," Sheridan breathed as his mouth left her lips and moved over her face. "Father Simon told me not to give up hope."

Sean inhaled her scent deeply; there were times when he never thought he would smell it again. Tears were still in his eyes as he kissed her neck, her cheek.

"I am so sorry to have caused you such torment," he murmured. "To ask for forgiveness seems wholly insufficient."

She shook her head, touching his face as if still convincing herself that he was real.

"There is nothing to forgive," she insisted softly. "I told everyone that I would not believe you had died unless they provided me with proof. Until I had your dead body within my grasp, there was still hope. I never let it die."

He smiled faintly, kissing her again just because he could. "I never let it die, either."

As she gazed back at him, her expression suddenly turned wistful. "Tell me what happened after I left you. Why did you not send me word before now?"

He sighed, shifting so that she was more comfortable. But it only managed to bump her belly against him and he looked down at her swollen midsection, putting his hand reverently against her stomach. He seemed to lose his composure again as the tears welled once more.

"A baby," he said, caressing her rounded belly. "Guy told me. I could not have imagined such a blessing. 'Tis a miracle."

She smiled weakly, watching his awe-struck expression. "The physic says that he believes it to be twins."

Sean's eyebrows flew up. "Twins?" he repeated, awed. "Sweet Jesus, is he sure?"

"He seems to be."

"Do you feel all right?"

She laughed joyously. "Now that you are in my arms, I feel wonderful," she sobered. "Please tell me what happened after we parted at the Tower."

He continued to rub her belly, distracted by the surprise of her pregnancy and struggling to focus on her question.

"The Marshall took me from the Tower to a manor he owns in north London," he replied softly, looking up from her belly and focusing on her face. "I lost consciousness at some point very soon after you fled with Guy and Father Simon. I do not remember anything until waking up almost a week later. For a very long time, I lingered near death. Gilby thought I was dead many times over but somehow I always managed to prove him wrong. When I had been infirm for about a month, a nasty infection set in and I was incapacitated for almost two months. Gilby never left my side, doing everything he could to be rid of the infection. But my body was so weak by that point that he could not rid me of it entirely. It kept coming back."

Sheridan listened with tremendous sympathy, kissing his hand, his cheek, as he spoke. "My poor Sean," she murmured. "But I am so thankful that you did indeed survive."

He wriggled his eyebrows wearily. "It was a long road, believe me."

"But why did Gilby not send word to me? I would have come to be with you during your illness."

He looked at her sheepishly; now came the meat of his confession. "I would not let him," he told her. "I was convinced that I was going to die and I did not want him to notify you that I had survived my initial injury only to receive word that some random poison had just as quickly claimed my life. It was selfish of me, I know, but I did not want to put you through that hell. Better that you believed I died on that fateful night than suffer emotional highs and lows of health issues that seemingly had no end."

She sighed faintly, understanding his reasons but distressed by them nonetheless. "I love you, Sean," she insisted softly. "I was my right to know."

"I realize that. But I suppose in my own mind I was trying to protect you."

"So you would permit me to believe you were dead so I could marry Guy and get on with my life?"

"Something like that," he murmured, feeling stupid even as he said it. "But the months passed and I slowly grew stronger. And along with my health, my resistance against the king returned."

She looked at him, shaking her head after a moment. "Always the king," she murmured. "You were on your death bed yet still you thought of the rebellion."

He lifted an eyebrow. "You must remember that the last nine years of my life have been dedicated to the opposition against the king. I did not want to waste my hard work. I did not want the Shadow Lord's reputation to be in vain."

She understood somewhat. "So what did you do?"

He sighed, pulling her on to his lap so he could feel her belly against him. His chin rested on her shoulder as he spoke.

"I joined the barons in Runnymede last month for the signing of what they are calling the Magna Carta," he told her. "It is a document that is meant to give rights and fairness to all. It is meant to end tyranny."

Her eyes widened. "I was supposed to be at that meeting but could not travel because of the baby. Do you mean to tell me that you were there?"

"I was."

"Jocelin was there in my stead. Did you not see him?"

He shook his head, thinking on the document he had helped author yet would never receive credit for. He wasn't even sure he would ever tell Sheridan. Perhaps some things were better left unsaid.

"I knew he was there but I did not want to reveal myself," he replied. "I did not want him to be the one to tell you that he saw me there, alive, when I had not yet contacted you."

Sheridan's thoughts turned from the great Magna Carta signing, something which the entire country was now aware of, to the fact that Sean had been well enough to travel to the signing. But still, he did not contact her and his behavior was puzzling. More than that, it was hurtful.

"I fail to understand why you did not send word to me when you were well enough to move about," she said honestly. "You should have."

He kissed the shoulder that his chin was resting on. "I did send word as soon as I was strong enough to do so," he murmured. "Assuming you were with Guy, I had Gilby send word to Abergavenny in late May. It took time for the missive to reach the Marches, but Guy was not there. His father sent word to him at Lansdown, prompting Guy to meet me in London. I told him to bring you but he did not. He explained why. So I accompanied him back to Lansdown."

It was a complicated series of events that took time to execute but the explanation made sense. She understood everything perfectly and suddenly, the delays and illnesses didn't seem to matter any longer. He was here and he was real and such happiness as she had never known swept her. She put her hands on his face, focusing on his clear blue eyes.

"And so you are here," she said softly. "Now what do you intend to do?"

He smiled, his eyes glimmering. "I intend to claim my wife and wait for the birth of my sons."

"And after that? What about your commitment to William Marshall and the resistance against the king?"

He shook his head. "With the signing of the Magna Carta, I am finished," he told her. "I have given enough to king and country. From now on, my devotion is to my wife and family. The Marshall has had enough of my time. The rest of it is yours."

Tears filled her eyes again. "Swear it."

He kissed her gently. "I swear on my oath as a knight that my devotion is to you and no other. I will never leave you again."

She threw her arms around his neck again and held him tightly. Sean swallowed her up in his big arms, silently thanking God that he had been given another chance at life with Sheridan. He would not take it for granted.

When Father Simon, Alys, Gilby, Neely and Guy finally joined them at the lake a nominal amount of time later, there was joy in the reunion. Even Sheridan's mother embraced him like a long-lost son. The very cause that had drawn them all together had indelibly linked them for life and a tremendous bond had been forged, never to be broken.

For nine years, Sean had been hated and feared. But now, he felt nothing but love and companionship. Even from Guy, who had become more of a friend than a rival. On the trip from London to Lansdown, they had made their peace and Guy eventually became Sean's brother-in-law. It made the nine years as the king's shadow a horror of the past, like a faded memory. It simply didn't matter anymore.

The Shadow Lord died on that cold January night; Sean de Lara, however, did not. He lived through the Magna Carta and the cause that he had fought so hard to ensure. He lived through Lansdown and Trelystan and the other holdings he had procured. He lived through the Chronicles that his wife had kept for safekeeping and in the love he had for her. Most of all, he lived through the nine children that he and Sheridan eventually had. The beautiful twin girls born in October of that year were only the beginning.

The de Lara legacy lived on.

☙ THE END ❧

Author Notes

Kathryn Le Veque has been a prolific writer of Medieval Romance Novels for twenty years. When most of her novels take around three months to complete, *Lord of the Shadows* took three years because the original ending concluded with Sean's death. Not exactly the happy ending that most romances have, but more than that, it was difficult to accept his death even though that was the natural progression of the story. So Kathryn put the story away for three years, finally rewriting the ending with a much happier finish.

If you are a fan of Kathryn's novels, you will notice the surname de Lara – in fact, Sean is the great-great-great-great-great grandfather of Tate de Lara of the novel "Dragonblade". In fact, the surname de Lara is very common throughout Kathryn's novels, as are many other surnames. Most of Kathryn's characters are related, or otherwise know each other – case and point: Sean's brother, Kevin, is a secondary character in the novel "Archangel", and Sean and Kevin's father makes an appearance in that novel as well.

Many of these characters are actual historical figures – Gerard d'Athée, for instance, really was a strong arm of King John. He was, in fact, mentioned in the Magna Carta. Jocelin, Bishop of Bath, is real as well.

The Marcher Lords of de Lara Series also contains the novel Dragonblade. Sean de Lara from Lord of the Shadows, is the ancestor of Tate de Lara, the hero of Dragonblade.

Dragonblade

Kevin de Lara, the brother of Sean de Lara, is a secondary character in Archangel.

Archangel

For more information on other series and family groups, as well as a list of all of Kathryn's novels, please visit her website at www.kathrynleveque.com.

Bonus Chapters of the exciting Medieval Romance LESPADA to follow.

1264 A.D. – Davyss de Winter is the champion for King Henry III, a powerful and arrogant man that descends from a long line of powerful knights. He is also a much-sought after man and has had more than his share of female admirers, including a besotted baron's daughter who bore him bastard twins.

His mother and family matriarch, the Lady Katharine de Warrenne de Winter, loses patience with her son's behavior and betrothes him to a woman she hopes will tame his wild ways. She selects a young woman from a lesser noble family with no political ties or ambitions, a perfect match for her son's prideful personality.

Enter the Lady Devereux d'Arcy Allington; a young woman of astounding beauty, she wants nothing to do with Davyss. When Davyss, in protest of the marriage, sends his sword Lespada to the marriage ceremony, Devereux is beyond offended. Livid, she battles tooth and nail, refusing to marry a sword by proxy, until Lady Katharine intervenes. Cornered, Devereux is forced to marry Lespada because her groom refuses to show up for the ceremony. When Davyss gives in to his curiosity and meets his wife for the first time, he is overwhelmed with her beauty.

Roughly consummating the marriage, he has set the tone for what both Davyss and Devereux believe will be a loveless, hateful marriage. But when Davyss begins to realize what he's done, he swallows his considerable pride and is determined to get to know the woman he married, a woman of grace and compassion like nothing he has ever known before.

Though trials and tribulations, Davyss and Devereux's bond only strengthens. When Davyss is involved in the Battle of Evesham against Simon de Montfort, Devereux faces her own life and death situation.

Lespada is a love story for the ages.

CHAPTER ONE

"And what is better than wisdom? Woman.
And what is better than a good woman? Nothing."
Geoffrey Chaucer c.1343 – 1400

London, England
The Ides of March, 1264 A.D.

THE EVENING WAS still and hushed, the hour late. The sounds of the gentle waters of the Thames drifted over the moonlit houses, roofs, and avenues like the caressing soothe of a lullaby. Hardly a soul stirred on the dirty, dangerous streets. Even the Tower of London was bathed in nocturnal peace, a bastion normally wrought with violence and tension. But the tranquility belied the chaotic heart beating within the fortress, with friction pulsing through halls like the veins of a living body.

It was a foregone conclusion that a variety of factions resided within the old stone walls of the Tower, and these days were particularly strained. There were those allied with the king, and there were those against. The ancient fortress had seen its share of political strife and the future could only threaten more of the same. Though the evening was peaceful and the mood still, there was an underlying element of pandemonium that threatened to explode. Each man and woman at the Tower lived moment by moment in anticipation of this. It was an exhausting existence.

But not all allowed themselves to be sucked into the tension that surrounded them. In the tower wing on the eastern wall, two brothers shared a fire and a carafe of blood-red wine from Sicily. These men were key components to the political strife enveloping the Tower, and one man in particular. He was the one with the heavy yellowed vellum in hand, his jaw ticking with disbelief as his eyes perused the writing.

"I do not believe it," he growled.

"Believe what?" asked the other.

The man continued to stare at the missive until finally settling it in his lap. There was a long sigh.

"Mother."

"What has she done now?"

Davyss de Winter handed his brother the message. Hugh took the vellum, reading the contents hesitantly as if fearful of what it might say. When he came to the end, he closed his eyes in acquiescence. The vellum collapsed in his lap.

"God give us strength," he muttered. The deep brown eyes opened to look back at his brother. "She has been threatening you with this for months. I did not believe her to be serious."

Davyss gazed steadily at his younger brother, a knowing smile playing on his smooth lips. "You should know her better than that, little brother. The Lady Katharine Isabella Rowyna de Warenne de Winter never threatens. Her oath is more trustworthy than that of any knight I know." He took back the vellum, eyeing it with something of regret. "I just thought it would be later rather than sooner."

"What are you going to do?"

Davyss glanced at the missive one last time before setting it aside. It had been a harried day and this had been the first chance he'd had to sit in one place and unwind. Yet in his position, relaxation could be deadly. He didn't think he'd truly relaxed in fifteen years.

"I am not entirely sure that I have a choice in the matter. Should I refuse, she will deny me my inheritance. She has told me thus."

"So you will do it?"

Davyss fell silent. His thoughts revolved around his overbearing mother, ill with age and bitter with life, and the inheritance that was his due. Nearly everything the de Winter family had come from his mother's side, including the castle in which she currently resided. As the only sister of the Earl of Surrey, she had been granted Breckland Castle in Norfolk by her brother. It was a glorious stronghold, well regarded and well-fortified near the dense Thetford Forest.

The de Warenne fortune came with it from his mother's sire. Davyss had worked too hard in the course of his thirty-four years to watch it all slip away to Hugh because he was too stubborn to do as his mother bade. It wasn't often that she dictated to him, but when she did, she meant it. He understood her want for her heir to marry and bear offspring to carry on the name. It wasn't unreasonable. He just wished he had some say in the matter.

He heard his brother snort. He glanced at him. "What is it?"

Hugh's handsome face was contorted in a smirk. "I suppose I find all of this ironic."

"How?"

Hugh snorted again, just for effect, and rose from his over-stuffed leather chair. He moved to the hearth and tossed another hunk of peat onto the blaze. Sparks flew up into the dim room.

"Because you are Henry's champion, for Christ's sake," he poked at the smoking fire. "The king of the mightiest country on earth turns to you for protection. Men are humbled at your feet and your reputation is second to none. A weak man did not achieve this. You have the will of the nation to command by sheer strength alone, yet your mother issues forth orders and suddenly, the champion is subdued like a submissive child."

The irony wasn't lost on Davyss. Hugh wasn't attempting to be condescending but that was the message.

"I cannot be selfish in this matter," he said simply. "I have the de Winter lineage to think of. I do indeed want sons to carry on my name"

"So you let dear Mummy arrange a marriage?"

Hugh was becoming taunting now. A long look from the quick-tempered Davyss quickly curbed any thoughts of furthering the torment. Under no circumstances would Hugh tangle with his older, and by far larger, brother.

"According to Mother, she is a woman of good bloodlines. Her father is Lord Mayor of Thetford and Sheriff of the Shire." He sounded suspiciously as if he was attempting to talk himself into the agreeable arrangement. "So I will marry her, she will bear my sons, I will stay in London and still collect my inheritance, and everyone will be happy. I see no issue with this."

Hugh didn't believe him, but he did not let on. When pushed to the breaking point, Davyss' temper was unpredictable and, at times, deadly. He had no desire to be cuffed. He sat back in his chair.

"So what is my new sister's name?"

Davyss stared into the fire, digging deep into his memory. His mother had told him, once, during the few discussions they had exchanged on the subject.

"The Lady Devereux Allington."

"Family?"

"Saxon lords. A grand sire, several generations over, was king of the ancient Kingdom of Dremrud. She comes with some wealth."

"What does she look like?"

Davyss lifted a dark eyebrow. "You can tell me that upon your return."

"Return from what?"

"My wedding."

CHAPTER TWO

Thetford, Norfolk

THE ONLY MAN not in attendance at the wedding was the groom.

Unwilling to leave London with the current political situation between Henry and the volatile Simon de Montfort, he remained at his post. Moreover, his absence was a statement to his mother that he could not be so easily pushed about. So he sent his knights, all five of them, to attend the marriage for him. Most importantly, he had sent his sword with Hugh. The lady would marry the weapon, by proxy, and become Lady de Winter. Davyss would therefore have a wife he'd never even met, a very neat arrangement for someone who did not wish to be married at all.

If the groom was reluctant, the bride was positively adverse. Hugh had been the first man to lay eyes on her, a petite woman with the body of a ripe goddess and luscious blonde hair that fell in a thick sheet to her buttocks. He had been momentarily dumbfounded by the glory of her face, so lovely that he was sure the angels were jealous. She had enormous gray eyes that were brilliant and bottomless, and a rosebud mouth that was sweet and delectable. But his glimpse of unearthly beauty had been fleeting as she slammed the door in his face. That action set the tone. The de Winter knights had, therefore, broken down the door and set chase to the fighting, scratching animal otherwise known as the Lady Devereux D'arcy Allington.

Hugh led the group with enthusiasm. One of the shortest knights, he was built like a bull. His dark hair, dark eyes and square jaw gave him a youthfully beautiful appearance and he was no stranger to women's attention. Usually, he could soothe any manner of female fits.

Much to his chagrin, however, his brother's betrothed had not fallen under his spell. As she fought him like a banshee, his enthusiasm waned and he backed off to let the rest of the group have a go at her. He was embarrassed she had not swooned at his feet but would not admit to it, not even to himself.

Sir Nikolas de Nogaret was the next in line to deal with the hysterical lady. A tall man with blue eyes and wide shoulders, he ended up with a black eye when the lady swung a broken chair leg at him. Sir Philip de Rou took over when Nik acquired the hit to his face; a slender, blonde man with a decidedly suave manner, Philip was as overconfident in his persuasive abilities as Hugh had been. The lady opened a door into his nose when he had chased her into a wardrobe and, in that gesture, damaged his fragile ego as well as his face.

With two knights down, the final pair took over. Sir Andrew Catesby and his younger brother, Sir Edmund Catesby, were ten years apart in age. Andrew and Davyss had fostered together and were the closest of friends.

Cool, calm, and exceedingly collected, Andrew stepped over Philip's prostrate form on his way to corral the lady and was met by a flying taper. Her aim had been true and almost put his eye out. Edmund, young and newly knighted, tucked in behind his older brother and used him as a shield. When the brothers finally cornered her in her father's chamber, it had been Edmund who had taken the glory of finally subduing her.

Victory was attained for the moment but there was more bedlam to come. Carting her, bound and gagged, to Breckland Priory had been no easy feat. Though small, she was oddly strong. The men didn't want to injure her but the woman struggled like a wildcat. They were frankly astonished at the resistance they met and tried not to look like vicious brutes as they carried her through the town. She screamed and fought as if they were taking her to be hanged. The entire berg turned out to watch and their procession transformed into a bizarre parade, with knights on foot carrying a reluctant captive.

Fortunately, they made it to the priory without anyone losing fingers. The lady's father, a short man with silver hair and gray eyes, followed them from the cottage and lingered near the door of the chapel as they lugged his daughter inside. He had readily agreed to the union between his only child and Davyss de Winter due to the prestigious connections with the House of de Winter, but now he wasn't so sure his decision had been a wise one. The knights were enormous men, built and bred for battle, and his stubborn daughter was caught in the middle of the storm. She was, in fact, the tempest. He said a prayer for her health as she was half-dragged, half-carried, to the altar.

The interior of the old priory was spartanly furnished and dimly lit, with long thin tapers trailing ribbons of smoke into the musty air. Massive columns supported the ceiling, flanking the central area for the congregation. A few priests lingered in the shadows, hiding behind the supporting pillars and watching the drama unfold. But their fears were for naught, for not one of them would be forced to execute the wedding Mass. Davyss' personal priest, a man named Lollardly, stood waiting to perform the ceremony.

Lollardly had seen battles, and participated in them, for nearly twenty years and had earned a reputation for himself as a fighting friar. But the brawl happening before him was something not even he had ever witnessed and he was, truthfully, astonished.

"Here, here, do not injure the lady," he commanded the knights. "Untie her, you animals. Have you no respect?"

Andrew and Edmund had Devereux between them. Ever the gentleman, and with a healthy respect for the clergy, Andrew gently righted her on her feet. Once balanced, she tried to run. Andrew grabbed her before she could get away and wrapped his big arms around her torso, holding her fast.

Devereux cursed him through the gag. Lollardly lifted a disapproving eyebrow, took a step forward, and pulled the sodden wad from her mouth.

"My lady," he said sternly. "I would suggest you calm yourself and fulfill your duty. Your behavior is harming none but yourself and you are creating an embarrassing spectacle."

Devereux licked her chapped lips, a gesture not missed by Hugh and Philip in particular. They were rather intrigued by the pink rosebud mouth, especially when it wasn't gnashing at them.

"You should be protecting me," she hissed at the friar. "How dare you ally yourself with these devils."

"Devils or no, they represent your husband and you will obey."

"He is not my husband yet."

Lollardly had little patience for the inane. Beautiful or no, the lady was ridiculous as far as he was concerned and he would waste no more time. He glanced at Andrew behind her.

"Let us kneel."

The knights dropped to a knee and Hugh produced the blade of his forefathers; Lespada, the sword of high warriors. It was a magnificent weapon that had seen many generations of de Winter men, now carried by Davyss. Andrew tried to force Devereux down but she stiffened like a board. Not wanting to create more of a scene, and slightly perturbed that he was not in complete control, Andrew tried a few methods to force her to kneel. The last resort was to throw his knee into the back of her right knee. The joint buckled enough to allow him to shove her down to the cold stone floor. He knew she must have cut her skin with the force of her fall but she did not utter a word of pain.

"Curse you," she hissed. "Curse all of you. I hope you burn in hell for this. I hope you rot. I hope you…!"

Andrew slapped a hand over her mouth, smiling thinly at the friar. "Proceed."

Lollardly lifted an eyebrow and began the liturgy. It really was a pity, he thought. Lady Devereux was a stunning example of the glory of womanhood. She also had the manners of a wild boar. Davyss would not be pleased.

The friar droned on in Latin. The lady's bright gray eyes blazed with fury, Andrew's hand still over her mouth. Somewhere in her glare, Lollardly could see the tears of fright, of sadness. Strangely, he saw no outright defiance, only self-protection. At least, he hoped that was what he saw. Given the opportunity, they could ease her fears to soothe her manner. But they could not curb blatant insubordination.

"Quod Jesus refero said unto lemma, liberi illae universitas matrimonium, quod es donatus in matrimonium," Lollardly intoned the liturgy, reading from the dog-eared mass book he had copied himself many years ago. Gently closing the book, he formed the sign of the cross over the lady's head.

"Bona exsisto vobis."

It was the union blessing. Devereux understood Latin and her loudly-thumping heart beat faster still. Andrew removed his big hand and Hugh placed the hilt of the sword in front of her lips.

"I will not kiss it," she said through clenched teeth.

Hugh tried to put the metal against her mouth in an effort to force her, but she would have no part in it. She bit her lips and lowered her head. Andrew, though it was not a gentlemanly gesture, grabbed the back of her blonde head and pulled her skull back. With a violent twist, she threw them both off balance and they tumbled to the ground.

"No!" she screeched.

The lady ended up on her back, with Hugh on top of her. The sword was in his hand. His weight, coupled with Andrew against her legs, rendered her immobile and Hugh found himself gazing into bright gray eyes.

The lady knew she was cornered. The knights had her and there was nothing more she could do, nowhere for her to go. She could feel herself breaking down, the fight in her veins leaving her. Still, she could not let go so easily.

"Please," she whispered in a strained tone. "Please do not force me to do this."

They were the first civilized words she had spoken. Her voice was like liquid sugar, soft and sweet and low. She was such a lovely creature that Hugh found himself listening to her. But he chased away his misgivings before they could control him.

"This is not my doing, my lady," he said neutrally. "Kiss the sword and we shall be done with it. Then I am to take you to London to meet your husband."

The lady shook her head. "But… but you do not understand. I will not. I cannot."

"Why?"

She wouldn't answer him and he was suddenly seized with anger. The fingers of his left hand bit into her upper arm. "Are you compromised?"

She gasped in shock at the suggestion. "No, my lord, I swear it," she insisted. "But… I will not marry de Winter."

Hugh gazed at her, baffled by her words, thinking it was surely another ploy. She was trying all avenues to resist this marriage. Before he could reply, however, a voice filled the stale air of the priory.

"Hugh!"

Lady Katharine de Winter strolled into the hall, leaning heavily on her cane. Behind her came a procession of properly submissive ladies in waiting with their severe wimples and pale faces.

"Get off of that woman, you beast," she told her son. "What are you doing to her?"

Hugh pushed himself off of Devereux, making sure that Andrew had a grip on her. His dark brown eyes warmed to his mother as he approached her.

"Darling," he kissed her on both cheeks. "How good to see you. You are as lovely as ever."

She let her youngest flatter her. "I can see that you waited for me." She cast a long glance in the direction of the lady, picking herself off the floor with Andrew's assistance. "What is she doing on the ground?"

Hugh took his mother's elbow and they began to walk towards the altar. "Nothing to worry over, Mother."

"Hmmm," Lady Katharine carefully inspected the disheveled woman from a short distance. "That is not what I think. I think someone has worked this young woman over." She paused before the knights, her sharp brown eyes scrutinizing every one of them. "Can anyone tell me what has truly happened here?"

Andrew had known Lady Katharine since childhood. His soft blue eyes twinkled at her. "The lady is reluctant to marry, my lady," he said. "We are simply helping her fulfill the pledge."

A withered eyebrow lifted. "Abusing the lady is not the same as helping her," she said flatly. Her wizened brown eyes peered more closely at the girl. "Lady Devereux, I have seen you since you were a child. I know your father. I have always known that you would be a match for one of my sons, although I sorely doubt the youngest is worthy of you and the oldest lacks the time and effort for the undertaking. Would you kindly explain why these men tell me you are reluctant to marry?"

Devereux faced the elderly woman with as much dignity as she could muster. From the instant she had been informed of her betrothal to Davyss de Winter until this very moment, the entire event had been a nightmare. Now, in front of these strangers, she must explain herself. She had no choice.

"I do not want to marry your son, my lady," she said quietly.

"Why not? And speak up, girl. My ears are not as they used to be."

Devereux started to reply, more loudly, but she glanced at the men surrounding her and the words died in her throat. She took a deep breath as she gazed into ancient, wise eyes.

"May I speak with you privately, my lady?" she asked.

Katharine cocked what was left of her eyebrow. "You will speak here. There is nothing you can tell me that these men cannot hear."

Something in the woman's attitude fired a spark in Devereux; there was no kindness, no compassion. Just like the men surrounding her. The realization fed her resistance and her attempt to be moderately tactful disappeared.

"Because your son supports a tyrant of a king," she said through clenched teeth. “I will not marry one so entrenched in oppression and politics.”

The knights stirred in outrage but none spoke; they would leave that to Lady de Winter, whose tongue could cut more deeply than the sharpest knife. The old woman’s eyes glittered with unspoken intensity as she sized up the blonde woman a few feet away; there was calculation to the gaze as she dissected the statement for both content and intent. She made her move accordingly.

“Your statement could be considered treacherous but I will give you the benefit of the doubt,” Lady Katharine replied after a moment. “Since I believe that every woman should be given the right to speak her mind, I will give you that same courtesy. Tell me, then, Lady Devereux, why you would make this slanderous and uneducated statement about my son?”

It was a direct slap but Devereux would not back down. She was not weak by nature and would not let this bird-like woman, no matter how powerful, push her around. Lady Katharine had already done quite enough of that when she forced Devereux’s father into a marriage contract. It had been a shock to Devereux those months ago when her father had informed her of the agreement. It made no sense, in any arena.

“It is not uneducated, my lady, I assure you,” she said as evenly as she could manage. “There is not a man, woman or child in this country who does not know the name Davyss de Winter. Everyone knows that he is the king’s champion and that men fear his power and wrath.” She took a step towards the frail old woman, her bright gray eyes glimmering with more curiosity than defiance. “I am the daughter of a minor noble. I have no great rank or power, nor do I come with a dowry of a thousand fighting men. I am not a particularly suitable match for your son and I would ask why you seem so determined for me to be his wife.”

Lady de Winter met Devereux’s gaze with equal force. “For precisely the reasons you have indicated,” she said quietly. “You are not politically connected. You cannot betray my son to an enemy who has coerced you or your father into submission. You do not come to this marriage with a secret agenda for power or money. You only bring yourself."

"That makes little sense to a politically connected family such as the de Winters."

Lady Katharine lifted a sparse brow. "It makes perfect sense. My son does not need a woman attempting to bend him to her will for her, or her family's, political gain," she paused a moment, studying Lady Devereux's exquisite face. The woman was genuinely beautiful in spite of the fact that she had been roughed over. "He needs someone strong and unconnected and true. He needs someone to keep his attention and show him that the true meaning of manhood comes from dedication to one woman, not the plaything of many. You are this person."

For the first time since being cornered in her father's home, Devereux felt her defiant stance waver. As Lady Katharine explained things, it made perfect sense. But it did not erase facts.

"How would you know that I am true?" she was genuinely curious.

The old expression was confident. "Because I have watched you grow up and, as I have said, I know your father. I have known your family for quite some time. You are aware of this, lady."

Devereux nodded faintly. "I know that you rule this shire. Your family has for generations. Everyone knows of the de Winter might."

"Then you are aware that I speak with some knowledge when I say that I know of you and of your character. You are the mistress of The House of Hope, a poorhouse that provides to the needy of the shire. You are held in high regard for your generosity and charity."

Devereux was growing increasingly perplexed. "Generosity and kindness do not necessarily seal a suitable match," she replied with less boldness and more awe. "The de Winter family came to these shores with William the Bastard. My family is Saxon, a conquered people. My mother died a few years ago and it has only been my father and I since that time. I tend the poor house and help my father manage the small village of people that depend upon us for their lives. A marriage into the House of de Winter is beyond my comprehension. I do not want to be involved in a family that so allies itself with the king."

"Why not?"

Her tone turned cold. "Because I do not believe in his absolute rule. I believe the country should be governed by the people as a whole, not by a monarchy that cares little for its subjects."

Lady Katharine almost looked amused. "Are you so sure of all things?"

Devereux was not so arrogant that she presumed to know everything. But she was resolute in her opinion.

"I am not, Lady de Winter," she said with some hesitation. "'Tis simply that I believe the Earl of Leicester is a man of the people, a man who understands how a country should be governed. It is his ideals that I support, not a king whose sense of entitlement is only exceeded by his arrogance."

One could have heard a pin drop in that cold, unfeeling chapel, surrounded by stone and effigies of barons long dead. Devereux was feeling increasingly uncomfortable as Lady Katharine simply stared at her. Then, something odd happened; the harsh glare faded from the old woman's eyes and she reached out, patting Devereux on her tender cheek.

"I like this one," she said to the men surrounding them. "Tell Davyss that I will expect him to treat her well. She will bear sons of character and strength." She refocused on Devereux, the twinkle in her eye once again hardening in a frightening manner. "You will now kiss the sword. Let us be done with this."

Devereux very nearly refused again; defiance shot up her spine and she could feel herself stiffen with the force of rebellion. But more than the threat from the knights and the physical battle that had consumed the majority of their acquaintance, the look in Lady de Winter's eyes suggested that she would not tolerate any further disobedience. Devereux didn't know why she suddenly felt herself submitting. The power in the old lady's eyes was unwavering and unkind. Devereux knew when she was beaten.

Lady de Winter did not wait for any words of agreement or refusal; she crooked a gnarled finger at Hugh, who brought about Lespada and held it to Devereux's lips. With her bright gray eyes still focused on the old woman she instinctively respected and naturally feared, she brushed the cold steel with her soft pink lips. Without any further struggle or fanfare, it was finally done.

And with that, Lady Katharine de Winter turned around and headed for the door of the priory. Hugh followed his mother to the entry, speaking softly with her and helping her through the portal as her ladies congregated around her. Then he turned around, his dark gaze suddenly focusing on something just over Devereux's right shoulder.

There was a figure in the shadows, something he'd not noticed until his mother just mentioned it. He instantly recognized the shape, and was silenced from speaking when a massive hand lifted to quiet him. It did not take Hugh long to deduce that his mother's arrival must have been a diversion so they would not have seen Davyss enter the priory; they had all been focused on the snarling bride and Lady de Winter, so much so that they would not have given thought to a vaporous figure in the darkness. And it was from that darkness that Davyss had witnessed the entire ceremony.

So his brother had decided to come after all. Hugh wisely assumed that the man would want time alone with his new bride, if for no other reason than to set her straight on the course their marriage would take after her natty little display of manners. Snapping his fingers at the knights, he jabbed a thumb at the door.

"Gather your mounts and secure transportation for the lady," he commanded. "I will join you in a moment."

Devereux was still standing near the altar with Lollardly; she was frankly a bit dumbfounded from her conversation with Lady de Winter. She was still trying to reconcile the event in her own mind. But the old priest eyed her critically as he moved past her and Devereux gazed back as if daring the man to speak harshly to her. She was still upset with him for going along with this travesty of a marriage ceremony.

Surprisingly, she did not try to run when the knights moved out. She stood where they had left her, watching her father bolt from the chapel and thinking the man to be a horrible coward. She knew he had only married her to de Winter to be part and parcel to the de Winter fortune. He was greedy that way. Feeling the least bit abandoned and, not surprisingly, exhausted in the light of her embattled wedding ceremony, she watched with some trepidation as the knights and the priest filed from the hall.

All except for Hugh; he marched upon her with an expression of hostility. Since all he had known from her since the moment of their association was violence, she hardly blamed him.

"You will wait here until we can bring about suitable transportation for the trip to Castle Acre Castle," he eyed her. "If you give me your word that you will not try to escape, I will not bind you."

She gave him a look that suggested she was bored with his statement. "If I wanted to flee, your bindings could not hold me," she fired back. "Go get your horses. I am not going anywhere."

"Do I have your word, lady?"

"I said it, did I not?"

"That is not an answer."

"It is enough of an answer for you. Do you doubt me?"

Hugh almost entered into an argument with her that would undoubtedly end in some manner of fist in his eye. But he caught himself in time, begging off for the sheer reason that Davyss was only a few feet away; he knew his brother would handle this banshee of a woman and they would all be the better for it. Still insulted with the fact that his charming and debonair self had not melted her with a first glance, he cast her a withering glare and quit the chapel.

When it was finally cold and empty, Devereux emitted a pent up sigh. Like a bubble of tension bursting, she suddenly felt deflated. She realized that tears were close to the surface but angrily chased them away, feeling despondent and disoriented.

She would wait for the knights to return to take her to her prison of Castle Acre Castle. It wasn't far from her berg, the great castle with the massive ramparts. Lady Katharine de Winter lived there at times; when she was not in residence, there were always groups of soldiers in and out of the place. Sometimes they would come into town and wreak havoc in the taverns. Devereux had spent her life knowing when to stay indoors and locked away when the soldiers were about. She had spent her life staying clear of the knights and other warriors who would, at times, pass through her town. She had never even seen her husband although she knew he had spent time at Castle Acre Castle periodically. She had often heard rumor to that effect. Now she was a part of that world she had attempted to stay clear of. She tried not to hate her father for it.

From the corner of her eye, she caught sight of the altar. It was beautifully carved and had the rarity of a cushion before it on which to kneel. Devereux found herself wondering where the priests were that usually inhabited this priory. She wondered if de Winter's knights had chased them off. With another heavy sigh, she made her way to the altar, gazing up at the gold-encrusted cross and wondering how drastically her life was going to change from this point.

Soft boot falls suddenly distracted her and she turned to see an unfamiliar knight entering the sanctuary. He was a colossal man, dressed from head to toe in armor and mail and weaponry. He was without his helm and as he emerged into the weak light, Devereux could see his very handsome features; his dark hair was in need of a cut, a bit shaggy and curly, and a dark beard embraced his granite jaw.

The longer she stared at him the more she realized that he was, in fact, extraordinarily handsome. It was something of a shock. Devereux continued to watch with a mixture of apprehension and fascination as the knight drew closer, his hazel eyes fixed on her flushed and weary face. It was a piercing gaze that sucked her in, holding her fast until she could hardly breathe.

"I apologize for disturbing you, my lady," he said. "Were you praying?"

His voice was deep and silky, like sweet wine. Devereux felt an odd flush of heat at the sound of his delicious tone, momentarily speechless as he gazed upon her. She managed to shake her head, however, and the knight came to stand several feet away. Even when he gazed toward the altar and crossed himself reverently, she couldn't take her eyes from him.

Davyss felt her stare, turning to look at her again. Christ, if she wasn't the most beautiful woman he had ever seen; even more beautiful at close range. She had long, straight blonde hair that was thick and silky, and eyes of the most amazing color. They were a shade of blue that was so pale that they were silver. Big and bottomless, he could see the fringe of soft lashes brush against her brow bone every time she blinked. And her face was sweet and round. He had witnessed the wedding ceremony from the shadows, stifling the roar of laughter as Hugh and Andrew had wrestled with her in an attempt to force her to kiss his sword.

But the more he watched, the more curious and strangely mesmerized he became with this woman who was now his wife. She was a hellion, a misfit, and he should have been disgusted with her behavior. But her spirit impressed him strangely, a woman who was not afraid to speak her mind or resist men twice her petite size. And when he witnessed the confrontation between her and his mother, calculated though it had been for his benefit, it had oddly cemented the deal. For some reason, he was no longer reluctant. But she clearly still was.

When the lady had finally kissed the sword to seal the marriage, Davyss realized he could no longer stay away. In spite of his own reluctance, he realized he had to discover her for himself.

"My lady is… weary," he cocked an eyebrow at her slovenly state. "May I assist?"

Devereux's bright gray eyes regarded him. "Nay, my lord," she turned away, her cheeks flushing and her confusion growing.

He continued to gaze at her, the marvelous blonde hair that cascaded from her head to her thighs. "Then why do you stand here if you are not praying?" he asked.

She shrugged weakly, refusing to look at him. "I was left here."

"By whom?"

She didn't reply. Davyss' eyes roved her body with interest, noting that she was deliciously curvaceous. She was petite in height, clad in some sort of rough garment, a leather girdle binding her small waist and emphasizing her full breasts. She looked like an angel but dressed like a peasant. He found himself shaking his head with awe, hardly believing this woman was his wife. She was a most startling paradox.

"You did not answer me," he said after a moment. "Who was foolish enough to leave you here alone?"

She sighed heavily. "Terrible men. Horrible men."

He raised an eyebrow. "Is that so? Why are they so terrible, other than the fact that they left you here alone?"

She turned to look at him, feeling that same odd heat she had experienced the very first time their eyes met. Even so, she found she could not tell him the whole situation. It was too embarrassing.

"They will return for me, I am sure," she said, avoiding his question. "They have probably gone to fetch my husband."

"And who is your husband?"

She made a face and Davyss had to conceal a smile. She looked like a child forced to swallow foul-tasting medicine. "Sir Davyss de Winter."

"Ah, yes," he nodded in acknowledgement. "De Winter."

Her expression darkened. "Then you know him?"

"A fair man."

"A fiend!"

"Is that so?" he realized he was very close to breaking a smile. "Why would you say that? I hear he is a wise and powerful man. Handsome, too."

Her eyes flashed. "This I would not know, my lord, for he does not even have the courage to face me."

"What do you mean?"

"I was only just married to him. But instead of showing me the respect of coming himself, do you know that he sent his sword in his place?"

It was at that moment that Davyss began to see that perhaps sending Lespada in his place had not been a wise decision. Whatever animosity the lady was feeling had been exacerbated by it. He began to regret his decision although, at the time, it had been the correct choice. Still, he could see she was very offended by it. For whatever reason, he felt the need to soothe her ruffled feathers.

"Would you sit, my lady?" he indicated one of two benches in the place. "I find I am exceedingly weary from my ride and wish to continue this conversation seated."

She lifted an eyebrow. "You look strong enough."

He fought off a grin and went to take the bench himself, thinking that she would follow him. He was wrong in that she did not and he almost laughed; clearly, nothing about Lady Devereux was predictable.

"You must understand that to marry to your husband's sword is a distinct honor," he said quietly. "The sword of a knight defines who he is as both man and warrior. It is as much a part of him as his heart or his head. When you are presented with the sword, he is offering you his very soul. When he presented you with his sword in his stead, he was asking you to become part of his life and his being."

Devereux's unhappy expression eased somewhat. It was apparent that she was thinking heavily on his words. After several moments, she simply shook her head.

"But I don't want to be part of the kind of life he leads," she said, all of the defiance out of her voice.

"Why not?"

She just looked at him. "You will forgive me, my lord, but that is truly none of your affair. I should not have said as much as I have only…."

"Only what?"

She shook her head again and turned away from him, moving away so she would not have to speak with him any longer. He watched her glorious hair, so beautiful and lush, the way it fell down her graceful back. After a moment, he stood up and wandered, slowly, in her general direction.

"I am sure had your husband known the offense you took at him not attending your wedding ceremony personally, he would have made the effort to come," he said in a low voice. "You must not judge the man too harshly. The sword is quite an honor."

She turned to look at him. "You will not come any closer, my lord."

He stopped. "Why not?"

"Because my husband's knights are near and should they see you in conversation with me, they might do you great harm."

He smiled faintly. "So you are concerned for me? You do not even know who I am."

Devereux looked him up and down, from the top of his dark head to the bottom of his enormous feet. He was tall and although she'd seen taller men in her life, the sheer width of the man's shoulders was astonishing. And his hands were positively enormous. He was an extraordinarily big man.

"You are a seasoned warrior," she said after a moment. "I can smell death on you. That is all I need to know."

His smile faded. "Your arrogance is astounding."

Her back stiffened with outrage. "Arrogance? You overstep yourself, sir."

He lifted an eyebrow. "That is because I have spent a mere two minutes speaking with you, enough to know that you are judgmental, closed-minded and arrogant. Do you believe you are so perfect, lady? Do you believe that you walk this earth with perfect thoughts and perfect deeds? Do you understand that it is men like de Winter who have fought and died a thousand times over so you may live in your nice manor home and lead a pleasant life in your pleasant little world? How dare you judge men for their determination that England should know a better future."

By the time he was finished, the gray eyes were wide with astonishment. "It is not arrogance I present but distaste for death and destruction," she explained earnestly. "Those men you speak of have killed innocents along with their enemies. They care not who they kill so long as they are victorious."

"And you believe de Winter to be this sort of man?"

"He is the king's champion. He did not achieve this position through grace and gentleness. What other sort could he possibly be?"

"If you have not met him yet, you might want to set your prejudice aside and come to know him before you pass judgment."

She opened her mouth to argue with him but thought better of it. She began to look at him strangely, as if paying closer attention to this knight who not only seemed to be exceedingly wise but also who seemed to know de Winter very well. A little too well, in fact; he seemed to be very defensive of the man. Furthermore, there was no earthly reason why he should be standing here, alone, speaking with her. Where were all of de Winter's knights while this was going on? Devereux was many things but she was not foolish; she began to suspect who the knight before her really was.

With that knowledge, she seemed to calm. An odd twinkle came to her eye. "Very well," she said. "Since you seem to know de Winter so well, then perhaps you will tell me what you know of him."

Davyss crossed his muscular arms and lifted an eyebrow thoughtfully. "Well," he said slowly. "As I said, he is a wise and powerful man. And very handsome."

"You said that."

"It's true."

"I am sure he is humble, also."

"Indeed."

"And chivalrous."

"Of course."

She shook her head sadly. "Then he will not want me," she turned away, a very calculated move. If the man was going to play games with her, then she was going to play to win. "I have none of those qualities. For certain, it is the entire reason behind my reluctance to marry him."

Davyss watched her luscious backside. "Is that so? Do tell and perhaps I can advise you."

She feigned distress, casting him a very sad glance over her shoulder. "I drink to excess. And I have been known to steal."

Davyss bit his lip; he almost burst out laughing. "Truly? A pity."

She was adding drama to her act now. "I have never been punished for my crimes because my father is Sheriff of the Shire and clearly, no one will accuse his only child of misdeeds. I have also been known to go on rampages and burn and pillage. That has to do with the excessive drinking, I think, but my father tried to have the priest purge me of these urges. He says the devil is in me. But… but the worst part is the children."

"What children?"

"My children," she wandered to the narrow window, gazing out into the greenery beyond. "I have six of them. All from different fathers." She suddenly whirled around and faced him. "Do you think he will still want me for his wife now?"

Davyss was very close to collapsing with laughter. It was difficult for him to speak and not sound like he was straining for every word. "Where are these children?"

She turned away with exaggerated distress. "All gone," she sighed. "I sold three into slavery, one to a passing nobleman, and two ran away. I think wild animals ate them."

Davyss had to turn away lest she see him grin. "I am sure it will matter not," he finally said. "At least he will know that you can bear him many strong sons."

Devereux whirled in his direction, her mouth opened in outrage. "What kind of man would want such a lowly woman?"

Davyss turned to look at her, rubbing his chin so she would not see the hint of a smile. "Me," he replied frankly. "I am Davyss de Winter and I am quite pleased with my acquisition."

Devereux didn't act overly surprised by the revelation. She leaned back against the wall, a soft breeze from the lancet window lifting her golden hair gently.

"I do not believe you," she said flatly.

He walked towards her, lifting his eyebrows. "'Tis true."

She shook her head. "Davyss de Winter is nine feet tall and breathes fire, so I have been told. You do not fit that description."

He grinned; he couldn't help it. "I assure you that I am he."

Devereux felt an odd flutter in her chest when he smiled; his teeth were big, straight and white and she could see, even with his beard, that he had big dimples in each cheek. If she thought the man to be handsome before, she could clearly see that her observations were correct; he was astonishingly so. The idea brought a strange quiver to her body. She folded her arms, protectively, across her chest as he drew close. Something inherent told her to protect herself from him.

"I was right," she said quietly, eyeing him as he came to a stop fairly close to her. "You are a seasoned warrior. I can smell death on you."

His smile faded. "Perhaps," he said. "It is regretful that you do not see marriage to me as an honor. Most women would, you know."

"Most women are given to silly romantic whims and dreams of god-like knights as their husbands," she said. "I, in fact, am not."

His smile was gone completely as his gaze moved over her, the lovely shape of her face and the delicate drape of her hair. "A pity you have such distain for those who are sworn to serve and protect you."

She shook her head. "You are not sworn to serve and protect me," she contradicted, a hint of irony in her tone. "You are sworn to serve and protect the king, sworn to carry out his commands right or wrong. Knighthood has the power to unite a country yet you do nothing more than squabble between yourselves and perpetuate war. It is those motives that I distain."

He was simply watching her now, analyzing her words, attempting to figure out what was at the heart of this woman that made her so bitter. There was something more than idealism there although he couldn't put his finger on it. He moved forward and grasped her gently by the elbow, encouraging her to come with him. Reluctantly, Devereux followed.

"Have you had much exposure to the knighthood, then?" he asked quietly as they moved through the empty church.

She faltered slightly. "My father has two knights who have served him for years as Lord Mayor and Sheriff of the Shire."

"Who are these men?"

"Older men who served King Henry. One of them used to serve Eleanor of Aquitaine."

"Are those the only knights you have ever known?"

She looked at him with those bright eyes. "Aye."

"Then your opinion of the knighthood is based solely upon these two men."

She paused, gazing up into his handsome face. "I am an active member of the community and take my duties as the daughter of the Sheriff of the Shire very seriously. I hear much and I see much. Do not think I live an isolated life, my lord. My opinion is based upon tales and information that has come to me over the years."

He looked down at her; she was such an exquisite creature but, truth be told, he was coming to feel some disappointment. She was not honored by the marriage, that much was clear; she also had a very bad opinion of his profession and, consequently, him. If he were to admit it to himself, it was somewhat of a blow to his self-esteem. He'd never met a woman who hadn't been overjoyed at a mere word from the mighty and powerful Davyss de Winter. Now he had married one who didn't care in the least. He tugged gently on her elbow to get her moving again.

"I would like to give you a bit of advice, my lady," he said as the door to the church loomed before them; he could see his men waiting outside. "I do not presume to discount your opinions because they are your own. They are not truth as I know it. But if I were you, I would think twice before insulting men who have spent their lives fighting and killing for their cause. The men that serve me are battle-born, hard to the core, and have demonstrated that fierceness in battle time and time again. The stories I could tell you about them would give you nightmares for the rest of your life. You have expressed your reservations to me so let that be the end of it. From this moment on, you are the wife of Sir Davyss de Winter, Champion to our illustrious King Henry and an honored knight of the realm. Whatever you think of me personally, I should like you to at least show some respect for that position. It is an important one. Is that clear?"

She paused just as they reached the door, the sunlight glistening off her miraculous hair as she turned to look at him. "Our parents made this arrangement, my lord, and for that fact alone, I will respect my father's wishes. My acceptance of this marriage has nothing to do with you or your standing. I do it because my father wishes it."

"And I do this because my mother wishes it."

"Then we are clear."

Davyss took her outside to his waiting men, who couldn't help but notice she was far calmer with him than she had been with them. They assumed Davyss had worked his usual magic and convinced the lady to be calm and compliant. He was particularly good at convincing women of his wishes.

The lady was mounted on Davyss' charger and he mounted behind her. With a piercing whistle from Davyss, the group thundered off in the direction of Castle Acre Castle.

CHAPTER THREE

"SHE DOES NOT want anything to do with me. Do you now see how miserable you have made us both?"

Lady Katharine sat patiently as her eldest son ranted. In the lavish solar of Breckland Castle with its massive walls and elaborate gardens, Davyss had been pacing around for over an hour. His source of agitation was his new bride, now locked in a chamber in the powerful keep of Castle Acre Castle. Davyss was afraid what would happen if he didn't lock her in, so he had bolted the door and headed for his mother's castle to let her know what, exactly, he thought of her little matchmaking scheme.

"It matters not how either of you feel," Katharine replied steadily, carefully stitching the petit poi in her hands. It was a colorful collection of birds. "You are married and that is the end of it."

Davyss' jaw ticked faintly. "It is not the end of it. She hates all I stand for, Mother. She will not be an agreeable or compliant wife in the least."

Katharine continued to stitch. "Is that what you were expecting?" she didn't look up from her hands. "Mere agreement and compliance?"

"What else is there?"

Katharine lifted her thin eyebrows. "There is much more, my son. Perhaps that is why I arranged this marriage so you would understand that there is more to life than kings and compliant women."

He faced her, a scowl on his face and his hands on his slender hips. "What are you talking about?"

Katharine glanced up at him, a hint of a smile on her old lips. "You have seen thirty years and four, Davyss. What have you learned in that time? That the more men you kill and the more power you wield, the more women will fall at your feet unconditionally? Have you ever had a conversation with a woman that was not foolish courtly flirting? Have you ever known a woman to show strength of character or courage in the face of adversity? Or do you simply view them as sheep as you select your dame du jour from the flock?"

His scowl was gone by now. After a moment, he sighed heavily. "I am sure you are driving at a point but I cannot see what it is."

"Aye, you can," Katharine set her needlepoint down. "I am trying to tell you that there is more to life than fighting, dying and cheap women, Davyss. You are a wise, intelligent man and God has given you excellent character and judgment. You are at an age where you need to understand that family is as important as those things you have fought all your life to achieve; a good wife, intelligent and strong without political aspirations, and sons to carry on your name. And, if you are lucky, you and your wife will be fond of each other like your father and I were. It makes life worth living to rise every morning to the face of someone you are very fond of. It means more than all the money and power in the world."

He lifted a dark eyebrow at her. "If you wanted me to experience a fond wife, then you have most definitely cursed me. She shall never be fond of me."

"She will make a man out of you."

Both eyebrows lifted in outrage. "Is that what you think? That I am not a man yet?"

Katharine's smile broke through. "You still have a great deal to learn. Telling a woman how powerful and handsome you are is not the mark of a true man."

He snorted and turned away. "I doubt there is anything my new wife could teach me."

The old woman's smile faded. "Allow me to tell you something about your new wife, Davyss, and perhaps you will understand what type of woman it is that you have married," she set the needlepoint on the table and leaned back in her chair. "From a young age, Lady

Devereux has known the true meaning of service and charity. Her mother started the poor house on the northern edge of Thetford several years ago and your wife helped her mother feed and shelter the needy. I have heard tale that she has gone without so that others less prosperous could know just a little. I began hearing rumors of this years ago so I started giving money to the poorhouse to continue the charity work that Devereux and her mother started. All the while, I kept my eye on this girl. I knew she had depth of character and morals that most women could only hope to bear. And I knew, someday, that I would marry one of my sons to her."

By this time, Davyss' belligerent expression was gone. "I know that place you speak of."

"Of course you do. You pass by it every time you come from London to visit me."

"They call it La Maison d'Espoir, I believe."

"Aye, they do. The House of Hope."

He actually looked surprised. "She is a part of that place?"

Katharine nodded, eyeing her son and realizing the information was having its desired effect. If nothing else, she knew her son well; he was hot-tempered and conceited, but he was not afraid to admit when he was wrong. It was a good trait.

"Not only is she a part of that place, but she has seen to its operation since her mother passed away," Katharine said. "Do you remember that epidemic that swept through the town about five years ago?"

He nodded. "I was in London at the time. I remember you told me of it."

His mother dark eyes were piercing. "Do you know that she nursed a great many people during that time?" When he shook his head rather weakly, she continued. "While others fled the area, including her father, your wife and her mother stayed to nurse the sick. Eventually Devereux and her mother were taken ill with the same affliction; the mother died but Devereux was spared."

Davyss stood there, staring at his mother as he processed what she had told him. Eventually he found a chair and sat, struggling to come to grips with the situation.

"Then I am sure she is selfless and true," he replied. "But she holds no respect for me at all."

"What do you think of her?"

"Are you seriously asking me that question after all I have told you?"

"I am asking what you think when you look at her. Is she beautiful?"

He thought on the silken blonde hair and gray eyes. "Aye," he admitted. "She is damn beautiful, in fact. I have never seen such beauty."

"And if you had seen her in London, would you have pursued her based upon her beauty alone?"

"Absolutely. She is a fine prize for any man. I will be the talk of court when people see the beauty of the woman I have married."

Katharine cast her son a rather disapproving look. "Based upon her appearance alone she is worthy to be seen on your arm, eh? Was there nothing else you found attractive about her?"

He pursed his lips irritably, thinking on their brief encounter. "She… well, she was rather humorous."

"Humorous?"

"She made me laugh."

"I see," Katharine looked down at her sewing so he would not see the smile on her lips; he sounded utterly distressed that the woman had the power to make him laugh. "So she is beautiful and humorous. And this distresses you because she does not view you in the same light?"

He could hear a mocking note in his mother's tone and he refused to look at her. "She despises me. She said as much."

Katharine shrugged. "Perhaps she will overcome that with time," she said softly. "Give her a reason to respect you, Davyss. Sometimes esteem is more than simply handling a sword better than most or bearing the honor of the king. It comes from the heart, not the hand."

He looked at her. "She is not perfect, either. She is proud and arrogant."

Katharine picked up her needlepoint and resumed. "Perhaps," she said faintly as she began to sew. "If I were you, I would try to get to know her before making such judgments."

He lifted an eyebrow, hearing his own words in them. Rising from the chair, he exhaled sharply and puffed out his cheeks. He wasn't sure what to think anymore.

"What would you suggest I do, then?" he ventured. "You started this. What brilliant stars of wisdom do you have for me in dealing with my new wife?"

Katharine scrutinized her son; he favored her with his dark hair and hazel eyes, something that his father had lamented. Grayson Davyss de Winter had been a handsome man, no doubt, but his son's handsome appearance had eclipsed him. Davyss was a spectacular example of the male species and he was well aware of the fact which was why, his mother suspected, he was so baffled at Lady Devereux's reaction to him. The possibility that the woman would not swoon at his feet had never occurred to him.

"Shave off that forest on your face and cut your hair," she told him. "You are not usually so shaggy in appearance"

"I have been traveling for weeks."

"That is no excuse for your lack of attention to your appearance," she sniffed. "You may want to bathe as well. I can smell you from here."

Davyss gave her a look that suggested he thought her to be ridiculous. "I apologize that I am so offensive."

His mother fought off a grin. "And bring her a gift," she said. "Go into my chamber upstairs and collect what you will for her."

"Like what?"

"Jewels. Clothing, if you think it will fit her. You just married the woman; ply her with gifts."

He puckered his lips wryly. "Anything else?"

Katharine shook her head and returned her attention to the needle in her hand. "You will have to figure it out for yourself."

He pursed his lips irritably, his gaze moving to the window that overlooked the bailey below. Business went on as usual below, in sharp contradiction to the unexpected turn his life just took.

"I do not need this additional burden," he muttered. "I have more pressing problems in London at the moment. I do not need the addition of a cantankerous new wife."

Katharine stopped sewing, casting him a sharp glance. "That is exactly what you need."

ও

THE ROOM WASN'T particularly large or well appointed. In fact, it was rather sparse with its single unused bed and old table. Having only heard of Castle Acre Castle, Devereux had been told it was a mysterious place, full of military implications, and now she found herself in the heart of it. It only heightened her sense of misery.

It was an enormous compound with massive ramparts built up around an enormous bailey to the south and a motte to the north. She'd never seen anything so large.

The group had entered the castle on the southwest side of town through a massive stone gatehouse, entering the complex that was vast and fortified. Several hundred soldiers were in residence at this time because of de Winter's presence and they were camped out in the enormous bailey, creating a quagmire of mud, chaos, men and animals. A vast great hall sat in the middle of the bailey along with several outbuildings. The whole area smelled like a swamp.

Built within a circle of ramparts to the north was a powerfully constructed keep, although the keep had been partially demolished by Henry II because it had been an unlicensed fortification eighty years prior. Lady Katharine's ancestor, William de Warenne, had built it during the conflicts between Empress Matilda and King Stephan, giving rise to a very fortified and illegal bastion. Henry, when he assumed the throne, went through the countryside destroying all of these unlicensed castles in the hopes they would never be used for an uprising ever again.

But somehow, he failed to demolish all of Castle Acre Castle's massive keep. Two stories of it still remained.

Davyss had brought her to the second floor of the crumbling keep and left her in one of the two chambers, bolting the door from the outside. He'd barely said a word and she, exhausted from her day of struggle and upset, hadn't shown any resistance. From the lancet windows to the north and west, she could see the small town beyond. It was a quiet place, certainly not as large as the berg she came from. Thetford was much bigger. As the day waned, her sense of homesickness and despair grew.

He left her with no food, no drink. Devereux spent a good deal of time and energy attempting to figure out how she could climb out of the windows and not kill herself, but the room was so barren that there was nothing she could make a ladder or a rope with. She could have jumped, of course, but it was several feet to the ground and she didn't want to break something. So she gave up on the idea of escaping and sat down in the chilly room, waiting for the moment when de Winter would decide to let her out again. She was thirsty and growing hungry. As the wait became excessive, so did her animosity.

It was late afternoon by the time she heard the door rattle. Startled from hours of silence and inaction, she instinctively leapt to her feet as the door opened. The first face she saw was that of the de Winter priest. She took a closer look at him, noting he had wild gray hair, wild gray eyes, and huge scarred hands. He didn't look like any priest she had ever seen. She couldn't help but notice he stood somewhat behind the door, as if using the panel as a shield against her.

"My lady," he greeted, eyeing her warily. "I came to see if you required anything to make your stay more comfortable."

She lifted a well-shaped eyebrow at him. "Can you seriously ask me that question as you look at this desolate room?" she wanted to know. "I have been locked in here for hours with no food, nothing to drink, and no comforts whatsoever. And you think to now come and ask me that question?"

He looked around the room, sighing faintly. Then he took a step inside and stopped using the door as a shield.

"Perhaps we started out on the wrong note," he said with some regret. "My name is Lollardly. We were not formally introduced earlier, but I am Sir Davyss' personal priest."

Devereux eyed him. "Is this how the de Winters normally treat women? Locking them in cold rooms with nothing of comfort?"

He grunted softly and scratched his head. "My lady, this was not my doing. It would be exceedingly more pleasant for us both if you would stop being so confrontational. I realize this day has been something of a shock for you but surely you know this was not my doing. I was following orders. If you choose to hate me because of my sense of duty, then so be it. But you should also realize that our association will be as pleasant, or as adversarial, as you make it. The choice is yours."

Devereux simply stared at him. Without a response, Lollardly saw no need to stay and he began to close the door quietly. Just before he closed it completely, Devereux spoke.

"Lollardly?" she said.

He stopped. "My lady?"

She took a step towards him, her expression a mixture of loathing and resignation. She finally settled for complete resignation.

"If it is not too much trouble, I should like something to eat," she said quietly. "I have not eaten all day. And perhaps a fire would be nice; it is cold in here."

Lollardly nodded firmly, as if she had just given him an intense command. "It shall be done, Lady de Winter," he said. "Anything else?"

She felt as if she had been struck by an unseen hand at the formal mention of her new title. It took her a moment to recover her shock and distaste.

"My things," she said. "Everything was left behind at my father's house. I will need my things."

Lollardly nodded. "A few of Davyss' knights rode for your father's home a few hours ago. They should be returning shortly."

She frowned at the thought of warriors handling her clothing and personal items. She hoped her father had sense enough to have his servants pack her trunks before the knights got their blood-stained hands on everything.

"Will there be anything else, my lady?" the priest interrupted her thoughts.

She eyed him, shaking her head after a moment. "Nay," she replied softly. "Except… well, if this is to be my bed, there is no mattress on it. I will need one."

"We are already seeing to that, my lady."

There was nothing more to say and he shut the door softly. She didn't hear the bolt slip through the bracket but she couldn't be sure that there wasn't a knight out there, just waiting for her to open it. If it was a test, she would pass it. Quite frankly, there was no use escaping and returning to her father. He would only turn her back over to her husband.

So she sat on the floor against the wall opposite the hearth and waited. Except for an occasional bird flying past the windows, her environment was largely silent. Her thoughts had settled somewhat from the turbulent day although her distain at what had happened was still a powerful thing. She mostly blamed her father but knew, deep down, that the man had only been doing what he thought best for his daughter. An advantageous marriage that had been proposed to him by Lady Katharine de Winter had been both a surprise and a blessing. Only a fool would have refused. If she was honest with herself, she understood why he did it.

Time was shiftless and shapeless up in her prison. She truly had no idea how much of it had elapsed when she heard the door latch give and the panel push open. An enormous man entered the chamber clad in a tunic, breeches and massive leather boots. Seated against the wall, Devereux watched with trepidation and curiosity as the man entered with a tray in his hand.

He was clean shaven with cropped dark hair. Devereux truly had no idea who the man was until he looked at her. Sultry hazel eyes and a face that surely Adonis was jealous of gazed steadily at her. He smiled faintly.

"My lady," he said in a soft, deep voice. "I have brought you something to eat."

She had to look again; realizing it was Davyss, she rose stiffly from the floor, inspecting him as if she was just seeing him for the first time. He was completely without armor, his face as smooth as a baby's bottom and his dark hair clean and cut. The rough linen tunic fit his powerful chest and enormous arms like the skin of a grape and she could see the muscles flexing as he moved. He had a tight waist, tight buttocks, and massively muscled thighs. And those hands… she imagined that his fist would be almost as large as her head. My God, she thought to herself. He was the most handsome creature she'd ever seen. But handsome or no, it did nothing to ease her animosity towards him.

"So you have come to feed your caged animal?" she moved towards him, slowly. "How chivalrous."

His smile faded. "I apologize for locking you in," he said. "You must understand that this is a military encampment. I have hundreds of men on the grounds that would not think twice before molesting a woman. What I did, I did for your safety."

She reached him and the food. "If that is true, then you should have had me bolt the door from the inside so no one could get in. As it was, you put the bolt on the wrong side of the door. Anyone could have unlocked it."

He shook his head. "The door was guarded on the landing. Moreover, had I told you the threat when I first brought you here, in your current hysterical state, I doubt you would have believed me. You would have disregarded my warning and tried to flee into an encampment of five hundred men who would have gladly taken you to sport."

She eyed him, attempting to determine if he was telling the truth. Unable to reach a conclusion, she reached out for a piece of hard, cold bread. She was starving and took a large bite.

"You could have at least left me with food and water," she scolded.

"This keep has been unused for years. I had to send my men to collect even basic necessities." He watched her stuff her mouth with the bread, feeling rather caddish about locking her up without any comforts. He moved swiftly for the door. "I have something for you. I shall return."

He slammed the door, leaving her rather startled at his swift disappearance. But her puzzlement at his departure did not outweigh her appetite and she returned to the food he had brought, set upon the old table. There was the bread plus a hunk of tart white cheese, two small apples and a handful of walnuts. There was also a cup of something, although she wasn't quite sure what it was. It smelled rank but she drank it anyway, thirsty, and realized it was old ale. She made a face of disgust.

She sat on the bed frame and finished off the bread, half the cheese and one of the little apples. By the time Davyss came back, she was in the process of trying to crack the walnuts by stepping on them. He saw what she was doing, picked the walnut off the floor, and cracked it with his bare hand. When he handed her the meat of the nut, Devereux tried not to look too astonished at brute strength.

"My thanks," she said, eyeing his massive hands and wondering what else he could crack with them.

He silently acknowledged her and proceeded to set a big satchel on the table next to the food tray. It was a leather bag with intricate embroidery on it and leather handles. He opened it up and proceeded to pull out the contents.

"Here," he handed her a great bundle of material. "This is for you."

Puzzled, Devereux unrolled the fabric and realized it was a surcoat. The material was fantastic; some kind of silk, it was dyed a brilliant blue yet when the light hit it, there were high-lights of black and iridescent green. Before she could thank him, he was piling more garments on her arms. Carefully, she began to lay everything out on the bed frame and realized, when he was finished, that she had four new surcoats, three delicate shifts, one heavy lamb's wool shift with gloriously belled sleeves and gold tassels, at least four scarves, two gold belts and several smaller pieces of jewelry. Astonished, she looked up at him.

"I… I am not quite sure what to say," she said. "I have never seen anything so glorious."

For the first time since they had met, Davyss felt like he had the upper hand. She was humbled, speechless, and he felt in control. He was also quite pleased by the awestruck expression on her face. He felt as if he had done something right.

"I hope they are to your liking," he said. "They are gifts on the event of our marriage."

Her expression went from awestruck to somewhat concerned. She actually looked worried.

"They are beautiful, of course," she said, daring to look up at him. "But I do not have any such gifts for you. I am not sure that it is fair for you to give me such riches and not expect something in return."

He smiled that brilliant, toothy smile and Devereux's heart began to race. The man was excruciatingly handsome and even she wasn't immune to it.

"Your beauty is gift enough, my lady," he said gallantly. "How fortunate for me to have married the most beautiful woman in England."

She didn't look particularly comfortable with that declaration. Seeing that his words did not have the desired effect, Davyss reached into the bottom of the satchel and pulled forth a small silk purse to retrieve another weapon in his flattery arsenal. He pulled forth a gold band with a massive yellow diamond in the center. It was a spectacular ring that glittered madly, even in the dim light. He held it out to her.

"This is the ring my father gave to my mother on their wedding day," he said. "My mother wanted you to have it. Would you honor me by wearing it?"

For the second time in as many minutes, Devereux was speechless. The ring was magnificent, larger and richer than anything she had ever seen. She knew the de Winters were wealthy but the concept truly had no meaning until this moment. For lack of a better response, she held out her hand to take it. But Davyss took her hand, flipped it over, and slipped the ring on the third finger of her left hand. It was a little snug, but the fit was secure. Devereux pulled her hand back to examine the beautiful piece.

"Again, I have nothing so magnificent for you," she said, with obvious humility. "I am not sure I can accept such extravagant gifts."

"Of course you can," he assured her. "I am your husband. It is appropriate that you should have these. A de Winter must be richly and lavishly dressed."

She looked at him. "Why is that?"

He snorted. "Because we are one of the most powerful families in England," he said as if she was in need of an education. "We must always be aware of that station and display it accordingly. Moreover, you have married the king's champion. You, my lady, must be the most beautiful and well-dressed woman in London. You must honor me in that regard."

She stared at him, beginning to see the egocentric man behind the handsome face. The man was full of himself; she'd seen a hint of it earlier in the chapel and she saw even more of it now. Her animosity and distaste for the union, so recently eased, suddenly returned with a vengeance.

"I see," she said. "So I must parade around like a peacock so that all men will look to you and envy your good fortune."

His brow furrowed slightly. "You have married well, my lady. Do you not understand that?"

She lifted an eyebrow. "And do you understand that I do not care?" she fired back. She grabbed one of the surcoats and shook it at him. "You ply me with gifts because you want me to be the best dressed, most beautiful woman in England, not because you are joyful at our marriage. All you have shown me so far is that you are only concerned with yourself and how I will make you the envy of all men. You have helped me to understand that my opinion of the knighthood was not wrong; those who participate in it are vain and self-centered. You only care for your own glory."

She tossed the garment down and turned away from him, wandering towards the lancet window where the sun was now beginning to set. Streams of pink and gold filtered in through the opening and cast beams of light on the floor.

Davyss stared at her, the gentle curve of her backside and that glorious hair that he felt the urge to run his hands through. He was struggling to see her point of view but found, at the moment, that he could not. He did not understand her resistance to that which he considered important and felt his irritation rise.

"I am sorry you do not appreciate the important station you have been given in life," he rumbled. "I was hoping you would at least understand what is expected of you."

She shook her head, unsure how to reply. The truth was that she was feeling hollow and hurt. They could not have been further apart in ideals if they had tried and the realization that she was married to such a man sank her spirits tremendously. She was going to be miserable the rest of her life and she knew it.

"You do not know me, my lord," she said quietly. "You do not understand what is important to me and I am sure you do not care. Give me time to adjust to your expectations because, I am sure, you will not adjust to mine. I do not expect it. If you want a wife in name only, then you must give me time to provide it."

He almost walked out of the room. He just didn't see any point in speaking further on the subject. But something made him stay; he wasn't sure what it was, but something deep inside told him not to leave her. Perhaps it was his mother's advice that did not allow him to move. Whether or not she was in the room, Lady Katharine was telling him to stay. Get to know her before you pass judgment. Crossing his enormous arms, he leaned against the wall thoughtfully.

"My mother told me get to know you," he said softly. "She told me that I must earn your respect. But I am not sure that is possible."

Devereux turned to him. "Why would you say that?"

He lifted his massive shoulders. "Because you have already formed your opinion of what kind of man I am. You did the moment you married me. I am not sure I can change that."

"You have given me little else to go on, my lord. The words out of your mouth are extremely pompous and your actions thus far have been self-serving."

He looked at her pointedly. "I have worked hard to achieve my station and reputation. I am not ashamed."

She gazed steadily at him, a faint sigh escaping her lips. "You do not have to be," she said. "But there is something called humility that is the most attractive quality anyone can possess. Do good deeds, earn your reputation, but be humble and gracious and endearing. Those qualities are more valuable than the greatest status on earth or the biggest chest of gold. It is those qualities that will cause people to bow at your feet and a wife to respect you. Does that make any sense?"

He could see she wasn't being condescending or confrontational. In fact, she spoke the words in a very gentle yet sincere manner. At that moment, he began to see something beyond the beauty. He saw something tender and benevolent. He wasn't used to those qualities in a lovely woman; he didn't think he'd ever seen it before. It made him uncomfortable, perhaps feeling exposed, but it also brought about greater interest. He wanted to see more.

"It does," he said after a moment. "But I am who I am, lady. I do not expect to change."

"I did not say change. Yet there is always opportunity to grow."

He grunted and averted his gaze as he kicked distractedly at the floor. He looked very much like he was fidgeting. "You sound like my mother. Did she tell you to say all of this?"

When he looked back up, she was smiling. Davyss had to catch his breath; he'd never seen her smile. Never in his life had he seen anything so lovely. She was an exquisite creature in any circumstance, but when she smiled, her entire face turned as radiant as the sun. It was breathtaking.

"Nay," she said with a chuckle. "I have only briefly spoken to your mother and it was not under the most pleasant of circumstances."

He pursed his lips wryly; then, he nodded and pushed himself up off the wall. "You sound just like her."

"Then she is a wise woman."

Davyss looked at her as if to retort but ended up chuckling. He made his way over to her. "Aye, she is, but do not attempt to out-smart her," he stopped a foot or so away. "She will beat you every time."

"I would never attempt to out-smart her."

"Good. And do not attempt to out-smart me, either, because that is not such a difficult task and if I lose I shall become very angry."

She fought off a grin. "Is that so?" she appeared to take his suggestion seriously. "What are the consequences, if I may ask?"

He frowned and shook his head, although there was clearly humor to it. "You would not like it."

"May I at least have a hint?"

"Are you sure you want one?"

Her grin broke through. "Is it so terrible?"

"I am not sure."

"Try."

He didn't know why he did what he did in that moment, only that it seemed like the most reasonable thing to do. Reaching out, he grabbed her by the arms and pulled her against him, planting his smooth lips firmly atop hers. When he felt her stiffen with resistance, he put his arms around her and held her fast. His embrace was warm, his hands caressing.

Devereux struggled to pull away from him, to turn her head, but every time she moved he seemed to be there, in all directions. His kiss went from firm and cold to gentle and warm. After several long seconds of defiance and struggle, she began to give in to the inevitable chemistry. The warmth, the magnetism, was irresistible and she naturally succumbed.

Davyss meant to dominate her and he had. She was small against his size and no match for his strength physically. But an odd thing happened; a gesture of dominance quickly turned into to something curious and warm. She was delicious and soft, and he took great delight in tenderly suckling her lips. When he felt her curious response, he licked her lips sensuously and gently plunged his tongue into her mouth. He could hear soft protests in her throat and she briefly struggled against him again, but just as quickly, she relaxed again. He held her closer.

He'd never known anything so sweet and pure. Because she had collapsed against him completely, his hands began to stroke her body, moving up her back and to her glorious hair. He entwined his fingers in it, feeling the silk against his flesh, and what had started out as an act of control was quickly becoming one of desire. Soon, the tables were turning and he was the one surrendering. He was losing his mind.

He lifted her up so that she was braced against him and he pushed her back against the wall. Trapped against the wall with his enormous body, Devereux had nowhere to go. His hands were everywhere and as caught up as she was in the firestorm of passion they were experiencing, she began to feel some fear when his hands moved, however tenderly, over her breasts. When she tried to protest, he merely covered her lips with his own. When she tried to physically remove his hands, he grabbed both her wrists and pinned her arms above her head.

Fear began to pound in her chest at the helpless position he had put her in. His mouth was on her neck, her face, and although there was large degree of excitement to it, she was still a maiden and everything he was doing to her was new. This wasn't anything she had ever experienced before. When he suddenly grabbed the top of her surcoat and ripped it wide-open, she shrieked. But he quickly covered her mouth with his, his tongue engaging in intimate delights, as her breasts sprang free and his hand began to grope her.

The fear bloomed and her struggles increased but he effectively had her trapped. There was nowhere for her to go. Davyss was out of control, his hand moving over her breasts and teasing her nipples into hard little pellets. When he lowered his head and capture a nipple between his lips, suckling firmly, Devereux felt excitement and desire such as she had never known shoot through her body. Bolts of lightning raced through her limbs and, for a moment, she stopped fighting him. He was warm, overwhelmingly manly, and passionate. As his mouth moved from one breast to the other, she gasped with pleasure. Whatever the man was doing to her was overpowering her senses and she began to surrender.

But that was until his roving hand ripped away the last of her surcoat and shift, leaving her entire body wide-open for his attention. The hand that was so powerfully yet tenderly caressing her breasts moved to the fluff of curls between her legs and stroked her intimately.

The fear was back in force with Devereux; she bucked with shock and he took it as desire. He wedged himself in between her knees and pried her legs open. His mouth was on hers again and she couldn't say a word; he heard the gasps and thought they were cries of passion when they were really cries of fright. He should have known the difference but he did not; when he finally inserted a finger into her warm, wet passage, Devereux screamed but he stifled her cries with his heated mouth. He stroked in and out of her, feeling her tight body, and it drove him mad like no other. He'd never been so aroused in his entire life.

With his free hand, he lowered his breeches, exposing his stiff and enormous erection. Quick as a flash, he let go of her wrists and grabbed her behind both knees, pulling her legs around his hips. Using his body, he kept her pressed firmly against the wall as hands held her pelvis against him, his arousal pushing insistently into her virginal passage.

Devereux was pounding on his enormous shoulder, terrified and aroused at the same time, as he thrust forward and almost seated himself completely on the first try. She cried out and he put his hand in her mouth to stifle her noise, his lips suckling her nipples as he firmly, carefully, withdrew himself and thrust into her again. She sobbed again and bit his hand, drawing blood, but he didn't feel it; he was only aware of his throbbing member enveloped by her tight, wet body.

And then he began to move. Slowly and carefully at first, withdrawing almost completely before pushing into her again. She was incredibly slick and his pace began to increase. His hands moved to her buttocks as he held her tight against him, his mouth on her neck and shoulders as she sobbed and weakly struggled. The more he moved within her, however, the more she seemed to surrender. With his hands on her buttocks, his mouth claimed her own and she showed the last shreds of her resistance. Soon, the hands bashing his shoulders stopped hitting him and fell still. His kisses eased into a tender and delicious assault and her hands, once still, began to caress his wide shoulders. She was starting to feel the power, too.

He stroked in and out of her, holding her beautiful body tightly against him as he moved. His mouth was everywhere; her lips, cheeks, neck, breasts. There wasn't any part of her upper body that had escaped his tender assault. As he suckled her nipples, he could feel her body drawing at him and he thrust hard, grinding his pelvis against hers and feeling her first release around his swollen member. As Devereux cried out softly, this time for an entirely different reason, Davyss thrust into her a few more times before finding his own blinding release. He spilled himself deep.

The room was full of the sounds of panting and sobs. Davyss' body was still pressing Devereux against the cold wall, his hands on her buttocks and his face buried in her neck. He originally thought her sobs were those of passion but it took him a moment to realize she was weeping deeply. It was not the sounds of joy. His head came up and he stared at her. An enormous hand flicked away a tear and she jerked her head away from him sharply.

"Stop," she wept. "Please… just stop."

He was genuinely concerned. "Why do you weep? Did I hurt you?"

She sobbed louder, putting a hand over her face so he could not see her confusion and fear. Davyss was truly at a loss; he squeezed her buttocks again, thrusting what was left of his arousal into her and gently kissing her neck. She gasped at the movement.

"Was that not to your liking, Lady de Winter?" he kissed her neck again. "We must consummate the marriage. Did you not enjoy it?"

She was weeping so hard that she couldn't speak. Davyss watched her face, thoroughly puzzled, before his gaze trailed down her slender white torso, inspecting his bride at close range. She had an incredibly beautiful body and already he could feel himself growing hard again. His hungry gaze moved to the junction where they were joined, the curls between her legs that were now mingled with his.

Her slender white legs, parted to receive him, drew his lust and he ran his hands down her thighs, feeling her stiffen to his touch. Caressing her buttocks again, he withdrew himself slightly with the intent of making love to her again but caught sight of a slight amount of blood on them both.

The sight was like throwing cold water on him. It took him a moment to realize that he had just consummated the marriage with his virgin wife and hadn't been entirely considerate about it. He'd treated her just as he treated any other woman he bedded. He should have been more thoughtful and compassionate, but the truth was that he'd been so overwhelmed with lust for the woman that he hadn't thought about anything other than quenching his own desire.

He hadn't thought of her feelings in the least; why should he? He was the great and powerful Davyss de Winter. He always took what he wanted and he had wanted her. But this was different; this wasn't some courtier or lady to be used and cast aside without thought. This was his wife, a good woman he'd been told, and he had just seriously abused that relationship. He'd thought only of himself. Pangs of remorse began to claw at him.

Carefully, he withdrew completely and set her on her feet. Sobbing, Devereux pulled the tattered ends of her surcoat tightly around her and stumbled away from him, pressing herself into the wall as close as she could get. The entire time Davyss reclaimed his tunic and secured his breeches, his gaze never left her. There was something in his expression, something unreadable and confused, that reflected the mood of the room. There was devastation here. He could feel it.

He left without another word.

Read the rest of **LESPADA** in eBook or in paperback.

About Kathryn Le Veque

Medieval Just Got Real.

KATHRYN LE VEQUE is a USA TODAY Bestselling author, an Amazon All-Star author, and a #1 bestselling, award-winning, multi-published author in Medieval Historical Romance and Historical Fiction. She has been featured in the NEW YORK TIMES and on USA TODAY's HEA blog. In March 2015, Kathryn was the featured cover story for the March issue of InD'Tale Magazine, the premier Indie author magazine. She was also a quadruple nominee (a record!) for the prestigious RONE awards for 2015.

Kathryn's Medieval Romance novels have been called 'detailed', 'highly romantic', and 'character-rich'. She crafts great adventures of love, battles, passion, and romance in the High Middle Ages. More than that, she writes for both women AND men – an unusual crossover for a romance author – and Kathryn has many male readers who enjoy her stories because of the male perspective, the action, and the adventure.

On October 29, 2015, Amazon launched Kathryn's Kindle Worlds Fan Fiction site WORLD OF DE WOLFE PACK. Please visit Kindle Worlds for Kathryn Le Veque's World of de Wolfe Pack and find many action-packed adventures written by some of the top authors in their genre using Kathryn's characters from the de Wolfe Pack series. As Kindle World's FIRST Historical Romance fan fiction world, Kathryn Le Veque's World of de Wolfe Pack will contain all of the great story-telling you have come to expect.

Kathryn loves to hear from her readers. Please find Kathryn on Facebook at Kathryn Le Veque, Author, or join her on Twitter @kathrynleveque, and don't forget to visit her website at www.kathrynleveque.com.

Made in the USA
Middletown, DE
25 January 2018